Octave Mirbeau

The *DIARY of a* *C*HAMBERMAID

translated by Douglas Jarman and with an introduction by Richard Ings

DEDALUS

Published in the UK by Dedalus Ltd, Langford Lodge, St Judith's Lane,
Sawtry, Cambs, PE28 5XE
email: DedalusLimited@compuserve.com

ISBN 0 946626 82 0

Dedalus is distributed in the United States by SCB Distributors,
15608 South New Century Drive, Gardena, California 90248
email :info @scbdistributors.com web site:www.scbdistributors.com

Dedalus is distributed in Australia & New Zealand by Peribo Pty Ltd,
58 Beaumont Road, Mount Kuring-gai N.S.W. 2080
email: peribo@ bigpond.com

Dedalus is distributed in Canada by Marginal Distribution,
Unit 102, 277 George Street North, Peterborough, Ontario,KJ9 3G9
email: marginal@marginalbook.com   web site: www. marginal.com

Dedalus is distributed in Italy by Apeiron Editoria & Distribuzione,
Localita Pantano, 00060 Sant'Oreste (Roma)
email: apeironeditori@hotmail.com

First published in France in 1900
First English edition in 1966
First published by Dedalus in 1991
New Dedalus edition in 2001

Translation copyright © Grafton Publishers 1966

Printed in Finland by WS Bookwell

A C.I.P. listing for this title is available on request.

The Diary of a Chambermaid - An Introduction

'What filth and decay there is under the pretty surface of our society!'
Jean Grave, editor of the leading anarchist journal, Le Révolté, on reading *The Diary of a Chambermaid*.

The Diary of a Chambermaid is probably the best known novel by the French writer, Octave Mirbeau. This is largely due to the interest of two giants of the cinema, Jean Renoir and Luis Buñuel, who based films on Mirbeau's popular and controversial satire. Both directors felt, in their own, very individual ways, a special affinity with this picaresque story of Célestine, a spirited chambermaid who keeps a diary charting her career in service. For the modern reader too, Mirbeau's tale is more than a confessional romp. It exposes the seamier aspects of an over-romanticised period in French history, the Belle Epoque, the era of the can-can, the Impressionists and high Parisian fashion, through the gradual corruption of its innocent heroine.

In Mirbeau's portrait of France at the end of the nineteenth century we can see a society at root not so different from our own. The gap between rich and poor - the central theme of this novel - is now writ large across the globe. The callousness of those who hold economic power is as vicious as ever. The earth itself seems consumed by a chemical rottenness that matches the human pollution Mirbeau exposed in his fiction and polemical journalism. The difference lies not in the problems, but in the poignant hopes and beliefs of

Mirbeau and many of his contemporaries which it is almost impossible for us to share: hopes of revolution, beliefs that society can be remade through political action.

Mirbeau's life spans a crucial seventy years, from the 'year of revolutions' across Europe in 1848 to the unimagined horror of the Great War. The issues that concerned Mirbeau throughout his maturity - state authoritarianism, militarism, anti-semitism, the powers of the Catholic Church - continued into the Vichy period and are alive today. For Mirbeau, anarchism - the philosophy developed by thinkers like Prince Kropotkin and Leo Tolstoy - provided the clearest analysis of social ills. Its visionary espousal of individual liberty spurred him politically and artistically. What George Woodcock has called 'a system of social thought, aiming at ... the replacement of the authoritarian state by some form of non-governmental co-operation between free individuals' became a lifelong credo.

In the thirty years between the founding of the Third Republic and 1900, when *The Diary of a Chambermaid* was published, France was convulsed by scandals that exposed tensions in society that remained unresolved well into the twentieth century. The most well known is the arrest and conviction of Captain Alfred Dreyfus in 1894 on charges of passing secrets to the German military attaché in Paris. The subsequent discovery that Dreyfus was innocent and that the army had attempted a cover-up might have been less significant had Dreyfus not been a Jew, the first to enter the General Staff. The stage was set for conflict between the republican supporters of Dreyfus - the so-called dreyfusards - and an alliance of dissidents dominated by Catholic royalists and anti-semitic 'patriots'. It is these latter elements that frequent Joseph's Cherbourg cafe at the end of Mirbeau's novel, which draws a disturbing picture of violent racism. For

Joseph, the only good Jew is a dead one - and that goes for Protestants and free-thinkers too. He carves his racist and patriotic slogans everywhere, 'even on the handles of the brooms'. This attitude resurfaced in the 1930's, when the French fascists vilified Leon Blum, the Jewish socialist leader of the Popular Front, with the slogan 'Rather Hitler than Blum'.

What is remarkable in an age that celebrates writers without taking them seriously is the vigorous engagement and influence of authors like Octave Mirbeau and Emile Zola in the thick of this political controversy. Zola's open letter to the President, 'J'accuse', has been called the prime catalyst in the whole affair, leading to the retrial and acquittal of Captain Dreyfus. Mirbeau consistently championed artists and writers whose work was attacked or suppressed by the authorities.

The battlelines evident in the Dreyfus affair had been drawn up much earlier, in the aftermath of the Revolution. On one side stood the republicans who wanted to consolidate their political victory by secularising the state, especially education. On the other side stood monarchists, Catholics threatened by the anti-clericalism of the Republic, and militarists who flocked to Boulanger's failed attempt to challenge the Republic in 1889. The revelations of government corruption in the Panama scandal in 1892 exposed another powerful and unpleasant trait of those opposed to the republic. Because the Panama Canal Company's Jewish financiers had bribed Republican officials to offer a large public loan to their ailing business, Jews became targets of a vitriolic campaign designed to discredit the 'patriotism' of the republican government. The fact that the vast majority of Jews belonged to the same working class as everyone else escaped the anti-semitic ideologues, who were later to claim that the Dreyfus affair had been a Jewish plot. This prejudice against the Jews puzzles Célestine, the heroine of Mirbeau's novel, even as she publicly affirms it: after all, whether Jews or Catholics, as masters and mistresses they have 'the same beastly natures, the same nasty minds'. If anything, Jews were more 'free and easy' with their servants.

Célestine often acts as Mirbeau's mouthpiece for his acid observations on the status quo. All his fiction is autobiographical, drawing on his development from the rural middle-class boy, educated by the Jesuits, who went on to study law in Paris, serve in the Army of the Loire and write for the monarchist press to the radical anarchist and best-selling novelist that he had become.

Reg Parr, author of the only considerable study of Mirbeau in English, pinpoints 1885 as the year when the thirty-seven year old journalist discovered Kropotkin's seminal anarchist work, *Paroles d'un Révolté* and Tolstoy's *Ma Religion*. 1885 was also the year when the government attacked the stage adaptation of *Germinal*, Zola's powerful novel about a miners' strike. Already a supporter of the avant-garde in the art world - Monet was, for example, a lifelong friend - Mirbeau finally made connections between his unease at government power and his libertarian instincts. The catalyst was anarchism and Mirbeau became the leading literary voice of the anarchist movement. Even when anarchism was tainted by the spontaneous terrorist bombings and assassinations of 1892 to 1894 (the so-called 'l'ère des attentats'), Mirbeau kept faith with its essential idealism and rationalism until the very end.

In the same way as Lu Xün, China's greatest modern writer, struggled for the same causes as the Chinese revolutionary leaders in the 1920s and 30s without compromising his independence, Mirbeau chose to speak the same language as many of the leading anarchists in France, people like Jean Grave and Sebastian Faure.

His fiction and his newspaper articles were welcome barbs in the flanks of what they considered a repressive regime. Mirbeau embraced the whole anarchist philosophy and its practical implications. He argued cogently against universal suffrage as an elective dictatorship, a method for the ruling classes to retain their power over the masses. He railed against the death penalty. He attacked the use of charity to keep the poor in their place. He condemned the arbitrary violence of the police and the parallel atrocities committed abroad in the French colonies. He discovered that everywhere he looked evil was paraded as good. Hypocrisy was Mirbeau's prime target; satire, sometimes so savage that it rebounded on him, was the chief string to his bow.

Mirbeau wrote several novels in the first flush of this conversion to anarchism: *Le Calvaire* (1886), *L'Abbé Jules* (1888) and *Sebastian Roch* (1890), all placing the individual against an implacable social order. *Sebastian Roch*, for example, describes the unhappy fate of a young man entrusted as a child to the less than tender mercies of Father de Kern at the Jesuit College of Vannes. The conflict between the hero's instinctive sense of justice and the religious and military indoctrination he is subjected to creates an unbearable tension that Mirbeau had only recently resolved for himself.

In 1899 Mirbeau returned to fiction, after years of dissident journalism and political activism, again out of anger at injustice. The Dreyfus affair found its literary metaphor in *Le Jardin des Supplices (The Torture Garden)*, a cruel tale that sets out to demonstrate Mirbeau's thesis that 'murder is the greatest obsession of mankind'. In this dystopian narrative Mirbeau links high society with depravity and torture, a theme he returned to in a more realistic vein in his following book *The Diary of a Chambermaid* (1900), where Célestine, in one memorable comment on the upper class, says: 'It is no exaggeration to say that the main aim of its existence is to enjoy the filthiest of amusements.'

Another link to the earlier novel is a disturbing emphasis on the darker sides of eroticism. While not taken to the logical extremes of de Sade or a later French writer, Georges Bataille, Mirbeau's treatment of sex and its relationship to corruption, cruelty and death did create controversy (and no doubt helped sales of his books). Célestine's vigorous sexual appetite - she admits, with typical candour, that she enjoys making love 'too much to be able to make a living from it' - seems healthier than the depraved tastes of her employers, with enough money and power to indulge their fetishes and fantasies. This makes her final capitulation all the more ironic, even tragic.

For a modern reader, though, the misogyny that runs through Mirbeau's writing must appear to weaken his reputation as a progressive radical thinker. Partly influenced by the fashionable symbolist cult of the femme fatale - Woman as evil seductress of Man's best instincts - Mirbeau also had an unhappy experience with an unfaithful mistress that apparently soured his view of women. However, in the person of Célestine he has created, whether he intended to or not, a strong and compassionate social critic at war with her oppressors. The fact that she succumbs in the end to the evil around her does not weaken the overall effects of her scathing and often riotously funny diagnosis of the petty-minded inanity and callousness of the bourgeoisie. Her fatal attraction to evil, despite her awareness of its moral and personal implications, is psychologically convincing. Deflowered at the age of twelve by a brutish foreman, whom she remembers 'with gratitude', she is ultimately drawn to men like Joseph, a wolfish rapist and proto-fascist, almost as a revenge on a society that offers her nothing beyond degradation and contempt.

The servant-master relationship and the scope it offers to an author to compare and contrast two classes runs through world literature and still fascinates: the Upstairs Downstairs school, one might call it. Seldom has the exploitation of the poor by the rich been explored as angrily as here: 'Solitude is ... living in other people's houses, amongst people who have no interest in you, who regard you as being of less importance than the dogs they stuff with titbits ... from whom all you get are, useless, cast-off clothes and left-over food, already going bad.' Servants are 'hybrid monsters', torn from their roots and never able to rise above their situation. And money rules all, money earned from exploitation. Célestine's last mistress owes her wealth to her father's unscrupulous scheme to help rich men's sons evade the draft by substituting the poor - a white version of the slave trade. As Célestine observes: 'I've never seen any money that wasn't dirty or any rich people who weren't rotten.'

Struggling not to become a victim, Célestine defends herself with what weapons she can lay her hands on: her sexual power over men, her intelligence, her bitter humour, her knowledge of the foibles of her employers. The price she pays is loneliness and a restless search for a better life: 'I have always been in a hurry to be somewhere else.' She can be perverse but she excites our sympathy to the end because we identify with her disgust - which is Mirbeau's as well - and with her love for life, which is thwarted at almost every turn by the relentless animosity of the ruling class. Only in the poignant episode with 'Monsieur George' does Célestine glimpse what could be. The cruel trick played on these lovers, when what should give life ends it, closes that avenue for ever. There are few options for women in Célestine's position.

Célestine's sensuality only came home to Luis Buñuel

after he had cast Jeanne Moreau in the role for his 1964 film adaptation of Mirbeau's novel. 'When she walks,' he recalled, 'her foot trembles just a bit on its high heel, suggesting a certain tension and instability.' It is easy to understand Buñuel's interest in *The Diary of a Chambermaid*, looking over his career as one of the great moralists of the twentieth century. Buñuel used surrealism to disturb and provoke, not simply to amuse. His translation of the novel's action to the 1920s drew conscious parallels between the dark side of the Belle Epoque and sinister rise of Fascism in the later period: from Dreyfus to Vichy. Like Mirbeau, Buñuel was an anarchist and delighted in satirizing the bourgeoisie. He too found sexual metaphors for repression - he makes a classic sequence out of Monsieur Rabour's foot fetish. Where Buñuel differs is in his transformation of Célestine into a moral avenger, secretly betraying Joseph to the police for his savage rape and murder of a young girl. Although the film ends with her marriage to an older, buffoonish version of Joseph - Captain Mauger - and Joseph's reported acquittal, Buñuel's conclusion is less bleak than Mirbeau's, evoking as it does the survival of the moral impulse.

In Jean Renoir's version, premiered in 1946, the moral heroism of Célestine is never in doubt. While Buñuel thrust doomed innocents into the den of bourgeois iniquity in films like The Diary of a Chambermaid and Viridiana, Renoir in the forties was focusing on how individuals defined themselves against, even outside the social order. Renoir's Célestine is an observer of corruption, not Mirbeau's participant. The fatal attraction of evil is replaced by moral repugnance. The Lanlaires' household is a trap - a 'tyranny of the enclosed', as one critic has it. The cathartic moment, when Célestine's sweetheart smashes a window to let symbolic light in, is matched by the mob celebrating Bastille Day, who settle accounts with Joseph. News of the liberation of Paris was coming in during filming and this might explain the optimistic interpretation Renoir makes of Mirbeau's much darker vision.

Mirbeau has been unjustly neglected. In France, his letters, plays and newspaper articles are now being reprinted. There are the beginnings of a reappraisal of his literary achievements and his influence on the shaping of modern French politics. It is intriguing to discover that he was hailed at the time as France's 'greatest secular writer' by no less a figure than Leo Tolstoy. Laurent Tailharde, an anarchist poet, memorialised his old friend's writing as 'chaotic, smouldering, fiery, maledictory, nothing less than an appeal for justice, a long cry for pity, gentleness and love'.

Like Shelley, whose radicalism is likewise underplayed today, Mirbeau was an impassioned artist, seeking to change the world through his writing. He used powerful exaggerations to illustrate the grotesqueries of Western civilisation, which was based, in his view, on an inversion of moral values. His purpose in laying bare the sick organism of French society was not to titillate, but to evoke in the reader a sense of outrage, a necessary impetus for change.

Richard Ings

FOREWORD

This book, which I have called *The Diary of a Chambermaid*, was in fact written by a chambermaid, a certain Mademoiselle Célestine R . . . When I was asked to revise the manuscript, to correct and re-write parts of it, I at first refused, for it seemed to me that, just as it was, with all its ribaldry, the manuscript had an originality, a special flavour, that any 'touching up' by me would only render commonplace. But Mlle Célestine R . . . was a very pretty woman. She insisted, and, being only a man, eventually I gave in.

I admit that this was a mistake. By undertaking what she asked of me, that is to say by modifying here and there the tone of the book, I am very much afraid that I may have diluted its almost corrosive elegance, weakened its melancholy power, and above all, transformed the emotion and life of the original into mere literature.

I say this in order to meet in advance the objections that certain grave and learned—and of course high-minded—critics will certainly not fail to make.

O.M.

14 September.

14 SEPTEMBER

Today, 14 September, at three o'clock in the afternoon of a mild, grey, rainy day, I have started in a new place, the twelfth in two years. Of course that's not counting all the jobs I've had previously. That would be impossible. Oh, I don't mind telling you I've seen the inside of a few houses in my time, and faces, and nasty minds . . . And there's more to come. Judging from the really extraordinary, crazy way that I've knocked about so far, from houses to offices and offices to houses, from the Bois de Boulogne to the Bastille, from the Observatoire to Montmartre, from the Ternes to the Gobelins, without ever managing to settle down any-where, anyone might think employers were difficult to please these days . . . It's incredible.

This time everything was fixed up through the small ads in the *Figaro*, without my having set eyes on my future mistress. We wrote to each other, and that was all: a risky business, which often holds surprises in store for both parties. True, Madame's letters were well-written, but they revealed a touchy, over meticulous nature. All the explana-tions she asked for, all the whys and wherefores . . . I don't know whether she's really a miser, but she certainly doesn't spend much on notepaper . . . She buys it at the Louvre. Poor as I am, that wouldn't suit me. I use fine scented paper, pink or pale blue, that I have knocked up at various places I've been in. I have even got some with a countess's coronet on it—that ought to have made her sit up.

Anyway, here I am in Normandy, at Mesnil-Roy. The house, which is not far from the village, is called The Priory. And that's about all I know of my future home.

Now that I find myself, as a result of a sudden impulse, living here at the back of beyond, I cannot help feeling both anxiety and regret. What I've seen of it frightens me a bit, and I wonder what is going to become of me. Nothing good, you may be sure; and, as usual, plenty of worries. Worry, that's the one perquisite we can always count on. For every one of us who is successful, that is to say marries a decent chap or manages to get herself an old one, how many of us are destined to misfortune, to be swept away into the whirl-pool of misery? In any case, I had no choice; and this is better than nothing.

It isn't the first time I've taken a place in the country. Four years ago I had one, though not for long . . . and in quite exceptional circumstances. I can remember it as though it were yesterday. The details of what happened may be rather sordid, even horrible, but I am going to describe them. And here I may as well warn anybody who thinks of reading this diary that, in writing it, I don't intend to hold anything back, either as regards myself or other people. On the contrary, I mean to put into it all the frank-ness that is in my nature and, where necessary, all the brutality that exists in life. It is not my fault if, when one tears away the veils and shows them naked, people's souls give off such a pungent smell of decay.

This is what happened then:

I had been engaged at a registry office, by a kind of housekeeper, as chambermaid for a certain Monsieur Rabour who lived in Touraine. Having come to terms, it was agreed that I should take the train at a certain time on a certain day for a certain station; and this was done as arranged. Having given up my ticket at the barrier, outside the station I found a coachman of sorts, a man with a red, loutish face, who asked me if I was M. Rabour's new chambermaid.

'Yes, I am.'

'Have you got a trunk?'

'Yes, I have.'

'Then give me the ticket for it and wait for me here.'

He went on to the platform where the porters treated him with considerable respect, addressing him in a friendly way as 'Monsieur Louis'. He found my trunk amongst a pile of baggage and got one of the porters to put it into the dog-cart which was standing in the station yard.

'Aren't you going to get up then?'

I took my place beside him on the driving seat, and we set off. The coachman began looking at me out of the corner of his eye, and I did the same. I could see straight away that he was nothing but a country bumpkin, little better

10

than a peasant; a fellow without the slightest style, who had certainly never seen service in a decent establishment. This was a bore for I love fine liveries—there's nothing I find more exciting than a pair of well-shaped thighs in close-fitting, white breeches. But this Louis just didn't know what elegance means. He had no driving gloves, and was wearing a suit of grey-blue serge, much too big for him, with a flat patent leather cap decorated with gold braid. Really, they're all behind the times in this part of the world. To crown everything he had a scowling brutal expression, though maybe he was not such a bad chap at heart. I know the type. When there's a new maid they start by showing off, but later on things get fixed up between them—often a good deal better fixed than they intended.

For a long time neither of us said a word. He was pretending to be a real coachman, holding the reins high in the air and flourishing his whip. Oh, he was a scream! As for me, I just sat there in a dignified way looking at the countryside, though there was nothing very special about it—fields, trees, houses, like anywhere else. When we came to a hill, he pulled up the horse to a walk and, with a mocking smile, suddenly asked me: 'Well, I suppose you've brought a good supply of boots with you!'

'Naturally,' I replied, surprised by such a pointless question, and even more by the curious tone of his voice.

'Why should you want to know? It's rather a stupid question to ask, my man, isn't it?'

He nudged me lightly in the ribs and, running his eyes over me with a strange expression on his face, a mixture of acute irony and jovial obscenity that puzzled me, he said with a sneer: 'Get along with you! As if you didn't know what I was talking about, you blooming humbug, you!'

Then he clicked his tongue and the horse broke into a trot once more. I was intrigued. What could all this mean? Maybe nothing at all. I decided the fellow must be a bit of a booby, who just didn't know how to talk to a woman and thought this was a way of starting a conversation. However, I felt it best not to pursue the matter.

M. Rabour's property was a fine big place, with a pretty house, painted light green and surrounded by huge flower-beds, and a pinewood that scented the air with turpentine.

11

I adore the country—though the funny thing is, it always makes me sad and sends me to sleep. I was more or less dopey by the time I reached the hall, where I found the housekeeper waiting for me. It was the woman who had engaged me at the registry office in Paris, after God alone knows how many indiscreet enquiries as to my intimate habits and tastes, which ought to have been enough to put me on my guard. But it is no use. Though every time you have to put up with some fresh imposition, you never learn from it. I hadn't taken to the housekeeper when I first met her; here I felt an immediate dislike for her, for there was something about her that reminded me of an old bawd. She was a big woman, not tall, but with lots of puffy, yellowish fat. Her greying hair was done in plaits, and she had a huge, bulging bosom and soft, moist hands, transparent like gelatine. Her grey eyes had a spiteful expression, cold, deliberate and vicious, and she looked at you in a cruel, unemotional way, as though trying to strip you body and soul, that was enough to make you blush.

She took me into a small sitting-room, and almost immediately left me there, saying she would let Monsieur Rabour know that I had arrived, as he wanted to see me before I started work.

'The master hasn't seen you yet,' she added. 'It's true I engaged you, but unless the master takes to you . . .'

I inspected the room. It was kept extremely clean and tidy. Brasses, furniture, floors, doors, were all scrubbed, waxed, polished till they shone like glass. Nothing trashy, no heavy embroidered curtains and hangings like one sees in some Paris houses, but a general air of wealth and solid comfort, of the regular, tranquil, well-to-do life they lived in the country. Crikey! How unutterably boring such an existence must be!

Monsieur Rabour came into the room, such an odd creature I could scarcely help laughing. Just imagine a little old man dressed up to the nines, freshly shaven and with pink cheeks like a doll's, very upright, very much alive, very attractive even, and skipping about like a grasshopper. He bowed to me and, with the greatest politeness, asked: 'What is your name, my dear?'

'Célestine, sir.'

'Célestine?' he repeated. 'Célestine? Bless me! A pretty name and no mistake . . . But too long, my child, much too long. If you have no objection I shall call you Marie. That's also a very nice name, and shorter. Besides, I always call the maids who work here Marie. It's become a habit that I should hate to give up. I would rather find somebody else.'

They've all got this strange mania of never calling you by your own name. So I was not really surprised, having in my time been called after every saint in the calendar. He went on:

'You don't mind if I call you Marie? That's agreed?'

'Certainly, sir.'

'Pretty girl . . . and good character. Excellent, excellent.'

He said all this in a spritely, extremely respectful way, and without putting me out of countenance by staring at me as though he were trying to see through my blouse and skirt as men usually do. Indeed, he had scarcely been look-ing at me. Since the moment he came into the room his eyes had remained obstinately fixed on my boots.

'Have you any others?' he asked after a short silence during which it seemed to me that his eyes had become strangely brilliant.

'Other names, sir?'

'No, my dear, boots,' and he kept licking his lips with the tip of his pointed tongue in the way cats do.

I did not answer immediately. I was amazed by this reference to boots, which reminded me of what that rascally coachman had said to me. What was behind it? After M. Rabour had put the question again I managed to reply, but I was flustered and my voice sounded hoarse like it does when you have to confess to the priest that you have committed sins of the flesh.

'Yes, sir, I have some others.'

'Polished ones?'

'Yes, sir.'

'Properly polished?'

'Of course, sir.'

'Good, good. Have you a brown pair?'

'No, sir.'

'But you must have brown ones. I shall give you a pair.

'Thank you, sir.'

13

'Good, good. Not another word.'

I was frightened, for a troubled look had come into his eyes, which were bloodshot with excitement, and drops of sweat were running down his forehead. Thinking he was going to faint, I was on the point of calling for help, but the crisis passed over and after some minutes he managed to say in a quieter voice, though there were still traces of froth at the corners of his mouth:

'It was nothing . . . it's all over . . . You must understand, my dear . . . I am a bit of a crank. But at my age that's not extraordinary, is it? For one thing, you see, I don't think it's right for women to have to clean boots, especially not mine. I have a great respect for women, Marie, and I won't allow it. So *I* shall clean yours . . . your dear, sweet little boots. *I* shall look after them. Now, listen carefully. At night, before you go to bed, you will bring your boots to my room and put them on the little table beside my bed, and in the morning, when you come to draw the curtains, you will take them away again.'

And as I appeared utterly amazed, he added:

'Come now, that's not such a tremendous thing to ask, is it? After all, it's quite natural, and if you're very good . . .' He quickly took a couple of louis from his pocket and handed them to me.

'If you're really nice, really obedient, I shall often give you such little presents. The housekeeper will pay you your wages each month. But I shall often give you little presents, 'Marie . . . just between you and me. And what do I expect in return? Come now, it's nothing so extraordinary. Is it really so extraordinary, my God?'

He was getting worked up again, and all the time he was speaking his eyelids kept fluttering like leaves in a gale.

'Why don't you say anything Marie? Speak to me . . . Don't just stand there—walk about a little so that I can see your little boots moving, coming to life . . .' He suddenly knelt down, kissed my boots, stroked them feverishly with his finger-tips, and began to unlace them. Then, still kissing and caressing them, he said in a plaintive voice like a child about to burst into tears:

'Oh, Marie, Marie, your little boots. Let me take them at

14

once, at once. I want them now, straight away. Give me them!'

I felt completely powerless, stupified with amazement scarcely knowing whether I was really alive or simply dreaming. All I could see of Monsieur Rabour's eyes were two little white globes, streaked with red, and his whole mouth was covered with a kind of white froth. In the end he took my boots off to his bedroom, where he shut himself up for the next couple of hours.

'The master is very pleased with you,' said the housekeeper, as she showed me over the house. 'You must try to keep things that way. You'll find you have a good place here.'

Four days later, when I went to his room at the usual time to draw the curtains, I almost fainted with horror. Monsieur Rabour was dead. He was lying on his back in the middle of the bed, his body almost completely naked, and one could sense immediately the stiffness of a corpse. The bedclothes were scarcely disturbed. There was no sign of a struggle, not the slightest trace of a convulsive death agony, of clenched hands straining to fight off death. Except for the hideous colour of his face, the sinister purple of aubergines, you would have thought he was asleep. But a ghastly sight, worse even than his face, made me tremble with fear. Clenched between his teeth was one of my boots, so firmly gripped that, having tried in vain to prise it loose, I was obliged to cut away the leather with a razor.

Now I don't profess to be a saint. I have known plenty of men and experienced at first-hand all the crazy and filthy things they are capable of. But men like this! No, really, such types shouldn't be allowed to exist. What on earth makes them want to think up such horrible things, when it's so nice, so simple to make love properly like everyone else?

I feel pretty sure that nothing of this kind is going to happen to me here. They are obviously quite a different sort of people. Though whether they will turn out to be any better remains to be seen.

One thing does really worry me, however. Perhaps I should have chucked up this beastly job for good . . . taken

15

the plunge and swapped a skivvy's life for a tart's, like so many of the girls I have known; girls who have 'fewer advantages' than me, even if I do say it myself. Though I am not what you'd call pretty, I have got something better than that: an appeal, a style, that plenty of society women and plenty of tarts have often envied me. A bit on the tall side, perhaps, but slim and well-made, with lovely fair hair and fine, deep blue eyes, saucy and enticing, and a bold mouth—and on top of that a sort of originality, a turn of mind at once lively and languorous, that men like. I could have been a success. But, apart from the fact that through my own fault I have missed some stunning opportunities that probably won't occur again, I've always been afraid; afraid, because you never know how things are going to turn out. I've come across so much wretchedness amongst such women . . . listened to such heartbreaking confidences! All those tragic visits to the hospital, that no one can hope to escape for ever. And, in the end, the sheer hell of St Lazare. The very thought of it is enough to give you the shivers. Besides, who knows whether I should have had as much success as a tart as I've had as a chambermaid? We have a special kind of attraction for men, that does not depend merely upon ourselves, however pretty we may be. It's partly a question, I realize, of the surroundings we live in—of the background of luxury and depravity, of our mistresses and the desire that they arouse. When men fall for us, it is partly our mistresses, and even more their mystery, that they are in love with.

And there's another thing. In spite of the free and easy life I have led, I have always fortunately had a very sincere religious feeling, that has saved me from going too far, held me back from the brink of the abyss. Oh, if it weren't for religion, for being able to go and pray in church on those dreary evenings when you feel morally down and out, if it weren't for the Blessed Virgin and St Anthony of Padua and all the rest of them, life would certainly be a great deal more miserable, that's certain. Without them, the devil alone knows what would become of you, or how far you would let yourself go.

Besides, and this is more serious, I haven't the slightest defence against men. I should always be sacrificing myself to my own open-heartedness and their pleasure. I am altogether too pleasure-loving . . . Yes, I enjoy making love too much to be able to make a living from it. I can't help it, but I couldn't ask a man for money when he had just given me such happiness, opened the radiant gates of ecstasy for me. They only have to begin talking to me, the monsters, and directly I feel the warmth of their breath and the pricking of their beard on the back of my neck, it's no use. I just go as limp as a rag, and they can do what they like with me . . .

So, here I am, at The Priory . . . waiting for what? Heavens above, I haven't the slightest idea. The most sensible thing would be not to think about it, but just wait and see what turns up. That way, perhaps, things work out best in the long run. Provided that tomorrow, at one word from the mistress and pursued by the pitiless bad luck that never leaves me, I don't have to chuck up the job once again. That would be a pity. For some time now I've been getting pains in the back of my stomach, my whole body feels worn out. My digestion's upset, and I'm losing my memory, and I've been getting more and more nervy and irritable. Just now, looking at myself in the glass, my face seemed to have a really fagged-out look and my complexion —the high complexion I'm so proud of—was as white as a sheet. Can it be that I'm getting old already? I don't want that to happen. But in Paris it's so difficult to look after oneself properly. There's no time for anything. Life is too feverish, too hurried—one is always in contact with too many people, too many things, too much pleasure, too many surprises. Yet you have to keep going just the same. Here, everything is so peaceful . . . And the silence! The air you breathe ought to be healthy and do you good. Oh if only I could relax a little, even if it does mean being bored to tears.

But the fact is I don't feel at all sure of myself. True, the mistress is quite nice to me. She was good enough to compliment me on my appearance, and to congratulate herself on the references she had received; though I don't like to think what she'd say if she knew they were false, or at best, just an act of kindness. What surprised her most is that I am so

17

elegant. Of course, to begin with, they're nearly always pleasant to you, the bitches. The newer the better, as they say. But before long the atmosphere begins to change—and that's another story we also know. Besides, she has cold, hard eyes that I don't fancy at all . . . the eyes of a miser, and as suspicious as a policeman's. I don't like her lips, either: thin and dry and covered with a white film. Nor the sharp, cutting way she has of speaking, that makes even a friendly word sound almost insulting or humiliating. All the time she was cross-questioning me, enquiring about my aptitudes and my past life, she was watching me like an old custom's officer, with that calm, sly impertinence they all have.

'Sure enough,' I said to myself, 'she's another of these lockers-up. I bet she counts how many lumps of sugar and how many grapes are left and, before she goes to bed, marks all the bottles. Oh well, it's just the same for a change!'

Still, I must wait and see, and not allow myself to be too much influenced by first impressions. Among so many mouths that have spoken to me, so many eyes that have tried to peer into my soul, perhaps—who can tell?—I shall one day find a friendly mouth and compassionate eyes. Anyhow, it costs nothing to go on hoping.

As soon as I arrived, still dazed after travelling for four hours in a third-class railway carriage, and without anyone in the kitchen even thinking of offering me a slice of bread and butter, Madame took me all over the house, from the cellars to the attics, to show me 'what was expected of me.' She certainly doesn't mean to waste either her time or mine. Oh, what a huge house it is, and every nook and cranny stuffed with furniture. To look after it properly would need at least four servants. In addition to the very large ground floor, which is extended on either side of the terrace by two little pavilions, there are two more storeys, so that I shall be continually running up and downstairs. Madame, who has a small sitting-room near the dining-room, has had the brilliant idea of putting the linen-room, where I shall be working, right under the rafters, next to our bedrooms. And then all the cupboards and wardrobes and drawers and storerooms, packed with every kind of junk—you can have

18

the lot as far as I'm concerned, for I shall never be able to find my way about.

Every few seconds Madame would point to something and say: 'You must take great care of that, my girl . . . That's very pretty, my girl . . . That's very rare, my girl . . . That cost a great deal, my girl.'

Of course she couldn't just use my name. Instead, she kept on with her everlasting 'my girl this . . . my girl that,' in that overbearing, hurtful tone of voice that is so disheartening, and sets such a distance, so much hatred, between us and our mistresses. After all, I don't call her 'my good woman.' And then this beastly habit she has of insisting that everything is 'very expensive.' It's infuriating. Everything that belongs to her, even the most miserable tuppenny-ha'penny things, is 'very expensive.' These women are so houseproud, you never know what they will find to boast about next . . . It's pitiful . . . After explaining to me how an oil lamp worked, just an ordinary lamp like any other, she insisted:

'You know, my girl, this lamp cost a great deal of money, and if it needs repairing it has to be sent to England. So treasure it like the apple of your eye.'

I should like to have replied: 'So what, old girl? How about your chamber-pot? Did that cost a great deal? Do you have to send that to London when it gets cracked?'

No, really, they've got a nerve, making such a fuss about nothing. And when I think that it's simply to humiliate and impress you!

After all, the house isn't all that grand . . . nothing to write home about, really. From the outside, standing amongst big clumps of trees and with the garden sloping gently down to the river and laid out in huge rectangular lawns, it does have a certain distinction. But inside . . . it's old and rickety and gloomy, and smells as though the windows were never opened. I can't understand how anybody can live in it. Nothing but poky little rooms, awkward wooden stairs that shake and creak when you tread on them and where you could easily break your neck, and long dark passages where, instead of fine, thick carpets, there are only badly-laid red tiles, polished again and again till they're as slippery as ice. The walls between the rooms are too thin, made of wood so dried out that the rooms echo like the inside of a violin.

Proper country style. And the furniture certainly isn't up to Paris standards. Room after room filled with old mahogany, old moth-eaten curtains, old worn-out, faded carpets, ridiculously uncomfortable armchairs and old worm-eaten sofas with no springs. How they must make your shoulders ache and take the skin off your backside! Just imagine, and me so fond of bright colours, and huge, springy divans where you can stretch out voluptuously on piles of cushions, and all the pretty furniture you can get nowadays, so luxurious and rich and gay. All this dreary gloom makes me feel melancholy. I'm afraid I shall never get used to such a lack of comfort and elegance, to all these crumbling antiques and old-fashioned designs . . .

The mistress doesn't exactly dress in Parisian style, either. She just doesn't know the meaning of *chic*, and has certainly never been near a decent dressmaker . . . A proper sight. Although she has certain pretensions about her clothes, she's at least ten years behind the fashion . . . and what a fashion! Mind you, she might not be so bad if she tried, at least not too bad. But what's really wrong with her is that she arouses no sympathy, there's nothing feminine about her. Yet she has regular features, pretty, naturally fair hair, and a good skin; though her colouring's a bit on the high side, as if she had some serious internal illness . . . I know her type only too well, and I'm never taken in by the brilliance of their complexion. Pink and white on the surface all right, but underneath it, rotten. They can't stand up to anything, and only keep going with girdles and medical bandages and pessaries, and every kind of secret horror and complicated mechanism. Of course, that doesn't prevent them putting on airs in public. Oh yes, if you please, very charming . . . flirting in corners, showing off their made-up skin, making eyes, waggling their bottoms, when all they're really fit for is to be preserved in spirits . . . A miserable lot. It's almost impossible to get on with them, I assure you, and there's no pleasure at all in working for them . . .

Whether by temperament or because of some organic indisposition, I should be very surprised if Madame was much good in bed. You can tell from the expression on her face, from her awkward gestures and the stiff movements of her body that she hasn't an idea about making love . . . and she certainly wouldn't know what it was to really let herself go. Her whole body has that sour, dried-up mummified quality that one finds in elderly virgins, though it's unusual in blondes . . . She certainly isn't the sort of woman you could imagine passing out at the sound of music, even music as beautiful as Faust, or fainting voluptuously into the arms of a good-looking man. Not on your life! She isn't, even, one of those very ugly women, whose faces are sometimes lit up by sexual passion with such radiant vitality and seductive beauty . . . Still, you can't always judge by appearances. Some of the grumpiest, most severe-looking women I've ever seen, women you would think were immune from the slightest feeling of love or desire, turned out to be regular trollops, prepared to go the whole hog with the footman or coachman.

Although Madame does her best to make herself agreeable, she certainly doesn't know how to set about it like some of those I've known. I should think she's a mean, grumbling sneak, with a nasty nature and a spiteful heart . . . the sort that would always be after you, plaguing the life out of you in every possible way . . . 'Can you do this? Can you do that?' Or, 'Do you break things? Are you careful? Have you got a good memory? Are you tidy in your habits?' On and on and on. And then 'Are you clean? I am very particular about cleanliness. There are some things I am prepared to overlook, but cleanliness I insist upon.' What does she take me for? A girl off the farm, or a country skivvy? Cleanliness indeed. I have heard that one before. They all say the same, but as often as not when you get down to brass tacks, when you lift up their skirts and have a look at their underclothes . . . why they are just filthy, enough to turn your stomach sometimes.

Anyway, I don't believe Madame is all that clean. When she showed me her dressing-room, I didn't see a bath or even a bidet, none of the things a woman needs if she's to look after herself properly. And certainly none of the knick-knacks and bottles and perfumed intimate things that I so much enjoy playing about with . . . I can scarcely wait to see her in her birthday suit . . . That'll be a sight for sore eyes. . .

That evening, as I was laying the table, the master came into the dining-room. He had just come in from shooting. He is very tall, with great broad shoulders, a huge black moustache and pale skin. Though his manners are rather heavy and awkward, he seems to be a decent sort. Obviously, he is no genius like M. Jules Lemaitre, whom I've waited on so often in Paris, nor a swell like M. de Janzé —Oh, he was a one! From his thick curled hair, his bull's neck, his athlete's calves and his full lips, very red and smiling, you can see he is strong and good-natured. I wouldn't mind betting he enjoys a bit of sex when he can get it! I could tell straight away, by his nose, with its sensual twitching nostrils, and by the brilliance of his eyes, gentle and gay at the same time. I don't think I've ever come across a human being with such eyebrows, so thick they're almost obscene . . . and such hairy hands. Like a lot of physically powerful but not very intelligent men, he's extremely shy.

He looked me over with a funny expression that was a mixture of kindliness, surprise and satisfaction, but which was also lascivious, though not impertinent; suggestive, though not brutal. It is obvious that he has not been used to maids like me . . . I have quite bowled him over already, made a deep impression on him. With some embarrassment he said: 'Oh . . . er . . . oh, so you're the new maid?'

Thrusting forward my bosom and lowering my eyes, and in my sweetest voice, at once saucy and modest, I answered simply: 'Yes, sir, I am.'

Then he stammered: 'So you managed to get here all right? That's good, very good.'

He would have liked to continue the conversation, but, being neither eloquent nor resourceful, could think of nothing to say. I was highly amused by his embarrassment. After a short silence he managed to bring out: 'So you come from Paris?'

'Yes, sir.'

'Good, good.'

Then, growing bolder: 'What's your name?'

'Célestine, sir.'

To hide his embarrassment he began rubbing his hands together, and then went on:

'Célestine? And very nice too, so long as my wife doesn't

insist upon changing it—it's one of her manias.'

To which I replied in a respectful and submissive tone: 'That is for Madame to decide, sir.'

'Yes, of course, of course. But it's such a pretty name.'

I almost burst out laughing. He began walking about the room, then, suddenly flinging himself into a chair and stretching out his legs, he looked at me as though to excuse himself and, in an almost pleading voice, asked: 'Well, Célestine—I shall always go on calling you Célestine— would you help me to pull off my boots? You wouldn't mind, would you?'

'Of course not, sir.'

'They are very awkward, you see . . . difficult to get off.'

With a movement that I did my best to make graceful and supple, even provoking, I knelt down in front of him, and while I was helping him pull off his boots, which were soaking wet and covered with mud, I was perfectly aware that he was delightedly smelling the back of my neck and that his eyes were following the outline of my bust and as much of me as he could see through my dress with growing interest. Suddenly he muttered:

'Bless me, Célestine, but you smell jolly nice.'

Without looking up, I said as artlessly as I could: 'What, me, sir?'

'Why, of course you. Damn it all, it's certainly not my feet!'

'Oh sir.' And I managed to put into this 'oh sir' at once a protest on behalf of his feet, and a kind of friendly rebuke for his familiarity—friendly to the point of encouragement. I think he understood, for once again, in a voice that trembled slightly, he repeated:

'Yes, Célestine, you smell jolly good, jolly good.'

Oh, so the big fellow was coming on a bit. I pretended to be slightly shocked by his insistence, and remained silent. Timid as he is, and knowing nothing of feminine wiles, he was upset, afraid lest he had gone too far, and hurriedly changed the subject, he said: 'I hope you're settling down here, Célestine?'

What an idea—'settling down' indeed, when I've scarcely been in the place a couple of hours. I had to bite my lip to stop laughing. The old boy's got some funny ways . . . really he's a bit stupid. But that's nothing to worry about. I don't dislike him. Even his vulgarity has a kind of strength, and there's a masculine smell about him, warm and penetrating like the scent of a wild animal, that I find rather attractive.

When we had finished taking off his boots, in order to leave him with a good impression of me I asked him in my turn: 'So you are fond of shooting, sir? Did you have a good day's sport?'

'I never have any sport, Célestine,' he replied, shaking his head. 'I only carry a gun as an excuse for walking—anything to get out of this house, where I'm bored to death.'

'So you find it boring, sir.'

Then, after a pause, he gallantly corrected himself:

'That is to say, I *used* to be bored, but now . . . at last . . . well . . .'

And with a stupidly touching smile, he continued:

'Célestine! Do you mind fetching me my slippers? I'm sorry, but . . .'

'That's what I'm here for, sir.'

'Yes, I suppose it is. You'll find them under the staircase, in the little closet on the left.'

By now I felt that he was ready to eat out of my hand. He's not one of the cunning ones, but the kind that surrendered at the first blow. You could do what you like with him . . .

Dinner, which was far from being luxurious and consisted of left-overs from the day before, passed without incident, almost in silence. The master ate ravenously, while Madame picked at her food sulkily, with a contemptuous expression on her face. But you should see the number of tablets, syrups, drops and pills that she gets through, a regular chemist's shop, that has to be laid out beside her plate at every meal! They scarcely spoke and, when they did, only about local affairs, which were of very little interest to me. One thing I gathered was that they do very little entertaining. It was obvious that they were not at all interested in what they were saying: they both had their minds fixed on me, and both of them were observing me, though with very different ends in view. The mistress, severe and stiff, contemptuous even, was more and more hostile and already thinking up all the dirty tricks she could play on me; the master never raised his eyes from his plate, but nevertheless they kept flickering in a very significant way, and every now and then, though he tried to conceal it, came to rest on my hands . . . I have never been able to understand what it is that men seem to find so exciting about my hands . . . I pretended not to notice what was going on, coming and going, dignified, reserved, attentive and remote . . . Oh, if only they could have seen into my mind and heard what it was saying, as I saw and heard what was going on in theirs.

I simply love waiting at table. That is where your employers give themselves away, revealing all the beastliness, all the squalor of their inner natures. Careful at first, and keeping an eye on each other, gradually they begin to expose themselves for what they are, without any pretence. They forget all about the servants lurking in the background, noting down every moral blemish, every iniquity, every secret scar, all the infamous and ignoble dreams concealed in the minds of respectable people. Collecting these revelations, classifying and labelling them against the day of reckoning when they will become a terrible weapon in our hands, is one of the great pleasures of our job, a precious revenge for all the humiliations we endure.

From this first contact with my new employers I was not able to gather any very distinct and positive impressions. But I did feel that things were not going well between them, that the mistress was boss, while the master counted for nothing, and was as scared of her as a child. Oh, it can't be much fun for the poor man. He certainly has plenty to put up with from her . . . I fancy I shall have a good time here now and then.

During dessert Madame, who throughout the meal had been continually sniffing at my hands and arms, said in a clear, peremptory voice: 'I do not like people to wear scent.'

And when I made no reply, pretending not to realize that she was speaking to me, she added: 'You understand, Célestine?'

'Yes, ma'am.'

I glanced stealthily at the poor master, who takes such pleasure in perfume, at least in mine. Apparently paying no attention, but at heart humiliated and hurt, he was sitting with both elbows on the table, watching a wasp hovering above the fruit dish. And, in the deepening twilight, a mournful hush fell upon the room, and something inexpressibly sad, some unspeakable weight, seemed to have descended upon these two creatures, till I found myself wondering what purpose they really served by their presence here on earth.

'The lamp, Célestine!'

Madame's voice, shriller than ever in the shadowy silence, made me jump.

'Surely you can see it's getting dark. I shouldn't have to remind you. Don't let this happen again.'

As I was lighting the lamp, the one that could only be mended in England, I felt like calling out to the poor master: 'Just you wait a bit, my beauty. Don't be so upset. I'll see you have your fill of the forbidden perfumes you like so much. You shall breathe them in my hair, on my mouth, on my breast, on every part of my body. We'll soon show the old misery what it is to enjoy ourselves, I promise you.'

And to give material form to my silent promise, as I put the lamp on the table, I was careful to brush gently against his arm. Then I withdrew.

The servants' quarters here are hardly what you'd call cheerful. There are only two others besides myself; a cook who never stops grumbling, and a gardener-coachman who never says a word. The cook's name is Marianne, the coachman's Joseph; wretched peasants, the pair of them. She, fat, soft, flabby, sprawling, the fleshy folds of her neck showing above a filthy kerchief that you'd think she used for wiping her saucepans, with enormous shapeless breasts under a kind of blue cotton blouse bespattered with grease, and a skirt too short for her, revealing thick ankles and broad feet clad in grey woollen stockings; he, in his shirtsleeves, with a green baize apron and clogs, clean-shaven, dried-up and nervy, with a hideous grin on his lips that splits his face in two from ear to ear, with a twisted walk and the sly movements of a sacristan. Such are my two companions.

As there is no servants hall, we take our meals in the kitchen, on the same table where, during the day, the cook does all her dirty jobs—cutting up meat and vegetables, gutting fish, with her fat round fingers like black puddings. It's really the limit.

This first evening, the heat from the fire made the atmosphere of the room stifling, and there was a continual smell of stale grease, rancid sauces and everlasting frying. All the time we were eating, a foul stench came from the saucepan where the dog's food was cooking, which caught you in the throat and made you cough . . . enough to make you throw up . . . They show more concern for the criminals in their prisons, and the dogs in their kennels . . . The meal consisted of fat bacon and cabbage, followed by stinking cheese, with only rough cider to drink . . . nothing else. The plates were earthenware, and as most of the glaze had worn off they smelt of burnt fat; and, to crown it all, the forks were made of tin.

Having only just arrived, I did not want to complain. But I didn't want to eat, either. There's no point in making my stomach worse, thank you very much. 'Why aren't you eating anything?' asked the cook.

'Because I'm not hungry,' I replied in a dignified tone of voice.

Whereupon Marianne grunted: 'I suppose her ladyship would prefer truffles?'

Keeping my temper, still snooty and standoffish, I said: 'It might interest you to know that I have at least eaten truffles, which is more than some people can say.'

That shut her up. Meanwhile, the coachman went on stuffing his mouth with huge chunks of fat bacon and watching me furtively. I don't know why, but the way this man looked at me was embarrassing, and his silence worried me. Though he was no longer young, I was astonished by the suppleness of his movements, swaying his hips when he walked like the undulations of a snake. But it's time I described him in more detail. His rough, greying hair, low forehead and slanting eyes, his prominent cheekbones and broad, powerful jaw, and his long, fleshy, jutting chin, all combined to produce a curious effect that I find hard to define. Was he a scoundrel, or was he just a simpleton? I couldn't tell. Yet the strange thing was that in some way the man impressed me, though eventually this obsession wore off. I realized that it had been just another of the thousand

27

and one tricks of my excessively romantic imagination, which makes me see both things and people as all black or all white, and which was now doing its best to transform this wretched Joseph into someone superior to the stupid lout, the dull peasant that he really was.

Towards the end of the meal Joseph, still without saying a word, took a copy of *Free Speech* from his apron pocket, and started reading it attentively, while Marianne, mollified by the two full carafes of cider she had drunk, became more agreeable. Sprawled in her chair, with her sleeves rolled up to the elbow and her cap askew on her tousled hair, she asked me where I came from, where else I had been in service, whether they had been decent jobs, and whether I was anti-Jewish. For a time we chatted away almost like friends. When it was my turn I asked her to give me some details about the household. Were there often visitors? And, if so, what kind? Did the master run after the maids? Had the mistress got a lover?

But heavens above! You should just have seen their faces, for Joseph's reading had been interrupted by my questions. They were utterly and completely shocked . . . One simply has no idea how backward these country people are. They know nothing, see nothing, understand nothing, and the most natural thing in the world absolutely flabbergasts them . . . Yet, despite his loutish respectability and the virtuous airs the cook gives herself, nobody is going to convince me that they don't sleep together. For my part, I must say, I should have to be really hard up to put up with a type like him.

'It's easy to see you're from Paris,' the cook sourly reproached me.

To which Joseph, nodding his head, briefly added:

'Sure enough.'

Then he turned to his paper again, while Marianne got up heavily from her chair and took the saucepan off the fire. Our conversation had come to an end.

My thoughts turned to the last place I had been in, and to Monsieur Jean, the footman, so distinguished with his black side whiskers and white skin, as carefully tended as a woman's. Oh, he was so nice and gay, Monsieur Jean, so natty, so refined, reading bits from the *Fin de siècle* to us of an evening, or telling us naughty stories, or giving us the latest news from the master's correspondence . . . Things are going to be very different here. How on earth did I manage to land up in a place like this, among such awful people, and miles from everything I like? . . . I could almost cry.

I am writing this in my bedroom, a filthy little room under the rafters, exposed to every wind, freezing in winter and stifling in summer. The only furniture is a wretched iron bedstead and a miserable unpainted wardrobe with a door that doesn't shut and no room to put all my things; and all the light I've got is a smoking candle that drips into a copper candlestick. It's pitiful! If I want to go on keeping this diary, or to read the novels I brought with me, or to tell my fortune with the cards, I shall have to buy candles with my own money. For as to pinching any from Madame, nothing doing, as Monsieur Jean used to say. She keeps them locked up.

Tomorrow I must try to sort things out a bit. If I nail my little gilt crucifix over my bed, and put the coloured china statue of the Virgin on the mantelpiece, with all my little boxes and trinkets and the photographs of Monsieur Jean, maybe it will make this garret seem a bit more cheerful and homely.

Marianne's room is next to mine, with only a thin partition between us, so that one can hear everything that is going on. I thought Joseph, who sleeps in the stables, might perhaps be paying her a visit. But no. For ages I had to listen to Marianne moving about her room, coughing and spitting, dragging chairs about, turning everything upside down . . . And now she's snoring. They must make love in the daytime. Far away in the country a dog is barking. It's almost two o'clock in the morning, and my candle is almost burnt out. It's time I got into bed, but I feel I shan't be able to sleep. Oh, I feel as though this miserable dump is going to turn me into an old woman before my time! And that's the truth!

15 SEPTEMBER

So far I haven't mentioned the name of my employers. It's a quite ridiculous name: Lanlaire . . . Monsieur and Madame Lanlaire . . . Monsieur and Madame Head-in-air Lanlaire! The sort of name you can't help making silly jokes about. As for their Christian names, they're even more ridiculous. The master's called Isidore, and she's Euphrasie! Really, I ask you.

At the draper's, where I've just been to match some silk, the woman told me a good deal about the set-up at The Priory. It was pretty awful. Though, to be fair, I must admit I've never in my life come across such an ill-natured gossip. If shopkeepers who rely upon their custom can talk about my employers like this, what on earth will other people have to say? Crikey! But these country folk are terrible scandal-mongers!

Monsieur Lanlaire's father was a cloth manufacturer and banker, at Louviers. He arranged a fraudulent bankruptcy and ruined all the small investors in the neighbourhood, for which he was sentenced to ten years' imprisonment. But considering all the forgeries, confidence tricks, thefts and other crimes he'd committed, he got off very lightly. He was still in prison at Gaillon when he died. But it seems that somehow or other he had managed to keep back 450,000 francs that ought to have gone to his creditors . . . And Monsieur Lanlaire inherited the lot! So you see, being a rich man is as simple as that!

The mistress's father was even worse, although he never did time but departed this life respected by all decent people. His stock-in-trade was human beings. The draper's wife explained to me how, in the time of Napoleon III, conscription was not obligatory for everybody as it is today. The conscripts were chosen by lot. But the sons of wealthy parents, if they happened to be selected, could buy themselves out. They would get in touch, either with an agency or some individual, who on payment of a premium, varying from 1,000 to 2,000 francs according to the risk involved, would find some poor devil who was prepared to take their place in the army for seven years, and, if there happened to be a war, die for them. In short, it wasn't only in Africa that there was a slave trade, only here, in France, it was white men who were bought and sold instead of black. We had markets for men instead of for cattle, though for a more horrible kind of butchery. This did not altogether surprise me, for the same sort of thing is going on today. After all, what are our registry offices and public brothels, if not markets for the sale of human flesh?

According to the draper's wife it must have been a very lucrative business, and the mistress's father, who had cornered the trade throughout the whole Department, showed considerable talent for it; that is to say, most of the premium went into his own pocket. Ten years ago, when he died, he was the mayor of Mesnil-Roy, deputy-justice of the peace, county councillor, chairman of the board of directors at the factory, treasurer of the welfare department, decorated by the Government and, in addition to buying The Priory for next to nothing, he left 1,200,000 francs, half of which went to the mistress, for her only brother turned out to be a bad egg and no one knew what had become of him. I don't care what anybody says, but that money's dirty money—if money can ever be said to be anything else. As far as I'm concerned, it's perfectly simple: I've never seen any money that wasn't dirty or any rich people who weren't rotten.

Anyhow, between them the Lanlaires—isn't it disgusting? —ended up with more than a million francs. Yet they're always trying to find ways of economizing, even though they probably never spend more than a third of their income. Always bargaining, haggling over every bill, going back on their word, refusing to stand by any agreement that isn't in writing and properly signed, so that you have to keep your eye on them continually and, whatever happens, never give them the slightest chance of going to law. Another thing, they take advantage of people by not paying their bills, especially small shopkeepers who can't afford a lawyer's fees, and any other poor devil who can't stand up for himself. Naturally, they never give away a cent except occasionally to the church, for they're very religious. As for the poor, they could be dying of hunger on the very steps of The Priory, and they wouldn't as much as open the door to them.

31

'I really believe,' said the draper's wife, 'that if they could steal money from the poor they would do it with pleasure, without turning a hair.'

And, as a monstrous example of their meanness, she added: 'Look, all of us round here who earn our living the hard way, when we give bread for the poor we buy the very best, it's just common decency, a question of self-respect. But that lot, the dirty misers . . . what d'you think they give? Why, not even white bread, my dear young lady, but just the ordinary black stuff the peasants eat. Isn't it scandalous . . . as rich as they are? Only the other day, Madame Paumier, the cooper's wife, heard Madame Lanlaire say to the vicar, who was giving her a scolding for being so stingy, "But what's wrong, Father? It's quite good enough for people like them!" '

Still, you ought to be fair, even to your employers, and though there may be only one opinion as regards the mistress, no one seems to have any grudge against the master. They don't dislike him. Everyone agrees that he's not stuck-up, and would treat people generously and do a lot of good if he was allowed to. The trouble is, he isn't. In his own house the master counts for nothing—less even than the servants, badly treated as they are, less than the cat, which does just as it likes. For the sake of a little peace and quiet, he's gradually given up all his authority, all his masculine pride, and it's Madame who controls, rules, organizes, administers everything. She's in charge of the stables, the poultry, the garden, the cellar . . . and she's always got something to complain about. Nothing ever goes right for her, and she's forever making out that she's been robbed. And she's as sharp as a knife . . . you'd never believe it! No one can play any tricks on her, for she's up to them all. It's she who pays the bills, draws the dividends, collects the rent and does all the business. She's as smart as an old book-keeper, as unscrupulous as a bum bailiff, and as tight-fisted as a moneylender. It's unbelievable! Naturally, it's she who holds the purse strings, and she never lets go of them . . . except to put away some more money. She leaves the master without a penny to his name, so that he's lucky if he has enough to buy his tobacco with, poor devil! With all that money, he's as hard-up as the poorest beggar in the neighbourhood. Yet he never jibs, never . . . he obeys her like one of the servants. Oh, it's funny to see him sometimes, looking all worried like a well-trained dog. If Madame happens to be out, and some shopkeeper calls with his account, or some broken-down beggar, or a messenger expects a tip, you just ought to see him! It would really make you laugh. He feels in his pocket, scratches his head, blushes, starts apologizing and then with the most pitiful expression says: 'Look, I am afraid I haven't any change . . . nothing but 1000 franc notes. Do you happen to have change for 1000 francs? No? Then I'm afraid you'll have to call again.'

A thousand francs indeed . . . why, he never has as much as a five-franc piece! If he only wants to write a letter, he has to go to Madame for the notepaper, because she keeps it locked up in a drawer and only allows him a sheet at a time, and grumbles about that. 'Heavens, you do get through some notepaper. Whatever can you be writing about to need so much?'

The only thing people reproach him for, the one thing they simply cannot understand, is his shameful weakness, allowing such a shrew to lead him by the nose. For everybody knows about it, you see . . . even if she wasn't always shouting it from the housetops . . . Of course, they don't mean anything to one another any more. For one thing, Madame, who has something wrong with her inside and cannot have children, just won't hear of sleeping with him, and that almost drives him out of his mind. On this particular subject there's a good story going the rounds.

One day, at confession, Madame explained the situation to the priest, and asked him if it would be all right for them to 'cheat'.

'It depends what you mean by cheat, my child?' the priest answered.

'Well, I don't exactly know, Father,' she said, highly embarrassed. 'But it seems there are certain caresses . . .'

'Certain caresses? But my child, surely you know that such caresses are a mortal sin?'

'That's just why I'm asking the Church's permission, Father.'

'Yes, yes, that's all very well . . . But how often?'

'My husband is a very robust man, a healthy man, Father. Perhaps twice a week . . .'

'Twice a week? That's much too often . . . sheer debauchery. However robust a man may be, he doesn't need certain . . . certain caresses twice a week.'

Then after pondering the question for a moment or two, he added: 'All right then, I will authorize it twice a week . . . but on certain conditions. Firstly, that you yourself get no pleasure from it . . .'

'Oh, but I swear I shan't, Father!'

'Secondly, that you donate the sum of 200 francs every year to the Chapel of the Blessed Virgin.'

'Two hundred francs?' gasped Madame, 'just for that? Why, it's out of the question!'

And she has never bothered her confessor again.

The draper's wife, who told me this story, concluded by saying: 'How on earth can such a decent man as Monsieur Lanlaire be such a coward with his wife, when she refuses to give him, not only money, but even pleasure? If it was me, I'd soon bring her to her senses . . . and that's a fact!'

So what happens? When Monsieur Lanlaire, who is a vigorous man and as fond of a bit of stuff as the next, wants to stand himself a little treat in that line, or even just to give some poor creature a present, he is reduced to the most ridiculous expedients . . . every kind of wangling and fiddling. And, when Madame finds out, it results in the most terrible scenes, rows that often go on for months at a time. So the master wanders about the countryside like a madman, waving his arms in the air, grinding clods of earth under his heel and talking to himself, come wind, rain or snow. And then, when he gets home in the evening, he's more timid than ever . . . more scared, more obsequious, more utterly crushed.

The most curious, and also the saddest, part of this story is that, despite all the recriminations of the draper's wife, despite all the infamous revelations, all the shameful filth that is hawked about from mouth to mouth, from shop to shop and house to house, I feel that the people of the village envy the Lanlaires even more than they look down on them. Despite their criminal idleness and all the harm they do to society, despite everything that is crushed beneath the

34

weight of their monstrous wealth, it is precisely their money that gives them a halo of respectability, even of importance. People are prepared to bow down to them, to greet them more readily . . . and how complacently they speak of this wretched dump, where they live in such spiritual squalor, as The Castle. If a visitor were to ask what places of interest there were to see in the neighbourhood, I feel convinced that even the draper's wife, despite all her hatred of them, would reply: 'We have a fine church and a fine fountain, but best of all, we have the Lanlaires, the Lanlaires who are worth a million francs and live in a castle. They are atrocious people, but we are very proud of them.'

The worship of money is the lowest of all human emotions, but it is shared not only by the bourgeoisie but also by the great majority of us . . . little people, humble people, even those who are practically penniless. And I, with all my indignation, all my passion for destruction, I, too, am not free of it. I who am oppressed by wealth, who realize it to be the source of all my misery, all my vices and hatred, all the bitterest humiliations that I have to suffer, all my impossible dreams and all the endless torment of my existence, still, all the same, as soon as I find myself in the presence of a rich person, I cannot help looking up to him, as some exceptional and splendid being, a kind of marvellous divinity. And in spite of myself, stronger than either my will or my reason, I feel, rising from the very depths of my being, a sort of incense of admiration for this wealthy creature, who is all too often as stupid as he is pitiless. Isn't it crazy? And why . . . why?

When I had left this horrible woman and her curious shop (where in any case I hadn't been able to match my silk), I thought despairingly of everything she had told me about my employers. It was drizzling, and the sky was as foul as the soul of this scandalmonger. I slipped on the muddy pavement and, furious with her and with my employers, furious with myself, furious with this provincial sky, with the mud in which I felt that my heart as well as my feet were immersed, furious with the incurable sadness of this little town, I kept repeating to myself: 'Oh well, so this is where you have landed up! This is really the last straw! Hell!'

Yes, I had made a proper mess of things. But there was worse to come. Madame dresses herself and does her own hair. She locks herself into her dressing-room, and even I am scarcely allowed in. God knows what she does there for hours and hours. This evening, unable to stand it any longer, I peremptorily knocked at the door and the following conversation ensued between her ladyship and myself:

'Knock, knock.'

'Who's there?'

Oh, that shrill, yapping voice . . . I'd like to shove it down her throat with my fist.

'It's me, Madame.'

'What do you want?'

'I was going to do the dressing-room.'

'It's been done. Go away, and don't come back until I ring for you.'

Which means that I'm not even a chambermaid here . . . I don't know what I am, or what I'm supposed to do. Dressing and undressing them, and doing their hair is the only part of the job I enjoy. I love laying out their nightdresses and playing with the frills and ribbons, fiddling about with their underclothes, their hats and lace and furs; rubbing them down after a bath, helping them to dry, powdering them, pumice-stoning their feet, perfuming their breasts— in short, getting to know them from top to toe, seeing them in all their nakedness. Like that, they cease to be just your mistress, and become almost your friend or accomplice, often your slave. Inevitably, in all sorts of ways, you become the confidante of all their sorrows and vices, of their disappointments in love, of the most intimate secrets of their married life, of their illnesses . . . not to mention the fact that, if you are clever enough, you acquire a hold over them in a thousand little ways that they don't even suspect. And there's much more to it than that: it can be profitable as well as entertaining. That's my idea of a chambermaid's duties. You would never imagine how many of them are— how shall I put it?—how many of them are really crazily indecent in their private lives, even those who, in society, are regarded as being most circumspect and severe in their behaviour, most inaccessibly virtuous. But in their dressing-rooms, when they let their masks fall, even the most impressive facades reveal themselves as cracked and crumbling.

I remember one woman I used to work for who had the most curious habit. Every morning before putting on her chemise, and every evening after taking it off, she used to stand naked for a quarter of an hour at a time, minutely examining herself in front of the mirror. Then, thrusting out her bosom and stretching back her neck, she would throw her arms in the air to make as much as possible of her flabby drooping breasts, and say: 'Look Célestine, they're still quite firm, aren't they?'

It was difficult not to laugh especially as Madame's body was really the most pathetic sight. By the time she had taken off her corsets, brassière and girdle and stepped out of her chemise, you almost expected it to dissolve all over the carpet. Belly, rump, breasts were like deflated wineskins, sacks that had been emptied, leaving nothing but fat, flabby folds of skin; and her buttocks were as shapeless and pock-marked as an old sponge. And yet, from all this formless ruin one pathetic element of charm survived, the charm, now little more than a memory, of a woman who had once been beautiful, and whose whole life had been devoted to the pursuit of love. Thanks to the providential blindness to which most ageing creatures are subject, she refused to accept the inevitable eclipse of her beauty. In a last appeal to love, she relied more and more upon expensive remedies and all the refinements of coquetry . . . And love responded . . . But what kind of love? That was the tragedy!

Sometimes she would arrive home just before dinner, out of breath and thoroughly embarrassed.

'Quick, quick . . . I'm late . . . Help me to change.'

Where could she have been, with that face so drawn with fatigue and those dark rings under her eyes, and so exhausted that all she could do was to fall like a log on the sofa in her dressing-room? . . . And the state of her under-clothes! . . . Her chemise crumpled and dirty, her petticoat hurriedly fastened, her stays all unlaced, her suspenders un-done, and her stockings in corkscrews . . . In her uncurled, hurriedly pinned-up hair there were sometimes bits of fluff from a sheet or a feather from a pillow, and the thick make-up of her lips and cheeks smeared by kisses, so that the wrinkles in her face stood out like cruel wounds . . .

In an attempt to allay suspicion, she would moan: 'I don't know what came over me . . . But I fainted . . . suddenly, while I was at the dressmaker's . . . They had to undress me . . . I'm still feeling terrible.'

Often, out of pity for her, I pretended to be taken in by these stupid explanations.

One morning while I was attending her the bell rang, and, as the footman was out, I went to open the door. It was a young man, a shady-looking specimen, gloomy and vicious, half worker, half layabout . . . one of those doubtful characters one sometimes runs into at the dance halls, who get their living from murdering people or from love . . . He had a very pale face, with a thin black moustache and a red tie. His shoulders were hunched up in a jacket too big for him, and he had the classical swaggering walk of his kind. With an air of troubled surprise he began by inspecting the luxurious furnishing of the hall, the carpets, mirrors, pictures and hangings . . . Then he handed me a letter for the mistress and, in an oily, drawling voice that was nevertheless a command, said:

'And see I get an answer . . .'

Had he come to settle an account, or was he only a messenger? I ruled out the second hypothesis—if he was here on behalf of someone else he would scarcely have such an air of authority.

'I'll see if Madame is at home,' I replied cautiously, twisting the letter in my hands.

'She's at home all right,' he said. 'I happen to know . . . So none of your monkey tricks. It's urgent.'

As she read the letter Madame turned almost livid and, forgetting herself in her sudden terror, muttered, stammered:

'He's here in the house? . . . You left him alone in the hall? . . . How ever did he find out my address? . . .'

Then, quickly pulling herself together and speaking as casually as possible: 'It's nothing . . . I scarcely know him . . . He's just a poor fellow, a very deserving case . . . His mother is dying.'

She hurriedly opened her desk, and with a trembling hand took out a 100-franc note: 'Give him this . . . Quick, quick, poor fellow!'

'Swine!' I couldn't help muttering under my breath. 'Madame is very generous today . . . Some poor people are lucky.'

And I stressed the word 'some' as bitterly as I could.

'Get along with you, quick,' she ordered, scarcely able to stand still . . .

When I got back, Madame, who is not very tidy and often leaves her things lying about all over the room, had torn up the letter, and the last scraps of it were already burning in the fireplace. I never knew for certain just who this fellow was, and I did not see him again. But what I do know, for I saw it with my own eyes, is that that morning Madame didn't stand looking at herself naked in the glass, nor did she want to know whether I thought her miserable breasts were still firm. She spent the rest of the day at home, restless and nervous, and obviously very scared . . .

From that moment, whenever Madame came in late in the evening, I was always terrified lest she'd been murdered in some brothel. And when I sometimes used to mention my fears in the servants' hall, the butler, a cynical, very ugly old man, with a birthmark on his forehead, used to growl:

'Well, so what? Of course that's how she'll end up sooner or later. What do you expect? Instead of chasing off after pimps, why doesn't the old cow stay at home and fix things up with a man she can trust, someone she can count on?'

'With you maybe?' I sniggered.

To which, as everyone burst out laughing, the butler, puffing out his chest, replied: 'And why not? I'd fix her all right . . . provided she paid me properly.'

He was really priceless, that man . . .

With my last mistress but one it had been a very different story . . . Oh, how we used to laugh about her, sitting round the table after the evening meal was finished. Nowadays I can see how wrong this was, for Madame was not really at all a bad sort. She was kind, generous and very unhappy . . . And she was always giving me presents . . . Sometimes, I must admit, we were really too beastly about her, but it's always those who treat us best that suffer most for it.

This woman's husband, a kind of scientist and member of some Academy or other, used to neglect her terribly. Not that she was ugly; on the contrary, she was extremely pretty. Nor that he ran after other women; in this respect his behaviour was exemplary. But being no longer young, and presumably not very keen on lovemaking—maybe it didn't even interest him—he used to let month after month go by without thinking of sleeping with his wife. She was in despair. Night after night I used to help her get ready for him . . . Transparent nightdresses . . . simply wonderful perfumes . . . everything. She used to say to me: 'Perhaps this evening he might come, Célestine? Have you any idea what he's doing?'

'The master is in the library . . . working.'

And with the same despondent gesture she would sigh: 'The library . . . always in the library! Still, perhaps he *will* come all the same . . .'

I used to finish titivating her, and proud of this sensual loveliness for which I was partly responsible, would look at her admiringly:

'Well, if he doesn't, all I can say is he'll be making a big mistake. Why, just to look at you this evening, Madame, would be enough to make him forget all his worries!'

'Oh, be quiet, be quiet!' she shuddered.

And the next day it would be the same old thing all over again . . . nothing but tears and groans.

'Oh, Célestine, he never came after all. I was waiting for him all night. I don't think he'll ever come.'

I did my best to console her: 'Oh, I expect he was worn out with work. These scholars, you know what they are . . . their heads are so full of other things they never have time for love. Have you ever thought of trying him with pictures ma'am? I've heard you can get some lovely ones . . . even the coldest fish couldn't resist them!'

'No, no, what's the use?'

'Well, suppose you tried changing the menu for dinner, ma'am? If you were to order highly spiced dishes, for instance, lobsters and that sort of thing?'

'No, no,' she would say, shaking her head sadly. 'It's nothing to do with that. It's simply that he doesn't love me any longer.'

Then, shyly, looking at me not with hatred but imploringly, she would ask: 'Célestine, I want you to be

quite frank with me . . . Has the master ever tried to get
you in a corner? Has he ever kissed you? Has he ever . . .'

'What an idea! . . .'

'But tell me, Célestine, be honest with me.'

'Certainly not, ma'am,' I exclaimed. 'The master has no
time for such things! Besides, do you really think, ma'am,
that I would do anything to harm you?'

'But you *must* tell me,' she begged. 'You're so beautiful,
your eyes are so full of love, you must have such a lovely
body.'

Then she would make me feel her breasts, her arms, her
thighs, her legs, comparing every part of our two bodies so
completely shamelessly that, blushing with embarrassment,
I began to wonder whether this was not just a trick on her
part, whether behind the grief of a deserted woman she had
not been concealing a desire for me. And all the time she
kept on murmuring: 'Oh God, God, it's not as though I was
an old woman. I'm not ugly, I'm not fat, my flesh is still soft
and firm. Oh, if you only knew. I feel so much love. My
heart's full of love!'

Often she would burst into tears, and throwing herself
on to the sofa, her head buried in a cushion to stifle her
tears, would stammer: 'Oh, never love anyone, Célestine,
never love anyone. It will only bring you unhappiness.'

Once, when she was crying more pitifully than usual, I
said to her sharply: 'If I were in your place, ma'am, I'd go
and find myself a lover. Madame is too beautiful to be left
like this . . .'

My words seemed to terrify her:

'Be quiet, oh, will you be quiet!' she exclaimed.

I insisted: 'But all Madame's friends have lovers . . .'

'Will you be quiet. Don't speak to me of such things.'

'But if Madame feels so loving . . .' and with calm
impertinence I mentioned the name of a very elegant young
man who often visited her: 'Oh, he's a duck of a man! Why
you have only to look at him to see how skilful and con-
siderate he'd be with a woman!'

'No, be quiet. You don't know what you're saying.'

'As you wish, ma'am. I was only thinking of your good.'

And persisting in her dream, while the master still sat in

41

the library adding up figures and drawing circles, she would repeat: 'But maybe tonight he will come.'

Every morning, over breakfast in the servants' hall, this was the sole subject of conversation. They would ask me for the latest news, and the answer was always the same: 'Nothing doing!'

You can just imagine what an opportunity it was for all kinds of coarse jokes and obscene allusions. They even used to lay bets as to when the master would pay her a visit.

It was after one of these futile discussions with the mistress, in which I always seemed to be in the wrong, that I gave her notice. I did it in a disgusting way, throwing up in her face, her poor bewildered face, all the poor little stories, all the intimate misfortunes, all the confidences, through which she had exposed her heart to me, her charming, plaintive, babyish little heart, so hungry with desire. Yes, everything. It was like throwing mud at her. Worse than that, I accused her of the filthiest kinds of debauchery, of every sort of ignoble passion. I really behaved horribly.

I don't know how it is, but there are times when I suddenly feel within myself a kind of need, a mania, to behave outrageously . . . A perversity, that drives me to turn the simplest things into irreparable wrongs. I can't help it . . . even when I am aware that I am acting against my own interests, that I shall only do myself harm. On this occasion I went much further. A few days after leaving Madame's service, I bought a postcard, and so that everybody in the house would be able to read it I wrote the following charming message. Yes, I actually had the nerve to say: 'This is to inform you, Madame, that I am returning to you, carriage paid, all the so-called presents that you have given me. I am only a poor woman, but I have too much self-respect, too much regard for decency, to keep all the filthy rags that you got rid of by passing on to me instead of throwing them into the gutter, which is all they were fit for. You need not imagine that, just because I am penniless, I am prepared to wear your disgusting petticoats, all stained with yellow where you've pissed yourself. I have the honour to be, Yours faithfully . . .'

So that was that. But it was stupid, and all the more so because, as I've said already, Madame had always been generous to me. In fact, only the next day I was able to sell the clothes she had given me—which, of course, I had never had any intention of returning to her—for 400 francs to a second-hand clothes dealer.

What probably made me do this was that I was furious with myself for having left an unusually agreeable job, the kind that we aren't often lucky enough to find, in a house that was run on lavish lines and where we were treated like lords. But hang it all, there's not always time to be fair to our employers. And if the decent ones have to suffer for the bad ones, so much the worse for them.

But, after all this, what am I going to do here? Stuck in the country with an old cat like Madame Lanlaire, it's no good dreaming of another such windfall, nor hoping for anything as entertaining. Here, it's going to be nothing but boring housework—and sewing, which I simply can't stand. Oh, when I think of the places I have had, it makes my position here seem even more dreary, unbearably dreary. I've a good mind to clear out, to make my final bow to this country of savages.

Just now I passed Monsieur Lanlaire on the stairs. He was going shooting. He looked at me roguishly and once again wanted to know whether 'I was settling down all right.' It's definitely a mania with him.

I replied: 'It's too early to say sir.' And added, saucily: 'And what about you sir? Have you settled down?'

He burst out laughing. Really, he's a good sort and knows how to take a joke.

'You *must* settle down, Célestine. You simply must settle down.'

Feeling in the mood to take liberties, I answered again: 'I'll do my best sir . . . with your help sir!'

From the sparkle in his eye I think he was on the point of making a pretty cheeky retort. But at that moment Madame Lanlaire appeared at the top of the staircase, so we made off in different directions. Pity!

That evening, through the drawing-room door, I heard Madame saying to him in the tone of voice you would expect: 'I disapprove of any familiarity with my servants.'

Her servants, indeed! As if her servants weren't also his! Oh well, we shall see.

18 SEPTEMBER

This morning, being Sunday, I went to mass. I have already explained that without being particularly devout I nevertheless believe in religion. For I don't care what anybody says, religion is always religion. Maybe the rich can do without it, but for people like us it's an absolute necessity. I know there are some people who make use of it in funny ways, and that there are plenty of priests and holy sisters who do very little credit to it. But that's not the point. When you are unhappy—and in our job we have more than our share of unhappiness—there's nothing like it for helping you to forget your troubles . . . religion and love. Though of course love brings a different kind of consolation. Anyway, even in the most un-Christian houses, I never miss going to mass. For one thing it's an outing, a distraction, time won from the daily grind of housework. But the main thing is the friends you meet here, all the stories you hear, and the chance of meeting people . . . Oh, if only, when I used to come away from the chapel of the Assumptionists, I had chosen to listen to the very odd psalms that quite respectable old gentlemen used to whisper in my ear, perhaps I shouldn't be here now!

Today the weather has improved and the sun is shining, one of those misty suns that make walking a pleasure and help you to forget your troubles. I don't know why, but this blue and gold morning makes me feel almost light-hearted. It is about a mile to the church, and you get there by a pretty little pathway, with hedges on either side. In the spring there must be lots of flowers, wild cherry trees and hawthorn. I love hawthorn . . . it has such a lovely scent and it reminds me of the time when I was a little girl. Apart from this, the country round here is much the same as anywhere else . . . nothing particularly exciting. There's a broad valley, and further on, at the end of the valley, sloping hills. A river flows through the valley and the slopes are covered with woods, veiled in transparent golden mist, that hides the view too much, though, for my taste.

It's a funny thing, but I still remain faithful to the country-side in Brittany . . . it's in my blood. Nowhere else seems to me so beautiful, nowhere else makes such an appeal to my heart. Even here, in the midst of the richest, most prosperous country in Normandy, I'm homesick for the heathland and the splendid tragic sea of the place I was born in . . . Just to think of it spreads a cloud of melancholy over the cheerfulness of this lovely morning.

On the way I met lots of other women. Prayerbook in hand, they were on their way to mass: cooks, housemaids and farm girls, coarse, heavy women, slowly dawdling along like cattle. It was a scream to see them all dressed up in their Sunday best, looking just like parcels! They smell strongly of the countryside, and it was obvious they had never been in service in Paris. They looked at me with curiosity; a wary, though not unfriendly curiosity. You could see they were jealous of my hat, my clinging dress, my little beige jacket and my rolled umbrella in its sheath of green silk. They were astonished that I was dressed like a lady, and especially that I wore my clothes in such a smart, coquettish way. With gaping mouths and staring eyes they nudged each other, drawing attention to my extravagance and *chic*. But I just walked on, fluttering and elegant, boldly holding up my dress, which made a swishing noise as it rubbed against my petticoats, high enough to show off my small, pointed boots . . . After all, any girl likes to be admired.

As they passed me I could hear them whispering to each other:

'It's the new maid at The Priory.'

One of them, short, fat, red-faced and asthmatic, with legs spread out like those of a trestle to support her immense belly, approached me with a coarse, slimy smile of someone who likes her drink.

'So you're the new maid at The Priory? And your name is Célestine? And you arrived four days ago from Paris?'

She already knew as much about me as I did myself. But what most amused me about this pot-bellied creature, this perambulating wineskin, was her musketeer's hat, a huge black felt, whose plumes fluttered in the wind. She continued:

'My name's Rose, Ma'amselle Rose. I work for Monsieur Mauger next door to you, a retired captain. Perhaps you have seen him?'

'No, Mademoiselle.'

'I thought you might have caught sight of him over the hedge that divides our two properties . . . He's always working in the garden . . . He's still a fine figure of a man, you know.'

We slowed down, for Mademoiselle Rose was almost out of breath. She was whistling like a broken-winded horse, and at each breath her bosom rose and fell, rose and fell.

'It's my asthma, you know . . . Everybody has something wrong with them these days . . . It's something awful,' she went on jerkily, wheezing and spluttering.

'You must come and see me, my dear . . . If there's anything you need, advice or anything . . . don't hesitate. I'm fond of young people . . . We'll have a little glass of something and a nice chat . . . A lot of the girls in the neighbourhood come to see me . . .'

She stopped for a moment to get her breath, and then in a lower voice, speaking confidentially, she said:

'And look, Mademoiselle Célestine . . . If you like, it might be advisable to have your letters addressed to us, for I ought to warn you Madame Lanlaire reads other people's letters, whenever she can lay her hands on them. On one occasion she only just escaped being summonsed for it. So I repeat, don't you hesitate.'

I thanked her and we started walking again. Though she was rolling and pitching like an old ship in a high sea, Mademoiselle Rose seemed to be breathing more easily and she continued her stream of gossip:

'Of course, you'll find it a big change here. In the first place, my dear, they just can't keep a maid at The Priory . . . Regular as clockwork . . . When it's not Madame who gives them the sack, it's Monsieur who puts them in the family way. A terrible fellow, that Lanlaire . . . Pretty or ugly, young or old, it's all the same to him . . . and every time, a baby. Oh, that house is well-known . . . anyone will tell you the same. Not enough to eat, no free time and worked to death . . . And nothing but scolding and nagging . . . A hell of a place! But you can see at a glance . . . a nice, well brought-up girl like you certainly wasn't made to work for skinflints like them.'

Everything the draper's wife had told me was now repeated by Mademoiselle Rose, but with even more distressing variations. So overpowering was her need to talk that she forgot all about her illness: ill-nature proved to be stronger than asthma . . . Her disparagement of The Priory went on and on and on, mixed up with all sorts of intimate details about local affairs. Although I knew most of it already, Rose's stories were so gruesome, and her way of telling them so discouraging, that I felt my sadness returning, and I wondered whether it wouldn't be better to leave at once. What was the use of going on, if I knew myself to be defeated in advance?

Some of the other women had now joined us out of curiosity, crowding round and greeting each fresh revelation with an energetic 'Quite true . . . That's right enough,' while Rose, who had now her second wind, chattered away tirelessly.

'Now Monsieur Mauger, there's a really decent man for you . . . and nobody else to worry about, my dear. It's almost like being the mistress there. A retired army captain, you see . . . so what else would you expect? He hasn't the slightest idea of running a house. All he wants is someone to look after him and spoil him a bit . . . to have his clothes properly seen to . . . his little ways respected, and now and then one of his favourite dishes for supper. If he didn't have somebody to look after him that he could trust, he'd have everybody sponging on him . . . God knows there are plenty of thieves in this part of the world!'

From the intonation of her voice and the way she screwed up her eyes it was clear enough how matters stood in the captain's house.

'After all, could you expect anything else? A man living on his own, who still has his little ideas . . . There's plenty of work to be done all the same. We're going to get a young lad to give a hand.'

She's lucky, this Rose . . . I've often thought of working for an old man. It may be disgusting, but it's a nice quiet life and there's always the future to look forward to. That doesn't mean it wouldn't have its difficulties, with a captain who 'still has his little ideas' . . . They must be a funny sight, the two of them under the same eiderdown . . .

We had to walk right through the village . . . Not exactly exciting; nothing like the Boulevard Malesherbes. Dirty, winding narrow streets, houses that look as though they're about to fall down, dark houses with rotten old beams and high gables, with the upper storeys bulging like in the old days . . . And the people you see . . . ugly, so ugly! I didn't set eyes on a single decent-looking fellow . . . The local industry is making felt slippers, and most of the shoemakers, who hadn't been able to finish their quota for the factory during the week, were still at work. Behind the windows I could see their poor, sickly faces and bowed shoulders as they fixed the leather soles with their blackened hands. It all added to the mournful sadness of the place. You'd have thought you were in a prison.

And there, standing at her door, smiling and waving to us, was the draper's wife.

'So you're off to the eight o'clock mass? I went at seven. But you've plenty of time, won't you come in for a minute?'

Rose thanked her, but did not stop. And when we were out of earshot she warned me against the woman, a nasty creature who spoke ill of everybody . . . a regular plague! Then she started singing the praises of her master again, and the easy life she led there. I asked her:

'So the captain has no family then?'

'No family?' she exclaimed in a horrified voice. 'Why, you're certainly wrong there, my dear. Oh, there's a family all right, and no mistake! Crowds of nieces, penniless good-for-nothings and misery-mongers who used to swindle him and steal from him right and left. You should just have seen, it was really abominable. Oh, but it didn't take me long to sort that lot out! I wasn't going to have those pests cluttering up the house. If it hadn't been for me, my dear young woman, the captain would have been on the rocks by this time! Now, he's only too pleased with what I did.'

I pressed my point with an irony which however escaped her.

48

'Then I suppose, Mademoiselle Rose, he'll have put you in his will?'

'Naturally the captain will do as he pleases,' she replied cautiously. 'He's a free man, and certainly I'd be the last person to try to influence him. I wouldn't ask him for a thing —not even when he forgets to pay me my wages. I only stay with him because I'm devoted to him. But *he* understands how things are, *he* knows who loves him and looks after him without a thought for themselves, who makes a fuss of him . . . You mustn't think he's as stupid as some people round here would like to make out, especially Madame Lanlaire. Why the things she says about us! On the contrary, Mademoiselle, he's a very shrewd man with a will of his own. Yes, indeed!'

With this eloquent defence of the captain we had reached the church. Rose never left my side. She insisted upon sitting next to me, and began mumbling prayers, genuflecting and crossing herself. And what a church! With those huge beams supporting the roof, it's more like a barn than anything else. And the congregation coughing and spitting, banging into the pews, dragging chairs about, you'd think you were at the village inn. All you could see were faces brutalized by ignorance, and embittered mouths soured with hate. Nothing but wretched creatures who have only come there to pray for God's help against someone else. I found it impossible to collect my thoughts, and a horrible chill seemed to envelop me. Perhaps it was because there was no organ. It may sound an odd thing to say, but I just cannot pray without an organ. The sound of an organ thrills my whole being, does something to me like when you are in love. If only I could always listen to the sound of an organ, I really believe I'd never want to commit another sin. But here, instead of an organ, there was an old lady sitting in the choir, with blue spectacles and a wretched little black shawl over her shoulders, painfully picking out the notes on a wheezy, out of tune piano . . . And the continual noise of all these people, coughing and spitting, so that you could scarcely hear the intoning of the priests or the choirboys chanting the responses. And what a horrible smell . . . A mixture of manure, cowsheds, earth, dirty straw and wet leather . . . A funny kind of incense! Really, it's awful the way these country people are brought up.

It seemed as though the service would never end and I was beginning to get bored. What worried me most was finding myself among such commonplace, ugly people, who scarcely seemed to notice me. Nothing nice to look at, no well-dressed women to take my thoughts off things and cheer me up. I'd never realized so clearly just how much elegance really means to me. Instead of being stimulated, as they always were in Paris, all my senses protested. In an attempt to distract myself I carefully studied the movements of the priest. But no thank you! He was just a strapping great fellow, still quite young, with a coarse, brick-red face. With his tousled hair, great hungry jaw and greedy lips, and little obscene eyes with black circles under them, it didn't take me long to place him. He enjoyed his food all right . . . and in the confessional, fumbling at your petticoat and making dirty remarks! Noticing that I was watching him, Rose leaned over to me and said beneath her breath:

'It's the new curate . . . I can recommend him. There's no one like him for hearing confessions. The rector's certainly a very good man, but most people find him too strict . . . Whereas the new curate . . .'

She made a clucking noise with her tongue and returned to her prayers, her head bowed over the back of a chair. Well, he certainly wouldn't suit me, this new curate, with his dirty, brutal appearance. You would take him for a carter rather than a priest. What I need is a little delicacy, a little poetry, something other-worldly . . . and nice, white hands. I like men who are gentle and stylish, men like Monsieur Jean.

After the service, Rose invited me to go with her to the grocer's, explaining to me in a mysterious way that it was just as well to keep in with her, and that all the servants round about curried favour with her.

Another little dumpling—this is certainly the place for fat women—she had a freckled face and lustreless, tow-coloured hair, so thin that you could see half of her scalp through it, and done up in a ridiculous little bun on top of her head. At the slightest movement, her bosom seemed to flow beneath her brown cloth bodice like liquid in a bottle. She had red-rimmed, bloodshot eyes, and a mouth so ugly that every smile was a grimace . . . Rose introduced me:

'This is the new maid at The Priory, Madame Gouin. I brought her to see you . . .'

The grocer's wife scrutinized me closely, and I noticed that her gaze was fixed with embarrassing persistence on my belly. She said in a toneless voice:

'You must make yourself at home here, Mademoiselle. A fine-looking girl . . . A Parisian I wouldn't wonder?'

'That's right, Madame Gouin, I come from Paris.'

'Obviously, you can tell straight away. You don't have to look twice to see that. I like Parisian women, they know what life is. I myself was in service in Paris when I was young. I used to work for a midwife in rue Guénégaud, a Madame Tripier . . . I daresay you know her?'

'No . . .'

'Oh well, never mind. After all that was a long time ago. But come in, Mademoiselle Célestine.'

She ushered us ceremoniously into a room behind the shop, where four other servants were already seated round a table.

'I'm afraid you're in for trouble, my poor girl,' murmured the grocer's wife, offering me a seat. 'It's not just because they've stopped dealing with me, but I can assure you that The Priory is a hellish place . . . hellish. Isn't that true?' she said, turning to the others.

'It certainly is!' they replied unanimously, All with exactly the same gestures and the same expressions on their faces.

'Thank you very much, but I certainly don't want to serve people who haggle over every little thing . . . always screeching like so many polecats that you're robbing and cheating them. They can go where they like for all I care.'

'That's right,' echoed the chorus of servants, 'Let them go where they like.'

To which Madame Gouin, addressing herself particularly to Rose, added in a firm tone of voice: 'Well, no one can say I run after them, can they Mademoiselle Rose? We don't have to rely on them, thank God.'

Rose contented herself with shrugging her shoulders, in such a way as to convey all the concentrated spleen, rancour and scorn that she felt. And her huge musketeer's hat accentuated the strength of her feeling with a wild flourish of black feathers. Then after a silence she added: 'But let's say no more about them. Every time I mention them I get the gripes.'

In the midst of the laughter another of the girls, a swarthy, skinny little creature, rat-faced and with spots all over her forehead and running eyes, exclaimed:

'Sure enough, let's drop the subject.'

Whereupon, the stories and the gossip started again—all those unhappy mouths spewing out an uninterrupted flood of filth like so many drains. The room seemed to be infected by it. The impression was all the more disagreeable because the room where we were sitting was so dark that their faces appeared to be fantastically deformed. The only light came from a narrow window which opened on to a damp, muddy yard, a kind of well, between walls covered with leprous mosses. A stench of pickling brine, of fomenting vegetables and sour herrings hung about, impregnating our clothes. It was intolerable. Then each of these creatures, slumped on their chairs like bundles of dirty linen, insisted on raking up some new scandal or crime. I was cowardly enough to try to join in their laughter, to applaud their stories, but I experienced a sense of atrocious and unbearable disgust. I could feel the nausea rising in my throat, cloying my mouth. I wanted to get away but I could not move, and I stayed there like an idiot, slumped in my chair like them, making the same gestures, listening stupidly to their shrill voices, which affected me like the gurgling sound of dishwater emptying itself down the kitchen sink.

I realize that it is necessary for us to defend ourselves against our employers, And I am certainly not the last one to do so, I can assure you. But no . . . this was really going too far . . . these women were hateful to me. I detested them, telling myself that I had nothing in common with them. Education, contact with elegant people, being used to beautiful things, reading the novels of Paul Bourget, have saved me from utter depravity. This was something quite different from the witty and amusing cattiness that goes on amongst servants in Paris!

It was definitely Rose who had the greatest success. Eyes fluttering, lips moist with anticipation, she began yet another story:

'Why that's nothing compared with Madame Rodeau, the lawyer's wife . . . Oh, there are some nice goings-on there, I can tell you.'

'I thought as much,' said one of them. While another declared: 'Though she's for ever running round with the clergy, I've always thought she was a filthy pig.'

They were all turned towards Rose, their eyes bright with anticipation. She began:

'The day before yesterday Monsieur Rodeau went out for the day, to the country, according to him . . .'

In my honour, and to put me in the picture as regards Monsieur Rodeau, she said parenthetically:

'A shady character, this Monsieur Rodeau, a lawyer who is really scarcely Christian . . . Always up to some fishy business or other. That's why I made the captain withdraw some shares he was looking after for him . . . But it's not *him* I'm concerned with for the moment.'

Having concluded her parenthesis, and turning to the company at large, she continued:

'Well, so Monsieur Rodeau was away in the country . . . What he's always running off to the country for I'm sure I don't know. Anyhow, as soon as he'd gone, Madame Rodeau sent for the little clerk, young Justin, on the pretext of sweeping out her bedroom . . . And there she was with scarcely a stitch on, and a funny look in her eyes like a bitch on heat. She called him over to her and started kissing and caressing him, and then, pretending to be looking for fleas, she started undressing him. And you know what she did then? Why, she suddenly flung herself upon him, the ghoul, and took him by force. Yes, by force, my dears . . . If I was to tell you just how she took him . . .'

'Oh, go on, tell us,' the dark girl begged, her rat's nose twitching with excitement.

They were all anxious to hear but in a sudden excess of modesty, all Rose would say was: 'It's not fit to be repeated in front of young girls like you!'

Her answer was greeted by a chorus of disappointed exclamations, and she went on, in a voice alternating between indignation and concern:

'A kid of fifteen, if you'll believe it . . . As pretty as a picture . . . and innocent as a new-born babe! To do a thing

53

like that to a child, a woman must be vicious through and through! . . . It seems that when he got home he was trembling all over, and crying fit to break your heart. What d'you make of that?'

There was an explosion of indignation, an avalanche of foul language. Rose waited until calm had been restored, and continued: 'His mother came to ask me about it . . . you may well imagine I advised her to sue the lawyer and his wife.'

'And quite right too!'

'Well, the mother hummed and ha'd and couldn't make up her mind, but in the end decided not to . . . It's my belief that the priest, who goes to dinner every week at the Rodeaus, took a hand in things. Anyhow the poor woman was scared. If it had been me . . . of course I'm religious, but no priest would have stopped me. I'd have made them cough up all right, hundreds and thousands, 10,000 francs at least . . .'

'That's right, that's quite right.'

'Heavens, fancy missing an opportunity like that!'

And the brim of the musketeer's hat flapped like a tent in a storm.

The grocer's wife said nothing. She appeared embarrassed, doubtless because the lawyer was one of their customers. Neatly interrupting Rose's flood of abuse, she said:

'I was hoping Mademoiselle Célestine would drink a glass of *cassis* with us all. And you, Mademoiselle Rose?'

Her invitation calmed everybody's anger, and while she was taking from a cupboard a bottle and glasses, which Rose arranged on the table, their eyes lit up and they licked their lips greedily.

As we were leaving, the grocer's wife said to me with a friendly smile: 'You mustn't worry because your people don't shop here . . . You must come and see me again.'

I walked home with Rose, who continued to acquaint me with the doings of the neighbourhood. I should have thought her stock of infamies was exhausted, but not at all. She kept recalling or inventing new ones, each more dreadful than the last. Her capacity for calumny appeared to be endless, her tongue ran on and on without a pause. Neither man nor woman escaped. It's amazing how many people she managed to condemn in so short a time. She accompanied me as far as the gate of The Priory. Even then she couldn't make up her mind to leave me, but went on talking, overwhelming me with her friendship and devotion. My head was splitting after all I had had to listen to, and the sight of The Priory filled me with a sense of discouragement. Its great lawns without a single flower-bed, and that huge building looking like a barracks or a prison, where an eye seemed to be spying upon you behind every window.

The sun had become warmer, the mist had disappeared, and the distant countryside was more clearly visible. On the hills beyond the plain I could see little villages, lit up by the sun's golden light, and with gay red roofs; the river in the valley, yellow and green, shone here and there with a silvery gleam, and a few clouds formed delicate patterns in the sky. But I found no pleasure in looking at all this. I had only one desire, a longing, an obsession, to escape from this sun and valley and hills, to get away from the hideous voice of this huge woman who was torturing me and driving me crazy.

At last she seemed on the point of leaving me, and taking my hand with her fat fingers, which protruded from a pair of mittens, she shook it affectionately.\

'So you see, my dear,' she said, 'Madame Gouin is a very agreeable woman and very skilful. You must keep in touch with her.'

But still she lingered. Then, in a more mysterious voice, added: 'You'd never imagine the number of young women she has helped! Immediately they notice anything they go and consult her. You can trust her completely, I assure you. Out of sight out of mind . . . She's a very clever woman.'

Fixing me with shining eyes and with a curious tenacity, she repeated: 'Very clever and skilful and discreet! She's the providence of the whole neighbourhood. So, my dear, don't forget to come and see us when you can, and visit Madame Gouin regularly. You won't regret it. So good-bye for now!'

She had gone. I watched her with her rolling walk, passing the wall, passing the hedge and suddenly turning into a footpath where she finally disappeared.

I passed Joseph, the coachman-gardener, who was raking the gravel paths. I thought he was going to speak to me, but he only looked at me obliquely and with a curious expression that made me almost shudder.

'Nice weather this morning, Monsieur Joseph.'

Joseph muttered something under his breath. He was furious with me for walking on the path he had just raked. What an odd man, and what bad manners! Why does he never speak to me, or answer when I speak to him? When I got back to the house Madame was obviously annoyed. She greeted me unpleasantly and at once began nagging me:

'In future I must ask you not to stay out so long.'

I would like to have answered her back, as I was irritated and annoyed, but fortunately I managed to contain myself and only mumbled something under my breath.

'What's that you're saying?'

'I didn't speak.'

'A good thing for you . . . And another thing, I forbid you to go out with Monsieur Mauger's servant in future. She's not at all the sort of person you ought to know . . . Look, because of you, everything is behind-hand this morning.'

I said to myself: 'Oh shut up, I've had about as much of you as I can stand . . . I shall see who I like, and speak to whom I like. I won't have you laying down the law, you old cow.'

Just to hear her shrill voice, to encounter again those spiteful eyes and overbearing manner, was enough to efface immediately the impression of disgust that Rose and the grocer's wife had made upon me. They were right, and so was the draper's wife. They were all right. And I vowed to myself that I'd see Rose as often as I wished, that I'd go back to the grocer's and I'd make that filthy draper's wife my best friend . . . if only because Madame tried to forbid it. And I kept repeating to myself savagely: 'Cow, cow, cow!'

But I should have felt much more relieved if only I'd had the courage to shout this insult straight in her face . . .

In the afternoon, after lunch, Monsieur and Madame Lanlaire went out for a drive in the carriage. The dressing-room, the bedroom, Monsieur Lanlaire's study, every sideboard, drawer and cupboard, were locked. Just as I thought. Oh well, there's no chance of reading any of their letters, or of making up a nice little parcel for myself.

So I stayed in my room writing to my mother and Monsieur Jean and reading *The Family*. It's a nice book and well-written. Yet it's a funny thing, though I like listening to dirty stories, I don't enjoy reading them. The only books I enjoy are those that make me cry.

For dinner that evening there was stew . . . it struck me that the master and mistress were very distant with each other. The master ostentatiously read his paper, crumpling it and rolling his kind, gentle eyes. Even when he's in a temper his eyes remain kind and timid. Eventually, in an attempt to make conversation, but with his nose still buried in his paper, he exclaimed: 'Well I never, there's another woman been cut to pieces.'

Madame made no answer. Sitting very upright and stiff in her austere, black silk dress, her brow furrowed and a hard look in her eyes, she continued to day-dream . . . But what was it all about? Perhaps she was sulking because of me . . .

26 SEPTEMBER

For the last week I haven't been able to write up my diary at all . . . By evening I have been worn out and exhausted and my nerves all on edge. All I can think of is to get to bed and go to sleep. To sleep . . . if I could sleep for ever! What a hole this is, my God! It's almost impossible to convey the least idea of what it's like.

For one thing. I'm always having to run up and down these confounded stairs just to satisfy the mistress's whims. And before you've had time to sit down for a moment in the linen-room to get your breath back a bit, ting-a-ling-a-ling, and off you go again. Even when you're not well, the bell never stops. And when I'm like that I get pains in my back that almost double me up, and tear my insides till I could almost shriek. But, of course, that doesn't matter to her . . . Ting-a-ling-a-ling . . . no time to be unwell, no right to be in pain. Illness is a luxury that's reserved for our employers. As for us, we just have to keep going, and look snappy about it . . . keep going till we drop. Ting-a-ling-a-ling . . . And if you don't answer immediately the bell goes, scolding, bad temper, scenes . . .

'Wherever have you been? Can't you hear? Are you deaf? I've been ringing for you for the last half-hour. It's most aggravating.'

And, usually, all it boils down to is this. You hear the bell and jump up from your chair like a jack-in-a-box, and all she wants is a needle! You go and find one . . . and then, 'Fetch me some cotton.' You take her the cotton and then she wants a button . . . and when you've found that, all she can say is: 'What have you got there? That's not the kind I wanted. Really, you never understand a thing! It's a linen button I need, No. 4 . . . and hurry up about it!'

So off I go to look for a No. 4 linen button—cursing and swearing to myself. And after all this coming and going, up and downstairs, Madame changes her mind and decides she wants something else, or maybe nothing at all.

'All right, then, let me have the needle and button . . . I'm in a hurry.'

My back's breaking, my knees are as stiff as wood, I'm just about at the end of my tether. And then, of course, Madame is satisfied . . . that's all she wanted. And to think that there's a society for the protection of animals! In the evening, when she comes to the linen-room to see how I've been getting on, she starts raving:

'How's this? What on earth have you been doing with yourself all day? I don't pay you just to lounge about, you know!'

I answer rather shortly, revolted by her injustice: 'But you keep interrupting me all the time, ma'am.'

'Interrupting you? Me? . . . To begin with, I forbid you to answer back. I'm not interested in your observations, you understand? I know what I'm talking about . . .' And then slamming of doors and endless grumbling, on and on and on. You can hear her yapping all over the house, in the passages, in the kitchen, even in the garden . . . hour after hour.

The fact is, I just don't know what to make of her. Whatever can have got into her to make her so irritable all the time? If I were sure of being able to find another place, I'd just walk out on her like that. Not long ago, I was having a worse time than usual. The pain was so acute that I felt as though an animal was tearing at my insides with its teeth and claws. When I got up in the morning I had already fainted from loss of blood. I just don't know how I had the courage to keep on my feet and drag myself about. Now and then, going upstairs, I was obliged to stop and cling on to the banisters in an effort to get my breath again and not fall down. I was green in the face, and my hair was soaked with cold sweat. I could have howled, but I can put up with pain and I pride myself on never complaining in front of my employers. Madame came upon me when I really thought I was going to faint . . . everything was spinning round me, banisters, staircase, walls.

'What's the matter with you?' she said harshly.

'Nothing, Ma'am,' and I tried to pull myself together.

'If there's nothing the matter with you, then why are you behaving like this? I can't bear having people around me, carrying on as though they were at a funeral. You have the most disagreeable expression when you're working.'

In spite of the pain, I could have smacked her face . . .

Amidst all these trials, I can't help thinking of other places I've been in. Today, the one I most regret is Lincoln Street. I was second housemaid there, and had practically nothing to do. Most of the day we used to spend in the linen-room, a magnificent linen-room, with a red felt carpet and big mahogany cupboards from floor to ceiling, with brass locks. We used to spend most of our time there, laughing and talking nonsense, reading, or taking off Madame's parties, looked after by an English housekeeper, who used to make tea for us with the special breakfast tea that Madame bought in England. Sometimes the butler—he knew his way around all right—used to bring us up all sorts of delicacies from his pantry, cakes, caviare on toast, slices of ham.

One afternoon, I remember, they'd made me put on one of the master's very smart suits—Coco we used to call him amongst ourselves. Naturally we were playing all sorts of naughty games, and sometimes went a bit too far, I don't mind saying. I looked so funny dressed up as a man, and it made me laugh so much that I couldn't help myself, I wet myself in Coco's best trousers . . .

Oh, that was the sort of place to have!

I am beginning to know the master quite well. People are quite right when they say he is a decent, generous man, for if it weren't for that he'd be an absolute swine, an utter rogue. His desire, his passion for being charitable leads him to do things that aren't at all right. However praiseworthy *his* intentions may be, that's by no means the case with other people, and the results are often disastrous. It must be admitted, his kind-heartedness was the cause of a lot of dirty little tricks . . . like this one, for instance: Last Tuesday, a poor chap, a Monsieur Pantois, brought some wild rose bushes that the master had ordered—without telling Madame, of course. It was already getting dark. I had gone downstairs for some hot water to wash a few things through. Madame had gone into town and wasn't home yet. I was chatting with Marianne, the cook, when Monsieur Lanlaire, in one of his jovial, expansive, noisy moods, brought old Pantois into the kitchen and told us to give him some bread and cheese and cider, and he stayed there chatting with him. The old chap was so worn out, so thin and badly dressed that I was sorry for him. His trousers were in rags, his cap absolutely foul; and through the open neck of his shirt you could see the skin of his chest, wrinkled and cracked like old leather. He began to eat greedily.

'Well dad,' exclaimed the master, rubbing his hands. 'That feels a bit better, doesn't it?'

And the old man, his mouth full of food, thanked him: 'It's very good of you, Monsieur Lanlaire. Since four o'clock this morning, when I left home, I haven't tasted a bite of food . . . not a thing.'

'Eat up then, Monsieur Pantois, enjoy yourself!'

'It's very kind of you, Monsieur Lanlaire. You must excuse me . . .'

The old man was cutting himself huge slices of bread, which took him a long time to eat, for he had no teeth. When he had satisfied his hunger, Monsieur Lanlaire said: 'And what about the rose bushes, Monsieur Pantois? They're all right, are they?'

'Well, some are and some aren't. You might say they're a pretty mixed lot, Monsieur Lanlaire. You can't just pick and choose, you see. And besides, Monsieur Porcellet wouldn't let me take any from his wood, so it meant going a long way to find them, a very long way. Why, I had to go as far as the forest of Raillon, more than fifteen miles from here. That's the honest truth, Monsieur Lanlaire.'

While the old man was talking the master sat down beside him. Cheerfully, almost jokingly, he patted him on the back, and exclaimed:

'Fifteen miles! Get along with you, you old devil. You're still strong, still a young man.'

'Not as young as all that, Monsieur Lanlaire . . . not by a long chalk!'

'Go on with you,' Monsieur Lanlaire insisted. 'Strong as a horse, and always cheerful into the bargain . . . they don't make your kind any longer, Pantois. You're as tough as nails.'

The old man shook his bald head, which was the colour of old wood, and repeated: 'Not as young as all that . . . my legs are beginning to go, Monsieur Lanlaire, and I'm losing the strength in my arms. And my back, oh my damned back! I've lost all my strength. And then the wife being sick and always in bed . . . and the price of medicine being what it is! Life isn't easy, you know. Not at all easy. If only you didn't grow old . . . that's the worst part of it, you know, Monsieur Lanlaire. That's the worst of all.'

Monsieur Lanlaire smiled and, making a vague gesture, replied philosophically:

'Well, of course. But what d'you expect, old man? That's life. We can none of us expect to be as strong as we used to be. That's how things are.'

'Sure enough, and the only thing is to make the best of it.'

'There you are.'

'The end's the end, and that's that. That's the truth, isn't it Monsieur Lanlaire?'

And after a pause, he added in a melancholy tone of voice: 'We all have our worries, though, Monsieur Pantois.'

'True enough . . .'

They fell silent. Marianne was cutting up herbs. In the garden night was falling. The two huge sunflowers that you could see through the open door were losing their colour, drowned in shadow. And old Pantois was still eating. His glass was empty. Monsieur Lanlaire filled it, and suddenly descending from his metaphysical heights he asked,

'And what are they fetching this year, rose bushes?'

'The roses, Monsieur Lanlaire? Well, this year, taking them by and large, rose trees are worth about twenty-two francs a hundred. It's a bit dear, I know. But I can't make it any less, and that's God's truth!'

Like a generous man who feels himself to be above all questions of money, Monsieur Lanlaire interrupted the old fellow, who was on the point of entering into detailed explanations to justify himself.

'That's all right, Monsieur Pantois . . . I quite understand. Have I ever bargained with you? I tell you what, I'll give you twenty-five francs a hundred instead of twenty-two. How's that?'

'Oh you're too good, Monsieur Lanlaire.'

'No, no, I'm simply being fair. I'm all on the side of the labouring man, damn it all!'

And banging his fist on the table he went on: 'What did I say? Twenty-five francs? Hell, no. I'll pay you thirty francs . . . you understand, Monsieur Pantois, thirty francs?'

The old man raised his poor, astonished, grateful eyes towards Monsieur Lanlaire.

'I heard all right . . . It's a real pleasure to work for you, Monsieur Lanlaire. You know what work is . . .'

Monsieur Lanlaire cut short his thanks, and went on:

'And I'll pay you . . .now let's see . . . today's Tuesday. I'll pay you on Sunday. How does that suit you? I'll bring it over to you . . . it will be an excuse for a little shooting. Agreed?'

The light of gratitude shining in the old man's eyes died away. He was troubled and upset, and had stopped eating.

'Well, yes, but . . .' he said timidly. 'But if you could manage to settle up tonight? That'll help me a lot, Monsieur Lanlaire. And I'd be satisfied with twenty-two francs.'

'You're joking, Monsieur Pantois,' the master replied with superb assurance. 'Of course I'll pay you straight away, if that's what you want, good God. I was only thinking that it might be an excuse to come over and see you.'

He felt in his trouser pockets, patted his jacket and waist-coat and then, with an appearance of surprise, exclaimed: 'Well, there now! It looks as though I haven't got any change on me, nothing but confounded 1,000-franc notes.' And, with a forced and really sinister laugh, he asked: 'I wouldn't mind betting you haven't got change for 1,000 francs, Monsieur Pantois?'

Seeing that Monsieur Lanlaire was laughing, old Pantois thought it was only proper for him to do the same, and he replied gaily:

'Ha, ha, ha! Why I've never so much as seen one of those confounded notes.'

'Right then, I'll see you on Sunday!' Monsieur Lanlaire concluded. He poured himself out some cider, and was clinking glasses with Monsieur Pantois, when Madame, whom no one had heard approaching, entered the kitchen like a gust of wind. Oh, you should have seen her face when she caught sight of the master, seated beside the poor old man and drinking with him!

'What's the meaning of this?' she said, her lips white with anger.

Monsieur Lanlaire could only stammer and stutter: 'It's the rose trees . . . You know, my love . . . Monsieur Pantois has brought me some rose trees. All of ours were taken by the frost . . .'

'I didn't order any rose trees. We don't need rose trees here,' she said in a cutting tone of voice.

And that was all. Then she turned on her heel and went out, slamming the door. In her anger she had not even noticed me. The master and the poor old man, who had both risen to their feet, remained awkwardly staring at the door through which Madame had just disappeared. Then they looked at each other, still not daring to say a word. Monsieur Lanlaire was the first to break this painful silence.

'Right, then, till Sunday, Monsieur Pantois.'

'Till Sunday, Monsieur Lanlaire.'

'And see you take care of yourself, Monsieur Pantois.'

'And you, Monsieur Lanlaire.'

'Thirty francs then . . . I shan't go back on my word . . .

'That's very kind of you, sir.'

And the old man, with his bowed back and trembling

legs, opened the door and was swallowed up in the darkness of the garden.

The poor master . . . I bet he was in for a good dressing-down. And as for old Pantois, if he ever gets those thirty francs, well, he'll be lucky.

I'm not saying that Madame was right, but I think it was wrong of the master to be on such familiar terms with some-one so much beneath him. That's not the way to behave.

I quite realize he doesn't have much of a life either, and has to make the best he can of it, which is not always so easy. If he gets home late from shooting, soaked through and covered with mud and whistling to keep his courage up, he can be sure the mistress will be waiting for him.

'This is a nice way to behave, leaving me alone all day like this . . .'

'But you know, darling . . .'

'Shut up.'

And she sulks at him for hours on end, hard-faced and with a nasty expression on her mouth, while he runs after her, trembling with fear and murmuring excuses: 'But darling, you know very well . . .'

'Leave me alone for heaven's sake! You'll drive me mad!'

So naturally, next day the master stays at home. But that doesn't suit her either.

'Why can't you find something to do, instead of roaming about the place like a lost soul?'

'But darling . . .'

'You'd be much better out of doors. Why don't you go shooting? You exasperate me. You get on my nerves. For goodness sake, be off with you!'

With the result that he never knows what to do, whether to go out shooting or stay at home. It's difficult for him, but as Madame does nothing but nag him whichever he does, he clears out as often as possible. That way, at least he doesn't have to listen to her shouting at him . . . Really, you can't help feeling sorry for him!

The other morning, as I was going to spread some wash-ing on the hedge, I saw him in the garden. He was actually gardening . . . during the night the wind had blown down some dahlias, and he was staking them.

Quite often, when he doesn't go shooting before lunch Monsieur Lanlaire does some gardening—at least he pretends to be doing something, messing about in the flower beds. It means he escapes for a bit from the boredom of being indoors, and there's no one to row at him. As soon as he gets away from Madame, he's another man, his whole face lights up and his eyes shine. His naturally gay nature gets the upper hand. Really he's not at all an unpleasant man. Though he scarcely talks to me any more indoors, and pretends not to notice me, outside he never fails to say a pleasant word or two . . . once he's made sure, of course, that Madame isn't spying on us. If he's afraid to speak, he just looks at me with eyes that are more eloquent than words. It amuses me to excite him in every sort of way, and, though I've not yet definitely made up my mind about him, to make a real appeal to his feelings. As I passed him in the alley, he was working, stooped over his dahlias, with his mouth full of raffia. I said to him without stopping: 'I see you're hard at work this morning, sir.'

'Yes,' he replied 'These damned dahlias, you see . . .' He was inviting me to stop for a minute.

'Well, Célestine, I hope that by this time you've begun to settle down!'

Always the same question, always the same difficulty in finding something to talk about. To please him, I replied with a smile:

'Oh yes, sir, I'm certainly beginning to.'

'Fine! That's not so bad . . . not bad at all.'

He stood up to his full height and looking at me very tenderly, repeated, 'Not bad at all,' thus giving himself time to think of something more interesting to say. He removed the raffia from his mouth, tied it around one of the canes and, standing with his legs apart and both hands on his hips, and with a frankly lascivious look in his eyes, exclaimed: 'I wouldn't mind betting you Célestine, that you used to get up to some nice tricks in Paris, what? Didn't you, now?'

This was quite unexpected, and I could scarcely help laughing. But I modestly dropped my eyes and, pretending to be annoyed and trying to blush in a seemly manner, I exclaimed with a reproachful air: 'Oh, sir!'

'What's wrong?' he insisted. 'A fine-looking girl like you . . . and with those eyes! You used to have some fun all right, don't tell me. Damn it, I'm all for people amusing themselves. I believe in love!'

He was getting strangely worked up. I recognized the signs of physical excitement. He was on fire . . . his eyes were blazing with desire. I thought it was about time to cool him off a bit, and, in a dry but at the same time very lofty tone of voice I said:

'You're mistaken, sir. You're not talking to your other chambermaids. You should realize that I'm a decent girl, sir.' And in a very dignified voice, just to show how much his behaviour had upset me, I added:

'It would serve you right, sir, if I were to complain to the mistress . . .' and I made as though to leave him.

He quickly caught hold of my arm and muttered: 'No, no.'

How I managed to get through all this without exploding, how I managed to stifle the laughter that was almost choking me I really don't know. Monsieur Lanlaire looked absolutely absurd. Livid, his mouth wide open, his whole appearance expressing simultaneously stupefaction and fear, he was reduced to silence and could only scratch the back of his neck.

Nearby there was an old pear tree, with twisted branches covered with lichen and moss, from which a few pears hung within reach. From the top of a chestnut tree a single magpie was chattering ironically. Crouched behind the box-wood border the cat was playing with a bumble bee. For Monsieur Lanlaire the silence was becoming more and more painful. At last, after the most strenuous efforts, efforts that caused him to pull the most grotesque faces, he asked:

'Do you like pears, Célestine?'

'Yes, sir.' But I did not lower my guard, and my reply expressed a haughty indifference. Afraid of being caught by his wife, he hesitated for a moment, then suddenly, like a boy stealing apples, picked a pear and handed it to me. Oh, it was pathetic! His legs were almost giving way under him, and his hand was trembling.

'Here, Célestine, hide that in your apron . . . She doesn't let you have these in the kitchen, does she?'

'No, sir.'

'Right, well I'll give you some more . . . some time . . . Because . . . because . . . I want you to be happy here.'

The sincerity and strength of his feeling, his awkwardness, his clumsy gestures, his frightened words, and also his male strength, all this touched me. I softened the expression of my voice, veiled the hardness of my eyes, and in a voice that was at once ironical and caressing, I said:

'Oh, sir! What if Madame were to see you?'

He was still agitated, but as we were separated from the house by a thick screen of chestnut trees he pulled himself together, and seeing that I had become less severe, he explained boastfully, making extravagant gestures with his hands.

'So what? . . . Madame indeed? What do I care about Madame? After all, she's no right to be always plaguing me . . . I've had just about enough of Madame, more than enough . . .'

Gravely I said: 'You shouldn't say such things, sir. You're not being fair. The mistress is a very kind woman.'

'Very kind?' he exclaimed. 'Her? Oh my God! But don't you realize she's spoilt my whole life? I'm not a man any more. I'm just nothing at all . . . no one around here gives a damn for me, and all because of my wife. She's a . . . she's a . . . yes, Célestine, she's a cow, a cow!'

I began to lecture him, speaking gently, hypocritically praising Madame's energy and orderliness, all her domestic virtues. But my praises of her only exasperated him more.

'No, no, she's a cow, a cow!'

However I managed to calm him down. Poor master! It was simply marvellous how easy it was to do anything I liked with him. With a mere glance I could transform his wrath into tenderness. Presently he stammered: 'Oh you're so kind . . . you're so nice! You must be such a good woman, whereas that cow . . .'

'Come, come, sir!'

He stopped short. Heartbroken, shamefaced, completely at a loss, he just didn't know what to do with his hands or eyes. He stood staring at the ground, at the old pear tree, at the garden, without seeing a thing. Utterly defeated, he began untying the raffia from the cane, stooped once more over the fallen dahlias, and in a suppliant, infinitely sad voice, murmured:

'Look, Célestine, what I said to you just now, I didn't really mean it. I meant to say something quite different. I meant to say . . . Oh it doesn't matter. I'm an old fool. Don't be angry with me, and above all, don't tell Madame about it . . . You're right. Fancy, if someone *had* seen us, here in the garden.'

I escaped as quickly as I could so as not to laugh. Yes, I wanted to laugh, and yet a quite different feeling was singing in my heart . . . something—how shall I put it?—a motherly feeling. True, I shouldn't like to sleep with Monsieur Lanlaire . . . but one more or less, what difference would it really make? I could give the poor old chap some of the pleasure he's deprived of, and I should enjoy it as well, for in love it's perhaps even better to give happiness to others than to receive it yourself. Even when our own bodies don't respond to their caresses, what a pure and delightful sensation it is to see some poor devil lying enraptured in our arms? Besides, what a joke it would be to spite Madame . . . I must think about it.

He went on: 'You're so sweet . . . and yet the funny thing is you're only a servant.'

He came closer to me and speaking to me very quietly: 'If only you would, Célestine.'

'Would what?'

'If only you'd . . . you know what I mean . . . Of course you do.'

'If you are suggesting that I should go behind the mistress's back and allow you to take liberties with me . . .'

He mistook the expression on my face . . . and, his eyes starting out of his head, the veins on his neck all swollen and his lips moist and foaming, exclaimed in a stifled voice:

'Curse it all! Yes, yes, that's just what I do mean.'

'You don't know what you're saying, sir.'

'I just can't stop thinking of it, Célestine.'

He was scarlet in the face.

'Oh, if you're going to start all that again . . .'

He tried to seize my hand, to draw me towards him . . .

'Yes,' he spluttered. 'Yes, I am. I can't help it . . . because . . . because . . . because I'm crazy about you,

Célestine. I can't think of anything else. I can't sleep. I feel . . . quite ill . . . And there's nothing to be frightened of. Don't be afraid of me. I'm not a brute. I . . . I won't give you a child . . . God no, that I swear! I . . . I . . . we . . .'

'Another word, sir, and this time I really will tell Madame . . . Why, what if someone were to see you now in this state in the garden?'

Monsieur Lanlaire did not go out all day. Having tied up his dahlias, he spent the entire afternoon in the woodshed, savagely chopping up wood for more than four hours. In the linen-room, however, hearing the metallic sound of the sledge ringing on the wedges, I experienced a sense of pride . . .

Yesterday Monsieur and Madame Lanlaire spent the whole afternoon at Louviers. The master had an appointment with his lawyer, Madame with her dressmaker . . . some dressmaker, indeed!

I took advantage of this brief respite to call on Rose, whom I had not seen again since that famous Sunday. Besides I certainly had no objection to meeting Captain Mauger.

He turned out to be a regular crackpot, such as you wouldn't see in a day's march. Imagine, a carp's head, with a moustache and a long, grey beard. Very dried up, very nervous and on edge, he can't stand still for five minutes at a time, and he's forever at work, either in the garden or in a small room where he does carpentry, singing military songs and imitating the sound of a bugle.

It's a pretty garden, old-fashioned and divided up into square beds, where he cultivates old-fashioned flowers, the kind that one only comes across nowadays in country gardens belonging to aged parsons.

When I arrived, Rose was comfortably installed in the shade of an acacia tree, sitting at a rustic table where she'd put her work-basket. She was darning socks, while the captain, wearing an old policeman's cap, knelt on the grass, mending the holes in a garden hose.

I was warmly welcomed, and Rose sent a little servant girl who was weeding a bed of asters to fetch a bottle of cherry brandy and glasses. After I had been introduced, the captain asked me:

'Well? So the Lanlaires haven't sacked you yet? You ought to be proud of yourself, working for such a remarkable scoundrel. You have my heartiest sympathy, my dear young lady.'

He went on to explain that once upon a time he and Monsieur Lanlaire had been good neighbours and inseparable friends. But a discussion about Rose had led to a deadly quarrel. Monsieur Lanlaire had reproached the captain for not keeping up his position, and allowing his servant to eat at the same table. Interrupting his account of the quarrel, the captain appealed to me:

'To eat with me, if you please! And what if I wanted her to sleep with me? Surely I've got the right to do as I please? Is it any business of his?'

'I should think not indeed, captain.'

In a tone of extreme modesty Rose sighed:

'A man living on his own . . . surely it's the most natural thing in the world?'

After this famous discussion, which had almost ended in blows, the two one-time friends spent their time playing tricks on each other and issuing summonses. They hated one another bitterly.

'For my part,' declared the captain, 'every stone I can find in the garden I throw over the hedge into Lanlaire's. If they happen to fall on his cloches and frames, I just can't help it, or rather, I'm delighted . . . the swine! Still you'll find out for yourself . . .'

Spotting a stone on the pathway, he rushed to pick it up, crept up to the hedge like a hunter stalking his prey and, with all his strength, hurled the stone into our garden. There was a noise of splintering glass. Triumphantly he returned to where we were sitting, and bursting and spluttering with laughter, hummed to himself:

'Every time we break a pane, Call the glazier in again . . .'

Gazing at him with a maternal expression, Rose said to me admiringly: 'Isn't he funny? And so young for his age . . . Just a boy!'

When we'd finished our glass of cherry brandy the captain wanted to show me round his garden. Rose

70

apologized for not coming with us, because of her asthma, and warned us not to be away too long. 'Besides,' she said jokingly, 'I shall be keeping an eye on you.'

The captain showed me his flower-beds, edged with box and filled with flowers. He told me the names of all the finest ones, remarking each time, 'You wouldn't find anything to compare with those in that pig Lanlaire's garden. Suddenly he picked a little orange-coloured flower, most unusual and charming, and turning the stalk gently in his fingers asked me: 'Have you ever tried eating these?'

I was so surprised by this ridiculous question that I couldn't answer. The captain insisted:

'I have. It tastes delicious. I've tried all the flowers you can see. Some are excellent, others not so good and some are no good at all . . . You see, I eat anything!'

He winked, clucked his tongue, patted his stomach and, in a challenging tone of voice, repeated more loudly: 'I just don't mind what I eat.'

The way in which the captain proclaimed this strange profession of faith made it clear that his greatest pride in life was to eat anything. I thought it would be amusing to flatter his vanity and replied:

'And you're quite right, captain.'

'Certainly,' he said, not without pride. 'And it's not only plants that I eat . . . It's animals as well . . . animals that no one else has eaten, that they haven't even heard of. I eat absolutely anything.'

We continued our walk amongst the flower-beds, down narrow alleys hung with clusters of flowers, blue, yellow, red. As he looked at them the captain seemed almost to shudder with delight. His tongue, passing over his cracked lips, made a moist little sound.

'I'm going to tell you something,' he continued. 'There's not an insect, not a bird, not even an earthworm that I haven't eaten. I've eaten polecats, snakes, rats, crickets, caterpillars. I eat anything. Why, I'm well-known for it round here. If anyone finds an animal, dead or alive, and they don't know what it is, they say: "Better take it to captain Mauger". So they do, and I eat it. In winter, especially when there's a hard frost, we get some very rare birds here. They come from America, or maybe further still. People bring them to me and I eat them. I bet there's not another man in the world who has eaten as many things as I have. I eat anything.'

Having seen all over the garden we went back to sit under the acacia tree. I was just getting ready to say good-bye when the captain suddenly cried:

'Wait, there's something I must show you, something very curious, that I'm sure you've never seen.' And in a stentorian voice he shouted: 'Kléber! Kléber!' explaining to me that this was his ferret, a phenomenal creature.

He called again, 'Kléber, Kléber!' And there on a branch right above us, showing between the green and golden leaves, was a little pink muzzle and two tiny black eyes, very alive and watchful.

'I knew he couldn't be far away. Come on, Kléber. Here!'

The ferret climbed along the branch, reached the trunk and cautiously descended, digging its claws into the bark. Its body, covered with white fur with tawny patches, moved with the subtle, graceful undulations of a snake. It reached the ground and, in a couple of bounds, was on the captain's knee, who began stroking it with a delighted expression.

'There's a good Kléber. There's my pretty little Kléber!'

He turned to me: 'Have you ever seen such a tame ferret? He follows me all over the garden, like a little dog. I've only got to call him and he comes at once, wagging his tail and his head in the air. He eats with us and sleeps with us— in fact I love the little creature as much as anybody in the world. D'you know, Mademoiselle Célestine, I have refused three hundred francs for him? But I wouldn't let him go for a thousand francs. No, not for two thousand. Here, Kléber.'

The animal raised its head and looked at its master, then climbed on to his shoulder and, with a charming little movement, curled itself round the captain's neck like a muffler. Rose said nothing, but she appeared to be on edge.

A monstrous idea suddenly entered my head. I said: 'I'll bet you, captain, you'd never eat your ferret.'

The captain looked at me, at first with deep astonishment, then with infinite sadness. His eyes grew quite round, and his lips began to tremble.

'What, Kléber?' he stammered. 'Eat Kléber?'

Obviously, though he was prepared to eat anything, this was something he had never thought of. It was as though a new world had suddenly opened before him.

'I'll bet you,' I repeated savagely, 'that you won't eat your ferret.'

Astonished and upset, shocked by some mysterious but invincible feeling, the old captain had got up from the bench where he had been sitting. He was seized by an extra-ordinary agitation.

'D'you mind repeating that?' he stammered.

For a third time, emphatically and pronouncing each word distinctly, I said: 'I bet you will not eat your ferret.'

'Not eat my ferret? What are you talking about? Are you saying that I won't eat it? Is that what you mean? Well, you're just going to see . . . I eat anything.'

He picked up the ferret, and, like breaking a roll of bread, he crushed the little creature's ribs, killing it before it could make the slightest movement. Then he threw it down on the path and shouted at Rose: 'There you are, you can make a stew of it for me this evening!' And he hurried away, gesticulating wildly, to shut himself up in the house.

For some minutes I stood there filled with unspeakable horror, utterly overcome by the revolting act I had just committed. I got up to go. I was very pale. Rose went with me and said, smiling:

'I don't mind at all what's just happened. He was getting too fond of that ferret, and I don't like him getting fond of things. Indeed, he thinks a great deal too much about his flowers already.'

After a short silence she added: 'But you know, he'll never forgive you for this. He's not the kind of man who likes to be challenged. An old soldier like him!'

Then, a few steps further on: 'You want to look out, my girl . . . they're already beginning to talk about you. It seems that somebody saw you the other day in the garden with Monsieur Lanlaire. It's very unwise of you, I assure you. He'll be sure to get you in the family way, if it hasn't happened already. So take care. With that man, re-member . . . one go, and hoopla, you've got a baby.'

Then, as she was shutting the gate behind me, she said:

73

'Oh well, so long! I suppose I had better go and make that stew for him . . .'

All the rest of that day I kept seeing the body of that poor little ferret lying in the dust on the path.

That evening at dinner, as I was serving the dessert, Madame said to me very severely:

'If you're fond of plums, you've only got to ask me and I'll see whether you can have some. But I won't have you helping yourself.'

I replied: 'I am not a thief, Madame, and I do not like plums.'

Madame insisted: 'I tell you, you've been taking them.'

I said: 'If you really believe I'm a thief, you have only to give me notice.'

She snatched the plate of plums out of my hands.

'The master had five this morning, and last night there were thirty-two. There are only twenty-five left, and that means you must have taken two of them. Just see that this doesn't happen again!'

It was true, I had eaten two. She must actually have counted them. No, really . . . in all my life . . .

28 SEPTEMBER

My mother is dead. I heard this morning in a letter from home. Though all I ever got from her was blows the news upset me, and I cried and cried . . . Seeing me in tears the mistress said: 'Come, come, what's all this about?'

And when I told her my mother had died, she went on, in her usual tone of voice:

'I'm sorry to hear it . . . but I'm afraid there's nothing I can do about it. Still, you mustn't let it interfere with your work . . .'

That was all . . . yes, really! She's not exactly overflowing with kindness . . .

What upsets me most of all is that I cannot help feeling there is some connection between my mother's death and the killing of the little ferret . . . that it is some kind of punishment from heaven. I keep thinking that if I hadn't made the captain kill poor Kléber, perhaps my mother would still be alive. In vain I tell myself that my mother must have been dead before the business with the ferret . . . It's no use, and the idea has haunted me all day.

I should like to have gone home . . . But Audierne is miles away, the end of the earth, and I just haven't got the fare. When I draw my first month's wages I shall have to pay the registry office their fee, and there won't be even enough to settle the little debts I had to run up when I was down and out.

Anyhow, what's the good of going? My brother's in the navy, in China I think, for it's ages since I last heard from him. And as for my sister Louise, where she's got to I'm sure I don't know. Ever since she left home, and went off to Concarneau with Jean the Duff, we never had another word from her. She must have been knocking about all over the place . . . God only knows! As likely as not she had ended up in a brothel. Or maybe *she's* dead as well . . . and my brother . . . so why go? There wouldn't be any point in it. I've got nobody there now. And my mother certainly won't have left me anything . . . her few clothes and bits and pieces of furniture won't even be enough to pay what she owes for drink.

It's funny, all the same . . . As long as she was still alive I scarcely ever thought of her . . . never wanted to see her again . . . The only times I ever wrote to her were if I changed my place, and then simply to give her my address. She used to beat me such a lot . . . and I was so miserable with her always drunk! Yet now, suddenly hearing she has died, my heart grieves for her, and I feel more alone in the world than ever.

I remember my childhood as clearly as anything. I can recall everything . . . all the things and people where I began my hard apprenticeship to life . . . Honestly, for some people there's too much unhappiness, and for others too little. There's no justice in the world.

I remember one night—though I must have been very little at the time—I remember us all being suddenly woken up by the lifeboat's siren. What a melancholy sound that used to be, in the middle of the night, with a storm raging! Since the previous day the wind had been blowing a gale, the harbour bar was all white with the crashing of waves, and only a few sloops had managed to get back to port. All the others must have been in terrible danger, poor devils! Knowing that my father was fishing in the shelter of the island of Sein, my mother had not been too worried, for she hoped he would have put into the harbour on the island, as he had often done before. Nevertheless, directly she heard the siren she got up, pale and trembling from head to foot, and hurriedly wrapping me in a huge woollen shawl set off for the pier. My sister Louise, who was already a big girl, and my brother, who was younger, followed her, and all three of them kept calling out: 'Oh blessed Virgin! Oh Jesus!'

The streets were full of people: women, old folk, kids. On the quay, where you could hear the noise of the boats grinding against the side, a crowd of frightened shadows were scurrying all over the place. But it was impossible to get on to the pier because of the high wind, and especially the waves that broke against its stone foundations and swept it from end to end with a roar like gunfire. My mother—'Oh blessed Virgin! Oh Jesus!'—took the footpath that runs along the estuary as far as the lighthouse. Everywhere was in pitch darkness, but now and then, in the distance, the sea was lit up by the flashes from the lighthouse, and you could see the huge white-capped waves rising and breaking. Despite their thundering crash and the deafening roar of the wind I fell asleep in my mother's arms. And when I woke up we were in a small room, where, through a forest of dark bodies and mournful faces and waving arms, I could see, lying on a camp bed and lit up by two candles, a corpse . . . a terrifying corpse, long and naked and stiff, the face crushed in, the limbs scored with bleeding gashes and covered with bruises. It was my father.

I can see him still. His hair was plastered to his skull, with strands of seaweed caught up in it, making a kind of crown. Leaning over him, men were rubbing his body with warm cloths and blowing into his mouth. The mayor was there, and the rector, a customs house officer and one of the harbour police. I was terrified and, struggling out of my shawl, I ran across the wet flagstones between the men's legs, wailing and calling for my father, for my mother. A neighbour took me away.

It was from that moment that my mother started drinking. To begin with she did her best to find work in the sardine factories, but, as she was always drunk, none of the owners would ever keep her on. So she stopped at home, steadily drinking, getting more and more miserable and quarrelsome, and when she had had her fill of brandy she would start beating us. God only knows how she didn't kill me! Whenever I could I escaped from the house, and spent my time playing about on the quay, plundering orchards or, when the tide was out, paddling in the pools. Sometimes I would take the road to Plogoff, and there, at the bottom of a grassy slope, sheltered from the sea wind and covered with thick bushes, I would be sure to find some of the lads from the village and, hidden amongst the hawthorn bushes, they would introduce me to their games . . . Often, when I got home in the evening, I would find my mother stretched out across the threshold, motionless, her mouth fouled with vomit and a broken bottle in her hand, so that I'd have to step over her body. And when she came to, it was terrible. She would be seized by a crazy passion for destruction, and without listening to my prayers and cries she would pull me out of bed and chase me round the room, trampling on me and banging me against the furniture, and shouting: 'I'll murder you, you little misery! I'll murder you!'

Many a time I thought I was going to die . . .

And then, to earn money for drink, she took to whoring. At night, every night, there would be a soft knock on the door, and a fisherman would come into the room, bringing with him the tang of the sea and a pungent odour of fish. He would get into bed with her, stay an hour, and then go away. And he would be followed by another, and the same business would be repeated. Sometimes they would start fighting, and the darkness would be filled with a terrifying clamour, so that often enough the neighbours would call the police.

Years passed like this. No one would have anything to do with us, me and my brother and sister. People would shun us in the street, and respectable folk would pelt us with stones to drive us away from their houses, whether we were on the look-out for something to steal or simply begging. One day my sister Louise, who by this time had also started going with the sailors, cleared out altogether. Then my brother got a job as cabin boy, and I was left alone with my mother.

By the time I was ten years old I was no longer chaste. My mother's example had initiated me into the meaning of sex; and, already perverted by all the games I'd been up to with boys, I had developed physically very early. Despite all the privations and beatings, the wonderful sea air had made me healthy and strong, and I had grown so fast that, by the time I was eleven, I had experienced the first shock of puberty. Though I still looked like a girl, I was almost a woman.

At twelve I was so completely, and no longer a virgin. Violated? Well, not exactly. Willingly? Yes, more or less . . . at least to the extent that the ingenuousness of my vice and the candour of my depravity permitted it . . . One Sunday, after high mass, the foreman at one of the sardine factories, an old man who stank like a billygoat and had filthy, shaggy hair all over his head and face, took me down to the shore by Saint-Jean. And there, beneath the cliffs, hidden in a dark cleft in the rocks where the seagulls used to make their nests and sometimes the sailors hid the flotsam they rescued from the sea, there, on a bed of stagnant seaweed, and without any attempt on my part to stop him, he seduced me . . . for an orange! He had a funny name: Cléophas Biscouille.

And here is something that I have never been able to understand, and have never found explained in any novel. Monsieur Biscouille was ugly, brutal and repulsive, moreover on the four or five occasions that he persuaded me to go with him to this black hole in the rocks, he never once gave me the slightest pleasure—on the contrary. Why is it then, that when I think of him—and I often do—I never feel like loathing or cursing him? I take pleasure in recalling him, and I experience an extraordinary sense of gratitude . . . a great tenderness . . . and, at the same time, a genuine regret, when I realize that never again, shall I see this disgusting creature, as he was then, beside me on that bed of seaweed . . .

While I am on this subject, despite my humble position,

perhaps I may be allowed to make a personal contribution to the life story of the great . . .

Monsieur Paul Bourget, the famous novelist, was the intimate friend and spiritual guide of Countess Fardin, where, last year, I was employed as housemaid. I was always hearing it said that he was the only man who really understood women's complex nature to its very depths, and many a time I had the idea of writing to him, in order to lay before him this particular example of passionate psychology . . . There is no reason for being too surprised at the seriousness of these preoccupations. They are not usual among servants, I agree. But, in the countess's drawing-room, everybody was for ever discussing psychology . . . It is generally accepted that our minds are influenced by those of our employers, and that what is said in the drawing-room will be repeated in the servants' hall. The only trouble was that, in the servants' hall there was no Paul Bourget capable of elucidating and resolving the feminine problems that we used to discuss there. Even the explanations of Monsieur Jean himself did not satisfy me.

One day, however, my mistress sent me with an urgent letter for the illustrious master, and he himself brought me the reply. This emboldened me to lay before him the problem that was tormenting me; though, of course, I attributed the scabrous story to one of my friends. Monsieur Bourget asked me. 'And what kind of a woman is your friend? A woman of the people? One of the poorer classes?'

'A maid like myself, sir.'

Monsieur Bourget assumed a most superior and disdainful expression. Heavens! He certainly doesn't like poor people!

'I'm not really concerned with such people,' he said . . . 'They are too small-minded, completely lacking in soul . . . They do not fall within the scope of my psychology.'

I realized at once that, in the circles in which he moved, no one with an income of less than 100,000 francs a year was expected to have a soul.

Monsieur Jules Lemaitre, on the other hand, another frequent visitor to the house, was quite different. When I put the same question to him, he replied with a friendly dig in the ribs: 'Well, Célestine my dear, all I can say is, your friend must be a nice girl, and if she's anything like as charming as you, I know precisely what I should say to her . . . Ha, ha!'

With his humorous expression, looking like a little hunch-backed faun, at least he didn't attempt to put on any airs. But there, he was really a decent sort. It's just too bad that now he's gone all religious!

With all this, I don't know what would have become of me in this hellish existence at Audierne, if the Little Sisters of Poncroix, finding me intelligent and pretty, had not taken charge of me out of pity. They made no attempt to take advantage of my youth and ignorance, nor of my difficult and shameful position, by shutting me away from the world so that I could look after them, as happens in so many convents of this kind, where human exploitation is carried to criminal lengths. They were poor, artless little creatures, timid and charitable; and, though they were certainly not rich, they were much too scared to beg in the street or to call upon the wealthy for subscriptions. Sometimes they were reduced to extreme poverty, but they just carried on as best they could, and amid all the hardships of their existence they always managed to keep cheerful, twittering away like so many little birds. There was something touching about their complete ignorance of life, which, today, when I understand their infinite goodness and purity better, moves me to tears.

They taught me to read and write, to sew and do house-work, and when I was more or less properly trained they found me a place with a retired colonel, who used to spend every summer with his wife and two daughters at a shabby little country house near Comfort. They were good people, I admit, but so sad! Oh, so sad! And crazy! Never a smile on their faces, nor a trace of gaiety in their clothes, which were always the most sombre black. The colonel had built himself a room under the rafters, and there he would stay all day by himself, turning boxwood eggcups on a lathe, or those 'darning eggs' that women use for mending their stockings. His wife was forever writing letters and petitions in the hope of getting a licence to sell stamps and tobacco, and the two daughters never seemed to do anything at all, hardly even speaking. One looked like a duck, and the other like a rabbit, and both of them were pale and thin, angular, like two wilting plants that were drying up under your eyes for lack of the sun and moisture and soil that they needed. Oh, how they bored me! . . . After sticking it for eight months, I just walked out on them one day, on a sudden impulse which I later regretted.

But all the same, this meant that now, for the first time, I was to know what it was to feel around me the seething life of Paris and the warmth of its breath, which filled my heart with new longings. Though I did not often go out, I was overwhelmed by admiration, and the streets, the shop windows, the crowds, the palaces, the dazzling carriages and elegantly dressed women entranced me. And, at night, when I climbed up to the sixth floor to go to bed, I used to envy the other servants in the house, enthralled by all the pranks they got up to and the marvellous tales I heard them telling each other. During the short time that I stayed in this job I was to see every kind of debauchery, as it was practised up there on the sixth floor . . . and, before long, I was playing my part in it, with all the competitive enthusiasm of a novice . . . Seduced by that deceptive ideal of vice and pleasure, what vague hopes I fed on, what dubious ambitions . . .

But there it is! When you're young, and know nothing of life, what else can you do but live on your imagination, on your dreams? . . . Dreams, indeed . . . stupidities! Oh, I drank my fill of them all right, as Monsieur Xavier used to say, a really perverted little rascal of whom I shall have more to say later on . . . And how I knocked about in those days—I was a regular rolling stone. It's frightening to think of it.

Though I'm still young, the things I have seen, and at close quarters, too. I have seen people stark naked, and smelt the odour of their linen, of their skins, of their very souls . . . And for all the scent they use, the smell is not at all a pleasant one, I assure you. What filthiness, what shameful vices and mean crimes disguised as virtue are hidden away by decent families in respectable homes. Oh, you don't have to tell me! It's no use their being rich, dolling

81

themselves up in silks and velvets, surrounding themselves with gilded furniture, using silver wash-bowls and generally showing off . . . I know them through and through. Beneath all the display their hearts are even more disgusting than my mother's bed used to be!

What a pathetic creature a poor servant-girl is, and how lonely! Even if she's one of a crowded, gay, noisy household, she is still always alone. Solitude is not just a question of living on your own, but of living in other people's houses, amongst people who have no interest in you, who regard you as being of less importance than the dogs they stuff with tit-bits, or the flowers they cherish like a rich man's child . . . People from whom all you get are useless, cast-off clothes and left-over food, already going bad. 'You can have this pear, it's rather over-ripe . . . Finish up that chicken in the kitchen, it's beginning to go off . . .'

With every word, they express contempt for you, their very gestures treat you like dirt: but you must never say a word—just smile and be thankful, or else you are considered to be ungrateful and ill-natured . . . Sometimes when I've been brushing my mistress's hair I've felt a mad desire to scratch her neck, savage her breasts with my nails.

Fortunately, you aren't always obsessed with such black thoughts . . . You must forget your worries and do your best to have as good a time as possible amongst yourselves.

This evening, after dinner, seeing me looking so sad, Marianne took pity on me and tried to console me. She went to the sideboard and fished out a bottle of brandy from a pile of old papers and dirty rags.

'You mustn't get so upset,' she said to me. 'Pull yourself together a bit, my poor girl, and try to cheer up.'

She poured me out a glass and, for the next hour, sitting with her elbows on the table and speaking in a drawling, mournful voice, she told me sinister stories of illnesses and lyings-in, describing in detail the death of her mother, her father and her sister. As time went on her voice grew thicker, and her eyes began to run. Draining the last drop from her glass, she repeated:

'It's no good upsetting yourself like this. Your mother's death . . . of course it's very sad. But what can you expect?

We're all of us only mortal. Oh my God, you poor kid!'

Then she suddenly started crying, and kept moaning through her tears: 'It's no good getting upset . . . It's no good getting upset . . .'

It started as a kind of lamentation, but her voice grew louder and louder and soon it turned into a hideous bray. And her huge round belly and enormous breasts were shaken with her sobs.

'If you make such a row, Marianne,' I said to her, 'the mistress will hear you, and come downstairs!'

But she paid no attention, and went on howling louder than ever: 'Oh, but it's so sad, so sad!'

With the result that I, too, feeling queasy from the drink and moved by Marianne's tears, began sobbing like a Magdalene . . . Still, she's not a bad sort . . .

But I hate it here, I hate it, I hate it. I would rather work for a *cocotte,* or try to find a place in America.

1 OCTOBER

Poor Monsieur Lanlaire! I think perhaps I may have been a bit too stand-offish with him the other day in the garden. Maybe I went too far. He's so simple that he may have thought he had offended me seriously, and that I'm hopelessly virtuous. He keeps looking at me with such a humble, imploring expression, as though he were trying to beg my pardon.

Though I've been behaving in a friendlier, more provocative way than ever, he has made no further reference to the subject at all, and he can't make up his mind to try some new attack, not even the classical tactic of asking me to sew on a button for him. A pretty vulgar approach, but surprisingly successful, all the same. God knows how many buttons I must have sewn on in my time!

Still, it's pretty clear he wants me more than ever, he's dying for it. The least thing he says to me is an admission, however indirect, but at the same time he's becoming shyer and shyer. He's afraid of coming to the point, in case it results in a final breach between us, and he no longer trusts my encouraging advances.

On one occasion, accosting me with a strange expression and a wild look in his eyes, he said:

'Célestine, you . . . er . . . you clean my boots beautifully . . . beautifully. Really, I . . . er . . . I don't think they've ever been cleaned so well . . . my boots, I mean.'

I thought this was really going to be it . . . but not at all. After puffing and blowing, and slavering at the mouth as if he were eating a huge juicy pear, he just whistled for his dog and went off.

But here's something even crazier. Yesterday, Madame went to market—she always likes to do her own shopping. The master had been out since dawn with his gun and dog. He got back early, having shot three thrushes, and immediately went up to his dressing-room to have a bath and change his clothes as usual. I must say he likes to keep himself clean all right, he's not afraid of water. I thought this was a favourable moment to try something that would make things easier for him. Leaving my work, I went to the door of the dressing-room and stood there listening for a moment. I could hear him walking about, whistling and singing to himself. Whenever he sings, he has the funny habit of mixing up all sorts of different songs. I could hear him moving the chairs about, opening and shutting cupboards, and then the sound of water being poured into the bath, followed by a succession of 'Ows!' and 'Ohs!' at the shock of the cold water. Then I suddenly threw open the door. And there he stood, facing me, dripping with water and shivering. Oh, if you could have seen him . . . eyes, head, body, suddenly motionless! Never in my life have I seen a man so utterly flabbergasted. Having nothing else to cover up his nakedness, with an instinctive movement of shame, that was incredibly comic, he used the sponge for a vine leaf. Confronted with this fantastic spectacle, it was honestly all I could do not to burst out laughing. I just had time to notice the tufts of hair on his shoulders and his chest like a bear's—Oh, he's a fine specimen of a man, all right. Then, naturally, I uttered a cry of shame and alarm as the situation demanded, and closed the door with a bang But I didn't go away, for I was certain he'd call me back . . . and then what was going to happen?

I waited for several minutes, but there was not a sound, not even the noise of dripping water.

'He's wondering what to do,' I thought, 'and daren't make up his mind. But he'll call me back.'

But it was no good. Soon I heard once more the splashing of water, and then the sound of him drying himself, rubbing himself strenuously, and of his slippers dragging across the floor. Then more moving of chairs, more opening and shutting of cupboards, and presently he started singing again.

'No, really! The man's a fool!' I muttered to myself, furiously angry. And off I went to the linen-room, having made up my mind never to allow him the pleasure of what, without the least feeling of desire on my part, I had sometimes dreamt of giving him out of pity.

All afternoon the master was very preoccupied. He came out into the yard, where I was emptying the cat's box on to the manure heap, and just as a joke, to see how embarrassed he would be, I apologized for what had happened in the morning.

'It doesn't matter,' he said. 'It doesn't matter at all . . . On the contrary . . .'

In the hope of keeping me there, he started mumbling all sorts of nonsense. But I cut him short in the middle of one of his endless sentences, and said in a cutting voice:

'You must excuse me, sir, but I'm much too busy to stay here chattering . . . Madame is waiting for me.'

'Damn it all, Célestine surely you can listen to me for just a second . . .'

'I'm afraid not, sir.'

As I reached the turn in the alley leading to the house I caught sight of him out of the tail of my eye. He hadn't moved. He was just standing there, with bowed shoulders, still gazing at the manure heap and scratching the back of his neck.

In the drawing-room after dinner the two of them had a furious row. I heard Madame say: 'I tell you, you are running after that girl.'

'Me?' he replied. 'Oh, for heaven's sake, what a crazy idea. Really, darling, a dirty little prostitute like that, a whore who has probably got every conceivable disease? No, no . . . that's really going too far!'

Madame went on: 'Do you imagine I don't know how you carry on? And your dirty tastes . . . All the women you run after, when you're supposed to be out shooting. Messing about with their filthy clothes and dirty little backsides!'

I could hear the floor of the drawing-room creak as the master strode backwards and forwards in a state of great indignation.

'Me? But you're just imagining things, my dear. Where on earth do you get hold of such ridiculous ideas?'

But Madame was not to be put off: 'And what about the little Gezureau girl, then? Only fifteen years old, you beast! And the 500 francs I had to pay out, just to save you from going to prison like your thief of a father.'

The master had stopped walking about. He had collapsed into an armchair, and was sitting there without saying a word. And Madame brought the discussion to a close by saying: 'Mind you, it's all the same to me . . . I'm not jealous. If you really want to, you can sleep with Célestine. All I'm concerned about is that it doesn't cost me any money.'

No, honestly! They disgust me, the pair of them . . .

Whether Monsieur Lanlaire really sleeps around with the peasant girls as Madame maintains I don't know. If he does, and enjoys it, I don't see why he shouldn't. He's a big strong man with a healthy appetite, and he needs it. And if Madame refuses to give it him . . . At least she has ever since I've been here, that I'm certain of, which is all the more extraordinary since they still share the same bed. A chambermaid with her wits about her and who has eyes in her head knows exactly what her employers are up to. She doesn't even have to snoop on them. Their dressing-room, bedroom, underclothes—all sorts of things—tell her quite enough. Since they are so fond of lecturing other people about their morals, and demand the most complete chastity from their servants, it is quite inconceivable that they should not be at greater pains to conceal the evidence of their own sexual manias. Indeed, on the contrary, some of them seem to enjoy drawing attention to them, either as a sort of challenge or from some strange kind of corruption. I am certainly no prude, and I enjoy a good laugh as much as anyone, but some of the couples I have known, often the most respectable ones, really have been the absolute limit.

In the past, when I first went into service, it used to have a funny effect on me when I saw them again . . . afterwards . . . next morning. I'd be quite upset, and when I took them their breakfast I could scarcely keep my eyes off them, gazing so insistently at their eyes, their mouths, their hands, that often the master or mistress would say to me: 'What's the matter with you, staring at us like that? Just keep your mind on what you're doing . . .'

Somehow, just to see them used to stir up all kinds of ideas, images—how shall I say?—desires, that plagued the life out of me, and being unable to satisfy these in the way I would have liked, I was driven to seek relief in frantic but unsatisfying bouts of self-abuse.

Nowadays, however, I have got used to it and habit, which reduces all things to proportion, has taught me a different, and I think a more sensible, reaction. When I see these faces, from which no amount of make-up, of toilet-water and powder can efface the ravages of the night, I just shrug my shoulders . . . But how they infuriate me, these respectable people, with their dignified airs and virtuous manners, their savage contempt for any wretched girl who happens to go wrong, and their everlasting nagging about our moral behaviour: 'Célestine, don't stare at men like that . . . Célestine, it is most improper, always gossiping in corners with the footman . . . Célestine, please understand that this house is not a brothel. As long as you're working for me and sharing my roof I simply will not allow . . .'

And so on and so forth.

Of course, none of this prevents the master, despite all his morality, pulling you on to a sofa or bed as soon as he gets the chance, and as often as not, in return for a fleeting moment of weakness, leaving you with a child on your hands. Then, of course, it's up to you to do what you can if you can . . . And if you can't, then you and the child can just starve, for all they care. It's no concern of theirs.

When I worked in Lincoln Street, for example, it used to

87

happen regularly every Friday—there couldn't be the slightest mistake about that. Friday was Madame's at home day, and swarms of women used to turn up, chattering, featherbrained, shameless creatures, plastered with make-up. A very posh crowd in short. And, of course, amongst themselves there would be plenty of filthy talk that used to excite the mistress. Then, in the evening, it was always the Opera and all that goes with that. Anyhow, whether it was this, that or the other that actually started it, what is quite certain is that every Friday night was *the* night. And what a night! You should have seen the dressing-room and bedroom next morning, furniture upside down, clothes strewn all over the place, and water from the wash-basins all over the floor. And the smell! Everywhere the powerful odour of human bodies mixed with perfume—though the perfume smelt delicious, I'll admit. In the mistress's dress-ing-room there used to be a huge mirror, from floor to ceiling. And, in front of it, you would find piles of cushions, all creased and battered, between tall silver candelabras covered with wax because the candles had been left to burn themselves out . . . Oh, they certainly liked their little gadgets, those two, God knows what they would have managed to think up if they hadn't been married.

Which reminds me of our famous trip to Belgium, one year when we were going to Ostend. At Feignies, we had to go through the customs. It was at night, and the master was so sleepy that he stayed behind in the compartment. So Madame and I had to go to the hall where the baggage was being inspected.

'Anything to declare?' asked a huge customs officer, who, seeing that the mistress was so elegant, was delighted at the thought of all the pretty things he could handle . . . There really are some of these officials for whom the chance of rummaging through a pile of vests and knickers belong-ing to a good-looking woman is a physical pleasure, almost amounting to an act of possession.

'No,' Madame answered, 'nothing to declare.'

'Would you mind opening this suitcase?'

Out of the six cases we had with us, he had picked on the

largest and heaviest, made of pigskin, with a grey cloth cover.

'But I tell you, I have nothing to declare,' Madame insisted irritably.

'All the same, open it,' the lout demanded, obviously incited by the mistress's reluctance to carry out a more thorough examination.

The mistress—why, I can see her now!—took her key-ring from her handbag and opened the suitcase. With a hateful appearance of pleasure the customs officer inhaled the delicious scent that escaped from it, and immediately started fumbling through the exquisite underclothes and dresses with his dirty, clumsy paws. Madame was furious, and protested indignantly, especially when, with obvious malevolence, the brute began turning everything upside down, crumpling up the clothes that we had so carefully folded and packed.

Then, just as it seemed that he had finished his inspection, he produced from the bottom of the trunk a long red velvet case and demanded: 'And this? What does this contain?'

'My jewellery,' Madame replied with complete assurance and not a trace of embarrassment.

'Do you mind opening it?'

'But what's the point? I've told you, it only contains my personal jewellery.'

'Open it.'

'No I have no intention of doing so. You are abusing your authority, and I refuse to open it . . . Besides I haven't got the key with me.'

By this time, however, Madame was beginning to show signs of extraordinary agitation. She attempted to snatch the disputed case from the inspector's hands, but he drew back, and said in a threatening voice: 'If you refuse, then I shall be obliged to call the chief inspector.'

'But this is preposterous . . . utterly shameful.'

'And if you can't produce the key we shall just have to force it.'

In a tone of growing exasperation Madame shouted: 'You have no right to do anything of the kind. I shall complain to our ambassador, to one of your ministers . . . I shall report the matter to the king who is a friend of ours . . I shall have you dismissed, do you understand? . . . You shall go to prison for this.'

Her angry words produced no effect, however, on the impassive customs house officer, who merely repeated with greater assurance: 'Will you open the case?'

Madame had turned quite pale and was nervously twisting her hands.

'No,' she said, 'I will not open it. I do not wish to, and in any case, I cannot.'

And for about the tenth time the stubborn official insisted: 'Open the case.'

This argument had led to a general interruption of the work, and a small crowd of curious travellers had gathered round us. As for me, I was intensely interested by the sudden change that had transformed this little drama, and especially by the mysterious case, which I did not recognize, and indeed, had never previously seen, and which I was quite certain had been packed without my knowledge. Once again, Madame now brusquely changed her tactics, adopting a much gentler, one might almost say an endearing manner towards the incorruptible customs official. Drawing closer to him, as though hoping to hypnotize him with the scent of her perfume, she begged him in a low voice: 'If you will just send all these people away I will open the case.'

The official, apparently thinking that Madame was trying to trap him, shook his obstinate, distrustful old head and said: 'I've had just about enough of this nonsense, and don't want any more of your eyewash. Open the case.'

And at last, blushing with confusion but resigned, Madame took a tiny key from her purse, a sweet little golden key, and trying to prevent the onlookers seeing what was in it, opened the red velvet case, which the customs officer held out to her, though still keeping a firm grip on it. Directly he saw what it contained, he leapt back with a gesture of dismay as though he were afraid of being bitten by a venomous snake.

'For Christ's sake!' he swore. Then, controlling his amazement, he exclaimed cheerfully: 'Why on earth couldn't you have told me in the first place . . . If I'd known you were a widow!'

And he closed the case, but not before the sniggers and whispers of the crowd, their offensive and even indignant remarks had made it only too clear to Madame that her 'jewels' had been seen by everyone.

She was extremely embarrassed. Still, I must admit, she showed considerable pluck under very trying circumstances, though she always had had plenty of cheek . . . She helped me to repack the suitcase which was in a terrible mess, and we left the customs shed to a chorus of whistles and insulting laughter.

I accompanied her to the sleeper, carrying her bag into which she had thrust the famous case. When we reached the platform she stopped a moment, and with the coolest impertinence said to me:

'Heavens, what a fool I was! I ought to have told him that it belonged to you.'

With equal impertinence I replied: 'I appreciate the honour, ma'am. You are really too kind. But, for my part, I prefer that particular kind of "jewel" in its natural state.'

'Hold your tongue,' said Madame, though not in the least put out. 'You are a little fool.' And climbing into the coach, she rejoined her Coco, who had not the slightest idea of what had been going on.

Apart from this, Madame never had much luck. Whether because of her cheek or as a result of her disorderly way of life, this sort of thing was always happening to her. I could give a number of examples, most edifying ones . . . But you reach a point when the feeling of disgust is too powerful, and you get tired of endlessly wading through filth. Besides, I think I've already said enough about this household, which I regard as the perfect example of moral degradation. I will restrict myself to a couple more instances.

In one of her drawers, Madame used to hide a dozen or so little books, bound in yellow leather with gilt clasps, as pretty as a young girl's prayer-book. Sometimes, on Saturday mornings, she would leave one of these by mistake on the table by her bed, or amongst the pile of cushions in the dressing room. They were full of the most extraordinary illustrations. And though I'm not exactly an innocent, I must say that only a whore would have found such absolute horrors amusing. Just to think of them makes me go hot all over. Women with women, men with men, the sexes all mixed up in crazy embraces and exasperated rut . . . Naked bodies rearing, bending, straining, wallowing, in heaps, in clusters, in processions welded together by fantastic caresses and complicated embraces . . . Mouths clinging to breasts and bellies like the suckers of an octopus, a whole landscape of thighs and legs, knotted and twisted like the trees of a jungle . . . Oh no, it was too much!

One day Matilda, the first housemaid, pinched one of them, imagining that Madame wouldn't have the nerve to ask her about it; though in fact she did. After searching everywhere for it, ransacking her drawers in vain, she asked Matilda: 'Did you happen to come across a book when you were doing the bedroom?'

'What book, ma'am?'

'A yellow one . . .'

'Do you mean a prayer-book ma'am?' Then, looking the mistress straight in the eyes, though without disconcerting her in the slightest, she added:

'Now I come to think of it, I did see a little yellow book with gilt clasps. It was on the table by your bed, ma'am.'

'Well?'

'I don't know what you could have done with it, ma'am.'

'You're sure you didn't take it?'

'Me, ma'am?' And with magnificent impertinence she went on: 'Surely, ma'am, you don't really imagine that *I* would read such books?'

Really, that Matilda was a scream . . . Madame simply didn't know what to say next. And afterwards, every day while we were doing the linen, Matilda would say:

'Attention please! We will now say mass.'

And she would pull out the little yellow book from her pocket and start reading from it, despite the protests from the English housekeeper, who would bleat: 'Will you be quiet! You are very naughty girls.' Though, nevertheless, she used to gaze longingly at the illustrations, her eyes magnified by her spectacles and her nose almost touching the page, as though she wanted to inhale its smell. What a time we used to have!

Oh, that English housekeeper! Never in my life have I

met such a drunk, and so funny with it. Whenever she'd
been drinking she used to become all tender, all amorous
and passionate, especially towards women. The vices that
she managed to conceal when she was sober beneath a mask
of comical austerity were then revealed in all their grotesque
beauty. But they were more cerebral than physical, and I
never heard of her actually practising them. As the mistress
used to put it, 'Miss was content to "practise" upon herself . . .' Indeed, without her, the collection of crackbrained,
dissipated humanity that distinguished this very modern
household would have been incomplete.

One night I was on duty waiting up for the mistress.
Everyone else in the house was asleep, and I was all on my
own in the living-room, trying to keep awake. Towards two
o'clock in the morning Madame arrived home. As soon as
the bell rang, I got up and went to her room, where I found
her taking off her gloves, staring at the floor, and laughing fit
to burst: 'Look!' she said, 'Here's Miss, completely drunk
again.' And she pointed to the housekeeper sprawled on the
floor, her arms flung out, one leg in the air whimpering, sigh-
ing and muttering unintelligibly.

'Come on. Get her up, and put her to bed.'

As she was very heavy and falling all over the place,
Madame did her best to help me, and it was only with the
greatest difficulty that we managed to get her on to her
feet. Clinging to the mistress's cloak with both hands, she
said: 'I don't want to leave you . . . I don't want to leave you,
ever. I love you terribly . . . you're beautiful . . . you're my
little baby . . .'

'Miss,' Madame replied, laughing, 'you're an old drunk.
Get to bed with you!'

'No, no, I want to sleep with you. You're beautiful, I love
you, I want to hold you in my arms.'

One hand still clutching Madame's cloak, with the other
she tried to stroke her breasts, at the same time thrusting
out her withered old lips in moist, noisy kisses . . .

'You pig, you pig . . . you're a naughty little pig, I want to
hold you in my arms, phew! . . .'

Eventually I managed to free the mistress from her
embraces, and succeeded in dragging her off to her bedroom. But now it was my turn. Though she could hardly

93

stand on her feet, she flung her arms round me and, much bolder than she'd been with Madame and much more precise in her movements, her hand began wandering all over my body. There was no mistaking what she was up to.

'Come on now, pack it up, you dirty old bag!'

'No, no, I want you, you're beautiful, I love you, really. Stay with me . . . Phew! Phew!'

I don't know how I should have managed to get away from her if, when we reached her bedroom, she had not been violently sick, with the result that her overwhelming passion was drowned in a flood of vomit.

Scenes like this Madame used to find very amusing, for her only real pleasure was the spectacle of vice, however disgusting.

On another occasion I surprised her in the middle of describing to a friend, in her dressing-room a visit she had paid the previous evening with her husband to a special kind of brothel, where she had watched two little dwarfs making love.

'You really ought to see them, my dear . . . You can imagine nothing more entrancing!'

Those who only see humanity from the outside, and allow themselves to be dazzled by appearances, can have no idea of how filthy and corrupt the great world, 'high society', really is. It is no exaggeration to say that the main aim of its existence is to enjoy the filthiest kinds of amusement. I have had plenty of experience of the middle class, and of the nobility, and only very rarely have I seen love that was accompanied by any noble feeling or real tenderness, the kind of self-sacrifice and pity that alone make it something great and holy.

Just one word more about this particular employer. Apart from receptions and formal dinner parties, Coco and the mistress were on very intimate terms with a smart young couple with whom they used to go to theatres, concerts, private rooms and restaurants and even, it appears, brothels. The husband was very good-looking, effeminate and scarcely a hair on his face; the wife, a handsome red-head, with curiously ardent eyes and the most sensual mouth I have ever seen. No one ever knew just what these two creatures actually were. When the four of them were dining together, it seems that their conversation often became so preposterous, so filthy, that the butler, who was certainly not easily shocked, could have thrown the food in their faces. He had no doubt whatever that there were the most unnatural relationships between them, and that they used to indulge in orgies like those illustrated in Madame's little yellow books. Such things may not be common, but they certainly happen all the same. And there are plenty of people who, though not driven to practise such vices by their passions, nevertheless indulge in them out of snobbery . . . because it is the smart thing to do.

Whoever would have imagined that Madame was capable of such abominations? For amongst her guests were archbishops and the papal nuncio, and every week *Le Gaulois* used to pay tribute to her virtues, elegance and charity, describing her *chic* dinner parties and her fidelity to the purest Catholic traditions of France. All the same, despite all the vicious practices that went on there, it was an easygoing, happy household, and the mistress never worried her head about the morals of the staff.

This evening we stayed in the kitchen longer than usual. I was helping Marianne do her accounts, for she could never manage them by herself. I realize that, like everyone else in such confidential positions, she is always on the scrounge, fiddling whatever she can. Some of her tricks even amaze *me*, but they have to be concealed. For if, as sometimes happens, her figures don't tally, Madame, who immediately spots any mistakes, is furious with her . . . Joseph is becoming a little more human with me. Now he even deigns to speak to me from time to time. This evening, for example, he did not as he usually does, go off to visit his dear friend, the verger. And while Marianne and I were busy with the books, he read his *Libre Parole*. It is his favourite paper, and he simply cannot believe that anybody could possibly read any other. I noticed that several times while he was reading he was observing me with a new expression in his eyes.

Having finished his paper, he insisted upon expounding

his political opinions to me. He is fed up with the Republic, which he maintains is ruining and dishonouring him. He is all for the use of force.

'Until we are prepared to draw the sword again, and let a little blood, we shall never get anywhere . . .' he said.

He is in favour of religion because . . . well . . . anyhow, he's all for it.

'Until religion has been restored in France as it used to be, until everybody is obliged once again to go to confession and to mass, we shan't get anywhere!'

On the wall of the saddle room he has stuck up pictures of the Pope and of Drumont, in his bedroom, Déroulède's, and in the loft, Guérin's and General Mercier's . . . 'Splendid fellows, patriots, real Frenchmen, what?' He religiously collects anti-Jewish songs, all the coloured portraits of generals he can lay hands on, and every possible caricature of the 'Yids', for Joseph is violently anti-Semitic, and belongs to every religious, military and patriotic association in the Department. He's a member of the anti-Semitic youth movement in Rouen and the old people's anti-Jewish society in Louvriers, as well as an infinity of groups, branches, cells, and so on. Whenever he speaks of Jews a sinister gleam comes into his eyes, and he makes ferociously brutal gestures. If he has to go into town he carries a club with him: 'As long as a single Jew remains in France we'll never know where we are,' and he adds: 'My God, if only I was in Paris! I'd kill some of these bloody Yids and tear their guts out! There's not much danger of any of the traitors trying to set up in Mesnil-Roy. Oh no! They know what they're up to, the crooks!'

His hatred extends to Protestants, freemasons and free-thinkers, as well as to all the rascals who never go to church and whom he regards as Jews in disguise. Though he doesn't belong to the clerical party, he is in favour of religion, and that's that.

As to the monster Dreyfus, he'd better not think of return-ing to France from Devil's Island. Oh no, indeed! And if there's any chance of that swine Zola coming to lecture at Louvriers, as has been rumoured, the sooner he changes his mind the better for him. They would soon settle his hash, Joseph would see to that. A miserable traitor who, for

600,000 francs, had betrayed the whole French army, as well as the Russian, to the Germans and the English! That's not just a yarn invented by the gossipmongers. Oh no, Joseph's quite sure of that. He has heard it from the verger, who heard it from the vicar, who heard it from the bishop, who heard it from the Pope, who had been told by Drumont . . . If any Jews care to visit The Priory, wherever they look they will see the words 'Long Live the Army! Death to the Jews!' inscribed by Joseph in the cellar, in the loft, in the stables, in the coach-house, on the lining of the harness, and even on the handles of the brooms.

From time to time, by a silent gesture or nod of her head, Marianne would signify her approval of these violent opinions . . . doubtless she also had been ruined and dishonoured by the Republic. She, too, is on the side of the clergy in favour of putting all Jews to the sword—though incidentally she knows nothing whatsoever about them except that something, some part of them, is missing.

And I, too, of course, am all for the army, for the country, for religion—and against the Jews. For amongst us servants, where will you find one, from the highest to the lowest, who doesn't profess this fashionable doctrine? You can say what you like about servants, they may have every defect under the sun, but one thing you have to admit, they are all patriots! And it's the same with me. No, politics are just not my cup of tea, and bore me to tears—and yet, only a week before taking on this job, I had bluntly refused to work for Dreyfus's lawyer, Labori, who wanted a housemaid. And all the other girls who happened to be in the registry office at the time also refused:

'What? That swine? No, thank you. Not on your life!'

But if I ask myself seriously why I am against the Jews, I simply don't know. I've worked for them in the past, before it was looked upon as being humiliating. And the fact is I could never see that there was anything to choose between Jews and Catholics. They both have the same vices, the same beastly natures, the same nasty minds. They're part of the same world, and the difference in religion counts for nothing. Perhaps the Jews put on a bit more swank, show off a bit more, like to make more fuss about all the money they spend. But despite all you hear about their gift for administration and their avarice, I maintain it's not at all bad working for them, for they run their households on much more free and easy lines than the Catholics.

But Joseph refused to listen to a word I tried to say. He just scolded me for being unpatriotic and not loving my country, and then, with a final prophecy of the massacres to come and a bloodthirsty description of skulls being smashed and guts strewn about the streets, he went off to bed.

Directly he'd gone Marianne brought out the bottle of brandy. We needed something to pull ourselves together and we talked about other things. Marianne, who confides in me more and more, told me a bit about her childhood, the difficult times she'd had as a girl and how, when she was working as a skivvy for a woman who kept a tobacco shop at Caen, she was seduced by a medical student . . . a slim, young lad, small and fair, who had blue eyes and a short, pointed, silky beard—'Oh, so wonderfully silky!' She became pregnant, and her mistress, who used to sleep with anyone, all the non-commissioned officers in the garrison, threw her out of the house! A mere girl, down and out in a big city, and a kid coming! As her boy friend had no money she experienced terrible hardship, and indeed would certainly have died of hunger if the student had not eventually found her a funny kind of a job in the medical school.

'Oh yes, goodness me,' she said, 'in the Boratory . . . I had to kill the rabbits and the poor little guinea pigs for them. It was really a nice enough job . . .'

And the smile that the memory of it brought to her great coarse lips struck me as being extraordinarily sad. After a silence I asked her:

'And the kid? What happened to that?'

Marianne made a vague, remote gesture, a gesture that seemed to be drawing back the heavy veil from the limbo where her child slept. And in a voice grown hoarse from drinking, she replied:

'Oh well . . . you know how it is. What else could I have done with it, for God's sake!'

'What? Like the little guinea pigs, you mean?'

'That's right,' and she poured herself out another glass of brandy.

By the time we went up to bed we were both a bit tight.

6 OCTOBER

Autumn has really come at last. The early frost has turned all the flowers in the garden brown. The dahlias, the same dahlias that witnessed the master's timid attempt at making love, are all scorched, and so are the big sunflowers that used to stand guard outside the kitchen door. Nothing is left in the desolate flower beds save here and there a few wretched geraniums and five or six clumps of asters, and they, too, are hanging their heads, already touched with the colour of decay. In Captain Mauger's garden, the borders which I saw just now over the hedge, are completely ruined, and everything is the colour of tobacco.

Everywhere the trees are beginning to turn yellow and lose their leaves, and the sky is gloomy. For the last four days we have been living in a thick brown fog, that smelt of soot and still hung about, even in the afternoon. Now it is raining, an icy, stinging rain, blown in sudden squalls by a sharp wind from the north-west.

For me, it is no joke. My bedroom is as cold as ice. The walls scarcely keep out the wind and the rain is coming in through cracks in the roof, especially above the sash windows that shed a meagre light into this gloomy attic and the rattle of loose slates, and the sudden gusts of wind, and the noise of straining beams and creaking hinges is deafening. Despite the urgent need for repairs, I have had the greatest difficulty in persuading Madame to call in the plumber tomorrow morning. And, so far, I haven't dared to ask for a stove, although, being very susceptible to the cold, I'm sure that if I have to live in this wretched dump throughout the winter it will be the death of me. This evening, in an attempt to keep out the wind and the rain, I have stuffed up the cracks in the windows with old petticoats. But, up on the roof, I can hear the weathercock, forever turning on its rusty pivot, and every now and then letting out such a shrill screech that you could almost think it was Madame having one of her rows.

Now that I've got over my first feeling of revolt, life here has become monotonous and stifling, but I'm gradually learning to put up with it without getting too miserable. No visitors ever come near the place—you'd imagine there was a curse on the house—and apart from the trivial incidents I have already mentioned nothing ever happens. Day after day it is just the same; the same jobs to be done and the same faces to look at. Death itself couldn't be more boring. But I'm beginning to be so numbed by it all that I put up with the boredom as if it were the most natural thing in the world. Even having to do without sex doesn't worry me too much, and I manage to bear the chastity to which I am condemned; or rather, to which I have condemned myself, for I have given up any designs upon Monsieur Lanlaire. I've definitely finished with him for good. He bores me, and I'm fed up with him for being such a coward as to talk about me in that preposterous way to Madame. Not that *he's* resigned himself or given me up. On the contrary, he's continually following me about, his mouth watering and his eyes starting out of his head more than ever. As I read in some book or other once, 'I am still the trough at which he feeds the pigs of his desire.'

Now that the days are drawing in, he stays in his study until dinner time, doing God knows what. He spends his time pointlessly going through old correspondence, marking up seed catalogues and chemist's advertisements, or listlessly turning the pages of books about shooting. In the evening, when I go in to close the shutters or make up the fire, you ought to see him. He gets up, coughs, sneezes, snorts, knocks into the furniture, upsets things, and in the stupidest ways tries to attract my attention. I could burst! But I pay no attention to him, pretending not to understand what all these childish antics are about. Then I leave the room, as haughty as you like, without saying a word and paying no more attention to him than if he was not there.

Yesterday evening, however, we did have the following brief exchange.

'Célestine!'

'What can I do for you, sir?'

'Célestine, you are being very nasty to me. What makes you so beastly?'

'Since you know that I am nothing but a prostitute . . .'

'Come, now . . .'

'A filthy tart . . .'

'Now really . . .'

'That I've got all sorts of foul diseases . . .'

'But for Christ's sake, Célestine, you've got to listen to me . . .'

'Shit!'

Yes, it is true. I let him have it just like that, straight in the face . . . I've had about as much as I can stand. It doesn't even amuse me any more to keep him on tenterhooks by flirting with him.

Nothing here amuses me—and what's worse, nothing really annoys me, either. Whether it's the air, or the country silence, or the coarse, heavy food, I don't know, but I'm sunk in a kind of lethargy, that has a certain charm all the same. At least it takes the edge off my feelings, deadens my dreams, helps me to put up with Madame's impertinence and her everlasting nagging. And for the same reason I am beginning to find some satisfaction in gossiping away the evenings with Marianne and Joseph. This strange creature no longer goes out as soon as we have finished supper; he definitely seems to prefer staying at home with us . . . What if he has begun to fall for me? Well, I should feel flattered. Yes, for God's sake, I've come to that! And then I read a lot, novel after novel. I have been reading Paul Bourget again, but I'm not as keen on his books as I used to be. They actually bore me, and I think he's a fake. They are inspired by a state of mind that I know all too well, having experienced it when I first came into contact with wealth and luxury, and was still dazzled and fascinated by them. But now I've got over that, and no longer find them so marvellous—though Bourget still does. I should never again be so daft as to ask him to explain anything psychologically, for now I know a good deal better than he does what goes on behind drawing-room doors and beneath lace petticoats.

What I cannot get used to is never getting a letter from Paris. Every morning when I hear the postman, I feel a little pang in my heart at the thought of how completely forgotten I am by everyone. That's how I measure the depth of my loneliness. In vain I have written to my old companions, especially to Monsieur Jean . . . urgent, heartbroken letters. In vain I beg them to think of me, to do something to get me away from this hole, to find me some kind of a job in Paris, however humble. But not one of them has replied. I could never have believed people would be so heartless, so lacking in gratitude.

And this is what makes me cling all the more tightly to what I have left: my memories, and the past. Memories in which, despite everything, the happiness outweighs the suffering . . . a past that restores my faith that I am not yet done for, that it is just not true that one false step can prove to be irremediable. And this is why, when the sound of Marianne snoring on the other side of the partition seems to typify everything I loathe about this place, I try to drown the ridiculous noise with the echo of my past happiness, passionately harking back to that past in order to create out of its scattered fragments the illusion that some future still awaits me.

As a matter of fact, today, 6 October, happens to be a date that is full of memories for me. Though it is five years now since the drama I am about to describe took place, I remember every detail of it vividly. It was a tragedy that ended in death, the death of a poor, tender, charming creature, whom I killed by giving him too much pleasure, too much life. And in all the five years since his death—a death for which I was responsible—this will be the first time that, on 6 October, I have not put flowers on his grave. Instead, I shall try to make him a more lasting wreath, one that will be better than decorating the wretched patch of earth where he sleeps in the cemetery, because it will cherish and keep alive his beloved memory. For the flowers of which this wreath is made I shall gather one by one from the garden of my heart—a garden that is filled not only with the wilting blossoms of debauch, but where the tall, white lilies of love also have a place.

It was a Saturday, I remember. At the registry office in the rue Colisée, where, for the past week, I had been coming regularly every morning in the hope of finding a situation,

I was introduced to an old lady in mourning. Never in my life had I encountered such a prepossessing face, such a gentle expression and simple manners. Never had I heard such encouraging words, and the politeness with which she greeted me warmed my heart.

'My child,' she said, 'Madame Paulhat-Durand (the woman who ran the registry office) has recommended you highly to me. From your appearance, I am inclined to agree with her—your frank, intelligent and cheerful demeanour pleases me. I need someone I can trust, and whose devotion I can count upon. Oh, I know that is asking a great deal— since you don't yet know me, there is no reason why you should feel devotion for me. I am going to explain to you exactly what the position is . . . But don't stand there, child . . . Come and sit down beside me.'

If anyone speaks kindly to me, if they do not regard me as a creature belonging to another world, something between a dog and a parrot, I am immediately touched . . . I immediately feel as though I were once again a child. All my bitterness and hatred, all my rebelliousness miraculously disappears, and I feel nothing but unselfish affection towards those who speak to me with humanity. I know from experience that only those who have themselves suffered can appreciate the suffering of others, even if they are socially inferior to them . . . There is always an element of insolence and remoteness in the kindness of those who have known nothing but happiness.

By the time I had seated myself beside her I already loved, really loved, this impressive old lady in her widow's weeds.

'The situation I'm offering you, my child, is not a very cheerful one . . .'

'Don't worry, ma'am,' I interrupted, with an enthusiastic sincerity that did not escape her. 'I will do whatever you ask of me.'

And it was true—I was ready for anything. She thanked me with a look of tenderness, and continued: 'Well, this is the position. Life has not treated me at all kindly. The only one of my family still left to me is a grandson, and his life is already threatened by the terrible illness that killed the others.'

As though fearing to utter the name of this terrible disease, she indicated what it was by placing her old, black-gloved hand on her chest and, with an even sadder expression, added: 'Poor child . . . he is a charming lad, really adorable, and I have set my last hopes on him, for if he were to die, I should be left quite alone in the world. And then what should I do with my life, dear God?'

Her eyes filled with tears, and she dabbed them with her handkerchief:

'The doctors assure me that he can be saved, that the infection is not yet serious; and they have prescribed a cure for him from which they expect great things. Every after-noon George has to bathe in the sea, though only a quick dip . . . then he has to be rubbed all over with a horse-hair glove to restore the circulation . . . then drink a glass of port wine, and finally lie down in a nice, warm bed for at least an hour. The first thing I should want from you, my dear, would be to see to all this. But what you must also under-stand is that the most important thing of all for him is youth, kindness, gaiety, life. Living with me, these are the things that he misses most. I have two very devoted servants, but they're old and sad, and a bit crotchety. George cannot stand them. As for me, with my white hair and always in mourning, I realize that I only distress him . . . and, what's worse, I know all too well that I often cannot hide my apprehension. Oh, I realize that this is perhaps scarcely the kind of role that a young girl like you ought to be expected to play towards a lad of George's age—after all, he's only nineteen, and it is bound to set tongues wagging. But I am not concerned with what other people think. I am only concerned with this poor, sick lad. And I have confidence in you . . . I am assuming that you are a good woman.'

'Oh yes, ma'am,' I cried, already convinced that I could be the kind of saint that this broken-hearted grandmother was hoping to find.

'As for him, poor child . . . In the state he is in, dear God! . . . Don't you see, that what he needs most of all, more than the seabathing and all the rest of it, is not to be left alone, always to have someone with him, with a pretty face and fresh, young laughter—someone who can rid his mind

104

of the idea of death, who can give him confidence in life . . .
Well, what do you think?'

'I accept, ma'am,' I replied, deeply moved, 'and you can
be quite sure that I shall do everything possible to look after
your grandson.'

It was agreed that I should enter upon my duties
immediately, and that we should set off next day for Houlgate, where the old lady had rented a fine villa on the sea-
shore.

His grandmother had not exaggerated, Monsieur George
was really a charming lad . . . His beardless face had all the
charm of a handsome woman's; and womanly, too, were his
indolent gestures, and the slim hands, so white and supple,
with the veins clearly visible. And what eyes! Eyes that
burned with a sombre fire, beneath eyelids ringed with blue
shadows as though the flame of his glance had singed them.
And what thought and passion they expressed, what
sensibility and intelligence, what a profound inner life,
despite the red flowers of death that already bloomed in his
cheeks . . . It seemed that it was not the illness he was dying
of, but the excess of vitality, the passion for life, that was
eating into his vital organs and withering up his flesh. Oh,
how charming he was to look at, and how sad! When his
grandmother took me to see him he was lying stretched out
on a sofa, holding in his long white hand a scentless rose.
He welcomed me, not like a servant, but as though I were
a friend for whom he had been waiting. And, from that first
moment, I felt myself drawn to him by all the strength of
my soul.

My arrival at Houlgate passed without incident. By the
time we arrived everything was ready. All we had to do
was to install ourselves in the villa, which was spacious and
elegant, full of light and gaiety, and separated from the
beach only by a broad terrace, with wicker chairs and gaily
striped awnings. Leading to the sea was a stone staircase
built in the sea wall, so that at high tide you could hear the
sound of the waves breaking on the bottom steps. Monsieur
George's bedroom was on the ground floor, with large bay-
windows looking out over a fine expanse of sea. Mine—one
of the best rooms in the house, with bright cretonne hangings—was separated from Monsieur George's by a passage

that led into a small garden with a few bushes and straggling rose trees. But to express in words the joy and pride, the pure and novel delight that I experienced at being treated like this . . . spoilt, invited like a lady to partake of all this luxury, to share, as I had so often vainly longed, the life of the family . . . all this is quite beyond me. Nor is it possible for me to explain how, by a wave of this marvellous fairy's wand, happiness had suddenly come to me so that, forgetting all my past humiliations, I could think only of the duties imposed upon me by being at last accepted as a human being. What I *can* say, however, is that in this moment I was really transfigured. Not only could I see from the mirror that I had suddenly become more beautiful, but also I knew in my heart that I was really a better woman. I discovered within myself inexhaustible springs of devotion and self-sacrifice, of heroism even, and I was dominated by a single thought: by my care and faithful attention, by every kind of ingenuity, to save Monsieur George from death.

I felt so strong a faith in my power to save that I would say to the poor old lady, always in despair and often spending the whole day weeping in the drawing-room:

'There, there, don't cry, ma'am. You'll see, we are going to save him . . . I give you my word, we shall.'

And indeed, at the end of a fortnight, Monsieur George was already feeling much better. There was a noticeable change in his condition. He had fewer attacks of coughing, and at longer intervals; his sleep and appetite were becoming normal. He was no longer having those terrible night sweats that used to leave him, next day, breathless and exhausted. Indeed, he had so far regained his strength that we were able to take long carriage drives, even to go for little walks, without tiring him too much. In a way, it was like a kind of resurrection. Since the weather was fine and the air, though tempered by a breeze from the sea, very warm, when we did not go out we would spend most of the day beneath the awning on the terrace, waiting until it was time to bathe . . . 'to have my dip', as Monsieur George used to call it. And he was gay, always gay, never referring to his illness, never speaking about death . . . I really believe that, during the whole of this period, he never once uttered the terrible word. On the other hand, he delighted in my chatter, often urging me on; while I, gaining confidence from the gentle look in his eyes and his kindly indulgence, talked to him about anything that came into my head, however silly or crazy. I told him about my childhood, my longings, my unhappiness, my dreams, my revolts, the various situations I'd been in and the cranky and squalid people I had worked for. And I made little attempt to hide the truth from him for, young as he was and though he had never been able to mix with people, with that insight, that marvellous intuition that sick people often have, he seemed to understand all about life. A genuine friendship had sprung up between us, partly as a result of his character, of his loneliness, but above all as a result of all the intimate little attentions with which I sought to bring comfort to his dying body. It made me happier than I can say, it helped to refine my mind through the continual contact with his.

Monsieur George adored poetry. For hours on end, lying on the terrace listening to the sound of the sea, or in the evening in his room, he would get me to read aloud to him poems by Hugo and Baudelaire, by Verlaine and Maeterlinck. Often he would close his eyes and lie without moving, his hands folded on his chest, so that, thinking he had fallen asleep, I would stop reading. But then he would smile, and say: 'Go on, little one, I am not asleep. I can listen to poetry like this and hear your voice better . . . You have a charming voice.'

At other times he would interrupt me. Then, after a moment's thought, he himself would begin to recite, slowly and drawing out the rhythms, the poems that he specially liked, and he would try—oh, how I liked that!—to make me understand them and to feel their beauty.

One day he said to me, and I have cherished his words like a relic:

'What is so sublime about poetry, you see, is that in order to understand and enjoy it there is no need at all to be highly educated. On the contrary, there are plenty of scholars who just can't understand it, and often they despise it out of vanity. All one needs to enjoy poetry is a soul . . . a little naked soul like a flower's. The poets speak directly to the souls of simple people, of the sad and the sick, and that's why their words are immortal. Do you realise that anyone with any sensibility already has something of the poet in him? Why, you, my little Célestine, often say things that are as lovely as poetry.'

'Oh, Monsieur George, don't make fun of me.'

'But I am not. And what is so wonderful is that you yourself are quite unaware that you're saying such beautiful things.'

For me those hours were unique. Whatever fate may have in store for me, as long as I live, they will sing in my heart. I experienced the sensation, unspeakably sweet, of becoming a new person, of sharing, so to speak, in the revelation of something new, of something hitherto unknown to me which was nevertheless me. And today, despite all my backsliding, despite the fact that the bad and angry side of me has once more gained the upper hand, if I still take a passionate delight in reading, if sometimes I feel an aspiration to things superior to myself and to the world in which I move, if in an attempt to recapture the spontaneity of my nature I have dared, despite my ignorance, to write this diary—all these are things that I owe to Monsieur George.

Yes, I was happy . . . happy above all to see this gentle invalid gradually reviving . . . putting on flesh and getting a better colour as he felt the new sap rising in his veins . . . happy for the joy and hope that the speed of his recovery was bringing back to the whole household, who began to look upon me as their fairy queen. For this miracle they attributed to me . . . to the way I looked after him, to my devoted vigilance, and still more, perhaps, to my constant gaiety, to my charming youthfulness and the surprising influence that I exerted over Monsieur George. His poor grandmother was always thanking me, overwhelming me with her gratitude and blessing—like a wet nurse to whom a dying baby has been entrusted, and whose pure and healthy milk has restored it to health, to health and laughter. Sometimes, forgetting her position, she would take my hands, stroking and kissing them, and with tears of happiness in her eyes, would say:

'I knew . . . As soon as I saw you, I was quite certain!'

And already the air was full of projects, of journeys in search of the sun, of rose-filled landscapes!

'You must never leave us, never, my child.'

The warmth of her feeling often embarrassed me, but in the end I came to believe that I deserved it. To have abused her generosity, as others might have done in my place, would have been infamous.

And what was bound to happen, happened.

On that particular day it was very warm, heavy and stormy. Above the smooth, leaden-coloured sea, the sky was full of huge stifling clouds, in which the storm crouched, ready to spring. Monsieur George did not want to go out, not even as far as the terrace, so we stayed in his room. More nervous than usual, owing to the electricity in the atmosphere, he did not even want me to read poetry to him.

'It would tire me,' he said. 'Besides, today I feel that you would read very badly.'

He went into the drawing-room and began doodling on the piano, but before long he returned to the bedroom and, in an attempt to distract himself, picked up a pencil and started to sketch me. But soon he gave this up, too, grumbling impatiently: 'It's no use, I can't. I'm not in the mood, and my hand is trembling. I don't know what's the matter with me, nor with you. You don't seem to be able to sit still.'

In the end he lay down on the sofa, by the huge window that looked out over an immense stretch of sea. In the distance, fishing boats, running before the threatening storm, were making for harbour at Trouville. With a listless expression, he stared out at their grey sails manoeuvring in the wind. It was true what he had said—I just could not stay still, but kept fidgeting about trying to think of something to occupy his mind. But I could find nothing, and my restlessness communicated itself to him.

'Why are you so restless, so on edge? Come and sit by me.'

I asked him whether he would like to be on one of those little boats.

'Don't talk just for the sake of talking . . . What's the good of asking such pointless questions? Come and sit here by me.'

No sooner had I done so than he complained that the

sight of the sea was unbearable, and asked me to pull down the blind.

'This half-light exasperates me. The sea is horrible. I don't want to look at it any more. Everything is horrible today. I don't want to look at anything at all except you.'

I gently scolded him: 'Now, Monsieur George, you're being very naughty. It's not right. If your grandmother were to see you in this state it would make her cry again.'

Raising himself a little on the cushions, he said:

'In the first place why do you keep calling me "Monsieur" George? You know I don't like it.'

'Well, I can scarcely call you Monsieur Gaston, can I?'

'You know quite well what I mean, you little wretch. Just call me plain George.'

'But I couldn't do that, I couldn't.'

And he sighed: 'Isn't it curious. Do you really want to be a poor little slave for ever?'

Then he fell silent. And we spent the rest of the day either in a state of nervous irritation or, which was even worse, in silence.

In the evening, after dinner, at last the storm broke. The wind rose to a gale, and the sea broke against the sea wall with a loud, lifeless thud. Monsieur George did not want to go to bed, because he felt it would be impossible to sleep, and he was afraid of the long night stretching before him. Lying on the sofa, with me sitting at a little table and a shaded lamp shedding its soft pink light around us, neither of us spoke. Though his eyes were brighter than usual, Monsieur George seemed to have become calmer, and the light from the lamp heightened the colour in his cheeks and threw into relief the charming outlines of his face. I was busy with some sewing.

Suddenly he said to me: 'Stop working for a bit, Célestine, and come and sit closer to me.'

I always fell in with his wishes, his caprices . . . He used to have these sudden outbursts of friendship sometimes, and I attributed them to his feeling of gratitude. Now, as usual, I did what he asked me.

'Closer, come closer to me,' he said. Then, 'Now, give me your hand.'

110

Without the least hesitation I let him take it, and he began stroking it.

'What lovely hands you've got! And your eyes too! Everything about you is lovely, everything.'

He had often spoken of my kindness, but never before had he told me I was pretty, at least, not in this way. Taken aback, but nevertheless delighted by his words, which he uttered in a serious, slightly breathless voice, I instinctively drew back.

'No, no, don't go away. Stay close to me, very close. You've no idea how much good it does me to have you near me . . . how it warms me. You see? I'm not nervous or upset any more. I'm not ill now . . . just content and happy . . . very, very happy.'

He put his arm round my waist, and gently pulled me down to sit beside him on the sofa. Then he asked:

'Do you mind being like this?'

I felt some misgiving, for his eyes were burning and his voice had begun to tremble . . . the trembling that I know . . . My God, how well I know it! . . . the trembling that always comes into men's voices when they feel the stirring of desire. I was deeply moved, and felt quite weak. My head was beginning to swim. But I was determined to defend myself against him, and above all, to defend him against himself, and I replied with a roguish smile:

'Yes, Monsieur George, I mind it very much . . . Let me get up.'

But without taking his arm away, he went on: 'No, no, please be nice to me.'

And in a voice that was unbelievably gentle and caressing he added:

'But you're frightened . . . What is there to be afraid of?'

At the same time he brought his face close to mine, and I could feel the warmth of his breath, which had a stale kind of smell like the incense of death. Seized by unspeakable anguish I cried out:

'Monsieur George, oh, Monsieur George, let me go! You will make yourself ill. I beg you, please let me go.'

Because of his weakness, the frailty of his limbs, I dared not struggle. I simply tried, with infinite care, to push away the hand with which, awkwardly, trembling with shyness,

111

he was trying to undo my blouse and feel my breasts. And again I said:

'Let me go! What you are doing is very wicked, Monsieur George. Let me go!'

The effort of holding me so close had tired him. The pressure of his arms grew weaker, and for a few seconds he had difficulty in breathing . . . Then his body was shaken by a dry cough.

'Now, you see, Monsieur George,' I said, as gently as a mother scolding her child. 'You wouldn't listen to me; now you've made yourself ill and we shall have to start all over again. A lot of good you've done yourself. Do, please, be sensible . . . please. If you were really good do you know what you'd do? You'd go to bed straight away.'

He took his hand from my waist, stretched out on the sofa and, while I was putting back the cushions which had fallen, murmured sadly:

'Yes, I know. You were quite right. You must forgive me.'

'There's nothing for me to forgive, Monsieur George. You must just keep calm.'

'Yes, yes,' he said, staring at a point on the ceiling where the lamp made a circle of moving light. 'It was crazy of me to have dreamt for a moment that you could love me . . . *me*, who have never known what love is . . . *me*, who have never had anything but suffering. Why should you love me? This ought to cure me of loving you . . . But when you are here, close to me, and I desire you . . . when you are here in all the freshness of your youth . . . with your eyes, your hands, those soft little hands, that seem to be caressing me when they are caring for me . . . Since I am continually dreaming of you, feeling within myself, in my whole soul and body, fresh strength welling up, a vitality I've never known before . . . that is to say, when I used to feel this . . . Anyway, what does it matter to you? I was crazy! And you? You? . . . No, you were right . . .'

I was very embarrassed. I did not know either what to say, or what to do. Powerful and conflicting feelings were tugging me in every direction, one impulse urging me towards him, but a sense of duty holding me back. And because I was not sincere, because I could not be sincere, torn as I was in the struggle between desire and duty, all I could do was to stammer:

'You must be sensible, Monsieur George. You mustn't think of such terrible things. It will only do you harm. Look, Monsieur George, you must try to be good . . .'

But he repeated: 'It's true. Why should you love me? You are quite right not to. You think I am a sick man. You're afraid that the poison of my mouth will poison you . . . that you will catch my disease—the disease I am dying of— from my kisses. You are quite right . . .'

The cruel injustice of his words pierced me to the heart.

'You mustn't say such things, Monsieur George,' I cried. 'It's horrible, it's wicked, what you're saying. I can't bear what you are doing to me. I can't bear it.'

I seized hold of his hands . . . they were moist, and burning hot. I stooped over him and his breath was like a furnace:

'It's horrible, horrible!' he continued. 'A kiss from you, that's what would restore me to life . . . would really mean my resurrection. Did you seriously believe in your sea-bathing and port wine and horsehair gloves? Poor little thing! It's your love I have been bathing in, the wine of your love I have been drinking, the irritant of your love that has caused new blood to course through my veins. If I have a new hold on life, if I have become strong again, it is because I have been looking forward to your kisses, longing for them, waiting for them . . . But I don't blame you for refusing. You are right to do so. I understand, I understand. You are a timid little creature, without courage . . . a bird singing first on this branch, then on that . . . and then, at the slightest noise, off you go!'

'It's terrible, what you're saying, Monsieur George.'

But he had not finished, and all I could do was to sit there wringing my hands.

'What's terrible about it? No, it's not terrible, it's true. You think I'm ill . . . Do you believe it's possible to be ill when one is in love . . . Don't you realize that love is life— life everlasting . . . Yes, yes, I understand. Though for me your kiss means life, you're afraid that for you it might mean death . . . Let's say no more about it.'

I could not listen any longer. Was it pity? Was it the

113

bitter reproaches, the savage challenge contained in his atrocious words? Or was it simply that I was suddenly possessed by impulsive, primitive desire? I have no idea. Perhaps it was something of them all. All I know is that I flung myself down beside him on the sofa and, raising his charming, boyish head in my hands, cried wildly:

'You've no right to say such things. See if I'm afraid, just see if I'm afraid!'

I pressed my mouth to his, grinding my teeth against his with such quivering passion that it seemed to me as though my tongue must penetrate his wounded lungs and draw forth all the poisoned blood and deadly pus. He flung his arms round me and held me close . . .

And what had to happen, happened . . .

Yet now, the more I think about it, the more I am convinced that what made me fling myself into George's arms and press my lips to his was first and foremost an overwhelming and spontaneous protest against the mean motives to which—it was a trick, maybe—George had attributed my refusal. Above all, it was an act of fervent piety, sure and disinterested, which meant: 'No, I do not believe you are ill . . . No, you are not ill . . .And the proof is that I'm not afraid to breathe your breath, to inhale it, to draw it deep into my lungs, till my whole body is saturated with it. And even if you were really ill, even if your illness was contagious and must kill whoever came near you, I would hate you to feel that I was afraid of catching it, or even of dying of it!'

Moreover, I did not foresee what must inevitably be the result of this kiss . . . that once I was in his arms, once I felt his lips upon mine, I should no longer have the strength to tear myself from his embrace . . . But there it is! Whenever a man holds me in his arms, my skin immediately starts burning, and my head spins and spins. I become intoxicated, mad, a wild thing, I can think of nothing but the satisfaction of my desire. All I can think of is him. And, docile and terrible, I let him lead me where he will, even into crime!

Oh, when I remember that first kiss of Monsieur George's! His awkward, charming caresses, the ingenuous passion of his every movement, and the look of wonder in his eyes as, at last, the mystery of woman and of love was unveiled for

114

him. In this first encounter I gave myself to him completely, with a zest that held nothing back, with that feverish, inventive delight that tames and overwhelms the strongest men, till they beg for mercy. But as the intoxication died away and I looked at the poor, frail boy lying in my arms, panting, almost swooning, I had a terrible feeling of remorse . . . the monstrous fear that I might have killed him.

'Monsieur George, Monsieur George! My poor boy, what have I done? I have made you ill.'

But, tenderly, trustingly, overwhelmed by gratitude, he snuggled up against me like a cat seeking protection and, with an ecstatic look in his eyes, murmured: 'I'm so happy . . . so happy . . . Now I don't mind dying.'

And when in desperation I began cursing my own weakness, he repeated:

'I am happy. Don't leave me. Stay with me all night. If you left me by myself I don't think I could bear the bitter sweetness of this happiness.'

While I was helping him to get ready to sleep, he had a bout of coughing. Fortunately, it did not last long. But short as it was it was heartrending. Could it be that after taking such care of him and curing him, I was now to be responsible for his death? I detested myself, and could scarcely hold back my tears.

'It's nothing,' he said, smiling. 'Nothing at all. You mustn't be upset when I am so happy . . . Besides, I'm not ill, I'm not ill. You'll see how well I shall sleep, with you here beside me. This is how I want to sleep, with my head on your breast, as if I were your child.'

'But if your grandmother rings for me during the night . . .?'

'No, no, she won't ring. I want to sleep like this, knowing you are beside me.'

Sometimes sick people are more sexually potent than other men, even the strongest. I think it must be because the idea of death, the presence of death, acts mysteriously as a terrible stimulus to their passion. During the fortnight that followed that marvellous, tragic night, it was as though we were both possessed by a kind of madness, as though our kisses, bodies, souls, were intermingled in an endless act of possession. We were in furious haste to make up for all the time we had lost. We wanted to live every moment of this love, this love which we both felt could only end in death.

'Again, again, again!'

By a sudden revulsion of feeling, I not only no longer felt remorse, but when Monsieur George's strength began to fail I discovered new and more effective caresses to revive him, to give him for a moment fresh energy. My kisses had the monstrous power of an aphrodisiac.

'Again, again, again!'

There was something sinister, madly criminal, in my love-making. Knowing that I was killing George, it was as though I were desperately striving to kill myself as well, in the same happiness, and of the same illness. I was deliberately sacrificing both his life and my own with a wild and bitter exaltation that enormously intensified our love. I inhaled, I drank death from his mouth, smearing my lips with his poison. Once, lying in my arms, when he was seized by a fit of coughing, more violent than usual, his lips were covered with bloodstained froth, and I took a clot of blood in my mouth and swallowed it as if it were the elixir of life.

It was not long before Monsieur George suffered a relapse. The crises became more frequent, graver and more painful. He began spitting blood, and had fainting fits that lasted so long it seemed he must be dead. He grew thinner than ever, his body wasted away till it was little more than a skeleton. Soon the joy that had returned to the household turned to bleak dejection. Once again his grandmother began spending all day in the drawing-room, weeping and praying, listening for every sound, waiting in anguish outside the door of his room lest a groan, a sigh might prove to be his last, might mean the end of the one dear, living creature still left to her. Whenever I left his room,, she would follow me all over the house, moaning:

'Why, oh, why, my God? Has it happened yet?'

Or she would say to me: 'You're killing yourself, my poor dear, you can't go on sitting up every night with George. I shall have to get a nurse to relieve you.'

But I refused, and she thought all the better of me for doing so, still hoping that, having already achieved one miracle, I might yet achieve another. And the thought that

116

it was I to whom she pinned her faith terrified me. As to the doctors she summoned from Paris, they were amazed by the swift progress of his illness, and by the terrible ravages it had caused in so short a time. Not for a moment did they, or anyone else, have the slightest suspicion of the shameful truth. All they could prescribe were sedatives.

The only person who remained gay and happy was Monsieur George, and his gaiety and happiness were unfailing. Not only did he never complain, but he was always overflowing with gratitude. He never spoke without expressing his happiness. Sometimes in the evening after an appalling bout of coughing, he would say to me:

'I am happy . . . you mustn't be so upset, you mustn't cry. Your tears can only spoil the marvellous joy I feel. Oh, I assure you, death is a small price to pay for this human happiness you have given me. Before you came I was lost, nothing could withstand the death that was already within me. You gave me back a radiant, blessed life . . . So don't cry, my sweet. I adore you . . . And I thank you.'

My passion for destruction had long ago left me. I felt terribly disgusted with myself, at the unspeakable horror of the crime I had committed. All that was left for me was the hope, the consolation or excuse, that I had caught George's illness, and that I should not outlive him. But when the horror had reached its height, when I felt myself hovering on the brink of madness, was when George, taking me in his dying arms and pressing his mouth to mine, still wanted to make love, still begged me for the love that I hadn't the courage or—if it were not to commit a new and more atrocious crime—the right, to refuse him.

'Give me your mouth again! Oh your eyes, your wonderful eyes!'

He was no longer strong enough to stand the shock of our embraces, and often he fainted in my arms.

And what had to happen, happened . . .

It was then October, the 6th October. Since the autumn had remained mild and warm that year, the doctors had recommended that the invalid should remain at the seaside till it was possible to take him south. Throughout the day Monsieur George had been calmer. I had thrown open the windows of his room and, having wrapped him up warmly,

117

pushed the sofa on which he was lying close to them, so that for a few hours he had been able to breathe the delicious air wafted from the sea. The life-giving sun, the pleasant salty smell, the fishermen searching for shell fish along the deserted beach, delighted him. Never had I seen him so gay. And this gaiety, on his emaciated face, the bones of which were almost visible through the skin, which every day became more transparent, produced so sharp an impression of morality that I could scarcely bear to look at it, and several times I had to leave the room lest he should see the tears streaming down my face. When I took up a book and suggested reading him some poetry, he refused.

'No,' he said. 'You are all the poetry I need, lovelier than any other.'

He had been forbidden to talk. The slightest conversation tired him, and often brought on an attack of coughing. Besides he was now almost too weak to talk. All that still remained to him of life, of thought and feeling, was concentrated in the eyes, where the flame of his spirit burned with an amazing, supernatural intensity. That evening, the evening of October 6th, he seemed to be no longer suffering any pain. Oh, I can see him now, stretched out in bed, propped up with pillows, his long, thin hands tranquilly playing with the fringe of the curtain, smiling at me and following every movement I made with a gaze which shone and burnt in the shadow like a lamp.

A couch had been made up for me in his bedroom so that I could rest and, pathetic irony, to spare our modesty a screen had been arranged so that I could undress. But I did not often sleep on the couch, for Monsieur George always wanted to have me beside him. He only felt really at ease, really happy, when I was close to him and he could feel my naked body against his. Having slept for a couple of hours, almost peacefully, towards midnight he woke up. He was feverish and his cheeks were flushed. When he saw me sitting beside him, with tears running down my face, he said in a gently reproachful voice:

'Now, now, you're crying again! Do you want to make me unhappy, to hurt me? Why haven't you gone to bed. Come and lie down beside me.'

I made no attempt to argue with him, for any opposition

118

upset him. The least feeling of constraint was enough to bring on a stroke, with formidable results. Knowing my fears, he took advantage of them. But scarcely had I got into bed, than his hand began exploring my body, his mouth feeling for mine. Timidly, though without daring to resist, I begged him:

'Not tonight . . . please.'

Scarcely listening, he replied in a voice trembling with desire:

'Not tonight? That's what you always say. But how can I know that there will be another night?'

Shaken by sobs, I exclaimed:

'Oh, Monsieur George, do you want me to kill you? Do you want me to suffer for the rest of my life, knowing that it was I who killed you?'

The rest of my life! Already I was forgetting that I wanted to die with him, to die for him.

'Monsieur George, Monsieur, have pity on me. I implore you!'

But already his lips were on mine . . . death was on my lips.

'Be quiet,' he panted. 'Be quiet! Never have I loved you as I do tonight . . .'

As our two bodies clung together . . . And as I felt desire stirring once more within me, it was a hideous pleasure to hear George's gasping cries, to feel beneath my weight the frail, almost fleshless bones of his body.

Suddenly his arms let go of me, and fell inertly on the bed. His lips were torn from mine, and a cry of distress burst from his upturned mouth, followed by a torrent of blood that spattered my face. I leapt out of bed, and caught sight of my reflection in a mirror, covered with blood. Panic-stricken, almost out of my mind, I was going to call for help, but the instinct of self-preservation, the fear that my responsibility for the crime would be exposed, every kind of calculating, cowardly motive, sealed my lips, held me back from the gulf of madness into which I felt myself falling. Suddenly I had realized, quite clearly, that my nakedness and the confused state of the room would make it obvious that George and I had been making love, and that it was quite out of the question to call for help.

What miserable creatures we are! To think that, at that moment, what I was most conscious of, stronger and more spontaneous than grief or dread, was this mean, ignoble concern for my own safety. Terrified as I was, I had the presence of mind to open the door of the drawing-room, then of the ante-room, and listen. Not a sound. The whole household was asleep. Only then did I return to the bed and lift George's body in my arms. As I raised his head and held it between my hands, sticky clots of blood were still flowing from his mouth, and the sound of his lungs emptying themselves into his throat was like that of water pouring from a bottle.

'George, George, George!' But he made no answer to my cries, for he no longer heard them, he was beyond the reach of any earthly appeal. I let go of his body, and it fell back on the bed. I let go of his head, and it sank heavily onto the pillow. I put my hand on his heart, but it had stopped beating.

'George, George, George!'

The horror of this silence, of those mute lips, of that motionless body . . . and of myself . . . was still strong. Broken with grief, overwhelmed with the terrible effort of trying to restrain it, I fell to the floor in a faint.

How many minutes I lay there, how many centuries, I have no idea. When I came to, one tormenting thought dominated all others: to get rid of all the evidence of my guilt. I washed my face and put on some clothes. I even found courage to tidy up the bed and the room, and only when this was all done did I rouse the household and break the terrible news.

Oh, that night! I suffered all the tortures of the damned . . . and now tonight, five years later, everything reminds me of it. The wind is howling as it did then, the night that I destroyed that beloved body. And the roaring of the wind in the trees reminds me of the roar of the sea, breaking on the rocks at the foot of that ever accursed villa at Houlgate. When we got back to Paris after Monsieur George's funeral, I refused to remain in service with his poor grandmother, despite her repeated entreaties. I wanted to get away, to escape the sight of her tear-stained face and the sound of her heart-rending sobs. Above all, I wanted to avoid her gratitude, the need she felt in the bewilderment of her grief, to keep thanking me for my devotion and heroism, to keep calling me her 'daughter . . . her dear little daughter', to keep overwhelming me with tenderness . . . Many a time during the next fortnight, since at her request I had agreed to stay on, I felt a longing to confess, to talk to her about all the things that were weighing on my soul and almost stifling me. But what was the use? Would it have brought her the slightest relief? It could only have added one more poignant grief to all her other griefs. Yet this terrible thought, the feeling of inexpiable remorse that, but for me, her beloved grandchild might still, perhaps, be alive . . . I knew I ought to admit everything to her, yet I lacked the courage to do so. So I left, taking my secret with me, venerated by her as a saint and laden with her gifts and with her love.

It happened that the very day I left, returning from Madame Paulhat-Durand's registry office, I met in the Champs-Elysées a valet with whom I had been in service in the same house for about six months. It was quite two years since I had last seen him. After greeting one another, he told me that, like me, he was looking for a situation, only being for the moment in funds he was in no great hurry to find one.

'Damned if you aren't as attractive as ever, Célestine,' said he, delighted to have met me again. He was a nice lad, gay, fond of a joke and always ready for a spree. He suggested that we should have dinner together, and, as I needed distraction, needed to drive away the mournful thoughts that were obsessing my mind, I accepted.

'That's the girl!' says he, and taking my arm, led me off to a wineshop in the rue Cambon. His heavy gaiety, his coarse jokes and vulgar obscenity in no way shocked me. On the contrary, I experienced a kind of sordid joy, a mean sense of security, at the thought of returning to a forgotten way of life. To be more explicit, I recognized myself, my whole life and outlook, in those tired eyelids and smooth, clean-shaven face, that displayed the same servile grin, the same lying wrinkles, the same taste for smut that one may find alike in an actor, a judge, or a valet.

After dinner we sauntered along the boulevards, and he took me to a cinema. I was feeling rather lazy, having drunk too much wine. In the darkness, as the French army was marching across the screen to the applause of the whole audience, he put his arm round me, and kissed the back of my neck so violently that he almost knocked my hat off.

'You're marvellous,' he murmured. 'And my God, you smell good!'

He took me as far as my hotel, and we stood there a few moments on the pavement, without saying anything and feeling rather stupid: he, tapping his boot with his cane, while I, with lowered head, my elbows close to my sides and my hands in my muff, was crushing a piece of orange skin with my toe.

'Well, so long then,' I said.

'Oh no,' said he. 'Let me come up with you. Be a sport, Célestine.'

Vaguely, more or less as a matter of form, I refused. But he insisted:

'Come on now, what's the matter with you? Suffering from heartache? Why, that's just the best time for it.'

He followed me. It was one of those hotels where no one pays much attention to who comes in at night. With its dark, narrow staircase, sticky banister, sordid atmosphere and fetid smells, it was something between an hotel for prostitutes and a thieves' hide-out. My companion coughed to reassure himself, while I thought to myself, my mind filled with disgust:

'What a miserable hole, compared with the villa at Houlgate or the warm flower-filled rooms at Lincoln Street.

I had no sooner got into the room and locked the door than he flung himself upon me, and threw me brutally on the bed, my skirts in the air . . . Really, what a bitch one can be sometimes!

So once again life had got hold of me again, with all its ups and downs, its eternal succession of faces, its stupid affairs that are over before they have begun . . . and its abrupt changes from a life of luxury to starving on the street.

What an extraordinary thing it is! I, who in the exaltation

of love, in my ardent longing to sacrifice myself, had sincerely and passionately wanted to die, was now, for several months, continually worried by the thought that I might have caught Monsieur George's disease. The slightest indisposition, and the most fleeting pain, filled me with terror. Often, at night, I woke up in a cold sweat, panic-stricken, and the power of suggestion would make me feel pains in my chest, and I would examine my sputum, imagining that I could see flecks of blood in it. From continually feeling my pulse, I made myself feverish; contemplating myself in the glass, I would imagine that I was becoming hollow-eyed, that my cheeks had the same deadly flush I used to see on Monsieur George's. Leaving a dance hall one night, I caught cold, and for the next week I was always coughing, so that I was convinced it was all up with me. I even burnt candles to St Anthony of Padua. But when, despite my fears, I found that I was as well as ever and still able to stand up to the double strain of work and pleasure, the mood passed.

Last year, on the 6th October, like every other year, I bought some flowers to put on Monsieur George's grave. It was in the Montmartre cemetery. As I was walking along the main avenue, I saw, a few steps ahead of me, his poor grandmother. Oh, how old she had become, and so had the two maids who were with her. Her body bent, and unsteady on her feet, she was walking slowly, supported by the two maids who were as bent and unsteady as their mistress. They were followed by a porter, carrying a huge wreath of red and white roses. Not wishing to overtake them and be recognized, I slowed down. Hidden by a high tombstone, I waited until the poor old woman had deposited her flowers and murmured a few prayers over her grandson's grave. They returned, at the same slow pace, along the little path where I was standing, their clothes almost brushing against the stone that hid me. I crouched lower to avoid seeing them, for it seemed to me that it was my remorse, the shadows of my remorse, bearing down upon me. Would she have recognized me? I think not. They were walking without looking at anything, without seeing what was going on around them, and their eyes had the staring fixity of the blind, and though their lips were moving, no sound issued from them. They were like three ancient corpses, lost in the maze of the cemetery and seeking their graves. And I recalled that tragic night, and my face dripping with the blood that flowed from George's mouth. It made my heart go cold . . . But at last they were gone.

Where are they today, those pathetic shadows? Perhaps by this time they are really dead. Perhaps, after all their wanderings, they have at last found the silence and the peace that they were seeking.

Does it matter? It was really an odd idea of hers, that poor old woman, to choose me as sick nurse for such a young and handsome youth as Monsieur George. And honestly, when I think back over that time, what most astounds me is that she never suspected anything, never saw anything, never had the faintest inkling of what was happening! Yes, it's obvious now that all three of them must have been pretty simple-minded . . . After all, didn't they still believe in people!

Today, I saw Captain Mauger again, over the hedge, crouched over a newly-dug flower bed and planting out some pansies and wallflowers. As soon as he saw me he left his work and came over to the hedge to talk to me. Apparently he no longer bears me any grudge for the death of his ferret. Indeed, he seems quite cheerful. Bursting with laughter he informed me that that morning he had caught the Lanlaire's white cat in a snare. Probably he looks upon the cat as his revenge for the ferret.

'That makes the tenth that I've bumped off, as easy as that,' he explained, tapping his thigh and rubbing the earth from his hand. 'I've had enough of him scratching up the earth in my frames, the brute, and ruining my seed beds . . . How if I was to catch that Lanlaire and his missus in a snare, eh? The pigs! Ha, ha, ha! Not a bad idea, what?'

The thought of it convulsed him with laughter for a moment, then suddenly, his eyes sparkling with malice, he asked:

'Why don't you put some itching powder in their beds, the brutes? Damn it, I could give you a whole packet of it.

Now that would be an idea! By the way, you remember Kléber, my little ferret?'

'Yes, what about it?'

'Well, I *did* eat him, you know.'

'I bet it wasn't very tasty?'

'Phew, it was like eating rabbit that's gone bad.'

And that was all the funeral service the poor animal ever got.

The captain also told me that, the previous week, he had caught a hedgehog under a pile of wood, and was beginning to tame it. He calls it Bourbaki . . . That also would be an idea! An intelligent, extraordinary creature who eats everything!

'Heavens, yes,' he exclaimed, 'that damned hedgehog will eat steak, mutton, fat bacon, Gruyère cheese and jam, all in the same day. He's marvellous, you simply can't satisfy him. He's like me, he eats anything.'

At that moment the little servant went by, wheeling a barrowful of stones, old sardine tins and a heap of kitchen waste to throw on the rubbish heap.

'Come here a minute!' the captain hailed her. And when, in reply to his questions, I had told him that Monsieur Lanlaire was out shooting, and his wife had gone to town and Joseph was shopping, he began hurling all the stones and every bit of rubbish, one after the other, into our garden, shouting at the top of his voice: 'Take that, you swine; take that, you miserable brute!'

Before long a freshly-worked plot where, the day before, Joseph had sown some peas, was covered with stones and rubbish. When he had emptied the barrow, the captain expressed his delight by hooting and waving his arms in the air. Then, twirling his old grey moustache, he said with a triumphant leer:

'Mademoiselle Célestine, you're a fine-looking girl, by God! Come round and see me sometime, when Rose isn't there, what? That *would* be an idea!'

What a man! He's convinced he's still capable of anything.

27 OCTOBER

At last I've had a letter from Monsieur Jean, a very dull one. To read it you would never imagine we had been on such intimate terms. Not a word of friendship or tenderness, not a single memory! All he talks about is himself. Yet if he is to be believed it appears that Jean has become quite a personage. You can tell that from the condescending, almost scornful, attitude he adopts towards me throughout the letter. He just wants to impress me. I always knew he was vain—and him such a good-looking fellow!—but never like he is now. Oh men, they're all the same! Always trying to show off!

It seems that Jean is still first footman at Countess Fardin's, and that, at the moment, the Countess herself is perhaps the most talked-of woman in France. Besides being a footman, Jean has taken to going to political meetings and become a Royalist conspirator. He attends demonstrations organised by the Coppée, Lemaitre and Quesnay de Beaurepaire, and he is conspiring with General Mercier to overthrow the Republic. The other evening he accompanied Coppée to a meeting of the Patrie Française. He proudly sat on the platform behind this mighty patriot, and was even allowed to hold his overcoat for him all evening. So now he can boast of having held the overcoats of all the greatest patriots of the day! That will be a great thing in his life . . . Another evening, coming out of a meeting called by Dreyfus's supporters, to which the Countess had sent him to boo the speakers and 'beat up the cosmopolitans', he was hauled off to the police-station for shouting 'Death to the Jews!', 'Long live the King!', 'Long live the Army!' But the countess threatened to have a question asked in the Chamber of Deputies, and he was immediately released. She even increased his wages by twelve francs every month for this doughty feat of arms . . . His name was mentioned in *Le Gaulois* by Monsieur Arthur Meyer, and also appeared in a subscription list opened by *La Libre Parole* on behalf of Colonel Henry, to which he had contributed 100 francs . . . Coppée has put forward his name for office, and has made him an honorary member of the Patrie Française, one of the top-drawer organizations. All the servants in the great house belong to it, along with all the counts, marquesses and dukes. When he came to lunch yesterday, General Mercier said to him: 'Well, my good Jean?'—Good Jean, my foot! And in an article in the *Anti-Juif*, 'Yet another victim of the Yids', Jules Guérin wrote: 'Our valiant anti-Semitic comrade, Monsieur Jean', etc. etc. Finally, Monsieur Forain, who now almost lives in the house, asked Jean to pose for a drawing which was to represent the Spirit of the Fatherland . . . he said Jean had 'just the phiz for it'.

It is amazing what handsome tips he is getting these days in addition to all the flattering honourable mentions, just from mixing with such illustrious folk. And, if everything seems to suggest, General Mercier decides to call him as a witness at the trial of Zola which the General Staff intends to arrange before long, that will be his crowning glory. For, in the best society, the giving of false evidence is at present all the rage. To be selected as a false witness not only means immediate fame, but is looked upon as the equivalent of winning first prize in the State lottery. Monsieur Jean is quite convinced that he is making a growing name for himself in the Champs-Elysées district. When he goes to the café in the rue François I to play cards, or takes the countess's dogs out for their evening piss, he is the object of universal curiosity and respect . . . and the dogs as well, presumably!

That is why, now he has achieved a notoriety that must inevitably spread from the quarter to the whole of Paris, and from Paris to the whole of France, he has decided to take out a subscription for the *Argus de la Presse*, as the countess does. When anything really important appears about him, he will send it on to me. That's the best he can do for me, for I must understand that he just hasn't the time to bother with me. Later on, we'll see . . . 'when we are in power', as he remarks casually. Everything that has happened to me is my own fault . . . I have never known how to behave myself properly . . . I have never stuck to anything . . . I have given up the most excellent situations without any advantage to myself. If I hadn't always been so undisciplined, perhaps I, too, might have been on good terms with General Mercier, Coppée and Deroulède . . . And, perhaps, in spite of being only a woman my name might have been mentioned in *Le Gaulois*, which is so important for all the other people in service. And so on, and so on.

By the time I had finished reading this letter I was almost in tears, for I feel that Monsieur Jean has pretty well broken with me, and that I cannot count on him any longer . . . nor on anyone else? He doesn't even mention the girl who has taken my place . . . Oh, I can just see them, the pair of them, in the room I used to know so well, kissing and cuddling, and going off together like we used to to theatres and dance halls. I can see him in his oilskin mac, coming back from the races after losing all his money, and saying to this other woman, as he so often said to me:

'Lend me your jewels and watch, will you, so that I can pop them?'

Unless, of course, in his new role as politician and Royalist conspirator he has now got other ambitions, and instead of carrying on with the maids has affairs with their mistresses. But he'll get over it one of these days.

Is it really my fault, what has happened to me? Perhaps. Yet it seems to me my whole existence has been weighed down by some fatality I have never been able to control, and that this is why I have never been able to keep the same job for more than six months. If I was not sacked, it was I who gave notice because I couldn't stand it any longer. It's a funny thing, but it is also sad . . . I have always been in a hurry to be 'somewhere else'. I have always set my hopes on this chimerical 'somewhere else', seeing it through the eyes of poetry as a deceptive mirage of far-off things . . . especially since the time I have spent at Houlgate with poor Monsieur George. Ever since then I have felt a restless longing, a painful need, to reach out towards unattainable ideas and forms. I think that all too brief glimpse of another world was fatal to me, and that since it was impossible for me to get to know it better it would have been better for me not to have known it at all. All these roads leading to the unknown are simply a deception! You set out again and again, but it is always the same . . . See that dusty horizon, there in the distance . . . blue and pink, fresh and luminous as a dream? How good it would be to live there. But you draw nearer, you arrive, and all you find is sand and stones and cliffs, desolate as the walls of a town. Nothing else . . . and above the sand and stones, a grey, opaque, lowering sky, a sky into which the day sinks in despair and where the light weeps soot. Nothing else, nothing at all of what you set out to find. Moreover, I no longer know what it is I am hoping to find . . . I no longer even know who I am.

Servants are not normal social beings, not part of society. The lives they lead are disjointed, and they themselves are made up of bits and pieces that do not fit together. They are worse than that, they are monstrous hybrids. They have ceased to be part of the common people from whom they spring and they will never become part of the bourgeoisie whom they live amongst and wait on. They have lost the generous responses, the native strength, of the people they have rejected, and have acquired the shameful vices of the bourgeoisie without the necessary means of satisfying them; they have adopted their vile feelings, their cowardly fears, their criminal appetites, without the background, and therefore without the excuse, of their wealth. Living in this 'respectable' bourgeois world, simply from breathing in the fatal atmosphere that rises from this putrid drain, they lose all sense of spiritual security, and cease to be aware of their own separate existence. They wander like ghosts of themselves amongst a crowd of strangers, and when they search their memories all they can find there is filth and suffering. They are always laughing, but the laughter is forced; and, since it does not spring from joys encountered or hopes realized, it always wears the bitter grimace of revolt, the cruel sneer of sarcasm. Nothing is so heart-rendingly ugly as this laughter—it burns and withers . . . Perhaps it would have been better if I had cried! Yet I don't know . . . Anyhow, to hell with it!

But here, nothing happens . . . And I cannot get used to it. It is this monotony, the absolute immobility of life here that I find hardest to bear. I want to get away from here. Get away? But where, and how? And since I have no idea, I just stay where I am.

Madame remains exactly the same: distrustful, methodical,

hard, rapacious, not a single generous impulse, utterly lacking in spontaneity and with never the slightest gleam of happiness on that stony face. The master has fallen back into his old ways, and from his shifty look I imagine that he bears me a grudge for having been so hard on him; but his grudges are not dangerous. After lunch, armed and gaitered, he goes off shooting, gets back at nightfall—though he no longer asks me to help him pull off his boots—and at nine o'clock goes off to bed. He is as loutish as ever, a vaguely comic creature . . . and he's putting on weight. How on earth do rich people manage to resign themselves to such a dreary existence? Sometimes I wonder whether, perhaps, I might have made something of him. But he never has a penny, and he certainly wouldn't have given me the slightest pleasure. And since Madame's not jealous . . .?

The terrible thing about this house is the silence. I just cannot get used to it, creeping about, 'walking on air', as Joseph says. Often, in these dark, cold passages, I feel like a ghost, a spectre. It's absolutely stifling here . . . yet I stay put!

My one distraction is visiting Madame Gouin, the grocer's wife, after mass on Sundays. Though she disgusts me, boredom outweighs disgust, so I continue to go. At least we are amongst ourselves there, and can gossip and play the fool and have a drink. At least there is an illusion of life, and it is a way of passing the time. The other Sunday, as I had not seen the rat-faced girl with the running eyes for some time, I asked about her.

'Oh, it's nothing . . . nothing serious, at least,' said the grocer's wife, in a tone which she tried hard to make mysterious.

'Is she ill, then?'

'Yes, but it's nothing. In a couple of days she will have quite got over it.'

And Mademoiselle Rose glanced at me in confirmation, with an expression that seemed to say: 'You see? What did I tell you? She's a very clever woman.'

While I was there today, I heard from the grocer's wife that yesterday the gamekeepers had found in the forest of Raillon, hidden amongst the brambles and dead leaves, the body of a little girl, horribly violated. It seems she is the daughter of one of the roadmen, known in the village as 'little Clara'. She was a bit simple-minded but a sweet little thing . . . not yet twelve years old. As you can imagine, it's an absolute godsend for a place like this, where you are reduced to chewing over the same old gossip week after week. And of course, they were all hard at it already.

According to Rose, who always knows better than anyone else, little Clara had had her stomach slashed with a knife, and the finger-prints on her neck and throat, where she had been strangled could still be clearly seen. Her private parts were terribly torn and swollen, as if she had been forced— the comparison was Rose's—'with the handle of a wood-man's axe'. One could still see, from the crushing and trampling of the undergrowth, the place where the crime had taken place. It must have happened at least a week ago, for the corpse was almost completely decomposed.

Despite the genuine horror inspired by this murder, I could tell that for most of these creatures rape, and the obscene pictures that it evokes, were not exactly an excuse for, but at least an attenuation of the crime, since rape is at least a form of love. They had every kind of explanation for it. Someone remembered how little Clara used to spend entire days in the forest, going there in spring to pick lilies of the valley and anemones to make into bouquets for the ladies of the town, or gathering fungi to sell on Sundays in the market. And in summer, there would be mushrooms, and other kinds of flowers. But what could she have been doing in the forest at this time of the year, when there was nothing to find?

One of them said sententiously:

'What I don't understand, is why her father didn't seem to be worried about her disappearing? It might have been him that did it.'

To which another, equally sententious, replied:

'But if he'd wanted to do such a thing he wouldn't have had to take her into the forest, surely?'

Mademoiselle intervened:

'The whole thing is very fishy! But I . . .' And, with the air of someone who is in possession of terrible secrets, she continued in a lower voice: 'Well, of course, I don't actually know, and I wouldn't like to say for certain, but—and she broke off, leaving our curiosity in suspense.

'But what? What then?' everyone demanded, craning their necks and with mouths agape.

'Well . . . I shouldn't be at all surprised . . . if it was'—by now we were all on tenterhooks—'if it was Monsieur Lanlaire . . . Anyway that's what I think,' she concluded with a ferocious expression.

While some of them protested and others suspended judgment, I insisted that Monsieur Lanlaire was quite incapable of such a crime and explained:

'What, him, poor man? Christ, he'd be much too scared.'

But Rose insisted even more venomously:

'Incapable? Fiddlesticks! What about the Jézureau girl? . . . and the little girl at Valentin? . . . and the Dougère child? You're forgetting them. Incapable, indeed!'

'They were quite different . . . It wasn't the same thing at all.'

Despite their hatred for Monsieur Lanlaire, they were not prepared to go as far as Rose and actually accuse him of murder. Violating little girls who consented to be violated was one thing. But to kill them? Oh no, that was unthinkable. But Rose angrily persisted. Foaming at the mouth, striking the table with her huge, soft hands and throwing herself about in her chair, she exclaimed:

'But I tell you, it *was* him. I'm certain of it.'

Whereupon Madame Gouin, who up to now had remained neutral, declared in her colourless voice:

'In matters of this kind, one can never be certain. But as regards the Jézureau girl, I can assure you it was the purest fluke that he didn't kill her.'

Despite this authoritative opinion and Rose's unwillingness to drop the question, one after the other they reviewed the crime. And there was certainly no lack of suspects— anyone they happened to dislike, anyone they were jealous of or had a grudge against, came under suspicion. Finally, the pale little woman with the rat face suggested:

'You know those two Franciscan monks who were here last week? Well, I didn't like the look of them at all, with their dirty beards and begging from everybody . . .Why shouldn't it have been one of them?'

But while the rest of us continued to accuse everybody in turn, Rose stubbornly repeated: 'But I tell you—it was him.'

On the way back, I stopped for a moment in the saddle room where Joseph was polishing the harness. Above some shelves containing neat rows of blacking bottles and tins of saddle soap, a picture of Drumont was pinned to the wooden partition, and to make it more imposing, Joseph had recently decorated it with a laurel wreath. On the opposite wall, a portrait of the Pope was almost completely hidden by a horse blanket hanging from a nail. One shelf was filled with anti-Semitic pamphlets and patriotic songs, and amongst the brooms in a corner of the room stood Joseph's club.

Abruptly, and from no other motive than curiosity, I asked Joseph:

'Have you heard about little Clara's body being found in the forest? And that she had been raped before she was murdered?'

Joseph was unable to repress a gesture of surprise. Or was it surprise? For, furtive as this movement was, it seemed to me that at mention of little Clara he had actually shuddered, though he quickly pulled himself together.

'Yes,' he said in a firm voice. 'I know. Someone in the village told me this morning . . .'

And, calm and indifferent again, he continued methodically polishing the harness with a big black rag. I noticed the strength of his arms, and was impressed by the supple power of his biceps and the whiteness of his skin. I could not see his eyes beneath the lowered lids, for he kept them obstinately fixed on his work. But I saw his mouth, that great wide mouth, and his enormous jaws like those of some cruel and sensual animal. And my heart seemed to miss a beat.

'Does anyone know who did it?' I asked.

Shrugging his shoulders, Joseph replied in a voice that was half joking, half serious: 'Tramps, I expect . . . some of those dirty Jews.'

And after a short silence, he added: 'But they'll never get

picked up, you just see! They've got all the magistrates bribed.'

He hung up the harness he had finished polishing on its hook and, pointing to the picture of Drumont beneath his laurel wreath, he added:

'There's the fellow we need . . . he'd sort them out!'

I don't know why, but when I left him I had a curious feeling of uneasiness . . . There's one thing, this business of Clara is going to give everybody something to talk about for the next week or so.

Sometimes when Madame is out, and I feel more than usually bored, I go to the garden gate, where Mademoiselle Rose comes to meet me. Always on the watch, she never misses a thing, and notes all our comings and goings. She has grown fatter and softer than ever, and redder in the face. Her gross lips hang more loosely, and her bodice can scarcely contain that vast surge of her bosom. More and more she is haunted by obscene thoughts . . . that's all she can ever think about, all she lives for. Every time we meet, she immediately glances at my belly, and the first thing she says in that greasy voice of hers is: 'Remember what I told you. Directly you notice the first sign, go to Madame Gouin's straight away, straight away.'

It's an absolute obsession with her, a mania. It irritates me and I reply:

'But why should I notice anything? I don't even know anybody here.'

'Oh,' says she, 'but it's a misfortune that can happen so quickly. A moment's carelessness, only too natural under the circumstances, and there you are! Sometimes you don't even know it has happened. Why, I've seen plenty of them just like you, quite certain everything was all right . . . until it was too late. But with Madame Gouin you can rest easy. Why, she's a blessing to the whole district.'

And as her imagination kindles, she grows uglier than ever, her whole body heaving with sensuality.

'Round here at one time, my dear, the whole place was simply full of children, the town was lousy with them. It was a perfect scandal! The streets used to be swarming with them, like chickens in a farmyard . . . squalling at every door, kicking up a row . . . kids wherever you looked. But nowadays, I don't know whether you've noticed, you scarcely see one.'

Then, with a slimy smile, she went on: 'Not that the girls don't have just as much fun. My goodness no! On the contrary. You don't go out in the evening, but if you were to walk down the chestnut avenue any evening about nine o'clock, you'd see for yourself. Why, there's a couple on every bench! People can't get along without it. But it's a nuisance to have swarms of children shitting about all over the place. Well, now they don't have them . . . they just don't have them any more. And it's Madame Gouin they have to thank for it. Of course, it's not very pleasant, but it's soon over . . . If I was in your place, I wouldn't hesitate, dear. A pretty girl like you, so distinguished-looking, and with such a lovely figure . . . Why, having a kid would be sheer murder.'

'Oh, you needn't worry. I have no intention of having one.'

'Of course, of course, no one wants to have one . . . only . . . tell me something. Do you really mean old Lanlaire has never tried it on?'

'Certainly not.'

'Well, I must say that surprises me, with his reputation. Not even that morning in the garden, when he had his arms round you?'

'I assure you . . .'

Mademoiselle Rose shook her head. 'I can see you don't mean to tell me . . . You don't trust me. Well, that's your business, only I know what I know.'

In the end I got annoyed and exclaimed: 'Oh, for goodness sake! Do you imagine I sleep with everybody, even with dirty old men?'

In a chilly tone of voice, she replied: 'All right, my girl, but there's no need to get your rag out. Some of the old ones are just as good as the youngsters. I know it's none of my business . . . That's what I said, didn't I?'

And in a nasty voice, more vinegar than honey, she wound up: 'After all, that may well be. Doubtless Monsieur Lanlaire prefers them not quite so old. Everyone to his taste, my girl.'

Some peasants passed along the road and hailed Mademoiselle Rose respectfully: 'Good morning, Mademoiselle Rose. And how's the captain these days?'

'Very well, thank you. He's just drawing some wine.'

Then some gentry went by and they, too, saluted Mademoiselle Rose, respectfully: 'Good morning, Mademoiselle Rose. And the captain?'

'Splendid, thank you. Most kind of you, I'm sure.'

Next came the village priest, walking slowly, and shaking his head. At the sight of Mademoiselle Rose he bowed, smiled, closed his prayer book and came to a halt:

'Ah, there you are, my child! And how is the captain?'

'Thank you, Father, going along nicely. At the moment the captain is busy in the cellar.'

'That's good, that's good. I hope the gardening's going well, and that he will have some nice flowers for us again for Corpus Christi?'

'Why, of course he will, Father.'

'Give him my best wishes then, my child.'

'And the same to you, Father.'

And as he turned away and opened his prayer book again, the priest called over his shoulder: 'Good-bye, then, good-bye! What a pity we haven't got more parishioners like you.'

And I returned to the house feeling sad and discouraged, and filled with hatred. Leaving the abominable creature to enjoy her triumph, greeted by everyone, respected by everyone, fat and happy . . . hideously happy. Before long I expect the parson will put her on a pedestal in the church, like a saint, with a candle on either side and a golden halo . . .

28 OCTOBER

One person who intrigues me is Joseph. He behaves in the most mysterious manner, and I have no idea of what's really going on at the bottom of that crazy, taciturn heart. But it is certainly something out of the ordinary. Sometimes he stares at me with such terrifying fixity that I have to drop my eyes. He has a way of walking, with slow, gliding steps, that frightens me . . . you'd think he was dragging a weight chained to his ankles, or at least the memory of it . . . Is it

prison he's remembering, or a monastery? Both perhaps . . .
His back also scares me, and that thick, powerful neck, like
a piece of old leather, with the hard tendons standing out
beneath it like knotted ropes. On the back of his neck I
have noticed a lump of hard muscle, like you find in wolves
and other wild animals that carry their prey in their jaws.

Apart from his hatred of the Jews, which indicates a love
of violence and taste for bloodshed, on the whole he is
rather reserved about other questions. Indeed, it's difficult
to know what he thinks. Unlike most servants, he doesn't
display that combination of noisy boasting and professional
humility that is typical of them; nor do you ever hear him
complaining about his employers and running them down.
He respects them without servility, and seems to be devoted
to them without ostentation. He never grumbles about
work, however irksome. He's extremely ingenious, and can
turn his hand to anything, even the most difficult and unusual jobs. He treats the Priory as though it belonged to
him, looks after it, guards it jealously and is ready to defend
it. He's always driving away beggars and tramps, distrustful and threatening as a mastiff. He's like one of those old-
time retainers from before the Revolution . . . Locally,
people say, 'You don't find servants like him nowadays . . .
he's an absolute treasure'; and they are always trying to
persuade him to leave the Lanlaires. He's had plenty of
good offers from Louviers, Eldeuf and Rouen, but he always
turns them down, without boasting about it . . . My goodness, no! . . . He's been here fifteen years, and looks upon
the house as his own; and as long as they want him he'll
stay. Even Madame, suspicious as she is and always ready
to see the worst in everybody, has complete confidence in
him. She may not trust another soul, but she certainly trusts
Joseph, and counts on his honesty and devotion. 'A treasure!
He'd go through fire for us!' says she. And, despite her
meanness, she overwhelms him with presents and little acts
of generosity.

All the same, I distrust the man. He makes me uneasy,
and at the same time interests me prodigiously. Sometimes
I have seen really terrifying things lurking in the obscure
depths of his eyes. Since I have become interested in him,
he no longer strikes me as being a coarse, stupid, loutish

137

peasant, as I used to think when I first got here . . . I ought to have examined him more carefully. Now I regard him as being unusually subtle and crafty . . . better than subtle, worse than crafty . . . I don't quite know how to sum him up. Moreover, as a result of seeing him every day, I no longer find him so old and ugly. Habit has the same effect on people as on things: it is like a fog that gradually obliterates the features of a face and hides its defects. After a while you don't seem to notice that a hunchback has got a hump! . . . But there's something else—all the new and deeper sides of Joseph that I'm beginning to discover. And they disturb me profoundly. For a woman, what constitutes masculine beauty is not the regularity of purity of a man's features. It is something much less obvious, and much more difficult to define . . . a kind of affinity, a sexual ambience, pungent, terrifying and intoxicating, which, for some women, becomes an irresistible obsession. And it is precisely this ambience that I am conscious of when I am with Joseph. The other day I was admiring the way he picked up a barrel of wine, playing with it like a child with a rubber ball. His exceptional strength, the suppleness of his movements, the formidable thrust of his loins and the athletic power of his shoulders set me musing. This strange and morbid curiosity, a mixture of fear and attraction, that the enigma of his shiftiness, of his grim silences, and impressive glances arouses in me is intensified by his muscular strength and bull-like solidity. Though I can't properly explain it, I feel that between Joseph and myself there is some secret relationship, a moral and physical bond, that binds us a little closer every day.

From the window of the linen room where I work I sometimes watch him in the garden. There he is, crouching down with his face almost level with the ground, or perhaps kneeling by the wall with the espaliers on it . . . and suddenly he has disappeared . . . vanished into thin air. Before you can turn your head, he's just not there. Does he sink into the ground? Can he pass through walls? . . . No and then I have to go into the garden to give him a message from Madame. I can't see him anywhere, and I call him.

'Joseph, Joseph, where are you?'

No answer. I call again:

'Joseph, Joseph, where are you?'

And suddenly, without a sound, Joseph appears before me from behind a tree or a vegetable bed. He's just there, like sunlight, with his grim, closed face, his hair plastered to his skull and his hairy chest showing through the open neck of his shirt . . . How does he manage it? . . . Where has he come from?

'Oh Joseph, you frightened me . . .' and the terrifying smile that plays on his lips and in his eyes gleams like the swift flash of a knife. I think this man must really be the devil himself! . . .

Little Clara's rape has become the talk of the neighbourhood, and whetted everyone's curiosity. People snatch the papers from each other's hands to read about it. *La Libre Parole* roundly denounces the Jews, and asserts that it is a ritual murder. The magistrates have arrived, and are carrying out enquiries and taking statements; dozens of people have been interrogated. But nobody knows anything. Rose's accusation of Monsieur Lanlaire has got around but no one believes it—they just shrug their shoulders. Yesterday the police arrested a poor pedlar, but he had no difficulty in proving that he was not in the neighbourhood at the time of the crime. The father, having been inculpated by all the gossip-mongers, had been completely exonerated . . . all the reports on him were completely favourable. So the police have been unable to find the slightest evidence to work on. Apparently the crime had impressed the magistrates by the amazing skill with which it was carried out . . . probably by professionals from Paris. It also appears that the public prosecutor is conducting the case in a very leisurely fashion, mainly as a matter of form. There's nothing particularly thrilling about the murder of a poor man's daughter . . . So probably nothing will be discovered, and before long, like so many others, the case will be classified as 'unsolved'.

I shouldn't be surprised if Madame thought her husband was guilty . . . It may be a joke, but she ought to know him better than anyone else. Ever since she heard the news she has been behaving most oddly. The way she keeps looking at her husband isn't natural. I have noticed during meals that, every time the bell rings, she gives a little start . . . Today, after lunch, when the master said he was going out, she stopped him.

'Surely you might just as well stay at home? What need is there for you to be always going out?'

She even strolled in the garden with him for a good hour. Naturally the master is quite unaware of what's going on; he eats and smokes as usual, and certainly doesn't lose a moment's sleep . . . What a blockhead the man is!

I have always been interested in what they find to say to each other, those two, when they are alone . . . Yesterday I was listening at the drawing-room door for over twenty minutes . . . I heard the master rumpling his paper, and Madame was sitting at her desk doing her accounts.

'What was it I let you have yesterday?' Madame asked.

'Two francs . . .'

'You're quite certain?'

'Of course, love . . .'

'Well, I am thirty-eight sous short . . .'

'I can assure you *I* haven't taken them . . .'

'Oh no, of course not. It must have been the cat!'

And that is all they had to say to each other.

Joseph doesn't like us to talk about little Clara in the kitchen. If Marianne or I try to do so he immediately changes the subject, or else withdraws from the conversation. The whole business annoys him . . . I don't know why, but the idea has occurred to me—and the more I think about it the more I am convinced—that it was Joseph who did it. I have no proof . . . and the only evidence in support of my suspicion is the look in his eyes and the slight gesture of surprise that escaped him, when, coming back from the grocer's and finding him in the saddle room, I suddenly mentioned little Clara's name, and told him about her having been murdered and raped . . . Yet this quite intuitive suspicion has increased, until it has become a possibility, almost a certainty. Of course, I may be quite wrong . . . I try to convince myself that Joseph really is a 'treasure'. I keep telling myself that I often imagine the craziest things, and allow myself to be influenced by the romantic perversity that I know to be a part of myself . . . But it's no use. In spite of myself, the impression persists. It doesn't leave me for a moment, and it is rapidly taking on the hideous, nagging form of a fixed idea . . . I have an irresistible desire to ask him:

'Tell me, Joseph, was it really you who raped little Clara in the wood? Was it you, you old swine?'

The crime was committed on a Saturday . . . I remember that at about the same time Joseph had been to collect some leaf mould from the Raillon woods. He was away all day, and only got back with his load late in the evening. This is what makes me certain. And by an extraordinary coincidence, I also remember there was a certain agitation in his behaviour, a more than usually worried look in his eyes, when he came in that evening. At the time I paid no particular attention. Why should I? Now, however, I can't help recalling these details . . . But was it actually on the Saturday of the crime that he went to Raillon? . . . I've tried in vain to fix the exact date . . . Besides, did he really have the uneasy gestures, the guilty looks, that now seem to me to prove his guilt? Or can it be that I am desperately trying to convince myself that there was something strange and unusual about him, to insist, unreasonably and against all appearances, that it was Joseph, this 'treasure', who really did it? . . . It annoys me not to be able to reconstruct what actually took place in the forest, though at the same time it strengthens my convictions . . . If only the inquest had revealed that freshly made cart tracks had been found in the dead leaves and undergrowth near the corpse . . . But no . . . it revealed nothing of the kind . . . merely that a little girl had been raped and murdered. That was all . . . And yet it is precisely that this impresses me so deeply— the murderer's cleverness in not leaving behind the slightest evidence of his crime, his diabolical invisibility. It is because of this that I feel, can actually see, the presence of Joseph.

After a short silence, completely on edge, I suddenly summoned up courage to ask outright:

'Joseph, which day was it that you went to collect leaf mould in the forest? Do you remember?'

Quite unperturbed, Joseph slowly raised his eyes from the

141

paper he was reading. Steeled against shocks, he said
casually:

'Why ever do you want to know?'

'To find out . . .'

He looked at me with a heavy, penetrating expression in
his eyes. Then, quite unaffectedly, like someone searching
his memory in an effort to recall a forgotten fact, he
answered:

'I'm damned if I really remember . . . But I'm pretty sure
it was a Saturday . . .'

'The Saturday that little Clara's body was found?' I
insisted, the urgency of my question giving an aggressive
edge to my voice.

He continued to stare at me, and there was something so
intense, so terrible in his gaze that, despite all my effrontery,
I was forced to lower my eyes.

'It's quite possible,' he said. 'Why, come to think of it, I'm
pretty sure it must have been that Saturday.' And he added:
'Oh, you damned women . . . haven't you got anything
better to think about? If only you read the papers you'd
realize that some more Jews have just been killed at
Algiers . . . that's at least of some interest.'

Apart from the expression in his eyes, he was perfectly
calm and at ease, almost good-humoured: he gestured
freely and his voice was quite steady. Then he relapsed
into silence and, picking up the paper he'd laid on the table,
returned to his reading again as though he hadn't a care in
the world.

I continued to brood over my thoughts, trying to recall
some indication of active ferocity in Joseph's behaviour
since I had been here . . . His hatred of the Jews, the way
he is always threatening to torture them, kill them, burn
them . . . But maybe that's simply bragging . . . Anyway it's
only politics . . . What I was looking for was something more
precise, something that would convince me I was not mistaken about his criminal temperament. Yet all I could
discover were a few vague impressions mere hypotheses,
which the desire, perhaps the fear, of obtaining irresistible
proof, made more important and significant than they
actually were . . . Desire or fear? Which of these two feelings is it that drives me on? I wish I knew.

But wait a minute . . . there is one thing, something quite horrible, and very revealing. It isn't something I've invented . . . I'm not exaggerating, and I didn't dream it . . . It happened like this. One of Joseph's jobs is to kill the chickens, rabbits or ducks for the house. He kills the ducks by driving a pin into their heads, the old Norman way. If he wanted to he could quite easily just knock them on the head, so that they didn't suffer. But he prefers to prolong their agony by refinements of torture. He enjoys feeling the quivering of their flesh and the beating of their hearts. He likes holding them in his hands, so that he doesn't miss a single stage of their suffering . . . One day I happened to be there when he was killing a duck. He held it between his knees, one hand round its neck, while with the other he drove a pin into its skull, twisting and turning it with a slow, regular movement like grinding coffee. And as he did so, he said with savage delight:

'You've got to make them suffer. The more they do, the better the flavour.'

The bird managed to free its wings, and began flapping them wildly. Although Joseph still had hold of it, its neck was writhing in a horrible spiral, and beneath its covering of feathers, the flesh kept twitching. Then Joseph threw it on the kitchen floor, and sitting with his elbows on his knees, his chin cupped in his hands, he watched, with an expression of ghastly satisfaction, the convulsive twisting and turning of the wretched bird, as it wildly scratched at the floor with its yellow feet.

'That's enough Joseph!' I exclaimed. 'Put it out of its misery. It's horrible making an animal suffer like that.'

But his only reply was:

'It amuses me . . . I like watching it.'

When I think of this, when I recall all the sinister details and even the actual words he said, I feel an even more irresistible desire to yell at him:

'It *was* you who raped little Clara . . . Yes, yes, now I am certain of it. It was you, you old swine.'

There's no doubt about it, the man must be an absolute swine. Yet this opinion I have reached as to his moral character, far from driving me away from him, far from creating a gulf of horror between us, has had the effect, I

143

won't say of making me fall in love with him, but at least of interesting me in him tremendously. It's a funny thing, but I've always had a weakness for brutes like him. There's something unforeseen about them that stimulates me . . . a particular kind of intoxicating odour, harsh and powerful, that excites me sexually. Yet however evil such brutes may be they are never evil in the way respectable people are. And what bores me about Joseph is his reputation for—and, indeed, unless you really know that look in his eyes, his appearance of—complete respectability. I should like him better if his brutality was frank and shameless. True, then he wouldn't have this aura of mystery, this fascination of the unknown, that so moves and disturbs and attracts me—for I must admit, the old monster does attract me.

Now I am beginning to feel easier in my mind, for now I know, with a certainty that nothing can ever shake, that it was he who raped little Clara in the woods.

For some time now I have realized that I am making a considerable impression upon Joseph's heart. His attitude towards me is no longer unfriendly. His silence isn't either hostile or scornful, even when he bites my head off, he does it with a kind of tenderness. He no longer looks at me with hatred—did he ever, I wonder?—and though there is still something terrible in the way he stares at me, it is because he is trying to get to know me, because he wants to put me to the test. Like most peasants, he is extremely suspicious and is afraid of trusting people in case they let him down. He must have plenty of secrets, but he hides them jealously behind a savage, scowling mask, in the same way that people lock up their valuables in an iron box, bolted and barred. Yet, when he's alone with me he's no longer so suspicious. Indeed, in his own way he is charming to me, and does everything he can to please me and show his friendship. He takes on some of the heaviest and nastiest jobs I am responsible for, and he does this quite unpretentiously, without any ulterior motive, without asking for gratitude or claiming anything in return. As for me, I tidy up his room, mend his socks and trousers, patch his shirts and put his clothes away in the wardrobe—and I don't

144

mind admitting I take more trouble for him than for Madame.

Looking at me with a contented expression, he says:

'That's very nice of you, Célestine . . . You're a good woman, a tidy woman. And I don't mind telling you, tidiness is worth a fortune. And when a woman's nice into the bargain and good-looking, what more could a man want?'

Until lately, we have only been able to talk in snatches. At night, in the kitchen with Marianne, conversation can only be quite general . . . There's never any intimacy between us, and even when I do find him alone it's almost impossible to get him to speak. He doesn't like long discussions, probably for fear of compromising himself. A couple of words here, a couple of words there, sometimes friendly, sometimes churlish, and that's all. But if he doesn't say much, his eyes are certainly not silent. They are continually looking me up and down, enveloping me, peering into my innermost depths, as though they were trying to turn my soul upside down to find out what is underneath it.

Yesterday was the first time we have had a long conversation. It was in the evening. The Lanlaires were already in bed, and Marianne had gone up to her room earlier than usual. I did not feel like reading or writing, and was bored with being on my own. Still obsessed by the thought of little Clara, I went over to the stable where I found Joseph seated at a little table, sorting seeds by the dim light of a lantern. His friend the verger was also there, standing beside him with a pile of brightly covered pamphlets under his arm. With his huge round eyes under the deep arch of his eyebrows, his flattened skull, and yellowish, coarsely-grained skin, he looked just like a toad; and when he moved, he seemed to hop like a toad as well. The two dogs were asleep under the table, rolled up in a ball, with their heads hidden in their fur.

'Oh, so it's you, Célestine,' said Joseph.

The verger tried to conceal the pamphlets, but Joseph reassured him:

'You can say what you like in front of Célestine . . . She's a sensible woman.'

Then, returning to their interrupted conversation, he went on: 'So that's understood then, old man? Bazoches . . .

145

Courtain . . . Fleur-sur-Tille . . . and you'll see they're delivered tomorrow, during the daytime? Try to get some subscribers . . . But, above all, make sure you call at every house, even if they're Republicans. Maybe they'll try to kick you out, but don't worry . . . just stick to your guns. If you manage to win over even one of the sods, that's always something. And don't forget, for every Republican you get a franc.'

The verger nodded his head by way of agreement. Then, having re-adjusted the pamphlets under his arm, he set off for home, accompanied as far as the gate by Joseph. When the latter returned he saw from my face that I was curious.

'Oh,' he said casually, 'only a few songs and pictures and some anti-Semitic propaganda we are distributing. I've got an arrangement with the clerical gentry . . . I work for them. And why not? Of course, we have the same outlook . . . but I admit, they also pay well.'

He sat down again at the little table. The two dogs, having woken up and sniffed about the room, had now settled down again, further away.

'Yes,' he repeated, 'the pay isn't at all bad . . . These parsons, you know, have got plenty of money all right.'

And as though he were afraid he might have said too much, he added:

'I'm only telling you this, Célestine, because you're a good woman . . . a sensible woman . . . Because I trust you. But it's strictly between you and me, you understand?'

After a silence, he said: 'What a good idea of yours it was, to come here this evening . . . Real nice . . . very flattering.'

I had never known him so friendly and chatty. I leant across the table towards him and, stirring the seeds he had been sorting out with the tip of my finger, and said flirtatiously:

'Well, as soon as we'd finished supper, you went off before we'd had time for a bit of a natter . . . Would you like me to help you sort your seeds?'

'Thank you, Célestine, but it's all done.'

He scratched his head and said, irritably:

'Blast it, I ought to go and see to the frames, or the mice will have the lot . . . No, I'm damned if I will . . . I've got to talk to you, Célestine . . .'

He got up, closed the door which he'd left half open, and led me into the saddle room. For a moment I felt scared. Suddenly I could see little Clara, whom I'd forgotten about, lying in the undergrowth, horribly pale and covered with blood . . . But the look in Joseph's eyes wasn't evil. Indeed, it was as though he was shy, though we could scarcely see one another in the dark room, which was lit only by the wavering sinister light from the lantern. Up to this point, Joseph had been speaking hesitantly, but now his voice became grave and assured.

'There is something I've been wanting to talk to you about, Célestine, for several days now,' he began. 'You see, it's like this. I'm fond of you . . . You're a good woman . . . a sensible woman. I feel I'm really getting to know you . . .'

I thought it best to put on a friendly, teasing smile, and replied:

'You must admit you've taken long enough about it . . . What used to make you so disagreeable to me always? You'd never speak to me except to chivvy me . . . Do you remember how you used to bawl me out, just for walking on a path after you'd been raking it? . . . A regular old misery you were.'

Joseph laughed, and shrugged his shoulders.

'Ah well . . . But damn it all, you can't be expected to tell what people are like straight away . . . especially women. They're the devil to understand. And after all you do come from Paris! But now I've got to know you.'

'If you know me so well, then tell me what sort of a person I am.'

Tight-lipped and with a serious expression, he declared:

'What sort of person? . . . Why, the same sort as me, Célestine.'

'As you?'

'Oh, not to look at, of course . . . But, at the very bottom of our hearts, you and me, we're just the same . . . That's a fact, and I know what I'm talking about.'

There was a moment's silence. Then he went on in a gentler voice:

'I'm fond of you, Célestine . . . And besides . . .'

'And besides?'

'I've also got a bit of money put away . . . Not much, but

147

damn it all a man doesn't expect to work in decent situations for forty years without managing to put a bit by, does he?'

'Certainly not,' I replied, more and more amazed at what Joseph was saying and the way he was behaving. 'How much have you saved, then?'

'Oh, a tidy bit.'

'Yes, but how much? . . . Show me.'

With a superior smile, Joseph replied:

'Why, you don't really imagine I keep it here, do you? Oh no! That's nicely tucked away where it can do a bit of breeding on its own . . .'

'All right. But how much does it come to?'

Then in a low voice, almost a whisper, he said:

'Maybe 15,000 francs . . . maybe a bit more . . .'

'Crikey! You've done pretty well for yourself, haven't you?'

'. . . or maybe a bit less.'

Suddenly, both the dogs raised their heads and sprang towards the door, barking. Seeing that I was frightened, Joseph reassured me.

'Don't worry,' he said, giving both animals a hearty kick in the ribs. 'It's only someone in the road. Listen! Yes, that's Rose coming home. I recognize her step.'

And sure enough, a few moments later, I heard the sound of footsteps and a gate being shut. The dogs stopped barking.

I was sitting on a stool in a corner of the saddle room. Joseph was walking up and down with his hands in his pockets, occasionally knocking the harness or the wooden partition with his elbow . . . We had stopped talking. I was feeling horribly ill at ease, wishing I had never come, while Joseph was obviously worried by something he still wanted to tell me. After a few minutes he made up his mind:

'There's something else I ought to tell you, Célestine . . . I come from Cherbourg, and Cherbourg's a pretty tough place, full of soldiers and sailors, and those damned lascars, always ready for a bit of fun. But it's a good place for business. Well, I happen to know that at this moment there's a pretty good opening at Cherbourg . . . a small café, in the best possible position, near the port . . . The soldiers

148

are drinking a lot these days . . . all the patriots are out on the streets . . . shouting and bawling, and getting up a thirst . . . This would be just the time to set up there. I reckon anyone could make money hand over fist . . . The only thing is you'd need a woman . . . a nice, sensible sort of woman . . . a woman that knew how to doll herself up a bit and could take a joke . . . You know what they're like, these army blokes . . . easy going, always ready for a laugh and a bit of fun . . . getting tight whenever they can . . . fond of a bit of sex and ready to pay for it . . . Well, what do you think about it, Célestine?'

'Me?' I exclaimed, completely bewildered.

'Yes, you. How do you fancy the proposition?'

'Me?'

I hardly understood what he was getting at, and was so everwhelmed with surprise that I couldn't think of anything else to say. But he insisted:

'Well, of course you . . . Who else do you think would do for the café You're a sensible woman . . . You know how to run things . . . You're not one of those stuck-up dames that can never take a joke . . . and you're a true patriot! Besides, you're pretty and charming . . . Your eyes are enough to drive the whole Cherbourg garrison crazy. That's true, isn't it? Ever since I got to know you properly and realized all the things you could do, the idea has continually been running in my head.'

'And what about you?'

'Me as well, naturally . . . We'd get married on a proper friendly basis . . .'

'So that's it,' I exclaimed indignantly. 'You want me to become a whore so as to earn money for you?'

Joseph merely shrugged his shoulders, and replied quite calmly:

'Everything would be absolutely on the level, Célestine . . . You know that, surely?'

Then he came over to me, seized me by the hands, squeezing them so hard that I could have screamed with pain, and murmured:

'I'm crazy to have you there, Célestine, in the café. Don't you realize, you've got right under my skin?'

And, seeing that I was nonplussed and rather frightened

by this outburst and could neither move nor speak, he continued:

'Besides, maybe it's more than 15,000 francs . . . more like 18,000, I wouldn't wonder. No one knows how much the capital has increased. And then think of all the other things you could have . . . jewels and such-like. Mark my words, you could be really happy in that little café.'

He took me in his arms and held me like a vice. I could feel his body against mine, trembling with desire. If he had wanted to, he could have taken me there and then, and I wouldn't have made the least effort to resist. But he went on telling me about his dream:

'A pretty little café, nice and clean, everything shining . . . There would be a great big mirror, and in front of it a fine-looking woman serving at the bar, dressed in Alsatian costume, with a silk blouse and broad velvet ribbons . . . Well, Célestine? . . . Just you think about it, and we'll discuss it again, some other time . . . We'll discuss it again.'

I couldn't think of anything to say . . . It was something I'd never dreamt of. And yet I didn't feel the least hatred for the man, or horror at his cynicism, though he was talking to me with the same lips that had kissed little Clara's bloody wounds, and was holding me to him with the same hands that had embraced and strangled her in the forest.

'We'll talk about it again some other time . . . I know I'm old and ugly, but when it comes to fixing a woman, Célestine, you mark my words, I know what I'm up to . . . But we'll talk about it again.'

Fixing a woman indeed! A pretty sinister way of putting it . . . Is it a threat or a promise, I wonder?

Today Joseph has remained as silent as usual. You'd never imagine there had been anything between us last night. He comes and goes, works, eats, reads his paper, just as though nothing had happened. I look at him and wish I could detest him . . . wish I could see his ugliness for what it is . . . Wish I could feel such profound disgust for him that I'd never go near him again. But it just isn't like that. No, the funny thing is that this man makes me shudder and yet he doesn't disgust me . . . And this is terrible, because I know it was he who killed little Clara in the forest, and raped her.

3 NOVEMBER

Nothing delights me so much as coming across the name of someone I've worked for in the papers. I experienced this pleasure as keenly as ever this morning when I read in *Le Petit Journal* that Victor Charrigaud has just published a new book, that it is a great success and that everyone is talking about it. It is called *From Five to Seven,* and it is causing a scandal . . . in the proper sense of the word. According to the article, it is a collection of studies of society, brilliant and slashing, which, beneath their lightness of touch, hide a profound philosophy . . . Of course they were bound to say that! And it goes on to praise Charrigaud, not simply for his talent, but especially because of his elegance, his distinguished connections and his salon . . . Oh, but I could tell you something about that *salon* of his. I was parlour-maid at the Charrigaud's for eighteen months and, God knows, I don't think I ever came across such a bunch of rotters!

Everyone knows Victor Charrigaud by name. He has already published a series of best sellers. He is extremely witty and extremely talented, but he had the misfortune to achieve success too early, and, with it, a fortune. His early work showed great promise. Everyone was struck by his powers of observation, his considerable satirical gift, and the relentless irony that enables him to unmask human folly. He was looked upon as one of those lively, unfettered minds for whom the social conventions represent nothing but cowardly evasions; a shrewd and generous spirit, who, instead of stooping to the humiliating level of prejudice, boldly aspired to the purest and noblest ideals. At least, this is what one of his friends used to tell me about him, a painter who had fallen for me and whom I sometimes used to visit. It is to him I owe, not only the foregoing opinion, but also the details that follow about the writings and life of this illustrious man.

Of all the human follies so mercilessly exposed by Charrigaud, the one he particularly concentrated on was snobbishness. In his lively, well-informed conversation, even more than in his books, he exposed this form of moral cowardice, and the intellectual sterility that lies behind it, with a savagely picturesque precision, a rough and ready philosophy, and brilliantly scathing witticisms which, as they rapidly passed from mouth to mouth, at once became classics . . . A whole amazing psychology of snobbishness could have been elaborated from the closely observed sketches, and the brilliant, curiously living portraits that his prodigious originality poured out in an inexhaustible stream . . . Thus one would have thought that if anyone was to escape this moral influenza, which has such a powerful grip on society, it would have been Victor Charrigaud, for who else was so effectively protected from the contagion by that admirable antiseptic—irony . . . But human nature is a continual surprise, compounded as it is of contradictions and folly . . .

Scarcely had he got over the first enchantments of success, than the snobbishness that existed within him—and this was why he had been able to depict it so forcibly—revealed itself, exploded, so to speak, like a motor car engine when the ignition is switched on . . . He began by dropping those of his friends whom he found to be tiresome or compromising and only retained those who, either because they were already recognized or because of their position in the newspaper world, could be useful to him and could further his youthful success by persistent acclamation. At the same time, he became intensely preoccupied with his clothes. He began wearing the most daring frock-coats, exaggerated eighteen-thirtyish collars and neckerchiefs, tight-waisted velvet waistcoats and showy jewellery, and would produce expensive gold-tipped cigarettes from a metal case encrusted with pretentiously valuable gems. Yet, in spite of all this, with his heavy movements and common pronunciation, he still retained the massive solidity of the Auvergne peasants amongst whom he had been born. Having so recently arrived in a world of elegance where he was out of his element, it was no use his studying the most perfect models of Parisian fashion: he could never attain the easy manner, the slender, upright carriage, that he so much admired— and so bitterly envied—in the young dandies who frequented the clubs and racecourses, the theatres and restaurants. And his failure was a continual source of bewilderment and dismay to him. For, after all, didn't he go to the best shops and most famous tailors? Weren't his boots and shirts made for him by the most outstanding masters of their craft? Yet when he looked at himself in the mirror, he could only curse himself despairingly.

'However much I doll myself up in silks and satins, I still only manage to look like an outsider. It just doesn't look natural!'

As for Madame Charrigaud, having hitherto dressed simply and discreetly, she also now took to wearing the most elaborate and showy get-up. Her hair was dyed too deep a red, her jewels were too big, her silks too rich, with the result that she looked like the queen of the costermongers, in all her imperial majesty at a Shrove Tuesday carnival . . . People often made fun of them, sometimes cruelly. Their friends, humiliated by so much luxury and bad taste, though also enjoying it, avenged themselves by saying:

'Really, for a man who prides himself on his irony, he doesn't have much luck!'

Thanks to one or two fortunate encounters, incessant diplomacy and even more incessant sycophancy, they began to be accepted in what they chose to regard as society, the world of Jewish bankers, Venezuelan dukes, archdukes on the run and elderly ladies crazy about literature, white slavery and the Academy . . . It became their one aim in life to cultivate and develop these new connections, with a view to achieving others even more enviable and exclusive, and so on and so on, in a continual ascent.

One day, in order to get out of an invitation that he had rashly accepted from an undistinguished acquaintance whom he did not want to break with completely, Charrigaud wrote him the following note:

> My dear fellow, We are most terribly sorry, but we simply must ask you to excuse us for Monday next. The fact is, we have just received, for that very evening, an invitation to dine with the Rothschilds, and as it is the first time we've been asked, you will understand that it is impossible for us to refuse. It would be absolutely disastrous. It's a good thing we know each other so well, since I'm sure that, far from being angry with us, you will share in our happiness and pride.

On another occasion, describing how he had bought a villa at Deauville, he said:

'As a matter of fact, I don't know who these people thought we were . . . Maybe they thought we were just journalists, Bohemians . . . but I pointed out to them that I had a lawyer . . .'

Gradually they managed to throw off all their old friends, people whose mere presence in their house was a constant and unpleasant reminder of the past, an admission that they were tainted with that mark of social inferiority—writing for a living. Charrigaud was also at considerable pains to quench the flame of intelligence that still occasionally lit up his mind, to stifle once and for all that damnable wit, which he thought had died a natural death, but which now and again terrified him by showing signs of reviving. He was now no longer satisfied to be invited by other people, but was determined to play the host; and a house-warming for a place he had just bought at Auteuil was to be the pretext for a dinner-party.

It was just about then that I started working for them . . . The dinner was not to be one of those intimate affairs, gay and unpretentious, which in the past had made their house a centre of attraction, but a really elegant, really solemn occasion, all starch and ice—in short, a select dinner-party, to which they would ceremoniously invite, in addition to one or two literary and artistic celebrities, a number of society people, not too fussy or conventional, yet sufficiently distinguished to reflect some of their lustre upon their hosts.

'It's perfectly simple just to invite people to a meal at a restaurant,' Charrigaud pointed out. 'The real test is to give a dinner-party in one's own home . . .'

Having considered the project for a considerable time, he finally made up his mind.

'The point is,' he decided, 'I don't think we ought to start by having nothing but divorced women and their lovers. But we must make a beginning, and there are some divorcees who are perfectly acceptable . . . even the strictest Catholic papers treat them respectfully . . . Later on, when our connections are more extensive and we are in a position to please ourselves, we can invite as many as we like.'

'You are right,' Madame Charrigaud agreed. 'For the present, the important thing is to restrict ourselves only to the most distinguished ones . . . After all, whatever people may say, divorce does present certain difficulties . . .'

'At least it has the merit of avoiding adultery,' scoffed Charrigaud. 'Adultery is such old hat . . . The only person who believes in it any more is friend Bourget. Christian adultery, of course, with all the appropriate English trappings . . .'

'What a bore you are with your malicious cracks,' Madame Charrigaud replied in a tone of nervous irritation. 'If you don't take care your witticisms are going to put an end to any chance of our having a proper *salon*.' And she added: 'If you really want to cut a figure in society, you had better make up your mind straight away, either to become an imbecile or to keep your mouth shut.'

After a number of attempts to draw up a list of guests, finally, as the result of a series of laborious combinations, they arrived at the following:

The divorced countess Fergus, and her friend, the economist and Deputy, Joseph Brigard; Baroness Henri Gogsthein, also divorced, and her friend, the poet, Theo Crampp; Baroness Otto Butzinghen and her friend, Viscount Lahyrais, well-known clubman, sportsman, gambler and cheat; Madame de Rambure, another divorcee, and her friend, Madame Tiercelet, who was in process of getting her divorce; Sir Harry Kimberly, symbolist composer and ardent pederast, and his golden-haired boy-friend, Lucien Sartorys, as pretty as a woman, supple as a suede glove and slim as a cigar; the two Academicians, Joseph Dupont de la Brie, a numismatist noted for his collection of obscene medallions, and Isidore Durand de la Marne, in private life a well-known retailer of other people's love affairs, but at the Institute an unimpeachable sinologist; the portrait painter, Jacques Rigaud; the psychological novelist, Maurice Fernancourt; and the society gossip-writer, Poult d'Essoy.

The invitations were sent out and, as by means of energetic negotiations, were all accepted . . . Only the countess Fergus showed some hesitation:

'Who are these Charrigauds?' she asked. 'Are they really possible? Wasn't he at one time involved in all sorts of business in Montmartre? I've heard it said that he used to sell obscene photographs that he had posed for himself . . .

As for his wife, the same sort of unpleasant stories were going around about her. Before they were married she seems to have been engaged in similarly sordid adventures. Why, I have even heard she used to be a model at one time, and pose in the nude. What a creature! . . . exposing herself stark naked in front of a lot of men . . . and not even her lovers, at that!'

Eventually, however, having been assured that Madame Charrigaud had only sat for her portrait, that Charrigaud was so vindictive that he was quite capable of putting her in one of his books, and that Kimberly would be there, she accepted . . . Oh, of course, if Kimberly had promised to come . . . Such a perfect gentleman, so refined, so utterly charming!

Though the Charrigauds were fully informed about these reservations and scruples, far from taking umbrage at them they congratulated themselves that they had been successfully overcome. Now all that remained was to watch their step and, as Madame Charrigaud put it, behave like genuine society people . . . This dinner-party, so marvellously prepared and organized, so skilfully arranged, was to be their first appearance in the latest avatar of their destiny . . . It therefore had to be an outstanding success.

During the preceding week the whole house was turned upside down. Somehow or other everything had to be smartened up so that nothing should let them down. To avoid embarrassment at the last moment, they tried out various combinations of lighting and table decorations—a matter on which the two Charrigauds quarrelled like fish-wives, for they had completely different ideas and tastes, she being inclined to sentimentality, he insisting that everything should be severe and 'artistic'.

'But that's perfectly ridiculous,' shouted Charrigaud. 'It looks like some little tart's place . . . We should never hear the last of it!'

'You're the one to talk,' retorted Madame Charrigaud, on the point of a nervous breakdown. 'You haven't changed at all . . . just the same lousy bar-room loafer . . . I've had as much as I can stand . . . I'm fed up to the teeth!'

'Oh, so that's how it is. Then what about getting divorced, my love? Yes, let's get divorced. At least we should then fit into the picture and not make our guests feel uncomfortable!'

There was a shortage of everything—silver, cutlery, plates, glasses . . . Well, they'd just have to hire some . . . Oh, and some chairs . . . there were only fifteen, and even those didn't match . . . In the end they decided to order the meal from one of the well-known restaurants on the boulevard.

'I want everything to be ultra smart,' Madame Charrigaud insisted, 'so that no one will recognize what it is they are eating. Minced prawns, cutlets of foie gras, game served to look like ham, ham like cakes, truffle *mousse,* cherries in cubes and peaches in spirals . . . In short, everything must be absolutely the last word!'

'Madame, don't worry about a thing,' the manager assured her. 'We can disguise food so skilfully that I'll wager nobody will have the slightest idea what they are eating . . . It is one of our chef's specialities.'

At last the great day arrived.

Charrigaud got up early . . . restless, nervous and on edge. His wife, who hadn't been able to sleep all night, exhausted by yesterday's shopping and all the preparations, could not sit still. Half a dozen times frowning, breathless, trembling all over, and so tired, she said, that her heart was in her boots, she made a final inspection of the whole house, aimlessly re-arranging the ornaments and furniture, wandering from room to room without any idea of what she was doing, as though she were crazy. She was terrified the cooks wouldn't arrive in time, that the florist would break his word, that the seating of the guests wasn't strictly according to precedence. And Charrigaud, wearing nothing but a pair of pink silk pants, trailed around after her, approving this, criticizing that.

'I've been thinking,' he said. 'Wasn't it rather an odd idea of yours to choose centauries for the table decorations? You realize that, by lamplight, blue just looks black! Besides, centauries are really just a kind of cornflower . . . It will look as though we've picked them ourselves in the country.'

'Cornflowers, indeed! You're absolutely maddening!'

'Yes, cornflowers. And as Kimberly said quite rightly, the other evening at the Rothschilds, cornflowers are simply not a social flower . . . Why didn't you order wild poppies as well?'

'For goodness sake, stop it!' Madame Charrigaud replied. 'You'll drive me crazy with all your idiotic ideas. What a moment to choose!'

But Charrigaud insisted: 'All right, all right, but you'll see . . . If only everything goes off reasonably well, my God, and there are no last minute snags! I hadn't realized that to get into society was such an exhausting and complicated business. Maybe it would have been better if we had been content to remain just ordinary hangers-on.'

'For heavens sake! Will nothing ever change you? You're not much credit to a woman, I must say!'

As they thought I was pretty, and extremely elegant into the bargain, they had decided to give me an important part in their comedy . . . To begin with I was to take charge of the cloakroom, and then help, or rather supervise, the four waiters . . . four huge lascars, with immense sidewhiskers, whom they had managed to engage at various registry offices.

At first everything went smoothly . . . though there was one false alarm. At a quarter past nine Countess Fergus had still not arrived. What if she'd changed her mind, and decided at the last moment not to come? It would be a humiliating disaster! The Charrigauds could scarcely hide their consternation, though Brigard did his best to re-assure them . . . This happened to be the day that the Countess had to preside at that admirable charity, 'Cigar ends for the Armed Forces', and sometimes the meetings went on very late . . .

'What a charming woman,' Madame Charrigaud cooed ecstatically, as though hoping that the compliment might magically hasten the arrival of the 'wretched countess' whom she was inwardly cursing.

'And so intelligent!' Charrigaud added, going one better, though feeling exactly the same. 'The other day, at the Rothschilds, I couldn't help feeling one would have to go back to the last century to find such perfect grace, such natural superiority . . .'

'Oh, further than that!' interposed Brigard. 'You see, my

158

dear Charrigaud, in every egalitarian and democratic society . . .'

He was about to embark on one of those half gallant, half sociological discourses that he peddled around from *salon* to *salon*, when Countess Fergus entered the room, imposing and majestic, in a black dress, embroidered with steel and jet that set off the plump whiteness and placid beauty of her shoulders. And with a sudden whispering and murmuring of admiration the company proceeded ceremoniously to the dining-room.

To begin with, the atmosphere of the dinner-party was distinctly frigid. Despite her success, or perhaps because of it, Countess Fergus was rather stand-offish, or at least unconsciously reserved. She seemed to affect an air of condescension at honouring the modest house of these 'nobodies' with her presence. Charrigaud was sure that she was examining, with discreet but barely concealed contempt, the hired silver, the table decorations, Madame Charrigaud's green evening dress, and the four waiters, whose long whiskers trailed in the food they were handing round. And he was filled with a vague sense of terror, an agony of doubt, lest perhaps something was wrong with them. It was a horrible moment!

After a few banal and laboured exchanges about the more futile events of the day, the conversation gradually became general, and eventually settled down to a discussion of standards of propriety in society. All these poor devils, these pathetic men and women, forgetting the looseness of their own lives, displayed a relentless severity towards anyone whom they suspected, not of any social offence, but merely of having, at one time or another, shown too little respect for those social standards which alone they regarded as binding. Living, in a sense, outside their own social ideal, thrust aside, so to speak, by a way of life whose proprieties and observances were their only religion, they seemed to imagine that, by expelling others, they themselves would be readmitted. Their approach to the question was really extremely comical. For them, the whole world was divided into two: those things that were 'done', and those that were not; those people it was permissible to entertain, and those who on no account could be invited into one's house . . .

And these two major-divisions of the world were again split up into an infinity of sub-divisions. Thus, there were some people with whom it was permissible to dine, and others whom one might only call on—and vice versa . . . those one might entertain at one's own table, and those who could only be invited—and then only on strictly prescribed conditions—to one's evening parties . . . Then there were those people whose invitations to dinner must be refused and whom one should on no account receive in one's own house, and others that it was permissible to receive but not to dine with . . . Or again, there were people one might invite to lunch but never to dinner, and yet others with whom one might dine in the country but not in Paris, and so on, and so on. And all this was based on precise and exacting precedents derived from the behaviour of the most exclusive circles of society . . .

'Subtlety,' declared Viscount Lahyrais, sportsman, club-man, gambler and cheat. '. . . that's what really counts. Whether anyone really belongs to society or not, depends entirely on his ability to observe these fine distinctions.'

I don't think I've ever listened to such dreary rubbish! Hearing them talk, I couldn't help being sorry for the wretched creatures.

Charrigaud ate nothing, drank nothing, scarcely spoke a word. But though he was not taking part in the conversation, its enormous, sinister stupidity weighed on him like lead. Pale and extremely nervous, he was keeping an eye on the waiters, scanning the faces of his guests for some indication of approval or irony, and, despite his wife's disapproving expression, mechanically rolling his bread into larger and larger pellets. When anyone asked him a question, he could only reply, in a startled, faraway voice:

'Certainly . . . Oh, certainly . . . certainly . . .'

Opposite him, very stiff in her green dress, glittering with the phosphorescent sheen of an infinity of green metal beads and wearing a plume of red feathers in her hair, Madame Charrigaud kept bowing to right and left, not saying a word, but smiling continually—a smile of such utter vacancy that she might have been wearing a mask.

'What an absolute gawk!' Charrigaud said to himself. 'What a stupid idiot! What a piss-begotten get-up!

Tomorrow, all through her, we shall be the laughing stock of Paris.'

And at the same time, behind her unchanging smile, Madame Charrigaud was thinking:

'What a perfect fool Victor is! . . . His behaviour's quite impossible . . . We shall never hear the last of him and his confounded pellets.'

Having exhausted the discussion of society, and after a short digression on the subject of love, they started talking about antiques. This was young Sartorys' great moment, for he had some unusually fine pieces and was reputed to be an extremely skilful and fortunate collector.

'But wherever do you find all these marvellous things?' asked Madame de Rambure.

'At Versailles,' replied Sartorys, 'in the houses of poetical dowagers and sentimental mothers-superior. You've simply no idea what treasures these old ladies have hidden away.'

Madame de Rambure insisted: 'But whatever do you do to persuade them to sell?'

Puffing out his narrow chest, with a cynical expression on his girlish features and obviously hoping to shock his audience, he replied:

'I begin by making love to them, and end up by introducing them to unnatural practices.'

There was some expostulation at this daring remark, but, as Sartorys was always forgiven, the majority of the guests decided to laugh.

'What do you call "unnatural practices"?' enquired Baroness Gogsthein, enjoying the scabrous situation and emphasizing the irony of her question by the bawdy tone of her voice. But, at a glance from Kimberly, Sartorys remained silent, and it was Maurice Fernancourt who, leaning towards the Baroness, said gravely:

'That really depends on which side Sartorys regards as natural.'

His remark caused a new ripple of laughter. Whereupon, emboldened by their success, Madame Charrigaud, addressing herself directly to Sartorys, exclaimed in a loud voice:

'So it's true, then? You really are one of those?'

The effect of her words was like a douche of cold water. Countess Fergus energetically fluttered her fan, and they all looked at one another with a shocked and embarrassed expression which nevertheless scarcely concealed a strong inclination to laugh. But Charrigaud just sat there, his fists on the table, his lips compressed, sweat running down his forehead, furiously rolling bread pellets, with a comically distraught expression . . . I don't know what would have happened if, at this tense moment, Kimberly had not taken advantage of the dangerous silence to begin an account of his recent visit to London.

'Yes,' said he, 'I spent a quite intoxicating week in London. Indeed, ladies, I took part in an unique occasion . . . a ritual feast to which the great poet, John Giotto Farfadetti, had invited a few friends to celebrate his engagement to the wife of his beloved Frederic Ossian Pinggleton.'

'Oh, but it must have been exquisite,' Countess Fergus simpered.

'You simply cannot imagine!' replied Kimberly, whose eyes and gestures, and even the orchid in his lapel, expressed a fervent ecstasy. 'Just think of it, dear lady, in the centre of a huge room, with the palest of blue walls, decorated with white and gold peacocks, an inconceivably exquisite oval jade table, on which stood plates of sweetmeats in harmonious shades of yellow and mauve, with a bowl of rose crystal in the centre, filled with Hawaiian preserves . . . and that was all! Dressed in long white robes, we moved slowly along the table, helping ourselves to a portion of these mysterious preserves, which we then conveyed to our lips with the golden knives we had been provided with . . . and that was all!'

'Oh, it sounds absolutely thrilling!' sighed the Countess.

'You cannot imagine! . . . But what was really most thrilling of all . . . what, quite truly, tore at my very heart-strings . . . was when Frederic Ossian Pinggleton intoned a bridal poem, jointly dedicated to his wife and his friend . . . I have never experienced anything so tragically, so super-humanly beautiful . . .'

'Oh, but I beseech you, my dear Kimberly,' yearned the Countess. 'Aren't you going to recite this marvellous poem for us?'

'That, alas, I cannot do . . . All I can hope is to convey to you its essence.'

'Of course, of course . . . the essence!'

In spite of his sexual predilection, which could scarcely be said to concern them, women were crazy about Kimberly, especially on account of his subtle gift for describing the most unusual sins and sensations. A sudden shudder of excitement ran round the table, and the very flowers, the women's jewels, even the glasses on the table, assumed attitudes of spiritual harmony. Charrigaud was convinced that he was going out of his mind, that he had landed in a madhouse. However, by sheer strength of will, he forced himself to say with a smile:

'But certainly . . . certainly . . .'

The waiters had just finished handing round something that looked like a ham, except that it was covered with a yellow sauce, swimming with cherries disguised as scarlet beetles. As for Countess Fergus, almost swooning, she felt herself already adrift in some extra-terrestrial region. Kimberly began:

'Frederic Ossian Pinggleton and his friend John Giotto Farfadetti shared a common studio, in which they performed their appointed tasks. One was a great painter, the other a great poet, one short and plump, the other long and thin, and both of them were dressed alike in homespun cloth and Florentine caps . . . and both of them, too, were equally neurotic, for their bodies, though separate, were inhabited by the same twin souls and lilywhite minds. In his poems Farfadetti described the marvellous symbols that his friend Pinggleton portrayed on canvas, with the result that the fame of the poet was inseparable from that of the painter and the world saluted the immortal genius of the two friends in a single act of adoration.'

Kimberly paused . . . There was a religious silence, and a divine presence seemed to hover over the table . . . Then he continued:

'Day was drawing in, and the early twilight filled the studio with floating, lunar shadows . . . Against the mauve walls, one could scarcely make out the long, undulating strands of green seaweed, that seemed to float in the current of some deep and magical stream . . . Farfadetti closed the vellum antiphonary, in which, with a Persian reed, he used to inscribe his immortal poems, while Pinggleton, putting

down his heart-shaped palette on an exquisite table, turned
his lyre-shaped easel with its face to the wall, and then, with
an air of noble exhaustion, the two men sank down side by
side upon a couch heaped with cushions, brilliantly
coloured as the plants that grow in the depths of the sea . . .'

'Ahem!' Madame Tierclet interjected warningly.

'Oh no, you needn't be afraid. It was nothing of that kind,
I assure you.' And Kimberly went on: 'In the centre of the
studio, a rich perfume rose from a marble basin, filled with
floating rose petals, while nearby, on a small table, a long-
stemmed narcissus drooped in a narrow vase, the neck of
which, shaped like the calyx of a lily, was a curiously perverted tone of green . . .'

'Quite unforgettable,' shuddered the Countess, in a voice
so low that it could scarcely be heard, while, with scarcely
a pause, Kimberly continued his story:

'Outside, the deserted street was utterly silent. From the
distant Thames could be heard the muted sound of sirens
and the panting voices of the river steamers. It was the hour
of the day when the two friends, at the mercy of their
dreams, were wont to maintain an ineffable silence . . .'

'Oh, I can just see them,' said Madame Tierclet
admiringly.

'And that "ineffable" is wonderfully evocative,' applauded
Countess Fergus. 'So utterly pure.'

Taking advantage of these flattering interruptions,
Kimberly swallowed a mouthful of champagne. Then,
satisfied that he was the centre of even more devout
attention, he repeated:

'An ineffable silence . . . But on this particular evening
Farfadetti murmured: "A poisoned flower blossoms in my
heart". And Pinggleton replied: "This evening a sorrowful
bird has been singing in my soul". The whole studio
seemed to respond to this unaccustomed conversation.
Against the mauve wall, from which the colour was fast
disappearing, one could have sworn that the golden seaweed ebbed and flowed, ebbed and flowed, in tune with the
rhythm of some unwonted undulation, for there is no doubt
that the human spirit can invest the souls of inanimate
objects with its own troubles, passions, fervours, its own
sins, its very life . . .'

'How true that is!'

Yet, though this exclamation was repeated on all sides, Kimberly did not allow it to interrupt the flow of his narrative. His voice merely took on a more mysterious note as he continued:

'That moment of silence was both poignant and tragic. "Oh my friend." entreated Farfadetti, "you who have given me everything . . . you whose soul is so marvellously akin to mine . . . you must yet give me a part of your very self, something without which I must surely die". "Is it my life you are demanding?" enquired the painter. "Take it, it is yours . . ." "No, something dearer still, your wife!" "Botticellina?" cried the painter. "Yes, Botticellina . . . Botticellina . . . flesh of your flesh, your soul's soul, magical solace of all your griefs!" "Botticellina . . . Alas, alas! This had to happen! For you and she are drowned in one another as in a bottomless lake, beneath the light of the moon. Alas, alas! This had to happen." In the gathering darkness, two phosphorescent tears fell from the painter's eyes, and the poet answered: "Listen, my friend! I love Botticellina, and she loves me, and yet, fearing to give ourselves to one another we are both dying of a love we dare not speak of . . . She and I, once part of the same living creature, have, for thousands of years been seeking one another, calling out to one another, and now, today, at last we have found one another . . . Oh, my dear Pinggleton, this life of which we are so ignorant has its own strange fatalities, terrible yet enchanting. Was there ever a more splendid poem than the one we are living this evening?" But all the painter could do was to repeat in a more melancholy voice, "Botticellina! Oh, Botticellina!" He rose from the pile of cushions upon which he had been reclining and began feverishly walking up and down the studio. Then, after some minutes of anxious cogitation he exclaimed: "Must it be that Botticellina, who once was mine, shall henceforward be yours?" "No, no! she shall be *ours*", replied the poet imperiously. "For God has chosen you as the being in whom that sundered soul, from which both she and I are sprung, should once more be re-united. If that should fail, Botticellina has the magic pearl that dissolves all dreams and I the dagger that delivers us from this

165

mortal coil . . . If you refuse, then death must consummate our love." And he added in thrilling tones that rang through the studio like a voice from the abyss: "That, perhaps, would be more beautiful still." "No," cried the painter, "you shall live . . . Botticellina shall be yours, as once she was mine. I will cut my flesh to shreds, tear out the heart from my breast, smash my skull against the wall, but my friend shall achieve happiness. I am not afraid to suffer. Suffering, too, can be a form of rapture!" "Yes, and the strongest, bitterest, most savage rapture of all!" Farfadetti exclaimed ecstatically. "I envy you your fate! . . . As for me, I think I shall die, either from the joy of loving or from the grief I cause my friend. The hour has come . . . Farewell!" He rose from the couch like an archangel and, at that very moment, the curtains quivered, then parted to reveal a shining apparition. It was Botticellina, draped in a diaphanous robe that gleamed like moonlight. Her loose hair glittered around her shoulders like flames of fire; in her hand she held a golden key; and ecstasy was on her lips, and the night sky in her eyes . . . As John Giotto flung himself upon her and disappeared behind the curtain, Frederic Ossian Pinggleton lay down once more upon the pile of cushions, brilliantly coloured as the plants that grow in the depths of the sea . . . And as he lay there, tearing at his flesh with his nails till the blood flowed in streams, the golden seaweed, now scarcely visible, gently stirred along the walls which gradually disappeared into the darkening shadows . . . And the heart-shaped palette and the lyre-shaped easel resounded with the strains of a bridal song.'

For a few minutes Kimberly remained silent. Then, as mounting emotion gripped the hearts of those seated around the table, he concluded:

'That is why I dipped the point of my golden knife in the preserves prepared by the Hawaiian virgins, in honour of a betrothal more magnificent than any known to this century, so ignorant of beauty.'

Dinner was over . . . The guests rose from the table in religious silence, but in the drawing-room everyone crowded round Kimberly to congratulate him. And, as the glances of the women converged upon him, lighting up his made-up face, they seemed to crown him with an ecstatic halo.

'Oh, how I should love Pinggleton to paint my portrait,' Madame de Rambure exclaimed passionately. 'I would give everything I've got for such happiness.'

'Alas, Madame,' replied Kimberly, 'since the sublimely unhappy occasion I have just described, it appears that Frederic Ossian Pinggleton has given up painting portraits of human beings, however charming, and now only portrays souls!'

'He is perfectly right . . . I should love him to paint my soul!'

'And what sex would it be?' Maurice Fernancourt enquired sarcastically, obviously jealous of Kimberly's success.

To which the latter replied simply:

'Souls, my dear Maurice, have no sex. They only have . . .'

'Hair on their chests!' Charrigaud whispered, but so quietly that the only person who could hear him was the psychological novelist, to whom at that moment he was offering a cigar. And as he led him off to the smoking-room, he muttered:

'Really, my dear fellow, it was all I could do not to start talking smut, at the top of my voice, in front of everyone. I was absolutely fed up with their souls, and the perverted love affairs and their magic Hawaiian jam. Yes, indeed, just to be able to talk filth for a quarter of an hour, to smother oneself with good, black, stinking muck, would be simply marvellous . . . and so restful . . . It would be some compensation for having to listen to all this nauseating tripe . . . Don't you agree?'

But the shock had been too powerful, and the effect of Kimberly's narration could not easily be shaken off. Nobody showed the slightest interest in vulgar terrestrial matters. Even Viscount Lahyrais, clubman, sportsman, gambler and cheat, felt as though he was beginning to sprout wings, and everyone felt the need to be alone in order to prolong or realize their dream . . . Despite all Kimberly's efforts, as he wandered about asking people if they had ever drunk sable's milk—'simply delicious, my dear'—the conversation could not be revived, and one after the other, the guests excused themselves and departed. By eleven o'clock the last of them had gone.

At last, finding themselves once more alone, the Charrigauds regarded one another for some time with bitter
hostility before exchanging their impressions. At last
Charrigaud exclaimed:

'Well, of all the miserable flops . . .'

'It was all your fault,' Madame bitterly reproached him.

'Well, I like that . . .'

'Yes, absolutely . . . You didn't make the slightest effort.
All you could do was to roll those filthy bread pellets, and
nobody could get a word out of you. You made an utter fool
of yourself . . . It was humiliating.'

'You can talk,' retorted Charrigaud. 'What about that
horrible green dress? And your everlasting smile? And the
brick you dropped with Sartorys? I suppose that was my
fault, too? And of course it was I who went on about the
wretched Pinggleton, and ate Hawaiian jam, and painted
people's souls? I, who was the lilywhite pederast?'

'Oh, I doubt if you're even capable of that!' screamed
Madame, beside herself with rage.

And they went on abusing each other at length, until at
last Madame Charrigaud, having put away the silver and
half-empty bottles in the sideboard, decided to go up to
bed, and locked herself in her room.

Left to himself, Charrigaud continued to wander around
the house in a state of extreme agitation, until suddenly,
catching sight of me in the dining-room, where I was tidying things up a bit, he came towards me, and putting his
arm around me, said:

'Célestine, do you want to be very nice to me? Would
you like to give me real pleasure?'

'Yes, sir.'

'Well then, my dear, just shout at me at the top of your
voice, ten, twenty, a hundred times, "Shit".'

'Really, sir! . . . What a strange idea . . . I should never
dare!'

'But do dare, Célestine, do dare, I implore you.'

And when at last I had laughingly done as he asked, he
said:

'Célestine, you've no idea how much good you have done
me . . . what immense pleasure you have given me. Why,
just to be able to look at a woman who isn't a soul, to touch

168

a woman who isn't a lily! . . . Give me a kiss!'

As if I'd think of such a thing, for heaven's sake.

But the next day, when they read in *La Figaro* a pompous account of their dinner-party, praising their elegant taste, and their witty and distinguished connections, they forgot all about their quarrel and could talk of nothing else but their great success. And they set their hearts on achieving still more illustrious conquests, attaining yet greater heights of snobbery.

'What a charming woman Countess Fergus is!' said Madame at lunch time, as they were finishing up the food left over from the dinner-party.

'And so spiritual,' Charrigaud added.

'And Kimberly! Have you ever met such a marvellous conversationalist? . . . And such exquisite manners!'

'Yes, one really oughtn't to make fun of him . . . After all, his vices are his own affair . . . nothing to do with us.'

'But of course . . . Why, if one were to start criticizing everybody . . .'

And for the rest of the day, in the linen-room, I have been amusing myself recalling all the ridiculous things that used to go on in that household . . . Madame's increasing passion for notoriety, to the point where she was ready to sleep with the first lousy journalist who promised to write an article praising one of her husband's books or to insert a paragraph about her clothes or her *salon*. And Charrigaud's smug complacency, knowing all about these goings-on, yet doing nothing about them. He would simply say, with complete cynicism, that at least it was much cheaper than fixing things up through the office. He had lost all sense of decency, and described such behaviour as '*salon politics*' or 'social diplomacy'.

Anyhow, now I must write to Paris for his latest book . . . though its bound to be rotten . . .

10 NOVEMBER

People have stopped talking about little Clara. As was expected, the case has been dropped. Joseph and the forest of Raillon will keep their secret for ever. From now on, the death of this poor little human creature will be as completely forgotten as that of a blackbird killed in a thicket. Her father goes on breaking stones by the roadside as though nothing had ever happened, and the town, after a moment's excitement and exhilaration, has resumed its normal appearance—a little drearier than usual because of the wintry weather. People stay at home more than ever, cooped up indoors by the bitter cold; and though now and then one catches a glimpse of pale, sleepy faces behind the frozen window panes, outside in the streets one scarcely meets anyone but an occasional ragged tramp or shivering dog.

This morning Madame sent me to do some shopping at the butcher's, and I took the dogs with me. While I was there, an old woman came into the shop and timidly asked for some meat:

'Just a small piece, enough to make some soup for the boy . . . He's ill.'

From a large copper bowl filled with offcuts and waste, the butcher fished out a wretched bit of meat, mostly bone and fat, and, having weighed it, briskly announced:

'Fifteen sous.'

'Fifteen sous for that?' exclaimed the old woman. 'Lord have mercy, that's impossible! And how do you expect me to make soup with that?'

'Suit yourself,' said the butcher, throwing the lump of scrag back into the basin. 'But don't forget, I shall be sending your bill today, and if it's not paid tomorrow, I shall have to put the bailiffs on you!'

'Let's have it, then,' said the old woman resignedly.

When she had left the shop the butcher explained to me:

'The fact of the matter is you'd never make any profit on a side of beef if the poor people stopped buying what you have to trim off . . . The trouble is, they're getting so fussy these days, the sods!'

And, cutting off two nice slices of lean meat, he threw them to the dogs . . . Obviously, a wealthy customer's dogs are not poor people!

At the Priory, various things have been happening, comedy succeeding tragedy . . . Fed up with the captain's exasperating behaviour, Monsieur Lanlaire, urged on by

170

Madame, has appealed to the local J.P. He is claiming damages for the smashing of his cloches and frames, and all the mess he has made of the garden. From all accounts, the meeting between these two old enemies at the magistrate's office was an epic encounter. They blackguarded each other like bargees. Naturally the captain denied on oath that he had ever thrown stones or anything else into the Lanlaire's garden, and insisted that, on the contrary, it was Lanlaire who had thrown them into his . . .

'Have you got any witnesses? Where are they, then? You're afraid of producing them,' bawled the captain.

'Witnesses?' Monsieur Lanlaire retorted. 'What more evidence do you need? What about the stones and all the other muck you keep showering on my property? All the old hats and worn-out slippers I'm forever picking up, and that everyone knows belong to you? . . .'

'You're lying.'

'And you're a dirty, good-for-nothing scoundrel . . .'

But since Monsieur Lanlaire was unable to produce any reliable witnesses, the magistrate, who in any case is a friend of the captain's, insisted upon him withdrawing the charge.

'And allow me to tell you, moreover,' concluded the magistrate, 'it is most improbable, indeed quite inadmissible, that a distinguished soldier, an intrepid officer, promoted from the ranks on the field of battle, would amuse himself by throwing stones and old hats on to your property like any street arab . . .'

'Exactly,' roared the captain . . . 'Why, the man's nothing but a miserable Dreyfusard . . . He's trying to insult the army . . .'

'What, me?'

'Yes, you. All you want, you dirty Jew, is to bring dishonour on the army . . . Long live the army!'

In the end, they nearly came to blows, and it was all the magistrate could do to separate them. Next day, Monsieur Lanlaire installed two permanent witnesses in the garden, behind a kind of wooden screen with holes cut in it so that they could watch what was going on. But it was a complete waste of money, for the captain got to hear of it and temporarily interrupted his stone-throwing . . .

171

I have talked to the captain once or twice over the hedge, for in spite of the cold he still spends all day working furiously in his garden. At present he's busy covering all his rose trees with grease-paper bags. He tells me all his troubles. Rose is suffering from an attack of influenza, on top of her asthma. Bourbaki has died . . . He got congestion of the lungs from drinking too much brandy. Really, he's out of luck. That villain Lanlaire must have cast a spell upon him. But he's determined to get the better of him, to rid the neighbourhood of him once and for all, and he has a marvellous plan that he wants me to put into practice.

'This is what you ought to do, Mademoiselle Célestine. You ought to issue a writ against Lanlaire, in the courts at Louviers, accusing him of indecent behaviour and attempted rape. It's a splendid idea . . .'

'But Monsieur Lanlaire has never tried to rape me, captain . . .'

'So what? You don't have to worry about that!'

'Oh, but I couldn't.'

'What do you mean, couldn't? Nothing could be simpler . . . Just issue the writ, and call Rose and me as witnesses. We'll bear you out, and solemnly swear we saw everything that happened . . . everything. After all, a soldier's word counts for something, you know, particularly these days. It's not just dog shit! . . . Besides, don't you see, if you do this it will be easy to get the little Clara case re-opened, and then we can involve Lanlaire in that, too . . . It's a splendid idea. Think about it, Mademoiselle Célestine, think about it.'

Oh, but I have so many other things to think about just now, far too many things . . . Joseph is pressing me to make up my mind. We can't wait much longer, he says. He has just heard from Cherbourg that the little café is to be sold next week . . . But I'm worried and upset . . . I want to, and yet I don't. One day I like the idea, and the next day I don't . . . The truth is, I'm frightened . . . I'm afraid Joseph is trying to get me mixed up in some really terrible business, and I can't make up my mind to go in with him. He doesn't try to force me, but he keeps putting forward arguments, tempting me with promises of freedom, of having fine clothes and being able to lead a secure and happy life.

'After all, I must buy the place . . . I can't afford to lose a chance like this . . . And supposing there's a revolution? Just think, Célestine . . . Why, we'd make a fortune straight away . . . There's nothing like revolution for stepping up the café business, you mark my words!'

'Buy it, then. If it's not me, you can always get someone else. . .'

'No, no, it's got to be you . . . I don't want anyone else. You've got right under my skin . . . But you don't trust me, do you?'

'No, Joseph, it's not that . . .'

'Yes it is. You are suspicious about me.'

How I had the courage to ask him at that moment, I simply don't know, but I did all the same.

'Well then . . . tell me something. Was it really you who raped little Clara?'

Instead of being shocked by my question, Joseph remained extraordinarily calm. He merely shrugged his shoulders and, hitching up his trousers, replied quite simply:

'There you are, you see . . . I knew that's what you were thinking about. I know everything that goes on in your mind.'

He spoke quite gently, but there was such a terrible look in his eyes that I was unable to utter a word.

'It's nothing to do with little Clara,' he went on. 'It's you we're talking about.'

He took me in his arms like he did the other evening . . .

'Why not come in with me, and we'll run the place together?'

Trembling from head to foot I managed to stammer out:

'But I'm afraid . . . I'm afraid of you, Joseph. Why am I afraid of you?'

He held me cradled in his arms and, without attempting to justify himself, perhaps pleased that he was able to frighten me, he said in a fatherly tone of voice:

'All right, all right, if that's what's worrying you . . . We'll talk things over later . . . tomorrow.'

There is a Rouen paper going the rounds of the town,

173

with an article in it that is causing considerable scandal amongst the devout. It is an amusing, rather bawdy account of something that happened quite recently at Port-Lançon, a pretty little place only a few miles from here. And the joke of it is, everybody knows the people concerned. It has given them something else to talk about for a day or two . . . Yesterday somebody brought Marianne a copy, and in the evening, after dinner, I began reading the famous article aloud. But no sooner had I begun than Joseph got up, very dignified and stern, even rather annoyed, and declared that he doesn't like dirty stories and can't stand people attacking religion.

'You've no business to be reading it, Célestine. It's not right.'

And off he went to bed. As the story is worth preserving, I am copying it into my diary. Anyhow, I may as well try to cheer up these dismal pages with a good laugh . . . So here it is.

The Dean in charge of the parish of Port-Lançon was a sanguine, active man, who had a great reputation in the neighbouring villages for his eloquence. Non-Christians and freethinkers used to attend his church on Sundays simply to hear him preach, excusing themselves because of his gifts as an orator.

'Of course we don't agree with what he says, but it's a pleasure to listen to a man like him all the same.'

And they only wished their Deputy, who never uttered a word, had the Dean's 'damned gift of the gab'. He was able to drive his point home. One of his pet subjects was the defects of lay education.

'What are they taught at school? Nothing at all. If you question them on any important subject, it's quite pitiful . . . They haven't the slightest idea what to answer.'

For this deplorable state of ignorance he blamed Voltaire, the French Revolution, the Government and the Drey-fusards—not publicly from the pulpit, but when he was with friends he could trust. For, despite his uncompromising religious views, the Dean had no intention of losing his salary. Every Tuesday and Thursday he used to gather as many children as possible in the presbytery courtyard, and then he would spend the next couple of hours trying, with amazing pedantry, to instill into them the most fantastic information in order to fill the gaps in their undenominational education.

'Now listen, children. Do any of you know where the earthly paradise was? If so, hold up your hands . . . Come on, now . . .'

But not a single hand went up, and in every eye gleamed a huge question mark. Whereupon, shrugging his shoulders, the Dean would shout:

'This is scandalous . . . What on earth do they teach you at school? It's a fine business, this undenominational education . . . free and compulsory, indeed! . . . Very fine! Well then, I'm going to tell you where the earthly paradise was. So listen carefully.'

And, speaking in the most categorical terms, he would continue:

'Whatever people may tell you, children, the earthly paradise was certainly not at Port-Lançon, nor anywhere else in the Seine-Inférieure . . . nor even in Normandy, or Paris, or France. And you won't find it in Europe, or Africa or America . . . or even in the South Sea Islands. Is that quite clear? You see, some people try to make out that the earthly paradise was in Italy or Spain, because those are the countries where oranges grow, the greedy guts! But they are completely wrong . . . For one thing, there weren't any oranges in the earthly paradise, only apples, unfortunately for us . . . Now, surely one of you can tell me where it was? Speak up.'

And when no one answered, he went on in a voice booming with anger:

'It was in Asia . . . for in Asia, in days gone by, there was never any rain, hail, snow, or thunder and lightning . . . Everything was always green and the air full of delicious scents, and the flowers used to grow as high as the trees, and the trees were as big as mountains. But today, it is not like that any longer. Because of the sins you have committed, there's nothing at all in Asia nowadays except the Chinese and the Cochin-Chinese and the Turks . . . black heretics and yellow pagans, who kill our holy missionaries and end up by going to hell . . . You can take it from me . . . And that

175

reminds me . . . do any of you know what faith is?'

With a serious expression on his face, as though repeating a lesson learnt by heart, one of the children began to stammer:

'Faith, Hope and Charity . . . It is one of the three theological virtues . . .'

'That's not what I asked you,' the Dean interrupted sternly. 'What I want to know is, what does faith mean, what does it consist of? . . . You see, no one knows that either. Well, faith means believing whatever you are taught by your parish priest, and not what you are told at school . . . School teachers don't know what they're talking about. They teach you about things that never really happened.'

The church at Port-Lançon is well-known to archaeologists and tourists, as one of the most interesting in this part of Normandy, where there is so much admirable religious architecture. In the west front, above the main entrance and delicately supported by a trefoil arcature, there is a superbly light and delicate rose window. The end of the north aisle, approached by a dark passage, is decorated with carvings of a more involved and massive style . . . Every kind of extraordinary creature, devils, symbolic animals and saints looking like ragamuffins, which, half hidden by the lace-like scroll work of the soffits, appear to be engaged in the most curious antics . . . Unfortunately most of them have been mutilated or lost their heads, for time and the prudish vandalism of priests have between them ruined these satirical carvings, which were once as gay and bawdy as a chapter of Rabelais. And since the crumbling stone bodies are now clothed with a gloomy covering of moss, it will not be long before it is impossible to distinguish anything but a desolate ruin . . . The building itself is divided into two by bold, slim arcades, while north and south the windows flame with radiance, and at the east end, above the altar, another huge rose window burns with the red glow of a setting sun.

The Dean's courtyard, full of ancient chestnut trees, communicates directly with the church by a small door, recently constructed, that opens into one of the transepts, the only key to which is shared between the Dean and

Sister Angela, who runs the almshouse. Thin and embittered, though still young in a crabbed and wilting way . . . strict, talkative, enterprising and a confirmed nosyparker, Sister Angela is the Dean's close friend and intimate adviser. They see each other every day, and are forever working out new combinations for the municipal elections, reporting to one another the secrets they have managed to unearth about the people of Port-Lançon, and planning ingenious methods of evading Government decrees and regulations in order to protect the church's interests. It was there that much of the worst scandal of the neighbourhood originated, and though everyone suspected as much, no one dared say so for fear of the Dean's biting wit and Sister Angela's notorious spitefulness, for she ran the almshouse just as she pleased and was both intolerant and vindictive.

Last Thursday, when the Dean was as usual in the courtyard inculcating the children with the most extraordinary theological notions, having explained what thunder, hail, wind and lightning were, he suddenly asked:

'And what about rain? Does anybody know what it is, where it comes from, who makes it? Of course, these modern scientists say that rain is due to condensation, but they are just liars and will tell you all sorts of things. They're wicked heretics, the devil's accomplices . . . But the truth is, children, rain is the wrath of God . . . God is angry with your parents, because for years they have been refusing to attend the Rogation processions . . . So he says to himself: "Right! If you are prepared to let your good parson lead the procession round your fields by himself, with nobody but the beadle and the choir, that's your look out. But I'm warning you, you'd better look to your harvests, you rascals!" And then he orders the rain to fall. That's what rain is . . . If only your parents would be good Christians, and carry out their religious duties properly, it would never rain again.'

As he was speaking Sister Angela suddenly appeared at the little door leading from the church. She was even paler than usual, and in a terrible state . . . her white headband had come undone and her coif was over one ear, it's two great wings were fluttering like a frightened bird's. As soon as she saw the schoolchildren, her first instinct was to go away again and shut the door. But the Dean, taken unawares by her sudden appearance and shocked by her pallor, was already advancing towards her, with contorted lips and agitated eyes.

'Send the children away immediately,' begged Sister Angela. 'At once. I have something to tell you.'

'Oh my God, whatever's happened? Eh? What? You are all upset.'

'Send the children away,' Sister Angela repeated. 'Something very serious has happened, very serious indeed.'

As soon as the last child had gone, Sister Angela sank on to a bench, where she sat for several seconds, nervously fingering her bronze crucifix and holy medals till they rattled against the starched bib in which her flat, spinster's chest was encased. The Dean, anxious to hear her news and speaking in a jerky voice, said:

'Quick . . . tell me what's the matter . . . You frighten me . . . What is it?'

'It's this,' she replied. 'Just now, as I was coming through the cloister, I saw a man on the church, stark naked!'

The Dean opened his mouth to speak, but for a moment he could only gaze at her convulsively. Then he stuttered:

'A naked man? . . . You mean to tell me, Sister, that you saw . . . on my church . . . a man . . . stark naked? On *my* church? You're quite sure?'

'Quite sure.'

'Is it possible that one of my parishioners should be so utterly shameless as to appear on the roof of the church stark naked . . .? I can hardly believe it!'

And, his face purple with rage, his throat so constricted that he could scarcely speak, he reiterated:

'Stark naked, on *my* church . . .? Oh, what terrible times we live in . . . But what was he doing there? Surely, not fornicating? . . .'

'But you don't understand,' interrupted Sister Angela. 'I never said that it was one of the parishioners . . . It is one of the statues.'

'What? One of the statues? Oh well, that's a very different matter, Sister.'

Considerably relieved by this information, but still breathing loudly, he added:

'Oh, but what a fright you gave me!'

Assured by his attitude, Sister Angela now became aggressive, and, compressing her pale lips, hissed venomously:

'So you think it doesn't matter, then? Are you suggesting that a man is any the less naked just because he's made of stone?'

'No, no . . . I never said that . . . Nevertheless, surely it's not quite the same thing?'

'But I can assure you, this stone man is a great deal more naked than you think . . . He's exposing his . . . his . . . An instrument of impurity . . . an enormous horrible, pointed instrument! Surely, Father, you don't want to make me sully my lips with an obscene word? . . .'

And she rose to her feet in a state of violent agitation. The Dean was utterly crushed by her revelation. His head was in a whirl and his imagination boggled at the thought of such depraved, such hellish sensuality . . . He could only mumble like a child:

'You're quite certain? . . . Huge and pointed? . . . But this is inconceivable. This is horrible, Sister . . . You are quite sure you actually *saw* this enormous, pointed thing? You couldn't have been mistaken? You're not joking? . . . Oh, no, it's inconceivable.'

Sister Angela stamped her foot angrily. 'And you mean to say that after all the centuries he's been there disgracing your church you've never noticed anything? Did it have to be me . . . a woman . . . a nun who had taken the vow of chastity . . . who had to draw attention to this . . . this abomination? Who had to come and tell you, "If you please, Father, there's a devil on the church"?'

Stirred by her passionate words, the Dean quickly pulled himself together and, in a determined tone of voice, answered:

'We simply cannot allow this scandal to last another day . . . The devil must be brought to his knees, and I myself accept full responsibility. Come back at midnight, when everybody in Port-Lançon is asleep, and show me where he is. I'll speak to the verger and tell him to get hold of a ladder . . . Is it very high up?'

'Yes, indeed . . .'

179

'And you're sure you can find it again, Sister?'

'I could find it blindfolded . . . I will meet you here at midnight then, your reverence . . .'

'God be with you, Sister!'

And, crossing herself energetically, Sister Angela opened the little door and disappeared . . .

It was a dark, moonless night. In the cloister the lights had long ago been put out, and the street lamps, swaying and creaking on their tall gallows, were only faintly visible. The whole of Port-Lançon was asleep.

'This is where it is,' said Sister Angela.

The verger set his ladder against the wall, close to a large window, the panes of which glowed faintly in the light from the sanctuary lamp, while the broken outline of the church stood out against a violent sky, studded here and there with the twinkling of a star. The Dean, armed with a hammer and chisel and carrying a dark lantern, climbed up the ladder, closely followed by Sister Angela, whose coif was concealed beneath a large black shawl. And as they ascended, the Dean mumbled the words of a prayer, to which Sister Angela supplied the responses:

'*Ab omni peccato—Libera nos, Domine—Ab insidiis diaboli—Libera nos, Domine—A spiritu fornicationis— Libera nos, Domine!*'

Reaching the top of the parapet, they stopped.

'There it is,' exclaimed Sister Angela, 'to your left.'

And overwhelmed by the darkness and the silence, she whispered hurriedly: '*Agnus Dei, quix tollis peccata mundi.*'

'*Exaudi nos, Domine,*' replied the Dean, shining his lantern on the maze of carvings, amongst which it was just possible to distinguish the apocalyptic figures of saints and demons, dancing and grimacing in the moonlight. Suddenly, as he caught sight of the impure image of sin, aimed directly at him, terrible and furious, the Dean let out a loud cry, while the nun, still clinging to the ladder, managed to stutter:

'*Mater purissima . . . Mater castissima . . . Mater inviolata . . .*'

'Oh, the swine, the filthy swine,' yelled the Dean, brandishing his hammer. And while, behind him, Sister Angela continued reciting the litany of the Blessed Virgin,

180

and the verger, huddled at the foot of the ladder, prayed in a whining voice, he struck the obscene image a resounding blow. Splinters of stone struck him in the face, and there was the sound of a heavy body crashing on to the roof, slithering towards the gutter, and finally falling with a thud into the cloister below.

The next morning as she was leaving the church after mass, Mademoiselle Robineau, a particularly devout lady, happened to notice on the floor of the cloister, an object which struck her as having the unusual form and curious appearance of those holy relics that one sometimes sees preserved in reliquaries. She picked it up and, after examining it carefully, said to herself:

'Probably it is a relic, a holy and precious relic, petrified in some miraculous spring . . . Indeed, God moves in most mysterious ways.'

Her first thought was to offer it to the Dean, but, on further reflection, she decided to take it home with her as a protection against sin and misfortune.

As soon as she got home, Mademoiselle Robineau went up to her room, and there, on a table spread with a white cloth, surmounted by a red velvet cushion with gold tassels, she carefully laid the precious relic. Then, covering it with a glass globe and placing a vase of artificial flowers on either side, she knelt down before this improvised altar and ardently invoked the unknown saint, to whom, in some remote period, this holy object had once belonged. But before long she began to feel worried. The fervour of her prayers, the pure joy of her ecstasy were increasingly disturbed by strangely human preoccupations. She was even assailed by the most terrible and piercing doubts. 'Can it really be a holy relic?' she asked herself.

And though she continued to say more and more *pater nosters* and *aves* she could not help indulging curiously impure thoughts and listening to a voice which, rising from within herself and drowning the sound of her prayers, kept repeating:

'Still, he must have been a fine figure of a man!'

Poor Mademoiselle Robineau. When she finally discovered

181

what the stone object really was, she almost died of shame and kept repeating over and over again:

'And to think how many times I kissed it!'

Today, November 10th, we were busy all day cleaning silver. This is quite an event, a traditional occasion like jam making. The Lanlaires have a magnificent collection of silver, including several antique pieces that are almost unique and extremely beautiful. Madame inherited it from her father who, according to some people, was holding it in trust; though others say that it was given him by a nobleman, as security for a loan. He wasn't satisfied with buying young men for military service, the old brute. He was up to anything, and one more swindle certainly wouldn't have worried him. If the grocer's wife is to be believed, the whole business of the silver was completely crooked, for it appears that Madame's father not only was repaid the full amount he had lent, but also managed to hang on to the silver. I don't know the exact circumstances, but there is little doubt it was a super swindle!

Naturally, the Lanlaires never use it. It is kept locked up in a cupboard in the pantry, in three large cases, lined with red velvet and fixed to the wall with strong iron staples. Each year, on the 10th November, the cases are brought out, and, under Madame's personal supervision, the silver is cleaned. Then, for another year, no one sees it again. You should have seen Madame's expression, at the thought of us being allowed to touch her silver. I've never seen a woman with a look of such savage cupidity!

Isn't it curious the way people like this hide everything away? Bury their silver, their 'jewels, their wealth, their happiness, and, instead of living happily and luxuriously, insist upon living as though they were hard up?

Having completed the job, and locked up the silver for another year, Madame at last cleared off, though not before she had satisfied herself that we had not taken anything. When she had gone Joseph said in a funny kind of voice:

'It's a splendid collection, you know, Célestine, especially the Louis XVI cruet. Jesus, but it's heavy . . . The whole lot must be worth at least 25,000 francs. In fact, no one can say what it *is* worth.'

And looking at me with a fixed, heavy stare, he added:
'Have you made up your mind to come with me yet?'

Whatever connection can there be between the Lanlaires'
silver and the Cherbourg café . . . I don't know why, but
the truth is, almost everything Joseph says scares me . . .

12 NOVEMBER

I said I was going to talk about Monsieur Xavier. I often
think of the little wretch! Of all the faces I have ever set
eyes on there are few that I recall as often as his, and when
I do, sometimes it makes me feel sad, sometimes angry . . .
Still, with that wrinkled, cheeky little face of his, he really
was jolly amusing . . . and utterly depraved! A regular
little bounder . . . A typical product of the times, as you
might say.

I had been engaged by a Madame de Tarves, who lived
in Varennes Street . . . a peach of a place . . . everything up
to the nines and excellent wages . . . a hundred francs a
month, free laundry, wine and so on. The morning I got
there, feeling very pleased with myself, Madame sent for
me to her boudoir . . . A marvellous room, walls covered
with cream-coloured silk . . . and Madame herself, tall,
heavily made up . . . skin too white, lips too red, hair too
fair . . . still pretty . . . rustling petticoats . . . and such
elegance, such a presence! Oh, there was certainly no
arguing about that . . .

I already had a good eye for such things. I had only to
walk into any Parisian household, and it was enough to give
me a pretty shrewd idea of the kind of people that lived
there and, though furniture can sometimes be as deceptive
as faces, I wasn't often far out . . . Here, in spite of the
lavishness of everything, I felt at once that something was
wrong, that relations were strained. There was an air of
hurried, feverish existence, of some kind of intimate, hidden
rottenness . . . though not so well hidden that I couldn't
detect the smell of it . . . That's always the same . . . Besides,
a new servant has only to exchange glances with the old
ones and a kind of masonic sign passes between them
—usually quite spontaneous and involuntary—that

immediately warns you of what to expect. As in all jobs, servants tend to be jealous of one another, and are prepared to defend themselves savagely against newcomers . . . I myself, although I'm so easy going, have had to put up with plenty of jealousy and dislike, particularly from the women, who are furious because I'm so attractive . . . Though I must say, in fairness to them, that the men have always made me welcome . . . perhaps for the same reason.

From the expression on the footman's face, when he first opened the door to me, I had clearly understood what he meant . . . 'It's a rum kind of a joint here . . . Not much security, but plenty of fun, all the same . . . You'll soon find your feet, my dear . . .' And by the time I reached Madame's boudoir I was therefore prepared for something out of the usual, at least to the extent that such vague and summary impressions can be relied upon. But, I admit, I had no very clear idea of what exactly I might expect.

Madame de Tarves was seated at a sweet little desk, writing letters. Instead of a carpet, the floor was covered with white astrakhan rugs, and, on the cream-coloured walls, I was struck by the coarse, almost obscene, eighteenth-century engravings that hung alongside antique enamels depicting scenes from the bible. There was a glass case, containing jewels, ivories, miniatures, snuff boxes and gay, charmingly delicate little Dresden figures; and a table, covered with costly toilet necessities made of silver and gold. On a sofa, between two mauve silk cushions, a little dog was curled up, a tiny ball of brown fur, silky and shining.

'So you're Célestine? That's right, isn't it?' enquired Madame. 'Well, that's a name I can't stand . . . I shall call you Mary . . . in English. Don't forget now . . . Mary. Yes, that's much more becoming.'

That's how it usually goes . . . We servants haven't even the right to use our own names, because there's nearly always one of the daughters, cousins, dogs or parrots that have the same one.

'Yes, ma'am,' I replied.

'Can you speak English, Mary?'

'No, ma'am . . . I told you before, when you asked me, ma'am.'

184

'Oh yes, of course . . . That's a pity . . . Turn round a little, Mary, and let me have a look at you!'

She examined me from every angle, front, back and sideways, murmuring to herself:

'Yes, not bad . . . pretty good.'

Then suddenly she asked:

'Tell me something, Mary . . . What about your figure? Would you say you were really well made?'

Her question surprised and upset me: I could see no connection between the fact that I was working for her and the shape of my body. But, without waiting for a reply, and coolly running her lorgnettes over me from head to foot, she said to herself:

'Yes, she seems to be pretty well made.'

Then, turning to me with a contented smile, she explained:

'You see, Mary, I can't stand anyone waiting on me unless they are well made . . . It's more becoming.'

But this was not to be the last of my surprises, for, continuing her minute examination of me, she suddenly exclaimed:

'Ah, your hair! You'll have to do *that* differently. Your present style isn't at all smart. You have lovely hair, and you ought to show it off to best advantage . . . The way a woman does her hair is always most important . . . See, like this . . . Yes, that's much better.'

And rumpling my hair over my forehead, she repeated:

'Yes, that's much better . . . She's charming. Look at me, Mary. Yes, quite charming . . . That's much more becoming.'

And she went on patting my hair, until I began to wonder whether she was either a bit cracked, or whether, perhaps, she had unnatural tastes . . . Honestly, that would have been about the last straw! . . . At last, when she had finished, and was satisfied about my hair, she asked:

'Is this your best dress you're wearing?'

'Yes, ma'am.'

'Well, for a best dress, I can't say it's up to much. I must let you have one of mine, and you can alter it . . . And what about your petticoat?'

She lifted up my skirt, and commented:

185

'Oh, I see . . . Not at all becoming . . . And your under-clothes?'

Annoyed by this impertinent inspection, I replied dryly: 'I'm afraid I don't know what Madame means by "becoming".'

'I want to see your underclothes . . . Go and fetch some . . . But first, let me see how you walk. Come back here . . . now turn around . . . again. Well, she walks all right. She's certainly got style.'

But, as soon as she saw my underwear, she pulled a face.

'What ghastly material! And your stockings, your slips? Terrible . . . As for those corsets, I simply couldn't allow anyone in my house to wear such things . . . Here, Mary, come and help me.'

She opened a red lacquer wardrobe and, pulling out a huge drawer full of perfumed frills and furbelows, she emptied them all out on the floor in a heap.

'You can have this one, Mary . . . No, you'd better take the lot . . . You may probably find you'll have to alter them a little, and some of them may need mending . . . but you can manage that. Take them all. You should find all you need there . . . enough to make yourself a pretty trousseau . . . Take the lot.'

There was, in fact, everything I could possibly want . . . silk corsets and stockings, shifts made of silk and finest cambric, the sweetest little knickers, charming fronts, and lovely, frilly petticoats. And the most delicious perfume, a mixture of delicate femininity and love, arose from this pile of lacy garments, which, like a basket of freshly gathered flowers, shimmered with every colour of the rainbow. I simply couldn't get over it, but stood there stupidly, delighted, though also embarrassed, by this gorgeous array of clothes—pink, mauve, yellow, red, with here and there a bit of more brightly coloured ribbon or delicate lace—while Madame sorted over these charming cast-offs, most of which had scarcely been worn, holding them up for me to see, suggesting which ones I should choose and indicating her own preference.

'I always like the maids who wait on me to be smart and elegant . . . and to smell nice. You are a brunette . . . Here's a red skirt that will suit you marvellously. But the fact is they all suit you admirably . . . You may as well take the lot . . .'

I was completely overwhelmed, and, not knowing what to do or say, I could only repeat mechanically:

'Thank you, ma'am. It's most kind of you, ma'am, thank you.'

But, without giving me time to pull myself together, Madame kept on talking and talking, alternately familiar, shameless, maternal . . . and sometimes like an old bawd.

'It's like cleanliness, Mary . . . taking care of your body . . . washing properly . . . That's one thing I insist upon above everything . . . I am most particular about it . . . It's almost a mania with me.'

And off she went into the most intimate details, continually using the word 'becoming', even when, to me, it seemed quite inappropriate. As we were finishing sorting out the underclothes, she suddenly said:

'A woman, no matter who she is, always ought to take care of herself properly . . . So you will always do as I do, Mary. It's important . . . Tomorrow you must have a bath . . . I'll show you where.'

She then took me into her bedroom, showed me the wardrobes and cupboards where her clothes were kept, and explained my duties, all the time keeping up a running commentary that struck me as being funny and quite unnatural.

'Now,' she said, 'I'll take you to Monsieur Xavier's room, for you'll be waiting on him as well, Mary . . . He's my son.'

'Yes, ma'am.'

Monsieur Xavier's bedroom was at the far end of the huge apartment, a charming room, hung with blue silk trimmed with yellow braid. There were coloured English engravings on the walls, depicting scenes of hunting and racing, carriages and castles, and the whole of one panel was taken up by a rack containing an elaborate panoply of riding crops, with a hunting horn in the centre between two pairs of crossed coach horns . . . On the mantelpiece, amongst all sorts of knick-knacks, cigar boxes and pipes, stood a photograph of a good-looking youth, young and clean-shaven, with the insolent features of a precocious dandy and the dubious grace of a young girl, which at once attracted my attention.

'That's Monsieur Xavier,' Madame informed me.

I could not help exclaiming, perhaps rather too warmly: 'Oh, isn't he handsome!'

'Now, now, Mary,' said Madame, though I could see from her smile that my words had not upset her. And she went on:

'Like most young people, Monsieur Xavier isn't very orderly in his habits, so I expect you to tidy up after him and see that his room is kept absolutely spotless. You will call him every morning at nine o'clock, and take him a cup of tea . . . At nine, you understand, Mary. Maybe he won't be too pleased to see you for he sometimes gets home very late. But don't let that worry you. A young man ought to be up by nine o'clock.'

She showed me where Monsieur Xavier kept his linen, ties, shoes and so on, accompanying each detail with some such remark as, 'My son is rather quick-tempered, but he's a dear boy all the same,' or, 'Do you know how to fold trousers properly? Monsieur Xavier is most particular about his trousers . . .' As for his hats, it was agreed that I should not be expected to see to them, since it was the footman's special glory to iron them every day. I found it extremely odd that, in a household where a footman was kept, it should be I who had the job of looking after Monsieur Xavier.

'It will be rather a lark . . . though perhaps not altogether becoming,' I said to myself, parodying my mistress's favourite expression.

The fact of the matter is, everything about this peculiar house seemed to me to be extremely odd.

That evening in the servants' hall I was to learn a good deal more.

'An extraordinary joint,' they told me. 'A bit of a shock to begin with, but you'll soon get used to it. Sometimes nobody in the house has a penny to bless themselves with. Then Madame starts running about all over the place, and when she gets back she's worn out and nervous, and starts using the foulest language . . . As for the master, he's forever on the telephone, shouting, threatening, begging, playing the very devil . . . And then the bailiffs! Often the butler has to pay the shopkeepers something on account, out of his own pocket, because they get so angry that they refuse to deliver anything. One day, in the middle of a party, the electricity and gas were both cut off! . . . And then, suddenly, the whole place is simply bursting with money again, though where it all comes from nobody actually knows . . . As for us servants, sometimes we have to wait months and months for our wages. True, we always end up by getting paid, but only as a result of all sorts of rows and swearing matches. You'd never believe . . .'

I could see that I had properly let myself in for it. Just my luck, when for once in a way I was getting really good wages.

'Monsieur Xavier didn't come home again last night,' said the footman.

'Oh well,' commented the cook, looking pointedly in my direction, 'maybe in future we shall find he does.'

And the footman went on to describe how, that very morning, one of Monsieur Xavier's creditors had called again and kicked up a hell of a row.

'It must have been some pretty dirty business, for the old man soon knuckled under, and agreed to pay him a huge sum at least 4,000 francs.'

'But was he furious!' he added. 'I heard him saying to Madame: "This simply can't go on any longer. He'll end up by dragging our name in the mud . . . in the mud".'

The cook, who seemed to be a philosophical body, merely shrugged her shoulders and said in a sneering tone of voice:

'A fat lot that'll worry them . . . It's having to pay out that they don't like.'

This conversation made me feel uneasy. It struck me vaguely that there might be a connection between some of the things Madame had said to me, and all the clothes she'd given me, and Monsieur Xavier . . . though I couldn't exactly see how . . . 'It's having to pay out that they don't like.'

That night I slept badly, haunted by the strangest dreams, impatient to see Monsieur Xavier. The footman wasn't exaggerating—it was a funny set-up all right!

Monsieur de Tarves was something in the pilgrim

business . . . I don't know exactly what, but some kind of president or director. He dug up pilgrims wherever he could, Jews, Protestants, tramps, even Catholics, and once a year used to conduct a party of them to Rome or Lourdes —at considerable profit to himself, of course. The Pope was delighted, and it was another triumph for religion. Monsieur de Tarves also had an interest in charitable and political organizations. The League Against Secular Education . . . The League for the Suppression of Obscene Publications . . . The Society for the Promotion of Religious Literature . . . The Association of Catholic Wet-Nurses for the Feeding of Working-class Children . . . I can't even remember them all. Then he was president of all kinds of orphanages, old boys' associations, schools of needlework, employment bureaux . . . anything like that . . . Oh he had plenty of jobs! He was a plumpish, lively little chap, always well shaved and very particular about his appearance, with the plausible, cynical manners of a sly, jolly priest. Now and then there were references to him and his organizations in the papers, some of them praising him for his humanitarian and devout way of life, others describing him as just an old crook. We servants used to get a lot of fun out of these contradictory reports, though it is usually regarded as rather flattering to work for people who get their names in the papers.

Every week, Monsieur de Tarves used to give a formal dinner party, followed by a reception attended by all kinds of celebrities—academicians, reactionary senators, catholic deputies, protestant priests, intriguing monks, archbishops and so on. There was one of them in particular, I remember, who always used to go out of his way to be nice to me . . . an aged Assumptionist father, whose name I forget, a poisonously sanctimonious old chap, who was always saying the most malicious things while maintaining an expression of the utmost piety. And all over the place, in every room, were portraits of the Pope . . . Oh, he must have seen some pretty funny goings-on in *that* household, the Holy Father!

I didn't take to Monsieur de Tarves. He had a finger in too many pies and liked too many people, and though no one knew half the things he really was up to, he was certainly an old shyster. The day after my arrival, as I was helping him to put on his overcoat, he asked me:

'Are you a member of my society? The Society of the Servants of Jesus?'

'No, sir.'

'Well, you ought to be, it's essential. I shall put your name down.'

'Thank you, sir . . . May I ask what the society is, sir?'

'An admirable society for rescuing unmarried mothers and giving them a Christian education . . .'

'But I don't happen to be an unmarried mother, sir.'

'That doesn't matter. It also provides for women who have been in prison, prostitutes who have turned over a new leaf . . . anybody, in fact. I shall certainly make you a member.'

Then he took some carefully folded newspapers from his pocket and handed them to me.

'Hide these, and read them when you are by yourself. You'll find them very interesting.' And, chucking me under the chin, he added: 'Tut! tut! tut! But she's an amusing little creature. Yes, indeed . . . very amusing.'

After he had gone, I had a look at the papers he had given me . . . *Le Fin de Siècle, Rigolo, Petites femmes de Paris* . . . Sheer filth, the lot of them!

Oh, these bourgeois! Always the same old comedy! I've come across a good many of them in my time, and at bottom they're all the same. For instance, there was a republican deputy I used to work for. He used to spend most of his time railing against the priests . . . And he didn't half think a lot of himself! . . . He wouldn't hear a good word about religion or the Pope, or the holy Sisters . . . Why, if anybody had paid any attention to him, there wouldn't have been a single church left standing, and all the convents would have been blown up . . . Yet every Sunday he used to go to mass, secretly, in churches where he wasn't known . . . If the slightest thing was wrong with him, he would immediately call in the priest, and he sent all his children to Jesuit schools. And just because his brother had refused to be married in church, he wouldn't speak to him . . . In one way or another, they are all just a bunch of hypocrites; disgusting, cowardly hypocrites.

191

Madame de Tarves also interested herself in good works. She was chairman of all sorts of religious committees and benevolent societies, and was always organizing charity bazaars, with the result that she was never at home and the household was left to get along as best it could. Often enough, after having been God knows where, she would arrive home very late, her underclothes all anyhow, and smelling of some scent that certainly wasn't her own . . . Oh, she couldn't fool me! I soon realized the kind of benevolent works she was engaged in . . . some pretty fishy committee meetings, if you ask me . . . But she was always nice to me . . . never a harsh word or a complaint. On the contrary, she would often get quite familiar with me, even friendly, so that sometimes, forgetting all about her dignity and my respect, we'd talk about everything under the sun . . . She would advise me about my personal affairs and encourage my coquettish tastes, smothering me with glycerine and eau-de-cologne, rubbing cold cream on my neck and shoulders and powdering my cheeks. And all the time she was performing these operations she would keep on:

'You see, Mary, a woman should always look after herself properly, and keep her skin soft and white. You've got a pretty face, so you must learn to arrange your hair to suit it . . . You have a very fine bust, so you ought to make the most of it. And your legs are magnificent, if only you would let people see them now and again . . . It's more becoming . . .'

On the whole I was content, yet somewhere inside me there remained a certain misgiving, an obscure feeling of suspicion. I could not forget the extraordinary stories that I heard from the other servants. Whenever I praised Madame, or told them about her many acts of kindness towards me, the cook would say:

'Yes, yes, that's all very fine . . . But you just wait and see what she's up to. What she wants is for you to sleep with that son of hers, so that he'll spend more time at home and not cost them so much, the old skinflints. She's already tried it on with plenty of others . . . Why, she's even tried it on with her own friends . . . married and unmarried. Yes, even girls, the old cow! Only Monsieur Xavier isn't having any . . . the lad prefers tarts. You'll see, you'll see.'

And then she would add, almost regretfully: 'Oh, if only I were in your place, I'd sting them . . . And I'd make no bones about it either!'

When she spoke to me like this I couldn't help feeling rather ashamed, but I tried to reassure myself by pretending that cook was jealous of Madame's obvious preference for me.

Every morning, at nine o'clock, I used to draw Monsieur Xavier's curtains and take him his morning tea. It's silly, but whenever I went into his room my heart used to start beating and I would feel quite apprehensive. For a long time he paid not the slightest attention to me. I used to hang about the room, putting his things ready, preparing his bath, trying to be as nice as I could and show myself off to advantage. But he never said a word to me, except to complain in a sleepy, grumbling voice that I'd woken him too early. His indifference vexed me, and I redoubled my efforts to attract his attention. Every day I expected something to happen, and Monsieur Xavier's silence, his complete lack of interest in my appearance, irritated me beyond measure. What I should have done if what I expected had actually happened, I just didn't bother to think. All I wanted was that it *should* happen . . .

He was really a very good-looking lad, much better than his photograph made him out to be. His light blonde moustache outlined the curve of his lips, which were red and full, just asking to be kissed. His eyes, light blue flecked with yellow, had a curious fascination for me, and when he moved he had the cruel, indolent grace of a girl or a wild animal. He was tall and slim, and extremely supple, and you could feel a kind of cynicism and corruption about him, that gave him an ultra-modern, very seductive elegance. Apart from the fact that I had taken to him the first time I saw him, and that I desired him for myself, the effect of his resistance to me, or rather his indifference, was that, before long, desire had become something stronger, and I fell in love with him.

One morning when I went into his room, I found Monsieur Xavier already awake and sitting bare-legged on

193

the side of his bed. I remember that he was wearing a nightshirt of white silk, with blue spots . . . One of his feet was tucked up underneath him and the other on the floor, so that his position was extremely revealing and not at all decent. Pretending to be shocked, I was about to withdraw. But he called me back:

'Hi, what's the matter? Come on in. What is there to be afraid of? Have you never seen a man before?'

He pulled a fold of his nightgown over his knee and, folding his hands on his lap and swaying his body, he sat watching me while I deposited the tray on the table in front of the fire, in such an impudent way that I couldn't help blushing a little. Then, for all the world as though this were the first time he had ever set eyes on me, he said:

'Why, you're a pretty smart girl . . .How long have you been in the place?'

'Three weeks, sir.'

'But that's marvellous.'

'What's marvellous, sir.'

'That this is the first time I've noticed how good-looking you are.'

Then, stretching out both his legs and patting his thighs, which were as round and white as a woman's, he exclaimed:

'Come here.'

As I went towards him I was trembling slightly. Without saying a word, he put his arm round me and, sniffing me all over, pulled me down beside him on the edge of the bed.

'Oh, Monsieur Xavier,' I whispered, struggling feebly. 'Please stop. What if your parents were to see you?'

But he only laughed.

'My parents? Oh, I'm absolutely fed up with them . . .'

This was one of his favourite expressions. When anybody asked him anything, he would say he was absolutely fed up, he seemed to be fed up with everything.

In order to delay the moment of the final assault, for his hands were already feeling impatiently for my breasts, I asked him:

'Tell me something, Monsieur Xavier . . . There's one thing that always intrigues me. How comes it that you are never to be seen at your mother's dinner parties?'

'Surely, sweetie, you wouldn't want me to . . . No, really! My mother's dinner parties bore me to tears.'

'And why is it,' I went on, 'that your room is the only one in the house where there isn't a portrait of the Pope?'

This question obviously delighted him. He replied:

'Well, my little pussy, you see I happen to be an anarchist . . . I've seen too much of all this religious business, all these Jesuits and priests. I'm absolutely fed up with them . . . Just imagine dining with a roomful of people like Mama and Papa. No, no, it's out of the question!'

By this time I was beginning to feel quite at ease with Monsieur Xavier, for I had discovered that, not only did he have the same depraved habits as the Paris corner boys, but he also spoke with the same drawling accent. I felt as though I had known him for years and years.

But now it was his turn to question me.

'Tell me something . . . Do you sleep with Papa?'

'With your father?' I cried, pretending to be scandalized. 'Oh, Monsieur Xavier . . . a saintly man like him?'

He burst out laughing at the top of his voice. 'But whyever not? He sleeps with every maid we have . . . He's crazy about maids. They're the only ones that excite him. Do you honestly mean to tell me you haven't slept with him yet? . . . You amaze me.'

'Well, I haven't,' I replied, also laughing. 'Though he did give me copies of *Le Fin de Siècle* to read, and *Rigolo* and *Les Petites femmes de Paris*.'

This seemed to make him almost delirious with pleasure, and with another burst of laughter he exclaimed:

'Oh, but Papa . . . he really is simply marvellous!'

And then letting himself go, he went on in the most comical tone of voice:

'It's just the same with Mama . . . Yesterday there was another awful scene with her. She said I was bringing dishonour on both of them. Would you believe it . . . And all this religion . . . and society . . . and all the rest of it. It's enough to make anyone die of laughter . . . In the end I just told her: "Look, my dear little mother, we'll make an agreement . . .The day you give up having lovers, I'll pull myself together". Pretty good, what? . . . Anyhow it made her shut up. No, no, they bore me to tears, my parents. I'm absolutely

fed up with them and their goings-on . . . By the way, you
know Fumeau?'

'No, Monsieur Xavier.'

'Yes, you must . . . Anthime Fumeau.'

'But I assure you . . .'

'A big fellow . . . quite young . . . very red cheeks and
ultra-smart . . . with the finest turn-out in Paris. Not to
mention an income of three million a year from Cabri tarts.
But of course you must know him . . .'

'But I tell you I don't.'

'You amaze me! Why everybody knows him . . . Fumeau's
biscuits! The man who was made a ward of chancery a
couple of months ago? Surely you must know who I mean?'

'But I haven't the slightest idea, on my word.'

'Oh well, never mind, little silly . . . Anyhow, last year I
played a wonderful trick on this Fumeau. Guess what? . . .
Can't you guess?'

'As I don't know him, how do you expect me to?'

'Well, it was like this, little pussy . . . I fixed things up
between Fumeau and Mama . . . Word of honour! A
brilliant idea, wasn't it? and the joke of it was that, in less
than two months, she had stung him for 300,000 of the
best! . . . It's as bad as Papa and his charities! Oh, those two
have got a nerve! But they know their way around all
right . . . if they didn't, we should all have been broke long
ago. We were up to our ears in debt . . . Even the priests
didn't want to know about it. What do you think of that?'

'Well, Monsieur Xavier, I think it's a very funny way to
treat your own family.'

'What do you expect, my love . . .? I'm an anarchist . . .
I'm fed up with the family.'

While we were talking he had succeeded in undoing my
blouse, an old one of Madame's that suited me down to the
ground.

'Now, Monsieur Xavier, you little devil! . . . That's very
naughty of you,' I exclaimed, pretending to defend myself
just for the look of things.

'Shut up,' he retorted, gently putting his hand over my
mouth. Then, throwing me back on the bed, he whispered,
'Oh, how lovely you smell . . . Just like Mama, you little
whore.'

Later that morning I noticed that Madame was at particular pains to be nice to me.

'I am very satisfied with your work here,' she said. 'I'm going to raise your wages ten francs a week.'

If she's going to give me a rise every time this happens, I thought to myself, I shan't be doing so badly . . . Most becoming, in fact . . .'

And yet, whenever I think of those days, I, too, am absolutely fed up. Monsieur Xavier's passion, or rather his weaknesses, for me, did not last long. He soon began to grow tired of me; and, in any case, my influence over him was never strong enough to keep him at home. Often, when I came into his bedroom in the morning, the bed was still neatly turned down and had not been slept in . . . He had spent the night on the tiles. The cook knew what she was talking about when she said he preferred tarts. But, on such mornings, the thought that he was still carrying on as usual, still enjoying the same pleasures, would give me a sudden pang of unhappiness, and for the rest of the day I used to be miserable.

The trouble was, Monsieur Xavier simply had no feelings . . . There was nothing the least poetical about him, like Monsieur George . . . Apart from sex, I scarcely existed for him, and as soon as it was over, he was off . . . without another thought for me. He never once expressed the slightest feeling for me, and he never used to talk to me nicely, like lovers do in novels and on the stage. Besides, our tastes were completely different . . . He didn't like flowers, for instance, except for the huge carnation he used to wear in his buttonhole . . . Yet it's so lovely, not just thinking of love-making all the time, but lying beside one another, whispering secrets, kissing, staring into one another's eyes for what seems like an eternity. But men are too coarse, they don't enjoy such things . . . and it's a great pity . . . As for Monsieur Xavier, the only things he enjoyed were vice and debauchery. Nothing else about love interested him . . .

'It's such a bore, you know . . . I'm absolutely fed up with poetry, and as to day-dreaming, I leave that to Papa . . .'

Immediately he was satisfied, I just became something quite impersonal . . . a servant, to be ordered about and bullied, with all the unconcern of an employer and the cynical impertinence of a street arab. For him, there was very little distinction between a beast of burden and a beast of love . . . Often he would say to me, with a smile at the corners of his lips that hurt and humiliated me:

'What about Papa? Is it true, you haven't slept with him yet? You amaze me.'

Once, when my tears were choking me so that I could no longer hide them, he lost his temper with me:

'Oh no, really! This is the absolute limit. If we're going to have nothing but tears and scenes, we may as well pack it up . . . I'm fed up with such nonsense.'

But I am not like that. When I am still under the spell of happiness, I like to hold the man who has given it me in my arms as long as I can . . . After the shock of passion, I feel the need—an immense, imperious need—for relaxation . . . just to lie there in a chaste embrace, exchanging kisses that are no longer a savage rending of the flesh, but an ideal, spiritually satisfying caress . . . I need to escape from the hell of sex, the frenzy of orgasm, into the paradise of ecstasy . . . into the delicious plentitude, the exquisite silence of ecstasy . . . But Monsieur Xavier was fed up with ecstasy. No sooner had he finished making love, than he tore himself from my arms, as though my embraces and my kisses had become physically distasteful to him. It was as though we had never been, if only for a moment, a part of one another; as if our sex, our mouths, our souls, had not momentarily been fused in the same cry, the same oblivion, the same exquisite death. And if I tried to keep him near me, holding him against my breast and clinging to him with my thighs, he would break free, brutally pushing me away, and leap out of bed . . . 'No, really, you're impossible' . . . and he would light a cigarette . . .

What distressed me most of all, was to realize that I left not the slightest trace of affection or tenderness in his heart, although I submitted to every sensual caprice, accepting, even outstripping, his wildest fantasies . . . and, God knows, some of them were as frightening as they were extraordinary. For though he was still only a kid, he was already utterly vicious, worse than an old man, more inventive and ferocious in his depravity than an impotent old man or a satanic priest.

Still, I think I might have gone on loving him, the little swine, and, despite everything, might even have become stupidly devoted to him . . . For, even now, I still can't help feeling some regret, when I think of that cheeky, cruel, pretty little phiz of his, and his perfumed body, and his sheer lechery, that sometimes horrified you, sometimes swept you off your feet. And I can still sometimes taste on my mouth, that has since been so often bruised by other men's kisses, the burning, acid savour of his lips . . . Oh, Monsieur Xavier, Monsieur Xavier!

One evening, when he had come home to change for dinner—and heavens, how lovely he used to look in evening dress!—while I was laying out his clothes in the dressing-room, he suddenly asked me, without the slightest hesitation or embarrassment, for all the world as though he were asking me to bring him some hot water:

'Do you happen to have a hundred francs you could lend me? . . . I simply must have them this evening, but I'll let you have them back tomorrow.'

As it happened, Madame had paid me that very morning, though whether or not he knew this I couldn't say.

'All I've got, I'm afraid, is ninety francs,' I replied, feeling a little ashamed, partly at the thought of him borrowing from me, but mainly I think, because I could not let him have as much as he wanted.

'That'll do,' said he. 'Let me have the ninety francs, and I'll pay you back tomorrow.'

He took the money, and having thanked me so casually that I was absolutely shocked, he then insolently held out his foot and brutally ordered me to tie up his shoe. 'And be quick about it,' he added, 'I am in a hurry.'

I looked at him sadly:

'Then you won't be dining at home this evening, Monsieur Xavier?'

'No, I'm having dinner in town . . .Hurry up!'

And, as I tied his shoes, I wailed:

'So you're going on the spree again, with that filthy woman of yours? And that means you'll stay out all night, leaving me here to cry my eyes out, I suppose? It's not very nice of you, Monsieur Xavier.'

'If you're just saying that simply because you've lent me ninety francs,' he retorted, in a hard, malicious tone of voice, 'you can jolly well have them back . . . Here, take them . . .'

'No, no,' I sighed, 'you know it wasn't for that.'

'Well then, leave me alone, for God's sake.'

He quickly finished dressing, and went off without kissing me or even saying good-bye.

Next day, he made no suggestion of repaying me, and I didn't like to refer to the subject. I was glad that he had accepted something from me . . . Oh, I know there are women who will kill themselves with work, who will sell themselves to the first passer-by in the street, who are ready to steal or even to kill, if only they can get money for the man they are in love with, so that he'll make a bit of a fuss of them . . . But had I really sunk to this? It is difficult to say . . . With men, there are times when I feel myself suddenly go all soft, soft as butter . . . lose all my will-power and all my courage . . . and just behave like a cow . . . Yes, like an absolute cow!

It was not long before Madame's attitude towards me changed. Instead of being nice to me, she became hard, exacting and cantankerous. I was a little idiot . . . I never did anything right . . . I was clumsy, dirty, badly brought up, forgetful and a thief . . . And her voice, which to begin with had been so gentle and friendly, was now as sour as vinegar; and when she told me to do anything, curt and humiliating . . . No more underclothes sessions; no more cold cream and rice powder; no more of those feminine confidences and intimate suggestions which, in the early days, I had found so embarrassing that I used to wonder, as indeed I still do, whether Madame didn't really prefer women . . . And as for the ambiguous friendship that had sprung up between us, which I had always felt to be fundamentally fake, since it had made me lose all respect for a mistress who was simply trying to reduce me to her own level of depravity, that, too, was over and done with . . . Knowing all about their preposterous goings-on, both in

200

public and behind the scenes, I sometimes used to let myself go, and we would end up by bawling each other out like a couple of fishwives.

'Where do you think you are?' she would shout. 'You talk as though you thought this was a whore house.'

What confounded cheek! . . . And I would answer:

'Well, so it is, whatever you may say. And as for you, if you really want to know . . . and that lousy husband of yours . . . Oh, la-la, as if everybody in Paris didn't know . . . why, anybody will tell you . . . this house is nothing but a brothel . . . and a good deal fouler than some brothels are, at that! . . .'

And so we would carry on, threatening and insulting each other in the kind of language you would only expect to hear in public brothels or on the lips of streetwalkers . . . And then, all of a sudden, everything would calm down again . . . As soon as Monsieur Xavier temporarily took a fancy to me again, everything would go all right for a time. And off we would go once more . . . the same sham familiarity and shamefaced plotting, the same gifts of clothes and fancy face creams—'so much more becoming!'—the same promises of higher wages and endless discussions as to the mysterious properties of the latest perfumes . . . Her whole attitude towards me was strictly determined by mine towards Monsieur Xavier . . . He had only to start making a fuss of me and immediately she would shower me with kindness. But directly the son showed signs of tiring of me again, the mother would once again start insulting me. I was completely at the mercy of his fluctuating feeling for me, endlessly tossed about by the intimate desires of a capricious, heartless kid . . . Anyone would think she was always spying on us, listening at keyholes, estimating the precise phase that our relations happened to be going through . . . But it wasn't really like that. It was simply that she had an instinct for vice . . . that she could smell it out, like a bitch sniffs the scent of game on the wind.

As to Monsieur de Tarves, somehow he managed to pick his way about amongst all these excitements, all this hidden family drama, alert, busy, cynical and infinitely comical. Every morning he would disappear like some pink-faced, clean-shaven, little faun, with his files under his arm and a brief-case stuffed with religious pamphlets and obscene literature, returning in the evening clothed in respectability and bursting with socialism and Christianity, but his step a little slower, his gestures not quite so unctuous, and his back slightly bowed from the burden of good works that he had performed during the day . . . And regularly every Friday the same ridiculous scene would be enacted between us.

'And what do you think I've got here?' he would say, pointing to his brief-case.

'Some kind of smut,' I would reply, laughing.

'No, no, not smut, just spicy . . .'

And he would give me a paper to read, hoping to bring me to the point where he could declare himself, content meanwhile just to smile at me with the air of an accomplice, chucking me under the chin and saying, as he licked his lips with the tip of his tongue:

'Well, well, well, she's a funny little thing . . . she certainly is . . .'

This ridiculous little game used to amuse me, and, without seeking to discourage his attentions, I made up my mind that at the first suitable opportunity I would give him a good dressing-down.

One afternoon, I was surprised to see him come into the linen-room, where I was listlessly day-dreaming over my work, for only that morning I had had a distressing scene with him and had not yet got over it . . . Monsieur de Tarves quietly closed the door, put his brief-case on the table near a pile of sheets and, coming up to me, took one of my hands and began patting it. Beneath their fluttering lids, his eyes were flickering like those of an old hen suddenly exposed to the sun, and, it was all I could do not to laugh.

'Célestine,' he began. 'I'd rather call you Célestine, if you don't mind . . .'

'Of course not, sir,' I replied, still struggling to keep a straight face, and rather on the defensive.

'Well, Célestine, I think you're charming . . .There!'

'Really, sir?'

'Quite adorable, as a matter of fact . . . adorable!'

'Oh, really, sir!'

And his fingers, trembling with desire as they traced the curve of my breast, began softly caressing my neck as though he were playing the piano.

'Adorable, adorable,' he murmured.

He tried to embrace me, but I pulled myself away to prevent him from kissing me.

'Don't go, Célestine. Please, please don't go! You don't mind me calling you *tu*?'

'No, sir . . . though I must say it rather surprises me.'

'Surprises you, you little flirt? Surprises you? . . . Oh, but you just don't know me!'

His voice was no longer dried up, and there was a trace of spittle at the corners of his mouth.

'Listen, Célestine, next week I am going to Lourdes . . . I shall be in charge of a pilgrimage . . . How would you like to come with me? I've got it all worked out. Would you like to? Nobody will find out . . . You can stay at an hotel, go for walks or whatever you like, and at night I'll come to you in your room, in your bedroom, in your bed, my little beauty. Oh, but you don't know me yet. You don't know what I'm capable of. I'm still as strong as a young man, and with all the experience of an old one . . . You'll see, you'll see . . . Oh, those great big naughty eyes!'

What surprised me was not so much the proposal itself— I'd been expecting it for a long time—but the unexpected form it had taken. However, I remained quite calm; and wanting to humiliate the old lecher, to show him that I hadn't been fooled by all the filthy tricks of himself and his family, I spat out:

'And what about Monsieur Xavier? It seems you're forgetting Monsieur Xavier. What's he going to do, while we're enjoying ourselves at Lourdes at the church's expense?'

A worried, sidelong expression, like the look of a wild animal that has been surprised, lit up in the depth of his eyes . . .

'Monsieur Xavier?' he stammered, 'why are you talking about Monsieur Xavier? It's nothing to do with him. It's none of his business.'

I returned to the charge, speaking even more insultingly:
'Oh, hasn't he indeed! Then just you tell me this, and I

don't want any of your monkey tricks, am I or am I not paid
to sleep with Monsieur Xavier? You know very well the
answer is "yes". Well, I do sleep with him . . . But you? . . .
Oh no, no, that's not part of the agreement . . . And shall I
tell you something else, my little man? You're just not my
type.' And I burst out laughing, straight in his face.

He turned absolutely purple and his eyes flashed with
anger, but he decided it was best not to become involved
in an argument in which I held all the trumps. He hurriedly
picked up his brief-case and slipped out of the room,
pursued by my laughter. Next day, without the slightest
provocation, he addressed a filthy remark to me. I flared
up . . . Madame arrived . . . and I completely lost my temper.
The scene that ensued between the three of us was so
terrifying, so utterly ignoble, that I won't attempt to
describe it. I accused them, in unmistakable terms, of all the
filthy, infamous tricks they had been guilty of, and
demanded that they should repay me the money I had lent
to Monsieur Xavier. At this, they began foaming at the
mouth. Whereupon, I picked up a cushion and, hurling it as
hard as I could at Monsieur de Tarves' head, shouted at the
top of my voice:

'Clear off with you! Get out of here immediately!'

Madame began screaming and threatening to scratch my
eyes out, while Monsieur de Tarves, hammering his brief-
case with his fist, yelled:

'I expel you from my society . . . You are no longer a
member . . . You fallen woman! You prostitute!'

But the end of it was that Madame kept back a week's
money that was due to me, refused to pay me the ninety
francs I had lent Monsieur Xavier, and insisted upon my
returning all the cast-off clothes she had given me.

'You're nothing but a bunch of thieves,' I screamed,
'Thieves and ponces! So you want a row, do you? Right you
are, then! Just you get on with it, you rotten bunch!'

And off I went, threatening to call in the police . . .

Alas, at the police station they pretended that it was
nothing to do with them, and when I spoke to a magistrate
about it he advised me to forget all about it, because, as he
explained:

'To start with, Mademoiselle, nobody is going to believe

204

you. And quite right, too, I assure you. For whatever would become of society if servants started getting the better of their masters? It would mean the end of society, Mademoiselle . . . It would be complete anarchy.'

I consulted a lawyer: he wanted a fee of two hundred francs in advance. I wrote to Monsieur Xavier: he did not answer . . . Then I added up my resources. All I had left was three francs fifty, and apart from that, the street . . .

13 NOVEMBER

And so I found myself at Neuilly, with the Sisters of Our Lady of the Thirty-six Sorrows, a kind of almshouse and registry office for servants combined. It was a fine, white building at the bottom of a huge garden, and in the garden, where there were statues of the Virgin Mary every fifty feet or so, was a little chapel, quite new and very handsomely appointed, that had been paid for by the alms of the faithful. It was surrounded by tall trees, and at all hours of the day you could hear the bells ringing . . . I like the sound of church bells . . . They remind you of things that happened long ago, that you've forgotten all about! . . . Whenever I hear them, I have only to close my eyes and I can see pictures of gentle landscapes, places I've never actually been to, perhaps, but which nevertheless call up memories of childhood and youth . . . the sound of Breton bagpipes . . . and across the heath, stretching away to the sea, crowds of people on holiday slowly winding their way . . . Ding-dong, ding-dong, ding-dong, ding-dong! . . . Not a very cheerful sound and in fact it has nothing to do with cheerfulness. Actually, it's rather sad . . . like love. But I love listening to it . . . In Paris, all one ever hears is the bugles of the turn-cocks and the deafening hooting of the trams.

At the Convent of Our Lady of the Thirty-six Sorrows they give you a bed in an attic dormitory, high up under the roof; and all you get to eat is meat that's been thrown out by the butchers and stale vegetables—and for that you have to pay twenty-five sous a day. That is to say, when they find you a place, they deduct the money due to them from your wages . . . And they pretend that's not charging anything for finding you work! Yet, on top of that, they expect you to work from six in the morning till nine o'clock at night, like the prisoners in a county jail. Never a day off, and the only recreation, meal-times and religious services. Oh, these good nuns certainly don't put themselves out much, as Monsieur Xavier would say . . . Their so-called charity is just a swindle . . . a proper have-on! But there it is—I've been a fool all my life, and I always shall be . . . All the bitter lessons I've had, all the misfortunes I've suffered, haven't been the slightest use to me. I have never learnt anything from them. For all my shouting and carrying on, in the end it always boils down to the same thing . . . I'm swindled by everyone.

Friends had often told me about these particular Sisters . . . 'Oh yes, my dear, you'll find plenty of really smart people there . . . countesses . . . duchesses . . . With any luck, they'll find you a marvellous situation.'

I thought it was true . . . And then I was so wretched that, like the fool I am, I kept thinking of the happy times I had spent with the Little Sisters of Pont-Croix . . . In any case, I had to find somewhere . . . and when you are broke it is no use being choosy.

When I got there, there were already some forty women and girls hoping to find jobs. Many of them had come from places as far away as Brittany, Alsace and the Midi, and had never previously been in service . . . awkward, clumsy creatures, with dirty complexions and a sly expression on their faces, who used to peer out over the walls of the convent at the mirage of Paris stretching away in the distance. But there were others, like me, who already knew their way around and just happened to be out of a job.

The Sisters asked me where I came from, what I could do, if I had good references, and whether I had any money left. I just codded them along, and they took me in without any further enquiries . . .

'Poor child, we shall have to see if we can't find her a good place.'

We were all their 'dear children'. And while we were waiting for the good situations they promised to find us, we 'dear children' were set to work according to our aptitudes. Some did all the cooking and housework . . .

others worked in the garden, where they were expected to dig away like navvies . . . while as for me, I was immediately given some sewing to do, because, as Sister Boniface said, 'I had supple fingers and an air of distinction'. My first job was patching the almoner's trousers, and darning a pair of underpants that belonged to a kind of friar, who happened to be in charge of a retreat in the Chapel . . . Oh, those trousers and pants! A very different cup of tea from Monsieur Xavier's, I don't mind telling you . . . Later on, the tasks I was entrusted with were not quite so ecclesiastical—like embroidering exquisite underclothes, which was much more up my street, or helping to prepare the elegant wedding trousseaux and expensive layettes that had been ordered by the rich and charitable ladies who supported the convent.

At first, after all I had just been through, there was something very comforting about the peace and silence of the place, despite the wretched food, and the almoner's trousers, and the lack of freedom, and the harsh exploitation that I was already beginning to suspect . . . I made little attempt to reason things out. I just wanted to pray. Remorse for my past behaviour or, rather, the feeling of exhaustion it had left me with, had aroused a fervent longing for repentance and forgiveness. Several times I made my confession to the almoner, yet though my intentions were quite sincere, when I thought of having to mend his filthy trousers, I couldn't help having the most irreverent and ridiculous ideas . . . He was a funny character, this almoner, round as a barrel, very red in the face, rather coarse in speech and manners, and smelling like an old sheep. He used to ask me the strangest questions, especially about the kind of books I liked reading.

'Armand Silvestre? Well, yes . . . I suppose so . . . Pretty smutty of course . . . I wouldn't exactly swop him for the *Imitation of Christ* . . . Still, he's not dangerous . . . What you mustn't read are blasphemous books . . . books against religion . . . Voltaire, for example. Never read Voltaire—that would be a mortal sin—nor Renan, nor Anatole France either . . . They are the kind of writers that are really dangerous.'

'What about Paul Bourget, Father?'

'Bourget? Well, he's certainly turned over a new leaf . . .

I wouldn't say no, I wouldn't say no. But he's not a genuine Catholic, not yet at least . . . He's still very muddled . . . He seems to me, this Bourget, rather like a wash-basin . . . Yes, that's it . . . a wash-basin that all sorts of people have been washing in, where you're apt to find olives from Mount Calvary floating about amongst bits of soap and hair . . . It would be better to wait a bit . . . And Huysmans? Well, he's a bit steep . . . Still, he's quite orthodox.'

Another time he said to me: 'Yes, I see . . . So you commit sins of the flesh. Well, that's certainly not right. Indeed, it's very wicked of you . . . Still, if you've got to sin, it's better you should do so with your employers—provided, of course, they're really religious people—than by yourself or with people of your own station in life. Sins of that kind aren't so serious . . . they don't upset God so much. Besides, people like that may very well have a dispensation . . . they often do, you know.'

But directly I mentioned the names of Monsieur Xavier and his father, he cut me short:

'Oh, no names, no names. I must ask you never to mention anybody by name . . . After all I am not a policeman. Besides, these people you refer to are rich and respectable, and extremely devout. By naming them, it is you who are committing a sin, because it means that you are rebelling against morality and against society.'

These ridiculous discussions, and especially the nagging all too human memory of his trousers, which I simply couldn't get out of my mind, considerably damped down my religious enthusiasm and longing for forgiveness. The work I had to do also got on my nerves. It made me feel a nostalgia for my proper job. I longed to escape from this prison, and to return to the intimacies of the boudoir. I yearned for cupboards full of perfumed underclothes, for wardrobes filled with taffetas and satins, for the soft feel of velvet and the sight of white bodies, relaxing in luxurious baths and half hidden by the soapy water. I missed all the gossip of the servants' hall, all the unexpected adventures that lie in wait in every bedroom, on every staircase . . . It's strange, because, when I am actually in a situation, such things disgust me, yet, as soon as I'm out of work, I miss them . . . And another thing—I was absolutely fed up with the jam we'd been getting for the last week . . . always the same, made of overripe gooseberries, simply because the Sisters had managed to buy a cheap lot at the Levallois market . . . Anything that could be saved from the garbage pail was good enough for us.

But what was really the last straw, was the quite obvious and shameless way they exploited us. It was such a perfectly simple trick that they scarcely bothered to conceal it. The only girls they found places for were those they themselves could no longer make use of. As long as it was possible to make any kind of profit out of them, by taking advantage of their talents, or strength, or lack of experience, they kept them prisoners. As the height of Christian charity, they had discovered a way of getting servants to work for them who would pay for the privilege of doing so, while at the same time robbing them, quite remorselessly and with incredible cynicism, of the modest resources they had managed to put by, having already made a profit out of their work . . .

I complained, feebly at first but later on more emphatically, that I had never once been summoned to the convent parlour. But to all my complaints these holy hypocrites merely replied:

'Have patience, dear child. We have you in mind for a very special situation, and we intend to find it for you. We know just what would suit you, but so far nothing has turned up . . . not what we would like for you . . . not what you deserve.'

Days and weeks went by, yet still none of the situations were good enough, 'special' enough for me . . . And all the while my debt to them was increasing.

Although there was a nun in charge of the dormitory, the things that went on there night after night were enough to make your hair stand on end. As soon as the sister had finished her rounds, and everybody was pretending to be asleep, white shadows would suddenly appear on all sides, gliding from cubicle to cubicle and disappearing behind curtains, and the whole room would be filled with the sound of stifled kisses, cries, bursts of laughter and whispering. My companions were completely unrestrained. In the dim, flickering light of the lamp that hung from the ceiling in the middle of the dormitory, many a time I witnessed scenes

209

of the wildest, saddest depravity . . . And all these holy nuns did was simply to close their eyes and ears, so that they should neither hear nor see what was going on. Anxious to avoid any scandal—for they would have been obliged to dismiss anyone caught in the act—they put up with these abominations by pretending to ignore them . . . And all the time my debt to them was increasing . . .

Fortunately, just when I was beginning to feel at the end of my tether, I was delighted by the arrival of one of my old friends, Clémence—Cléclé I used to call her—whom I had known when we were both working at a house in University Street. She was charming, all pink and white, and extremely fair, a regular little tomboy, full of life and gaiety. She was always laughing, for she managed to take things in her stride and to see the bright side of everything. Faithful and devoted, her one pleasure in life was helping other people. Though she was depraved to the very marrow of her bones, she was so gay, so utterly ingenuous and natural, that her depravity was in no way repugnant. Her vices were as natural to her as the flowers on a plant, or the cherries on a cherry tree. Chattering away like some sweet little bird, for a time she made me forget all my troubles, and calmed my feelings of revolt . . . As our cubicles were next to one another, on the second night she came into my bed . . . After all, what else could you expect? Force of example, perhaps . . . but also, perhaps, the craze to satisfy a curiosity that for a long time had been plaguing me . . . And, besides, with Cléclé it was a passion . . . ever since she had been seduced, four years ago, by one of her mistresses, a General's wife.

One night as we lay in each other's arms she began telling me in a funny little whisper about her last situation, with a magistrate at Versailles:

'You'd never imagine all the animals there were in that dump . . . cats . . . three parrots . . . a monkey . . . and a couple of dogs. And I was supposed to look after the lot. Nothing was good enough for them, though any old rubbish would do for us . . . the same thing day after day. But not for them . . . Oh no, they had to have bits of chicken, cream tarts, Evian water . . . Yes, honestly, my dear, they had to have Evian water to drink, the filthy brutes, because of the typhus epidemic at Versailles . . . And, though it was winter, Madame had the nerve to take the stove from my bedroom and put it in the room where the monkey and the cats slept. Would you believe it? . . . I loathed them, especially the dogs . . . There was one, an absolutely horrible old pug-dog, who was forever sniffing under my skirts. Oh, I don't mind telling you he used to get plenty of kicks for his pains . . . Then one day Madame caught me beating him, and you can't imagine the row there was. In less than five secs she'd given me the sack . . . And d'you know, my dear, that dog . . .'—she was laughing so much that she tried to stifle the sound by burying her face between my breasts—'well, that dog had exactly the same tastes as a man!'

Really, that Cléclé, what a scream she was! And so sweet! . . .

No one has any idea of all the worries that servants have to put up with, nor of the monstrous way in which they are continually exploited. If it's not the employers, it's the registry offices or some charitable institution—not to mention your fellow servants, for some of them are pretty foul. No one has the slightest concern for anyone else. Everybody lives, grows fat, amuses himself at the expense of someone more miserable and hard-up than himself. However much the scene may change or the background be transformed, however different or hostile the social setting, men's passions and appetites remain the same. Whether it is in a cramped, middle-class flat, or some banker's luxurious town house, you find the same beastliness, the same inexorable fate. When all's said and done, the truth is that a girl like me is defeated even before she starts, wherever she may go and whatever she may do . . . poor human dung, nourishing the harvest of life and happiness for the rich to gather and use against us . . .

There is supposed to be no more slavery nowadays. But that's all rubbish. What about servants? What are they, I'd like to know? In practice, they are simply slaves, with all that slavery entails—the moral degradation, the inevitable corruption, the spirit of revolt that breeds hatred . . . It is the masters who teach servants to be vicious. However pure and simple-hearted they may be when they start—and some of them are—they are soon corrupted by the depravity they come in contact with. They find themselves surrounded by vice, everything they see, breathe or touch is vicious. And so from minute to minute, from day to day, they begin to adapt themselves to it, for far from being able to defend themselves against it, they find themselves on the contrary, obliged to wait upon it, pamper it, respect it. And the spirit of revolt arises from the fact that they are powerless either to satisfy it or to break the shackles that prevent its natural development. It's really quite extraordinary. They expect us to have all the virtues, all the resignation, all the heroism and readiness for self-sacrifice, but only those vices that flatter their vanity and further their interests. And for this, all we get in return is their contempt—and wages that vary between thirty-five and ninety francs a month . . . No, it's fantastic! . . . And, on top of all this, we have to live in a state of perpetual struggle, of constant fear, between the semi-luxury of having a job one day, and, the next, having to face the squalor of unemployment; knowing that, whatever we do, we are always under suspicion, so that they are forever bolting doors, padlocking drawers, locking up cupboards, marking bottles, counting every cake and plum, and even have the nerve to search our pockets and our trunks as though they were detectives. There's not a single door or cupboard in the place, not a drawer or a bottle, that isn't continually shouting at us: 'Thief, thief, thief!' And, as if all this wasn't enough, we have to put up with the constant irritation of seeing the terrible inequality, the appalling contrast between our lot and theirs, so that despite their familiarity with us, despite all their smiles and little gifts, an impassable gulf exists between us and them, a whole world of unspoken hatred, of suppressed envy, of longing for revenge . . . a contrast that, at every minute of the day, is made more blatant and humiliating by the whims, and even by the kindnesses of these unjust, loveless creatures, which is what rich people always are . . . Do they ever, for one single moment, consider what bitter and legitimate hatred we must feel, how we must long to kill them . . . yes, kill them . . . when we hear them, in order to describe something low and ignoble, saying, with a disgust that denies all common humanity: 'He has the manners of

a servant . . . She is as sentimental as a servant girl . . .'
Under such conditions, what do they expect us to become?
Do these women really imagine that I, too, wouldn't like to
wear beautiful dresses, drive about in fine carriages, flirt
with my lovers . . . yes, and even employ servants? . . . And
then they lecture us about devotion, about being honest and
faithful . . . I only wish their words would choke them, the
cows!

Once, when I was in Cambon Street—God knows how
many situations I must have had!—the daughter of the
house was getting married, and her parents were giving a
big evening party at which all the wedding presents were
on show . . . enough to fill a furniture van. Just for a joke,
I asked Baptiste, the footman:

'Where's yours, then? Aren't you giving them a present?'

'Mine?' said Baptiste, shrugging his shoulders.

'Go on, what is it?'

'The only present I'd give them would be a can of lighted
petrol under their bed.'

It was a jolly good answer. But Baptiste was always one
for politics.

'And what about yours, Célestine?' he asked me.

'Me? Why this' . . . I replied, holding up my hands, with
the fingers curved like claws, and pretending to scratch
someone's face . . . 'My nails in his eyes!'

The butler, whom neither of us had spoken to, and who
was meticulously arranging flowers and fruit in a crystal
bowl, said calmly:

'I'd be quite satisfied if I could just sprinkle them with
vitriol instead of holy water when they were walking down
the aisle . . .'

And he stuck a rose between two pears.

The really extraordinary thing is that such acts of revenge
don't occur more often. When I think that a cook, for
example, holds the life of her employers in her hands every
day . . . A pinch of arsenic instead of the salt, a touch of
strychnine instead of vinegar . . . Why, it would be as easy
as wink! And yet it just doesn't happen . . . I suppose we
must have servility in our blood!

I am not an educated person. I just write what I think

213

and what I have seen . . . Well, what I say is, all this can't be right . . . I think that directly anyone takes someone else into his house, even if it's the most miserable devil alive or the lowest of whores, then they owe it to that person to look after them and make them happy . . . And I also maintain that, if our employers don't give us these things, then we have the right to take them, even if it means robbing them or even killing them . . .

Still, that's enough of that . . . It's stupid of me to worry about such things, for they only give me a headache and turn my stomach . . . I had better go back to my story.

I had the greatest difficulty in getting away from the Sisters of Our Lady of the Thirty-six Sorrows . . . In spite of my affair with Cléclé, and all the new and pleasant sensations it had given me, I felt myself growing old in that dump, and was itching to be free again. As soon as they were really convinced that I'd made up my mind to leave, the good Sisters started offering me place after place . . . According to them they would all suit me down to the ground . . . But I am not a complete idiot, and I soon know when anybody is trying to do the dirty on me. So I turned down all the situations they offered me, for in each case I found something that didn't suit me. You should have seen how upset they were, those blessed women . . . It was a scream! They reckoned that, by fixing me up with some sanctimonious old hag, they would be able to repay themselves for my keep out of my wages—with interest. And I was delighted to be able to turn the tables on them for once.

One day I notified Sister Boniface that I intended to leave that evening. She had the nerve to reply, raising her arms to heaven:

'But my dear child, that's impossible.'

'What do you mean, impossible?'

'Why, you just can't leave the convent like that, my child . . . You owe us more than seventy francs. You'll have to pay that back before you can leave.'

'And what with?' I enquired. 'I haven't got a farthing . . . Oh no, nothing doing!'

The Sister looked at me with hatred in her eyes and proclaimed, in a pompously severe tone of voice:

'But don't you realize, young woman, that that would be stealing, and that to steal from poor women like us is worse than any ordinary theft. It would be sacrilege, and God would punish you for it . . . Think what you are doing.' ·

Unable to suppress my anger, I shouted: 'Just you tell me this, then . . . Which of us two is the thief, you or me? Really, you're a wonderful bunch, you nuns!'

'Young woman, I forbid you to speak like that.'

'Oh, for heaven's sake, shut up! What on earth are you talking about? We do all your work . . . We slave for you from morning till night . . . We earn huge sums of money for you . . . And all you give us in return is food that a dog wouldn't look at . . . And, on top of that, now you expect me to pay you! Well, you've got another think coming . . .'

Sister Boniface had turned quite pale . . . I could see she was furious, simply bursting with coarse, filthy words that she was afraid to utter. So she merely stammered:

'Hold your tongue. You're a shameless, un-Christian girl, and God will punish you . . . You can go if you want to, but we shall keep your trunk.'

I planted myself right in front of her, defiantly, and looking her straight in the face, I said:

'I'd just like to see you! You try to keep my trunk and, before you know where you are, I'll have the police on you . . . And if religion means mending your filthy almoner's trousers for him, and stealing from hard-up tarts, and gloating over the horrible things that go on every night in the dormitory . . .'

By this time the sister was livid, and, in an attempt to drown my voice, she screamed:

'Just you listen to me, young woman!'

But I went on: 'Are you trying to pretend you know nothing about all the filthy goings-on in the dormitory? Have you got the guts to look me in the face and tell me you don't know? . . . You just encourage them because you're making money out of them . . .Yes, making money out of them!'

Trembling all over, out of breath, my throat dry, I nevertheless managed to complete my indictment:

'If religion means all this . . . If it's just a prison and a brothel, then all right, I've had about as much religion as I

215

can stand . . . My trunk, do you hear? I want my trunk, and you're going to give it to me right away.'

Sister Boniface was frightened.

'I refuse to argue with a fallen woman,' she said in a smug voice. 'It's all right, you may leave.'

'With my trunk?'

'With your trunk.'

'That's good . . . A pretty carry-on, just to get hold of your own belongings, I must say. Why, it's worse than going through the customs.' Cléclé, who had a little money put by, was very sweet and lent me twenty francs . . . I took a room in a lodging house in La Sourdière Street, and I stood myself an evening out at the Porte-Saint-Martin, where they were performing *The Two Orphans* . . . It might almost have been the story of my own life . . . And I enjoyed myself thoroughly, sobbing my heart out . . .

18 NOVEMBER

Rose is dead. Fate has certainly struck the captain's household. Poor fellow—first his ferret, then Bourbaki, now Rose! Two days ago, in the evening, she died of congestion of the lungs, after a short illness. She was buried this morning. I watched the funeral procession from the linen-room window as it passed along the road . . . The heavy coffin, carried by six men, was covered with wreaths and bunches of white flowers as though it were a young girl's. And it was followed by a considerable crowd—the whole of Mesnil-Roy—a long stream of people in black, chattering away, with the captain himself at the head, tightly buttoned into his black frock coat, and very upright and soldierly. And the solemn tolling of the church bell in the distance seemed to echo the tinkling of the little bell carried by the verger . . . Madame had forbidden me to go to the funeral, but I had no wish to anyway. I never liked this coarse, malicious woman, and her death leaves me quite cold. Still, I daresay I shall miss her, and perhaps now and then I shall regret not meeting her on the way to church. What a to-do there will be at the grocers!

I was curious to know what effect her unexpected death

had upon the captain, so, as my employers were out visiting, during the afternoon I walked as far as the hedge. The captain's garden was sad and deserted, and his spade stuck in the ground, suggested that he was not working. I don't suppose he'll come out this afternoon, I thought. He's probably shut up in his room, crying over his memories. Then suddenly I caught sight of him. He had taken off his frock coat and, dressed in his ordinary working clothes and wearing his old policeman's cap, he was furiously spreading dung on the flower-beds. I could even hear him humming a marching song in his deep bass voice. He left his barrow and came over to me, carrying his fork on his shoulder.

'It's a pleasure to see you, Mademoiselle Célestine,' he said.

I wanted to condole with him, to say how sorry I was, and I tried to find suitable words . . . But confronted by that ridiculous face of his it wasn't easy to express any genuine emotion, and all I could do was to keep on repeating:

'A sorry business for you, Captain . . . a sorry business . . . Poor Rose!'

'Yes, yes,' said he feebly.

His face was expressionless, and he gestured vaguely. Sticking his fork into the soft bit of ground near the hedge, he added:

'Especially as I can't manage on my own.'

'It certainly won't be easy to find anyone to take her place,' said I, emphasizing Rose's domestic virtues.

But, obviously, he wasn't in the least upset. Indeed, judging by the greater alertness of his movements and the lively look that had suddenly come into his eyes, one might almost have thought that he'd just got rid of a tremendous burden.

'Nonsense,' said he after a short silence. 'Nobody's irreplaceable.'

His philosophical resignation astonished me, even shocked me a little. Just for fun, I tried to make him understand all that he had lost through Rose's death.

'After all, she was used to all your little ways . . . understood all your tastes, all your whims! And then, she was so absolutely devoted to you.'

'Heavens, it just needed that . . .' he sneered. And, with a gesture that seemed to sweep away every objection, he went on:

'Do you really believe she was so devoted? . . . Look, there's something I'd like to tell you. I was fed up with Rose . . . not half! Ever since we took on a lad to help her, she didn't bother to do a thing in the house. Everything was going to pot . . . to pot! I couldn't even get her to boil me an egg the way I liked it . . . And scenes from morning till night, all over nothing . . . Every penny I spent she'd be on to me, scolding and shrieking. And if I so much as spoke to you, like I am now, I'd never hear the last of it, she was so jealous. The way she was carrying on, I tell you the place was no longer my own, damn it.'

He drew a deep, loud breath, like a traveller who had just returned from a long journey and, looking around him, he contemplated with a new kind of pleasure the sky, the empty flower-beds, the dark tracery of the trees against the light, and his little house . . . His delight, which was scarcely very complimentary to Rose's memory, struck me as being quite comic. Hoping to encourage his confidences I said, reproachfully:

'I don't think you're being very fair to Rose, Captain.'

'Look here, for God's sake,' he retorted vigorously, 'you don't know what you're talking about. You have no idea. She wasn't going to tell you all about the rows she kicked up . . . her overbearingness . . . her jealousy . . . her selfishness. I couldn't call a thing in the place my own any more. She thought she owned the lot. Why, would you believe it, I wasn't allowed to sit in my own wing chair any more. She was always taking it. And not only that, she took everything else. Just imagine, we weren't allowed to eat asparagus because *she* didn't like it . . . No, it's a good job she's dead! It was the best thing that could have happened to her for, one way or another, I'd decided not to keep her on . . . No, damn it, I wouldn't have kept her on much longer. She was driving me crazy. It was more than I could stand . . . But I'll tell you one thing . . . If I had died before she did, Rose would have been jolly well caught out . . . I'd got something up my sleeve that would have put her nose out of joint properly. I can tell you that!'

218

His mouth twisted into a smile that ended as a hideous grimace. And he continued, intercepting his words with damp little puffs:

'You know I'd drawn up a will leaving everything to her . . . house, silver, investments, the lot. She must have told you . . . She used to tell everybody. But what she couldn't have told you, because she didn't know about it herself, was that, two months later, I'd made a second will, cancelling the first . . . and in that I had left her nothing, damn it.'

And he burst out laughing . . . a strident laugh that scattered through the garden like a flock of twittering sparrows. Then he almost shouted:

'A good idea, what? Can't you just see her face when she discovered that I'd left my little fortune to the Academy? For that's precisely what I did, my dear Mademoiselle Célestine. I left everything I possessed to the Academy.'

Waiting until he had finished laughing, I asked him in a serious voice:

'And now what are you going to do, Captain?'

He stared at me for a moment or two with a slyly amorous expression, and then replied:

'Well, that's just it . . . It all depends on you.'

'On me?'

'Yes, entirely on you.'

'Whatever do you mean?'

There was another short silence, during which, drawing himself up to his full height and jutting his little beard at me, he seemed to be trying to envelop me in an ambience of seduction. Then suddenly he said:

'Come on now, let's get down to brass tacks . . . Putting it bluntly . . . one man to another . . . how would you like to take Rose's place? . . . It's yours for the asking.'

I was prepared for this attack. I had seen it maturing in the depths of his eyes, and I met it with a grave, impassive expression.

'But what about your will, Captain?'

'Good God, I'll tear that up.'

'But I can't even cook . . . ,' I parried.

'Oh, I'll do the cooking . . . and I'll make the beds . . . our bed, I mean. Why, damn it all, I'll do everything.'

His manner had become very amorous and there was a randy glint in his eye . . . It was lucky for me that there was a hedge between us, otherwise I'm convinced he would have flung himself upon me there and then.

'But there's more than one kind of cooking,' he explained in a hoarse, rattling voice. 'And the kind I want to do . . . Oh Célestine, I bet you know how to . . . I bet you can make it spicy . . . Oh, for God's sake . . .'

I smiled ironically and, shaking my finger at him as though he were a child, I said:

'Now Captain, now Captain . . . you're behaving like a dirty little pig!'

'Not little,' he retorted boastfully, 'a big one, a huge one, damn it! . . . And there's another thing, Célestine . . . I must tell you.'

He leant over the hedge, craning his neck, his eyes bloodshot. And in a lower voice he said:

'If you come to me, Célestine, you see . . .'

'Well, what then?'

'Why, it would drive the Lanlaires absolutely mad, don't you see?'

I remained silent, pretending to be pondering some problem . . . The captain grew more and more impatient, on edge, grinding his heel into the gravel path.

'Look, Célestine . . . Thirty-five francs a month . . . have your meals with me . . . share my bed . . . and a new will, damn it all! . . . What more could you want? Tell me . . .'

'We'll see about that later on . . . But, in the meantime, find somebody else, damn it all!'

And turning my back on him, I went off towards the house to prevent myself bursting out laughing.

So now I have two of them to choose from . . . the captain and Joseph. Either I can become the captain's servant-cum-mistress, with all the risks that entails, that is to say, to be always at the mercy of a coarse, unreliable, stupid man, and dependent upon every kind of unpleasant circumstance and prejudice; or else, by marrying Joseph, I can achieve a measure of tolerable freedom and respect, and live without being continually subject to other people's orders and all the hazards of existence . . . which would mean realizing at least part of what I have always dreamt of . . .

True, I should have preferred something on a rather grander scale. But, considering the few opportunities that are likely to present themselves to a woman in my position, I ought to be glad of what would, after all, be some alternative to everlastingly chopping and changing, to the monotonous succession of different situations, different beds, different faces . . .

Actually, I have already made up my mind to turn down the captain's proposal . . . It didn't need this last conversation with him to convince me that he is an utterly fantastic specimen of humanity, a grotesque and sinister crackpot. Apart from his sheer physical ugliness—and there's nothing to be done about that—there's not the slightest chance of exercising any moral influence over him. Rose firmly believed that he was completely under her thumb, but he was simply leading her up the garden . . . It's just as impossible to influence something that doesn't exist, as it is to act in empty space . . . Besides, the mere thought of lying in this ridiculous creature's arms, and kissing him, is simply laughable . . . not just because he disgusts me, for disgust presupposes the possibility of my doing it, but because I am perfectly certain I never could . . . If, by some fantastic miracle, I happened to find myself in bed with him, I know perfectly well that every time I tried to kiss him I should burst into uncontrollable laughter. One way and another I have slept with plenty of men—out of love or pleasure, boredom or pity, vanity or self-interest. It seems to me to be a perfectly normal, natural and necessary thing to do. I have no feeling of guilt about it, and there are very few occasions when it has not given me some pleasure . . . But, with a man as utterly ridiculous as the captain, I just know that it simply couldn't happen . . . it would be physically impossible . . . To me, it would seem completely unnatural . . . worse even than Cléc1é and her little dog . . . Yet, despite all this, the captain's proposal still gives me a certain satisfaction, almost a feeling of pride . . . Sordid as it is, nevertheless it is a tribute to me, and, as such, it gives me added confidence in myself and in my looks.

With regard to Joseph, my feelings are quite different. Joseph has got a real hold over my mind . . . He dominates and obsesses it . . . He alternately disturbs, enchants and scares me. True, he's ugly, brutally, horribly ugly. But when you examine this ugliness closely, there is something formidable about it that is akin to beauty, an elemental force that is more than beauty, beyond beauty. I don't at all under-estimate the difficulties, the danger even of living with such a man whether married or not . . . a man that I feel so deeply suspicious of, without really knowing him. But it is precisely this that attracts me to him, till I feel almost giddy . . . At least he is a man who is capable of achieving a great deal . . . of evil perhaps, but also, perhaps, of good. I just do not know . . . What does he want of me? What will he make of me? Shall I become the unwitting instrument of schemes I know nothing about, the plaything of his savage passions? Or does he simply love me . . . and, if so, why? . . . Because he thinks I'm good . . . or vicious . . . or intelligent? Or because I am no more bound by prejudice than he is? I just don't know . . . Besides the attraction of the mysterious and unknown, the sheer power of the man has cast a bitter, powerful spell upon me. And this spell—for that's what it is—is more and more getting on my nerves, reducing me to a state of physical passivity and submission. When I am near him my senses are on fire. I have a feeling of exaltation that I have never experienced with any other man. I feel a longing for him, more sombre, more terrible, more violent than the desire that swept me off my feet with Monsieur George . . . It is something different, something I can't properly describe, that takes possession of my entire being, spiritual and sexual, revealing instincts that I was previously unaware of, that must, unknown to me, have been asleep within me, and that no love, no shock of passion, had ever before brought to life. And when I remember what Joseph once said to me, I tremble all over:

'You're like me, Célestine . . . Oh, not to look at, of course! . . . But our souls, they are as alike as twins . . .'

Can it really be true? These feelings that I am experiencing are so novel, so insistent and tenacious, that they never give me a moment's respite. I am continually under the influence of their numbing fascination. Though I try to occupy my mind with other things . . . reading . . . walking in the garden when the Lanlaires are out . . . busying myself with mending when they're at home . . . it is no use! The thought of Joseph obsesses me. And this complete domination applies not only to the present, but also to the past. Between me and my whole past life, I am so forcefully aware of his presence, that it is as though I can see no one else, and the past with all its faces, ugly or charming, becomes more and more remote, emptied of all colour . . . Cléophas Biscouille, Monsieur Jean, Monsieur Xavier, William, whom I haven't mentioned yet, even Monsieur George, who I thought had left a mark upon my soul as indelible as the number branded on a convict's back, and all those others, to whom freely, gaily, passionately I have given some part of myself, of my trembling flesh and sorrowful heart, are nothing but shadows . . . Vague, flickering shadows, already disappearing, scarcely memories and soon to become mere troubled dreams . . . intangible, forgotten realities . . . smoke fumes disappearing into nothingness . . . Sometimes, in the kitchen after dinner, looking at Joseph and his criminal mouth, his criminal eyes, the heavy cheekbones and low, rugged brow thrown into relief by the light from the lamp, I tell myself:

'No, no, it isn't possible . . . I'm going crazy . . . I won't, I can't love such a man . . . No, no! it just isn't possible!'

But it is possible . . . It's true . . . And it's time I admitted it to myself, time I shouted aloud 'I love Joseph!'

Oh, now I realize why one should never laugh at love . . . Now I know why there are women, driven by the invisible force of nature, who yearn for the kisses of brutes, fling themselves heedlessly into the arms of monsters, moaning with pleasure, their faces contorted like satyrs and demons . . .

Madame has given Joseph six days' holiday, and tomorrow, on the pretext of family business, he is going to Cherbourg. He has decided to buy the little café, though for some months he won't be running it himself. He has a friend there he can rely on, who will look after it for him.

'You see,' he said to me, 'first of all it must be repainted from top to bottom, so that everything will be in first-class order, with a new sign "To the French Army" in gold letter-

ing. Besides, I can't give up my place here at present . . .
It's out of the question.'

'Why, Joseph?'

'Because it wouldn't do . . . not now . . .'

'But when do you intend to give in your final notice?'

Scratching the back of his neck, and glancing at me slyly,
he said: 'I don't really know . . . Maybe in six months' time
from now . . . It might be a bit sooner, it might be a bit
later. You can't tell . . . It all depends . . .'

I knew he didn't want to talk, but I insisted:

'All depends on what?'

It was some time before he answered. Then, mysteriously,
but at the same time with a kind of excitement, he said:

'Some business I have to see to . . . important business.'

'But what kind of business?'

'Business . . . And that's that.' He spoke sharply, not
exactly angrily, but as though he were on edge and refused
any further explanation.

What surprised me was that he had said nothing about
me. I was surprised and very disappointed. Could he have
changed his mind? Was he fed up with my curiosity, and
my continual hesitation? Surely it was quite natural, if I
was to share in the success or failure of the undertaking,
that I should be interested? . . . Had my suspicion, which I
couldn't conceal, that it was he who had raped little Clara,
decided him to break things off between us? . . . From the
sudden quickening of my heart, I felt that the conclusion I
had reached—though from coquetry, just to tease him, I
hadn't yet told him—was nevertheless the right one. To be
free, to sit behind the bar giving orders to other people, to
know that so many men were looking at me, desiring me,
adoring me . . . Was it to prove yet another of my dreams
that never came true? . . . I did not want Joseph to think I
was throwing myself at his head, but I did want to know
what was in his mind. Putting on a forlorn expression I
murmured:

'When you go, Joseph, I shan't be able to stand this house
another moment . . . I've got so used to you now . . . to our
little chats.'

'Well, there it is . . .'

'I shall pack it up as well.'

He made no reply but began walking up and down the saddle-room frowning and preoccupied, nervously twiddling a pair of secateurs in his apron pocket . . . There was a nasty expression on his face.

'Yes, I shall pack up and go back to Paris,' I repeated.

Still no word of protest, not even a pleading glance in my direction . . . He put some wood on the dying fire, then resumed his silent pacing . . . Why was he like this? Had he accepted our separation? Was that what he wanted? Had he lost all confidence in me, all his love for me? Or was it simply that he dreaded my rashness, my everlasting questions? . . . Trembling a little, I asked:

'Wouldn't you mind at all, Joseph, if we were never to see each other again?'

He continued to walk up and down, not so much as looking at me with that funny, oblique expression of his.

'Of course I should,' he said. 'But there it is. You can't force people to do something if they don't want to . . . Either they do or they don't . . .'

'But what have I ever refused to do, Joseph?'

Ignoring my question, he added: 'Besides, you've always had rotten ideas about me.'

'Me? Why do you say that?'

'Because . . .'

'No, no, Joseph, it's you that don't love me any longer . . . You've got some other idea in your head . . . I've never refused anything . . . I just wanted time to think about it, that's all. Surely, that's reasonable? You don't take somebody on for the rest of your life without thinking about it . . . On the contrary, you ought to be glad that I hesitated. It proves I'm not just a featherbrain, that I'm a serious woman . . .'

'You're a good woman, Célestine, and a sensible woman.'

'Well then, so what?'

At last he stopped walking about and, staring at me with a grave expression, still distrustful, yet very gentle, he said slowly:

'It's not that, Célestine . . . That's got nothing to do with it. I don't want to stop you thinking about it . . . For God's sake, think about it as much as you like . . . There's plenty of time. We'll talk it over again when I get back . . . But look, what I don't like is when anyone is too inquisitive. There are some things that don't concern women . . . There are some things . . .' And he concluded the sentence by shaking his head.

After a moment's silence, he went on: 'I think about nothing else, Célestine . . . I dream about you . . . You've got right under my skin . . . as true as God's in heaven. And when I say a thing once, I say it for keeps . . . We'll have another talk about it . . . But don't you be too inquisitive . . . What you do is your business, and what I do is mine . . . Like that, we shall get along fine.'

He drew closer to me, and took hold of my hand:

'I know I'm pig-headed, Célestine . . . I admit it. But that's not such a bad thing . . . It means I'm not one to change my mind . . . I'm crazy about you, Célestine . . . you, in our little café.'

The sleeves of his shirt were rolled up, and I could see the huge supple muscles of his arms, moving swiftly and powerfully beneath the whiteness of his skin . . . His forearms, and both biceps, were tattooed with flaming hearts and crossed daggers and a vase of flowers . . . A strong masculine odour, almost like the smell of a wild animal, rose from his broad chest, curved like a cuirass . . . Intoxicated by this strength, this odour, I leant against the wooden saddle-tree where he had been polishing the harness brasses when I first came in . . . Neither Monsieur Xavier, nor Monsieur Jean, nor any of the others, handsome and sweet-smelling as they were, had ever made such a profound impression on me as this already ageing man, with his narrow skull and cruel, animal face . . . And as I clasped him in my arms, pressing my fingertips into the steely bands of muscle, I said in a fainting voice:

'Joseph, you must take me now, my love . . . I, too, am crazy about you . . . You've got right under my skin as well.'

But he replied in a gravely, fatherly voice: 'No, it isn't possible . . . not now, Célestine.'

'Yes, Joseph, straight away, my dearest one.'

Gently he freed himself from my embrace: 'If it was simply for a bit of fun, Célestine, of course it would be all right . . . But this is serious, this is for keeps. We've got to behave right . . . We've got to wait until we're married.'

And there we stood, facing one another. He, with gleaming eyes and heaving chest . . . I, with my arms hanging slackly at my sides, my head buzzing, my whole body on fire.

20 NOVEMBER

Yesterday morning, as had been arranged, Joseph set out for Cherbourg. By the time I got down he had already left. Marianne, still only half awake, puffy-eyed and her throat full of phlegm, was drawing water from the pump. Joseph's plate was still on the kitchen table, and an empty jug of cider . . . I was anxious, but, at the same time glad that he had gone, for I felt that from today a new life was beginning for me. The sun was scarcely up and it was cold. Beyond the garden the countryside still slept beneath a thick blanket of fog, and in the distance I could hear the faint whistle of an engine coming from the invisible valley. That train bore both Joseph and my hopes for the future . . . I could not eat any breakfast . . . I felt as though a heavy weight was pressing on my stomach . . . The sound of the whistle died away . . . The fog was growing thicker, filling the garden . . .

But supposing Joseph didn't come back?

All that day I was listless and nervous, and extremely restless. Never had the house weighed so heavily upon me; never had the long corridors seemed to me so dreary, or the silence so icy; never had I so detested Madame's ill-tempered face and yapping voice. Work was out of the question, and I had such a violent row with Madame that for a moment I thought she was going to give me notice . . . I kept wondering how I was going to get through the week without Joseph . . . I dreaded the boredom of having meals alone with Marianne. What I needed was somebody I could really talk to . . .

By the time evening comes Marianne is generally pretty well stupefied with drink . . . She just sits there, with her fuddled brain and thick speech, her mouth hanging open, her lips shining like the worn edge of an old well . . . All you can get out of her is an occasional grumble, or a kind of childish whimper . . . Yesterday evening, however, she was less drunk than usual and, in the middle of her endless moaning, she suddenly announced that she was afraid she was pregnant . . . I ask you, Marianne in child . . . If that isn't the last straw! My first instinct was to laugh . . . Then I thought, what if Joseph is the father? And I felt a sudden pain, as though someone had hit me in the pit of the stomach . . . I remembered how, when I first got here, I had suspected that they might be sleeping together . . . But that was ridiculous and certainly not borne out by anything that had happened since. On the contrary . . . No, no, it was impossible . . . If Joseph had been having an affair with Marianne I must have known about it . . . I should have smelt it in the air . . . No, it wasn't that, it couldn't be that . . . And another thing, in his way, Joseph was too much of an artist . . .

'Are you sure you're pregnant, Marianne?' I asked her.

She pressed her hand against her stomach, her huge fingers sinking into the folds of flesh, like those of a badly blown-up rubber cushion.

'Not sure . . .' she said, 'just afraid.'

'And who's the man?'

She hesitated a moment . . . Then, abruptly, almost proudly, she declared:

'Why, the master!'

This time I couldn't help laughing. The master . . . that really was the last straw! Marianne took my laughter for a sign of admiration, and she, too, began to laugh.

'Yes, yes . . . the master!' she repeated.

But how was it that I had noticed nothing? How could anything so perfectly ridiculous have been going on, right under my nose, so to speak, without my having seen anything, or even suspected anything? . . . I began questioning her, and with a little pressing, she told me all about it, with the greatest complacency, and rather flattered.

'About two months ago,' she began, 'Monsieur came into the scullery one day, while I was washing up after lunch. It must have been soon after you got here . . . Yes, that's right, because he'd just been talking to you on the staircase . . . Well, when he came into the scullery, he was flinging his arms about, puffing and blowing . . . and you should have seen his eyes, all bloodshot and fairly starting out of his head . . . I thought he was going to have a stroke . . . Then, without a word, he just hurled himself on me . . . and it was pretty clear what he was up to . . . Being the master, you understand, I didn't dare try to defend myself . . . Anyway, you don't often get that kind of chance here! . . . It took me quite by surprise . . . though, mind you, I enjoyed it all right . . . After that he often used to come to the scullery . . . Oh, he's a lovely man . . . and so tender with it.'

'A bit of all right, what, Marianne?'

'Oh yes,' she murmured, her eyes full of ecstasy. 'Oh, a lovely man!'

Her huge soft face lit up with a sensual smile, and beneath her torn blouse, stained with grease and smoke, her vast breasts heaved . . .

'So you're quite happy about it?' I asked.

'Oh yes,' she replied. 'That is to say, I should be if I was quite certain I wasn't in the family way . . . That would be too bad, at my time of life.'

I did my best to reassure her . . . and, at everything I said, she just nodded her head . . . Then she added:

'All the same, just to put my mind at rest, I shall go and see Madame Gouin tomorrow.'

I felt genuinely sorry for this poor woman, with her dull brain, stuffed with hazy ideas . . . Pathetic, unhappy creature, whatever was to become of her? . . . To me, it was quite extraordinary, but love didn't seem to have even touched her with its radiance; there wasn't a trace of that halo that passion sometimes seems to create around the ugliest faces . . . She remained just as she'd always been . . . heavy, soft and dumpy . . . And yet I couldn't help feeling pleased that this happiness, that must have revivified that great body with the almost forgotten touch of a man's hand, had come to her through me. For had I not first aroused Lanlaire's desires he would never have chosen to satisfy them with this pathetic creature . . .

'You'll have to be very careful, Marianne . . . It would be terrible if Madame caught you,' I said affectionately.

'Oh, there's no danger of that,' she cried. 'He only comes when she's out . . . and he never stays for long . . . As soon as he's had it, he's off . . . Besides, the scullery door opens onto the backyard, and from there there's a door into the alley. At the slightest sound he can get away without anybody seeing him . . . But what's the odds? If Madame does catch us, that's that!'

'But she'd give you the sack, my poor Marianne.'

'Well, there it is,' she said, swaying her head from side to side like an old bear.

After a short silence, during which I tried to imagine these two poor creatures making love in the scullery, I asked:

'Is the master gentle with you?'

'Oh yes, ever so.'

'Does he talk to you nicely sometimes? What does he say?'

'Well, as soon as he comes in, he starts making love straight away . . . Then he says, "That's better, that's better", and puffs and blows a bit . . . Oh, he's really lovely . . .'

By the time we parted, I was feeling genuinely sorry for her . . . Never again should I laugh at her and, instead of pitying her, I felt a kind of sorrowful affection for her.

But it was myself I really felt sorry for, and when I got up to my room I was filled with a sense of shame, an immense dejection . . . One should never think about love . . . it's too sad, and all it leaves behind is absurdity, or bitterness, or just nothing . . . What remains to me today of Monsieur Jean, preening himself up there on the mantelpiece, in his red plush frame? Nothing, except for a feeling of disillusion that I could once have loved such a heartless, conceited idiot. Could I really have ever loved this fop with his white unhealthy face and black mutton-chop whiskers, and that absurd parting? His photograph irritates me. I simply can't stand those stupid eyes, staring at me all the time with that impudent flunkey's look of his. No . . . It may as well join all the others at the bottom of my trunk, until the time comes when I can make a magnificent bonfire of my whole detestable past.

I began to think of Joseph . . . Where would he be at this time of night? What would he be doing? Was he thinking about me? He was probably at the little café, looking around, arguing, taking measurements, trying to imagine how I should look, standing at the bar in front of the mirror and all those shelves full of sparkling glasses and brightly coloured bottles . . . I wish I knew what Cherbourg was like, with its streets and squares and harbour, so that I could imagine Joseph wandering about, conquering the town as he had conquered me . . . I was rather feverish, and kept turning over and over as I lay in bed. My thoughts were shuttling back and forth, between the forest of Raillon and Cherbourg . . . from little Clara's corpse to the café. And when, at last, after a distressing period of sleeplessness, I finally dozed off, it was with a picture of Joseph before my eyes, dour, uncouth, motionless, silhouetted against a dark, stormy background, criss-crossed with tall cranes and swaying masts.

Today, Sunday, I went into Joseph's bedroom. The two dogs eagerly accompanied me, and seemed to be asking what had happened to Joseph. The furniture consisted of a small iron bedstead, a big wardrobe, a kind of low cupboard, a table and two chairs, all made of unpainted wood; and there was a portmanteau, concealed behind a green cotton curtain to keep the dust off it. Though scarcely luxurious, the room was tidy and extremely clean. It had something of the stiff austerity of a monk's cell. On the whitewashed wall, between portraits of Déroulède and General Mercier, there were unframed pictures of the Blessed Virgin and the Saints, an Adoration of the Magi, a Massacre of the Innocents and a scene from Paradise. Over the bed was a large crucifix of black wood that could be used as a holy water stoup.

It was not very nice of me, I admit, but I couldn't resist a violent desire to search the place, hoping rather vaguely, to discover some of Joseph's secrets. But there was nothing mysterious about the room, no attempt to conceal anything. It was the sparsely furnished room of a man without secrets, a man whose life was completely straightforward, free of all complications . . . Though the cupboards and drawers all had keys, none of them was locked. On the table stood some packets of seeds, and a book called *Good Gardening;* and, on the mantelpiece, a prayerbook with yellowing leaves and a small notebook, in which he had copied out recipes

231

for making furniture polish and Bordeaux mixture, and the correct amounts of nicotine and iron sulphate to use. Nowhere could I find a single letter, nor even an account book . . . not a trace of any correspondence, business or political, family or personal . . . In the cupboard, amongst a clutter of discarded shoes and old sprinkler valves, were piles of pamphlets and several numbers of *La Libre Parole*. Under the bed there were some rat traps . . . I turned everything upside down, felt everything, emptied everything . . . clothes, mattress, linen, drawers . . . but there was nothing else! In the wardrobe everything was just as I had left it a week ago, when I had tidied it up with Joseph looking on . . . Could it really be possible that Joseph possessed nothing else? . . . That he simply managed to do without all the thousand and one intimate, personal little things that reveal a man's tastes and passions and thoughts? Yes, there was just one thing . . . At the bottom of the table drawer I found a cigar box, wrapped up in paper and tied round with four strands of tightly knotted string. With the greatest difficulty I undid the string, and there, packed in cotton wool, were five holy medals, a small silver crucifix and a rosary made of red beads . . . Always religion!

My search concluded, I left the room with a feeling of nervous exasperation at having found nothing that I had been looking for, nothing I wanted to know. Joseph certainly manages to infect everything he touches with his own impenetrability. His possessions tell you no more than he himself does, they are as inscrutable as his eyes or his forehead . . . Throughout the remainder of the day I could see, actually see before my eyes, Joseph's face, alternately enigmatic, sneering, churlish. And I seemed to hear him say:

'So your curiosity didn't get you very far, then, you little duffer . . . Oh, you can try again, you can search through all my underclothes, turn out my trunks, even peer into my soul, but you'll never find out anything!'

But I want to stop thinking about all that . . . and about Joseph . . . My head is aching so badly that I feel I'm going mad . . . We had better get back to my reminiscences . . .

No sooner had I left the convent at Neuilly, than I found

myself once again condemned to the drudgery of a registry office, although I had sworn I would never have recourse to one again. But when you are out of a job and haven't even got the wherewithal to buy yourself a meal, what else is there? . . . Friends? Old Comrades? Why, they don't even answer your letters . . . Advertisements in the papers? They cost a great deal, and simply lead to endless correspondence, endless journeys that get you nowhere . . . Besides, they are such a chancy business. And then, you have to pay in advance . . . and Clécle's twenty francs had soon melted away . . . Prostitution? Wandering about the streets picking up men, who as often as not are as hard up as yourself? My God, no! I don't mind doing it for pleasure, but not for money. I simply can't. Besides, I'm no good at it—I always get done down. I even had to hock the last few bits of jewellery I'd managed to hang on to, just to pay for a room and my keep . . . No, you can't get away from it—when you're down and out, the agencies are your only hope, even if they do rob and exploit you.

And they really are a filthy swindle, these registry offices . . . For a start, you have to pay ten sous down, just to get your name on their books . . . In return for which they give you the chance of some lousy job or other . . . Oh, yes, they've got plenty of them to offer, all right. And if you're not fussy, you can take your pick . . . Why, nowadays, every tuppeny ha'penny little shopkeeper likes to show off by keeping a servant . . . But the rotten part of it is, that if, after submitting to a humiliating cross-examination and even more humiliating haggling, you do at last manage to come to terms with one of these rapacious creatures, you have to pay the registry office three per cent of your wages for a whole year . . . If you can't stick the job for more than ten days, that's just too bad. The registry office doesn't worry, because they still draw their full commission . . . Oh, they know what they're up to all right. They know the kind of place they're sending you to, and that it won't be long before you're back again . . . Take my case, for instance. I had seven situations in four-and-a-half months . . . a run of bad luck . . . all quite impossible, worse than prison. Well, I had to pay the registry office three per cent on seven whole years' wages . . . that is to say, when you add the ten sous booking fee each time, more than ninety francs in all . . . And in the end I was simply back where I'd started! Do you call that fair? Isn't it sheer robbery?

But there, whichever way you turn, it's always the same, and naturally it's always those that have got the least that get robbed the worst . . . But what can you do about it? You can rage about it as much as you like, you can try to revolt, but in the end you just have to admit that it's better to be cheated than to starve, and die in the street like a dog . . . There's only one thing certain, and that is that the world's damned badly organized . . . It's a pity General Boulanger was defeated . . . At least he seems to have liked servants . . .

The registry office where I had been fool enough to put my name down was in a courtyard off Coliseum Street, on the third floor of a dark, old house, more or less working-class. Immediately inside the door, you went up a steep, narrow staircase, so filthy that you could feel the soles of your shoes almost sticking to the treads, and the banisters were slimy with damp. There was a horrible smell of sinks and lavatories, enough to dishearten anybody. I don't pretend to be all that fussy, but the very sight of that staircase turned my stomach. It used to make me feel so weak at the knees that I could scarcely bring myself to face it. All the hopes that had been singing in your heart on the way there, were immediately stifled by this thick, greasy atmosphere, the filthy stairs and the sweating walls, which you felt must be swarming with creeping insects and clammy frogs. Honestly, I should have thought ladies would have been afraid to visit such a filthy slum. In fact, however, it did not seem to disgust them at all . . . But there, is there anything that does disgust them these days? They'd never think of visiting such a house if it was a question of helping the poor, but to find themselves some wretched servant to plague they'd go anywhere.

This particular registry office was run by a Madame Paulhat-Durand, a tall woman, about forty-five years old, with black, wavy hair, which, despite the flabbiness of her body squeezed into a terrible pair of corsets, had not yet begun to go grey. Her face still showed traces of beauty, and what a presence, what an eye! . . . Crikey! I bet she used to have a good time, all right! . . . She dressed with austere elegance, always in a black taffeta dress, with a long gold chain gleaming on her formidable bosom and a black velvet scarf round her neck. And she comported herself with the utmost dignity. She lived with a local government clerk, Monsieur Louis—we only knew his Christian name —a funny little chap, extremely short-sighted, with mincing gestures, who never spoke a word. In his shabby, grey suit, that was much too large for him, he always looked extremely awkward . . . Sad, timid, stooping, and still quite young, he seemed to be resigned rather than happy. Yet Madame was so furiously jealous of him that he never dared to speak to us, or even to glance in our direction. When he got back from work with his brief-case under his arm, he would just touch his hat to us, without so much as turning his head, and then, dragging one leg slightly, he would disappear down the passage like a ghost. And how exhausted the poor fellow must have been, for every evening it was he who had to deal with all the correspondence, keep the accounts, and all the rest of it.

Neither Paulhat nor Durand was Madame's real name. Though she had adopted them because they went well together, they had apparently belonged to two gentlemen, long since dead, with whom she had once lived, and who had put up the money to set her up in business . . . Her real name was Josephine Carp. Like most of the women who run registry offices, she had once been in service. That was obvious from her pretentious behaviour, but though she aped the manners of the ladies she had once worked for, she could not altogether disguise her squalid and lowly origins. She had all the unmistakable insolence of a one-time domestic servant, but her insolence was reserved exclusively for us: towards her clients, she displayed an obsequious servility, strictly proportioned to their social standing and fortune.

'Oh, you never saw such a lot, my dear Countess,' she would say with a simpering smile. 'High-class maids they call themselves . . . that is to say, girls who just are not prepared to do a stroke of work, and whose morals I simply wouldn't care to vouch for. When it comes to women who really know their job, who are prepared to get down on their hands and knees and have been taught to sew, I just don't know where to find them any more . . . and nor does anyone else. That's what things are coming to nowadays.'

Nevertheless, she did a thriving business. Her clientele consisted mainly of people living near the Champs Élysées, mostly Jews and foreigners . . . Oh, the stories I could tell you.

The door opened into a passage, which led to the room where Madame Paulhat-Durand sat in state, wearing her everlasting black silk dress. On the left of the passage was the waiting room, a great dark cavern of a place, with benches round the walls and, in the middle, a table covered with a faded serge cloth. Nothing else. The only light in this room came from a high window, that ran the whole length of the wall between it and Madame's office, and the subdued, murky twilight was sadder than if we had been in complete darkness. Here we used to sit, through the long mornings and afternoons, a whole crowd of us, cooks and housemaids, gardeners and footmen, coachmen and butlers, passing the time away recounting our troubles, gossiping about our employers and dreaming about the wonderful situations we were going to obtain in some fairyland of freedom. Some of the women used to bring books or magazines with them, and devoured them passionately. Others wrote letters . . . And every now and then the murmur of conversation would be interrupted by the sudden appearance of Madame Durand, shouting angrily:

'Will you be quiet . . . It's impossible to hear ourselves speak in the office.'

Or, perhaps, she would call out somebody's name, and a girl would get up, smooth down her hair and follow her into the office, only to reappear a few minutes later with a disdainful expression on her face . . . either her references had been unsatisfactory, or they had been unable to come to terms about wages.

'The miserable old cat! A wretched dump . . . and not a chance of any perks . . . she does the shopping herself! . . . And four kids to look after into the bargain!'

All this punctuated with angry or obscene gestures . . .

One after the other we would be summoned to the office by Madame Paulhat-Durand's shrill voice, while her waxen skin turned greener and greener as she grew more and more angry . . . When it came to my turn I could tell at once the kind of woman it was, and that the situation wouldn't suit me. And then, for a bit of fun, instead of submitting to their stupid interrogation, I would start asking the questions myself . . . Oh, I didn't half pull their legs . . .

'Are you married, ma'am?'

'Of course . . .'

'I see. Then I expect you have children, ma'am?'

'Certainly . . .'

'And dogs?'

'Yes.'

'And you expect your maid to sit up at night?'

'When I go out for the evening, naturally.'

'And do you often go out in the evening, ma'am?'

And then, before she could reply, coolly looking her up and down, I would say in a disdainful tone of voice:

'I'm sorry, but I'm afraid the place Madame has to offer would not suit me . . . I am not accustomed to working in households like Madame's . . .'

And I would triumphantly turn my back on her, and leave the room.

One day, a small woman with outrageously dyed hair, her lips and cheeks plastered with make-up, insufferably overbearing and reeking of perfume, concluded a long series of questions by asking:

'And now about your personal behaviour . . . Do you invite your lovers to the house?'

'Do you, ma'am?' I replied, without turning a hair.

Some of the girls, not so hard to please as I am, or because they were too tired out and scared, would accept really lousy jobs, and when they came back to the waiting room the rest of us would jeer: 'Happy days . . . See you again before long . . .'

Sometimes, seeing us all slumped on the benches, sickly looking, round-shouldered, legs outstretched, pensive, stupid, chattering, waiting for our names to be called, Victoire, Irene, Zulma, it struck me that it was very like being in a brothel, waiting for a customer . . . Funny? . . . Sad? . . . I am not sure which. Though when I happened to express the idea aloud one day, there was a general burst

237

of laughter, and immediately everybody began discussing the pros and cons of such establishments . . . A huge, fat-faced creature, who was peeling an orange, said:

'Why of course you'd be better off . . . There's always plenty of grub . . . And you get champagne to drink . . . and swanky underclothes to wear, without any beastly corsets!'

Then a tall, dried-up woman, with very black hair and a bit of a moustache, and dirty-looking into the bargain, chipped in:

'And another thing . . . it must be a lot less tiring . . . By the time I've slept with the boss, and his son, and the *concierge,* and the footman, and the butcher's boy, and the blokes who come to see about the gas and electricity . . . not to mention all the others . . . why, by the end of the day, I've just about had it!'

'Oh, the dirty bitch!' voices proclaimed on all sides.

'All right, then! And what about the rest of you, my little angels?' retorted the tall dark girl, shrugging her skinny shoulders, and giving herself a resounding smack on the backside.

I couldn't help thinking of my sister Louise, who was probably still working in one of these brothels, and I tried to imagine the kind of life she would be leading. If she wasn't happy at least she didn't have to face poverty and hunger . . . And feeling more than ever disgusted with my own dreary, downtrodden, shiftless existence, always terrified by the thought of what tomorrow would bring, I couldn't help thinking: 'Yes, after all, perhaps we should be better off.'

Then the evening would close in . . . the dingy room would grow even darker . . . and gradually we would all fall silent, exhausted by too much talking, too much waiting. Then someone would light the gas in the passage and, regularly at five o'clock, we would see through the glass door the stooping silhouette of Monsieur Louis as he hurried past and disappeared . . . It was the signal to go home.

Outside, on the pavement, there would often be old women, hanging about touting for their private brothels. Beneath their highly respectable appearance, these miserable old bawds were all alike . . . butter wouldn't melt in their mouths. They would follow you, keeping at a

238

discreet distance until they came to some dark corner behind the massive buildings of the Champs Élysées, and, then, when there was no chance of police interference, they would accost you:

'Why not come to my place, dear? . . . Instead of all this worry about finding a job . . . You'd like it with me . . . First-class conditions, and plenty of money . . . and you'd be free.'

Dazzled by their marvellous promises, a good many of the girls used to accept the offers of these second-hand love merchants . . . It saddened me to see them go, and I often used to wonder what became of them . . .

One evening, one of these jackals, a fat, greasy creature, whom I had already told to clear off, eventually persuaded me to go to a café with her for a drink. I can still see her—soberly dressed, looking like some middle-class widow, with plump, sweaty little hands, covered with rings, and extremely pressing, she launched into a long, persuasive rigmarole. And when all her nonsense failed to make any impression upon me, she exclaimed:

'If only you'd give it a try, love . . . You don't need to look at you twice to see that you're a real little beauty . . . everywhere! Why, with a body like yours, it's a wicked sin to waste it on nobodies. A lovely girl like you could make a fortune in no time. Especially with a first-class clientele like mine . . . elderly gentlemen, you know . . . in good positions, and plenty of money to spend . . . Of course, sometimes you'd have to work pretty hard . . . I'm not saying you wouldn't. But just think of all the money you'd make . . . Why, all the very best people in Paris come to me . . . famous generals, distinguished lawyers, even foreign ambassadors.'

She drew closer to me and, lowering her voice, added:

'When I tell you that the President of the Republic himself . . . oh yes, love, on the level! That gives you an idea of the kind of house I run. There's not another in the town to touch it . . . Robineau's isn't a patch on my place . . . Shall I tell you something? . . . Yesterday the President was so well pleased that he promised he'd get my son made a member of the Academy . . . he's the chief solicitor for a religious educational establishment at Auteuil.'

And, staring hard at me, as though she would have liked to strip me body and soul, she repeated: 'Oh, if only you'd come to my place, what a success you could be.'

Then, in a more confidential tone, she continued:

'And there's another thing . . . Now and again we get real society women . . .sometimes alone, sometimes with their husbands or lovers, and all very hush-hush, of course . . . But there . . . in a place like ours, you have to be prepared for all sorts . . .'

I raised every kind of objection . . . that I wasn't sufficiently experienced, that I hadn't got the right kind of underclothes or dresses or jewellery . . . but the old hag waved them all aside:

'Oh, if that's all,' she said, 'you've nothing to worry about . . . We don't go in for fancy clothes, you see. All you need is a pair of decent stockings and your own natural beauty.'

'Yes, yes, I know, but still . . .'

'I assure you there's nothing for you to worry about,' she insisted amicably. 'Of course some of my best clients, especially some of the ambassadors, have . . . well, have their little fancies . . . you know how it is, at their age and with all that money . . . And what most of them seem to prefer is for the girls to be dressed like ladies' maids . . . tight black dress, white apron and a smart little lace cap . . . And, of course, pretty undies. That goes without saying . . . Look here, I'll tell you what, if you'll sign an agreement with me for three months, I'll give you the loveliest trousseau you can imagine, everything of the very best, enough to make the girls at the Théâtre-Français green with envy . . . Is it a bargain?'

I said I should have to think about it . . .

'That's right, you think about it,' this dealer in human flesh agreed. 'I am going to give you my address, and when you've made up your mind, all you have to do is to come along . . . I shall be only too delighted . . . And tomorrow, when I see the President of the Republic, I shall tell him all about you.'

We had finished our drinks. The old woman settled with the waiter and, taking a card from a little black notecase, she surreptitiously pressed it into my hand. After she had gone, I looked at the card. It bore the words:

Madame Rebecca Ranvet

Dressmaker

I saw some extraordinary scenes at Madame Paulhat-Durand's. Unfortunately it is impossible to describe all of them, so I have chosen one, as a typical example of what used to go on there pretty well every day.

I have already explained that there was a window with transparent curtains, running the whole length of the wall between Madame's office and the waiting-room. Well, in the middle of this window, there was a fanlight, which was usually kept shut. But one day happening to notice that, by mistake, it had been left unfastened, I decided to take advantage of the fact . . . Climbing up onto the bench, I found that with the help of a hassock I was able to see through it . . . I gently pushed it open, and this is what I saw.

A lady sitting in an armchair, with one of the girls standing in front of her, while, in a corner of the room, Madame Paulhat-Durand was sorting out some papers on her desk. The lady was from Fontainbleau, and she had come to find a maid. She must have been about fifty years old, and she looked like a well-to-do, middle-class woman, not easy to get on with, soberly dressed with a kind of provincial austerity . . . Puny and sickly-looking, and grey-faced from eating irregularly or not at all, the girl had a pleasant expression and, had she ever known a little happiness, might even have been pretty. Very neat and slim, she was dressed in a black skirt, and a tight-fitting black jersey showed off her small bosom. A pretty little white linen bonnet jauntily worn on the back of her head, displayed the fair curls clinging to her forehead.

After a detailed examination which she carried out in the most slighting and offensive manner, the lady at last began to question her:

'And how would you describe yourself? . . . A housemaid?'

'Yes, ma'am.'

'One would hardly think so, to look at you . . . What's your name?'

'Jeanne Le Godec . . .'

'What did you say?'

'Jeanne Le Godec, ma'am.'

The lady shrugged her shoulders.

'Jeanne?' said she. 'That's no name for a servant . . . If you came to work for me, I assume you would have no objection to changing it?'

'As Madame wishes . . .'

Jeanne lowered her head, clasping her two hands more tightly on the handle of her umbrella . . .

'Where are you from?'

'Saint-Brieuc . . .'

'Saint-Brieuc? . . .' The lady's normally disdainful expression became a hideous grimace. She screwed up her eyes and the corners of her mouth as though she had just swallowed a glass of vinegar . . . 'From Saint-Brieuc? So you're from Brittany? . . . I don't like Bretons. They're stubborn and dirty . . .'

'But I'm quite clean, I assure you, ma'am,' poor Jeanne protested.

'That's what you say . . . But we'll come to that later . . . How old are you?'

'Twenty-six.'

'Twenty-six? . . . Not counting the months you were at the breast, I suppose. You certainly look much older than that . . . There's no point in your lying . . .'

'I am not lying, ma'am. I assure you, I'm only twenty-six . . . If I look older, it's because for a long time I was ill . . .'

'So you've been ill?' replied the lady, with a harsh note of mockery in her voice. 'For a long time, yes? . . . I must warn you, my girl, that though the work is not arduous the house is a pretty large one, and I need a woman in robust health . . .'

In an attempt to remove the impression she had created, Jeanne declared: 'Oh, but I have got over it . . . I'm completely cured now . . .'

'That's your business . . . Besides, we haven't come to that yet . . . And what are you, a spinster? . . . married?'

'I am a widow, ma'am.'

'I see . . . But no children, I presume?'

And, since Jeanne did not immediately reply, the lady insisted: 'Well? I'm waiting . . . Have you any children, yes or no?'

'One little girl,' she admitted timidly.

Whereupon, frowning and waving her arms as though she were driving off a swarm of flies, the lady exclaimed:

'Oh but I certainly shan't allow a child in the house . . . not on any account . . . Where is she, this daughter of yours?'

'She's with one of my husband's aunts.'

'And what does this aunt do for a living?'

'She has a wine shop, at Rouen.'

'A deplorable trade . . . Drunkenness and debauchery are certainly a fine example for your little girl . . . Still, that's up to you. That's your business . . . How old is the child?'

'Eighteen months, ma'am.'

Madame gave a start, twisting herself violently in her chair. So shocked was she, so outraged, that she almost growled:

'Really . . . I ask you! . . . Fancy having children, when you can't even bring them up and keep them at home with you . . . These people are quite incorrigible . . . no self-control at all.'

She was looking so savagely aggressive that Jeanne began to tremble.

'I warn you,' she went on, almost spelling out each word, 'I warn you, that if you *do* come to me, you will certainly not be allowed to bring your daughter into the house . . . And I'm not going to have a lot of comings and goings, either . . . That's something I won't allow . . . Oh no, we can't have a lot of strangers, tramps, people I know nothing about . . . We already have to put up with far too much of that sort of thing . . .'

Despite this offensive harangue, Jeanne plucked up courage to ask:

'In that case, perhaps Madame would allow me to go and see my daughter once a year . . . just once?'

'No,' Madame replied ruthlessly. 'I never allow my maids to take holidays. That's one of my principles, and I intend to stick to it. I certainly don't pay servants so that they can always be going off on the spree, on the pretext of visiting

their daughters. That would be much too easy. Oh, no . . .
Have you brought any references?'

'Yes, ma'am,' Jeanne replied, taking from her pocket a
dirty envelope containing some yellow, crumpled papers
and handing them to Madame with a trembling hand . . .

Taking one of the references gingerly as though she were
afraid of dirtying her fingers, the lady unfolded it with an
expression of disgust and began to read aloud:

'I certify that the girl Jeanne . . .'

But she broke off abruptly, and looking at Jeanne even
more savagely, demanded:

'What's the meaning of this? . . . "Girl", it says here . . .
So you are not married after all? . . . You have a child, and
yet you are not married? . . . What's the meaning of this, if
you please?'

The maid explained:

'I'm sorry, ma'am . . . but you see I was married three
years ago, and this reference was given to me six years
ago . . . If you look at the date, ma'am . . .'

'Oh well, that's your business . . .' And the lady resumed
her reading: ' "that the girl, Jeanne Le Godec, worked for
me for thirteen months, during which time I had no
complaint to make of her work, her conduct or her
honesty . . ." Oh, these references are all the same . . . they
tell you nothing you want to know . . . no real information
at all . . . Where can I write to this lady?'

'She's dead, ma'am.'

'Oh, so she's dead, is she? . . . Heaven's above, you offer
me a reference, and then you tell me that the person who
gave it you is dead . . . That's pretty dishonest I must say.'

All this was said with a humiliatingly suspicious
expression in a tone of heavy irony. Then, taking up another
reference, she asked:

'And this lady? . . . I suppose she's also dead?'

'No, ma'am . . . Madame Robert is in Algeria, with her
husband . . . He's a colonel . . .'

'In Algeria,' exclaimed the lady. 'But, of course, she would
be . . . And how do you expect me to write to Algeria? . . .
First, they're dead, then they're in Algeria. So I suppose if
I want to know anything I must go to Algeria. An extraordinary business.'

244

'But there are others, ma'am,' pleaded the unfortunate Jeanne. 'As you will see, they can give you any information you require . . .'

'Yes, yes, I see you have plenty of others . . . which simply means you must have had plenty of other situations . . . far too many, if you ask me. At your age, that's charming! . . . Still, leave your references with me, and I will have a look at them later . . . Now for another matter . . . What are you trained to do?'

'Housework, sewing, waiting at table . . .'

'Are you good at darning?'

'Yes, ma'am.'

'Do you know anything about fattening poultry?'

'No, ma'am, that's not my job . . .'

'Your job, my girl,' said the lady severely, 'is to do what your employers tell you to . . . You seem to have a very rebellious nature.'

'Oh no, ma'am, I'm not one for answering back . . . not me.'

'That's what you say, naturally . . . But, like all the others, you get upset about nothing . . . Still, as I think I told plenty of work. You will have to get up at five . . .'

'In winter as well?'

'Certainly . . . In winter as well, indeed! There's just as much to be done in winter as in summer, isn't there? What a ridiculous question! . . . The housemaid is responsible for the staircase, the drawing-room and the master's study . . . and our bedroom, of course . . . And she has to see to all the fires. The cook does the hall, the passages and the dining-room . . . And remember, I insist upon cleanliness . . . I can't bear to see a speck of dirt anywhere . . . The door handles must be properly polished, as well as the furniture and mirrors . . . And then the housemaid is expected to look after the poultry . . .'

'But I don't know how to, ma'am.'

'Then you'll have to learn . . . And the housemaid does the washing and ironing—apart from the master's shirts—and the sewing—I don't have any sewing done outside except my costumes. She waits at table, helps the cook with the washing up and does all the polishing . . . I like everything to be kept thoroughly tidy . . . In fact, the three things

245

I am most particular about are tidiness, cleanliness, and above all, honesty . . . though, of course, everything is kept under lock and key. If you want anything you come to me for it . . . I detest waste . . . What do you usually drink in the morning?'

'Coffee, ma'am.'

'Indeed? . . . You certainly do yourself well. But, there, they all expect coffee these days . . . However, you won't get coffee with me. You'll have soup . . . It's much better for the stomach . . . What did you say?'

Jeanne had not spoken, though it was obvious she was trying to say something. Eventually she managed to stammer:

'Excuse me, ma'am, but may I ask what we get to drink with our meals?'

'You get an allowance of six litres of cider a week . . .'

'But I can't drink cider, ma'am . . . The doctor has forbidden it.'

'Well, I can't help that . . . You will get six litres of cider and, if you insist upon drinking wine, you must buy it yourself . . . That's up to you . . . What wages do you expect?'

Jeanne hesitated. She stared at the carpet, then at the clock. At last, her eyes fixed on the ceiling and twisting her umbrella nervously in her hands, she said timidly:

'Forty francs a month, ma'am.'

'Forty francs?' cried Madame. 'Why not ask for ten thousand francs, and have done with it? You must be crazy . . . Forty francs, indeed? Why, it's absolutely unheard of. In the old days, when you paid a girl fifteen francs, you used to get much better service than you do today . . . Forty francs . . . and you don't even know how to fatten poultry? . . . I'll give you thirty francs, and, in my opinion, even that is much too much . . . You won't have any expenses when you're with me. I shan't be fussy about your clothes, and you'll get your food and laundry free. And, I can assure you, you will be well fed . . . I do the carving myself.'

'I've been paid forty francs in all the other places I've been in . . .' Jeanne insisted.

But the lady had already risen from her chair, and in a dry, unpleasant voice she said:

'Well in that case you'd better go back to one of them . . .

246

Forty francs, indeed! What cheek . . . Here, take your references, your references from the dead, and be off with you.'

Jeanne carefully folded up the precious papers, put them back in the pocket of her dress, and then, in an unhappy, pleading voice, shyly said:

'If Madame could see her way to make it thirty-five francs . . .'

'Not a sou . . . Be off with you! You had better go and work for Madame Robert, in Algeria . . . There are all too many lazy good-for-nothings like you. Be off with you.'

Sadly, slowly, Jeanne turned and left the office, but not before she had curtseyed twice. I could see from her eyes and the puckering of her lips that she was on the point of tears.

As soon as she had gone, the lady exclaimed angrily:

'Oh, these servants. They're an absolute pest. It's hopeless trying to find anybody who is prepared to work nowadays.'

To which Madame Paulhat-Durand, who had meanwhile finished sorting her papers, replied with majestic and over-whelming gravity:

'I did warn you, Madame. They're all the same . . . They all expect to earn a fortune without doing a stroke of work . . . I'm afraid I have no one else for you today. The others are even worse. I must see if I can't find you something tomorrow. Oh, it's really heartbreaking, believe me . . .'

As I climbed down from my observation post, Jeanne Le Godec had just returned to the noisy waiting room.

'Well?' they asked her . . .

She went back to her place on the bench, at the far end of the room, and there she sat, with lowered head and folded arms, hungry, dejected, silent and, except for the nervous twitching of her feet, motionless.

But I saw even sadder things than this. Amongst the girls who used to attend Madame Paulhat-Durand's every day, I had noticed one in particular—firstly, because she was wearing the Breton head-dress, and secondly, because the very sight of her filled me with overwhelming sadness . . . A peasant, lost in Paris, in this terrifying Paris, forever swirling and jostling in feverish excitement . . . Could anything be more pathetic? Involuntarily, I was reminded of myself, and I felt deeply moved . . . Where was she going? Where had she come from? What had persuaded her to leave her native soil? What madness, what tragedy, what gales and tempests had driven this frail vessel to shipwreck here, in this roaring sea of humanity? Such are the questions I used to ask myself as, day after day, I watched this poor girl, sitting in her corner, horribly alone . . .

She was ugly, with that special kind of ugliness that excludes all idea of pity and arouses people to savagery, because they see in it an offence against themselves. However naturally ill-favoured a woman may be, it is only rarely that she achieves such utter and complete ugliness. Usually there is something about her, no matter what, her eyes or mouth, some sinuous movement of the body, a swaying of the hips, or, even less, a gesture of her arms, the turn of a wrist, the freshness of her skin . . . something at least that other people may contemplate without disgust. Even amongst the very old, a certain grace almost always survives their physical deformities, defies the death of what they once used to be. But this Breton peasant girl had nothing of this, although she was still quite young. Small, rather long in the body, but squarely built, with narrow hips and legs so short that she almost seemed to be a cripple, she reminded me for all the world of one of those images of barbaric, snub-nosed saints, rough hewn from great blocks of granite, that have stood for centuries in some wayside Breton shrine . . . As for her face, poor wretch . . . beneath a heavy forehead, eyes that seemed to have been rubbed out with a dirty thumb, and a hideous nose, flattened from birth, with a gash running down the middle and sharply turned up at the end, revealing two deep, round, dark holes, fringed with stiff hair. And, covering all this, a grey, scaly skin, like a dead grass snake's, that seemed, when the light shone on it, to be covered with flour . . . And yet this indescribable creature had one beauty that many women would have envied her—her hair . . . Her magnificent hair, thick and heavy, a glowing red, with gold and purple lights in it. Yet, far from mitigating her ugliness, this lovely hair only served to emphasise it, making it still more striking, still more irreparable.

And that was not all. Her slightest movements were clumsy and awkward. She couldn't move a step without knocking into something; if she picked anything up she was sure to drop it. Her arms caught in the furniture, sweeping away anything that happened to be in the way . . . When she walked, she trod on your toes, banged you in the chest with her elbows. And when she apologised in her rough, deep voice, her breath gave off a horrible odour of decay. From the moment that she first arrived in the waiting room, everyone had complained about it, and before long complaints had turned to grumbling insults . . . People booed and hissed at the wretched creature as she walked across the room, stumbling on her short legs, flung from one to another like a ball, until at last, at the far end, she managed to find a place on the bench. Even then, her neighbours drew themselves away from her with gestures of disgust, raising their handkerchiefs to their noses . . . And in the empty space thus created around her, the poor girl would sit, leaning against the wall, silent and accursed, with never a word of complaint or a gesture of revolt, without even seeming to be aware that she was the object of all this scorn.

Though sometimes just to be like the others I joined in this savage by-play, I could not help feeling a kind of pity for her. I realized that she was one of those beings predestined to suffer, a creature who, whatever she did, wherever she went, would always find herself rejected by man and beast . . . for there is a certain degree of ugliness, a certain kind of physical deformity, that even animals will not tolerate.

One day, overcoming my disgust, I went up to her and asked:

'What's your name?'

'Louise Randon . . .'

'I'm from Brittany, from Audierne . . . You're a Breton, too, aren't you?'

Surprised that anyone should wish to speak to her, and fearing that it might only be a joke or an insult, it was some time before she replied . . . I repeated my question:

'What part of Brittany do you come from?'

She looked at me and, seeing that I was not being unkind she answered:

'I come from Saint-Michel-en-Grève, not far from Lannion.'

Her voice was so horrible that I scarcely knew what to say next . . . hoarse and staccato, like a hiccough, with a rumbling accompaniment as though she were clearing her throat . . . At the sound of it I felt my sympathy for her ebbing away. But I went on:

'Are your parents still alive?'

'Yes, my father and mother . . . and I have two brothers and four sisters. I'm the eldest.'

'And what does your father do?'

'He's a blacksmith.'

'Is your family hard up?'

'My father owns three cottages and three plots of land, and he has three threshing machines as well . . .'

'So he's rich, then?'

'I'll say he's rich! . . . He farms the land himself and lets the cottages . . . And then he goes round the countryside threshing for the peasants. It's my brother that shoes the horses.'

'And your sisters?'

'They wear lovely caps, covered with lace . . . and embroidered dresses.'

'And what about you?'

'Me? Oh, I haven't got anything.'

I drew back a little to avoid the deathly odour of her breath. Then I asked:

'What makes you want to be a servant?'

'Because . . .'

'Why did you leave home?'

'Because . . .'

'Because you were unhappy?'

Speaking very quickly so that her words tripped over one another like the sound of falling pebbles, she replied:

'My parents used to beat me . . . and my sisters . . . they all used to beat me, and made me do all the work . . . It was me who had to bring up my sisters.'

'Why did they beat you?'

'I don't know . . . Because they wanted to, I suppose . . .

In every family, there's always one that gets beaten, because . . . Well, there it is.'

My questions did not seem to have upset her, and she was becoming more confident.

'And what about you?' she asked. 'Didn't your parents beat you?'

'Why, yes . . . Of course they did. That's the way things are.'

Louise had stopped picking her nose; her hands with their bitten nails were spread out flat on her lap. What with all the whispering that was going on around us, all the laughter and quarrelling, the others could not hear what we were saying. After a silence, I asked:

'But what brought you to Paris?'

'Well you see, last summer there was a lady from Paris at Saint-Michel-en-Grève, who used to go bathing with her children. I suggested working for her, because the servant she brought with her was caught stealing, and got the sack . . . And then she brought me to Paris with her, to look after her father . . . an old man, an invalid, with paralysis of the legs . . .'

'Then what made you leave? In Paris it's not easy . . .'

'Oh no,' she interrupted violently, 'I should never have left. It wasn't that . . . Only you see things didn't work out.'

Her lustreless eyes lit up with a gleam of pride, and she drew herself up. 'It was impossible,' she continued. 'The old man turned out to be a filthy old swine . . .'

For a moment I was utterly dumbfounded . . . Could it really be possible. Could anyone, even a sordid, miserable old man, feel the slightest attraction to this shapeless body, this monstrosity of nature? Imagine anyone trying to kiss her, with those terrible decayed teeth and that foul breath . . . Oh, what absolute beasts men are . . . I looked at Louise, but the light had already died from her eyes, and once again they had become grey, lifeless smudges . . .

'Was that a long time ago?' I asked.

'Three months . . .'

'And you haven't had another situation since?'

'Nobody seems to want me, I don't know why. When I go into the office, as soon as the ladies see me, they say, "Oh no, she certainly won't do" . . . Somebody must have put a curse on me . . . After all, it isn't as though I were ugly. I know how to do housework . . . I'm very strong . . . and I'm willing. If I'm too small, that's not my fault . . . No, I must be under a curse.'

'But how do you manage to live?'

'I'm in a lodging house . . . I do all the rooms, and mend the linen and so on . . . and they give me a mattress in one of the attics and a meal every morning . . .'

The thought that here, at least, was someone worse off than myself, revived my sympathy for her.

'Listen, Louise, dear,' I said, trying to make my voice sound gentle and convincing. 'It's very difficult finding work in Paris. There are a lot of things you have to know, and the employers are much more difficult to please than they are in the country. I'm worried about you . . . if I were in your place I should go back home.'

But the idea seemed to terrify her.

'No, no,' she said, 'never! If I went home, they'd say I'd been a failure . . . that no one would have me . . . And everybody would laugh at me. No, no, it's impossible . . . I'd rather be dead!'

At that moment the door of the waiting room opened, and the harsh voice of Madame Paulhat-Durand called out 'Louise Randon.'

'Is it me she's asking for?' asked Louise, trembling with fear.

'Yes, it was you . . . Hurry up. And this time, make up your mind you're going to succeed.'

She got up, striking me in the chest with one of her elbows, stumbled over my feet, knocked into a table and, swaying on her short legs, she disappeared through the door to an accompaniment of boos.

I climbed up on to the bench and pushed open the fan-light, anxious to see what happened . . . Never had Madame Paulhat-Durand's office seemed to me so utterly dreary, though God knows it used to freeze my heart every time I went into it. All that ghastly furniture covered with worn blue rep, and the big registration book in the middle of the table, with its cloth of the same blue material, covered with inkstains . . . And that desk, where Monsieur Louis' elbows had made pale, shining patches on the blackened wood . . .

And, at the far end, the sideboard, with its hideous array of glassware brought from abroad, and old-fashioned dishes . . . And on the mantelpiece, between two bronze lamps, among all those fading photographs, that infuriating clock, that seemed to make the time pass even slower with its maddening ticking . . . And the dome-shaped cage, with its two home-sick canaries puffing out their drooping feathers . . . And the mahogany filing cabinet, with its scratched sides . . . But I wasn't there just to make an inventory of this lugubrious, tragic room. In any case, I knew it only too well unfortunately, and often my crazy imagination used to see its bourgeois smugness as a fitting showcase for the display of human flesh . . . No, what I was there for was to see how these slave-dealers would treat poor Louise. . .

There she stood, near the window with her back to the light, quite still, her arms hanging at her sides. A heavy shadow cast a thick veil over the ugliness of her face, but emphasised the stocky, massive deformity of her body, and the hard light that lit up the falling strands of her hair at the same time revealed the twisted outline of her arm and throat, before losing itself in the black folds of her deplorable skirt . . . An old lady, sitting in a chair with her back turned towards me—a hostile, savage back—was examining her attentively . . .All I could see of this old woman was a black hat with ridiculous feathers, a black cloak trimmed round the bottom with grey fur, and the hem of a black dress, forming a circle on the carpet. What I noticed particularly was the hand, lying on her knee in a black silk glove and contorted with athritis, the fingers slowly extending and contracting, plucking at her dress like the claws of a bird of prey . . . Near the table stood Madame Paulhat-Durand, stiff and dignified.

There was really nothing very special about all this . . . three commonplace people in this commonplace setting. It was in no way particularly striking or moving . . . Yet, to me, the sight of these three people, silently observing one another, held all the elements of a tremendous drama . . . I felt that I was watching a social tragedy, more terrible, more agonizing, than any murder . . . And my throat was dry, my heart was beating furiously.

Suddenly the old lady said:

'I can't see you properly, my dear . . . Don't just stand there . . . I can't see you, I tell you . . . Walk to the other end of the room, so that I can get a proper look at you!' And then, in an astonished voice, she exclaimed: 'Good God, how tiny she is!'

As she said this, she turned her chair a little so that I could now see her profile. I should have expected her to have a hooked nose, with long projecting teeth and the round yellow eye of a hawk. But not at all . . . her face was tranquil, almost friendly. As a matter of fact, her eyes expressed nothing at all, neither good nor evil . . . She might have been a retired shopkeeper. In business, people acquire a special gift for controlling the expression on their faces, so that it is impossible to tell what is going on inside their minds. The more callous they become, the more the habit of making quick profits develops their ambition and all their lower instincts, the gentler, or rather the more neutral, becomes their expression. All the evil in them, whatever might make their customers distrustful of them, is either concealed within the depth of their being or else finds some totally unexpected physical expression. The hardness of this old woman's heart was not apparent in her eyes, her mouth, her forehead or the slack muscles of her face, but was all concentrated in the back of her neck . . . That was her real face, and it was a terrible one.

In obedience to the old lady, Louise had moved to the other end of the room. Her desire to please made her truly monstrous, utterly disheartening, and directly the light fell upon her the old lady exclaimed:

'Oh, but how ugly you are, my dear!' And turning to Madame Paulhat-Durand she added: 'Is it possible? Can such hideous creatures really exist?'

Solemn and smug as usual, Madame Paulhat-Durand replied: 'Certainly she's no beauty . . . but the girl is quite honest . . .'

'That may be so,' said the old lady, 'but she's really too ugly . . . Such ugliness is really quite offensive . . . What's that you're saying?'

Louise had not uttered a word. She had merely blushed a little, and lowered her head. A thread of scarlet had appeared, circling her lustreless eyes. I thought she was going to cry.

'Still, I suppose we'd better see . . .' the old lady went on, her fingers working furiously, tearing savagely at her dress.

She questioned Louise about her family, the situations she had been in, her experience of cooking, housework, sewing. Louise merely replied 'yes' or 'no', in her harsh, jerky voice, but the mean, meticulous, cruel cross-examination went on for some twenty minutes.

'Well, my girl,' the old woman concluded, 'one thing's perfectly clear: you are completely untrained . . . I shall have to teach you everything . . . It will be at least four or five months before you are of the slightest use to me . . . And then your looks . . . They can hardly be called prepossessing . . . That mark on your nose, was it the result of a blow?'

'No, ma'am, I have always had it . . .'

'Well, it's certainly most unattractive . . . What wages do you expect?'

'Thirty francs, ma'am . . . and free laundry and wine,' Louise declared in a determined voice.

The old woman almost leapt out of her chair.

'Thirty francs,' she screamed. 'But have you never looked at yourself in the glass? You must be insane! Why, nobody will employ you . . . If I take you on, it will simply be out of the goodness of my heart, because I'm sorry for you. And you ask for thirty francs! Well, there's one thing, you're not lacking in cheek. If that's the advice your friends out there have given you, you'd do better not to listen to them . . .'

'Quite true,' commented Madame Paulhat-Durand, approvingly. 'The trouble is, they all egg each other on . . .'

'Well then,' proposed the old woman, 'I shall pay you fifteen francs, and you'll pay for your own wine . . . It's really much too much, but I don't want to take advantage of your being so ugly and hard up . . .' And, lowering her voice so that it sounded almost kindly, she added: 'You must realise, my dear, this is a unique opportunity for you, such as you won't find elsewhere . . . I'm not like the others, you see. I'm quite alone . . . no family, no one. I look upon my maid as my family, and all I ask of her is to show me a little affection . . . She lives with me, shares my meals . . . Oh, I make a regular fuss of her . . . And then, when I die—and I'm a very old woman, and often ill—you can rest assured I shan't forget her, provided she has looked after me properly, been devoted to me . . . You're ugly, horribly ugly. Well, I must just get used to that . . . Besides, some of the pretty ones are wicked creatures, who are simply out to rob you. So perhaps your ugliness will be a guarantee for your behaviour . . . At least you're not likely to have men running after you . . . You see, I mean to be fair with you, and what I'm offering you, my child, is a fortune . . . more than a fortune . . . a family.'

Louise was shaken. Clearly the old woman's words had raised unexpected hopes, with her peasant greed, she was already dreaming of coffers filled with gold, fabulous legacies . . . And then, the thought of sharing her life with such a good mistress, eating at the same table with her, going for little outings with her in the town and neighbouring woods . . . all this dazzled her. But at the same time it all scared her, for her deeply ingrained mistrust cast a shadow of doubt over these shining promises . . . She could not make up her mind what to say or do . . . I longed to call out to her 'No, don't accept', for I could easily imagine the kind of existence that was being offered her, shut away, overwhelmed with work, continually scolded, never enough to eat . . . all the everlasting, brutal exploitation of the poor, patient defenceless creature . . . 'No, come away, don't listen to them . . .' But I never uttered the cry that was on my lips.

'Come a little closer, my dear,' the old lady ordered. 'Anyone would think you were afraid of me . . . Come now, there's nothing to be frightened of . . . It's a curious thing, you know, but already you seem to be less ugly . . . I'm already getting used to that face of yours . . .'

Louise slowly approached, holding herself stiff in a desperate attempt not to knock anything over, trying hard to walk elegantly, poor creature. But as soon as she came near the old woman pushed her away.

'My God,' she cried, screwing up her face, 'whatever's the matter with you? What makes you smell so terribly? . . . This odour of decay . . . it's frightful, unbelievable! . . . I've never known anybody smell like this . . . Have you got cancer? . . . Your nose, your stomach, perhaps?'

Madame Paulhat-Durand made a noble gesture.

'I did warn you, Madame,' she said. 'It's her one great defect . . . the only thing that has prevented her from finding a situation.'

But the old woman went on muttering: 'Oh my God, my God! Is it possible? Why, you'll poison the whole house . . . I couldn't bear you near me . . . This makes all the difference . . . And there was me, growing so fond of you! No, no. I may be kind-hearted, but it's simply not possible.'

She took out her handkerchief and began waving it in front of her face as though to purify the air, at the same time repeating: 'Oh, really, it is simply impossible.'

'Come, come,' Madame Paulhat-Durand intervened, 'make an effort . . . I'm sure this unfortunate girl will always be extremely grateful to you . . .'

'Grateful indeed! That's all very well, but gratitude isn't going to cure this terrible infirmity . . . No, indeed! In fact, the very most I could pay would be ten francs, not a penny more . . . You can take it or leave it . . .'

Up to this point Louise had succeeded in restraining her tears, but now she broke down.

'No, no,' she sobbed, 'No, I won't take it, I won't.'

'Listen, young lady,' observed Madame Paulhat-Durand drily, 'either you accept this situation or I shall take no further responsibility for you . . . You will have to go to some other registry office. I have done what I can for you, and you're certainly not much credit to my business . . .'

'That's perfectly true,' the old woman agreed. 'You ought to be only too grateful that I'm prepared to pay you ten francs . . . I offer them because I am sorry for you . . . Don't you understand that it's an act of charity, that I may well be sorry for later on.'

Then turning to Madame Paulhat-Durand, she added:

'It can't be helped . . . I'm like that . . . I simply can't bear to see people suffering . . . I'm quite silly when it comes to the misfortunes of others. And at my age I am scarcely likely to change . . . Come along now, child, you can come with me.'

At this point, an attack of cramp forced me to get down from my observation post. I never saw Louise again . . .

Two days later Madame Paulhat-Durand called me into her office and, after looking me over in a rather tiresome manner, said to me:

'Mademoiselle Célestine, I have a good situation to offer you . . . extremely good . . . The only thing is it's in the country . . . Oh, not very far . . .'

'In the country? . . . I don't fancy that much, you know . . .'

'People are quite wrong about the country,' she insisted. 'There are excellent situations to be found there.'

'Excellent? That's a good one,' I interrupted. 'In the first place there's no such thing as an excellent situation anywhere.'

Madame Paulhat-Durand gave me a friendly, simpering smile. I had never seen her smile like that before.

'I beg your pardon, Mademoiselle Célestine . . . there's no such thing as a bad situation.'

'Heavens, I know that . . . only a bad employer.'

'Not at all . . . only bad servants . . . You know very well I send you to the very best houses. It is not my fault if you choose not to stay there . . .'

Then, looking at me in an almost friendly fashion, she went on:

'Besides, you are very intelligent . . . you have a good appearance . . . you're pretty, with a good figure and charming hands, not ruined by hard work . . . And you certainly know how to use your eyes. Things might turn out very well for you . . . You might end up almost anywhere if you behave yourself . . .'

'Misbehave myself, don't you mean?'

'That depends how you look at it . . . I call it behaving yourself . . .'

She was beginning to relax. Gradually she was dropping her dignified mask . . . revealing herself to me for what she was, an ex-chambermaid, adept at every kind of monkey business. At that moment she had the suggestive eyes, the soft, lewd gestures, the typical slavering mouth, that are typical of every procuress, and which I had noticed in the case of 'Madame Rebecca Ranvet, Dressmaker . . .' She repeated . . .

'I prefer to call it behaviour.'

'So what?' said I.

'Look, Mademoiselle Célestine, you are no longer a child and you know your way around . . . We can talk frankly . . . The situation in question is with a gentleman living by himself, already getting on in years and extremely well-off, and it is not very far from Paris . . . You will be expected to run his house for him . . . be a kind of housekeeper, you understand? . . . Such situations require a certain tact, but they're much sought after and can be very profitable. There's an assured future in it for a woman like yourself, intelligent and charming and, I repeat, one who knows how to behave herself.'

It was what I had always dreamt of . . . how often I had set my hopes on an old man's infatuation for me, and now the paradise I had dreamt of was within my grasp, smiling at me, beckoning to me! . . . And yet, by some inexplicable irony of life, some stupid contradiction the cause of which I could not fathom, now that this happiness that I had so often longed for was mine for the asking . . . I turned it down flat.

'A dirty old man? . . . Oh no, I've had some, thanks very much . . . I'm absolutely fed up with men . . . young, old, the lot.'

For a moment Madame Paulhat-Durand was completely taken aback . . . this was the last thing she had expected. Then, recovering the austerely dignified manner with which, as she thought, she maintained a proper distinction between the correct middle-class woman she would like to have been and a Bohemian creature like myself, she added:

'Oh indeed, young woman . . . and what do you take me for? Who do you imagine you are?'

'I don't imagine anything . . . All I'm telling you is that I'm simply sick of men . . .'

'Do you realize who it is you are talking about? This gentleman happens to be extremely respectable . . . a member of the Society of Saint-Vincent-de-Paul, and at one time a royalist deputy . . .'

I burst out laughing.

'Oh, get along with you! Don't tell me . . . you and your Vincent-de-Pauls . . . Deputy indeed . . . Thank you very much.'

Then, abruptly, and without the slightest change of tone, I asked:

'What exactly is he like, this old man of yours? . . . After all, I don't suppose one more or less will make all that difference.'

But Madame Paulhat-Durand was not prepared to relent. In a severe tone of voice she declared:

'It's no use, young woman . . . I'm afraid you're not the serious, reliable type of woman this gentleman is looking for . . . I thought you might have been suitable, but obviously you are not to be trusted.'

I did my best to get her to change her mind but she remained implacable, and I returned to the waiting-room, feeling moody and depressed . . . Oh that dreary, dark waiting-room, always the same! All those wretched creatures sprawling about on the beaches, just bodies for sale, to satisfy the voracious appetite of the bourgeoisie . . . All that eternal ebb and flow of misery and filth, forever washing us up here, pitiable odds and ends from the shipwreck of humanity.

'What a strange creature I must be,' I thought. 'I long for things, so many, many things, just as long as they seem to me to be unattainable. And as soon as they are within my grasp, as soon as they begin to assume concrete shape, I no longer want them.' Certainly this was one reason for my refusal. But there had also been another . . . an irresistible desire to take Madame Paulhat-Durand down a peg, to revenge myself on this scornful, high and mighty creature by showing her up as a common or garden procuress.

I was sorry about the old man, who now had for me all the appeal of the unknown, all the attraction of an inaccessible ideal . . . And I amused myself by imagining what he would have been like . . . A natty, little old chap, with soft hands and a merry smile on his well-shaven pink and white face, gay, generous, easy to get on with, not too passionate and with none of Monsieur Rabour's perversions . . . An old boy that I could have ordered about like a little dog . . . ready to come when I called him, wagging his tail affectionately and gazing at me with submissive eyes.

'Beg . . . There's a good dog, beg . . .'

And then he'd sit on his little backside waving his front

paws in the air, while I gave him lumps of sugar and stroked his silky back. The thought of him no longer filled me with disgust, and I asked myself again:

'Must I always be such a fool? . . . A pet of a little man . . . a lovely garden . . . fine house . . . money, peace of mind, and an assured future . . . Fancy having refused all that without even knowing why! . . . And never knowing what it is I want . . . and never taking it when I have the chance. Though I have given myself to plenty of men, the fact is, when I am by myself, men scare me . . . worse even, they disgust me. But I only have to be with them, and I let myself be caught as easily as a sick hen . . . and then I'm capable of every folly under the sun. I can only resist things that won't ever happen and men I shall never meet . . . Something, I'm convinced, will always prevent me from being happy . . .'

The waiting room was stifling. The thought of that dingy light and those sprawling creatures made me feel more and more depressed. Something heavy and irremediable seemed to be hovering over my head . . . I left early, without waiting for the office to close, my heart heavy and my throat on fire . . . Outside I passed Monsieur Louis. Clinging to the banister, he was slowly and laboriously climbing the stairs . . . For a moment we looked at one another. He did not speak to me, nor I to him. But, though I could not find a word to say, the glance we exchanged expressed everything . . . He, too, was unhappy . . . I waited a moment for him to reach the top, then I rushed downstairs . . . Poor little sod!

In the street I paused for a moment, bewildered . . . I looked to see if any of the old bawds were waiting about. At that moment, if I had caught sight of Madame Rebecca Ranvet, Dressmaker, I should have rushed up to her and handed myself over . . . But none of them was there, and the passers-by, preoccupied and indifferent, had no thought to spare for my anguish . . . On the way home I stopped at a pub and bought a bottle of brandy, and, after wandering about for a time, I got back to my hotel, still feeling half dazed.

Later in the evening I heard someone knocking at the

door. I was stretched out on the bed, half-naked and muzzy with drink.

'Who's there?' I cried.

'Me.'

'Who's me?'

'The waiter . . .'

I got up, my breasts half exposed, my hair coming down and falling over my shoulders, and opened the door.

'What do you want?'

The waiter smiled . . . He was a great strapping fellow with red hair, whom I had often passed on the staircase. And he was staring at me with a strange look in his eyes.

'What do you want?' I repeated.

Still smiling with embarrassment, screwing up the bottom of his greasy apron in his huge fingers, he stammered:

'Mademoiselle . . . I . . .'

With an expression of gloomy lust he was considering my breasts, my almost naked stomach, the shift hanging round my waist . . .

'All right, come in then, you great brute,' I suddenly exclaimed. And, pushing him into my room, I shut the door behind us with a bang . . .

When they found us next day, we were in a terrible state, wallowing on the bed and still drunk . . . The waiter got the sack. I had never even discovered what his name was.

I cannot leave the subject of the registry office without mentioning another of the poor devils I met there . . . a gardener, who had lost his wife, four months previously and was looking for a job. Of all the pitiful faces I saw there, none was as sad, as utterly overwhelmed by life, as his. After being out of work for two months, his wife had died of a miscarriage, the very day before they were due to start a job at a country estate . . . she looking after the poultry, and he as gardener. Whether from bad luck, or whether because he was just fed up with life, he had been unable to find any other work since this misfortune befell him. Indeed, he had scarcely bothered to look for any. And what little money he had managed to save had quickly disappeared during the time he was without a job. Although he was very distrustful of everybody, I managed to get round him a bit. What follows is an impersonal account of the simple, human drama, which he described to me one day, when, feeling very upset by all his misfortunes, I had been more than usually sympathetic. Here it is.

After visiting the gardens, with its terraces and greenhouses, and having inspected the gardener's cottage which, thickly covered with ivy and virginia creeper, stood at the entrance to the park, they slowly returned, in a state of mingled hope and anxiety, and without speaking to one another, to the lawn where they had left the Countess. She was sitting fondly watching her three, fair-haired, pinkfaced children, who, daintily dressed, were happily playing on the grass, watched over by their governess. While still some distance away, the couple stopped respectfully, the husband bareheaded and cap in hand, his wife standing timidly beside him, ill at ease in her black straw hat and dark, woollen jacket, and twisting the chain of a little leather bag in an attempt to keep herself in countenance. Behind them, stretching far away into the distance, lay the undulating parkland, with its massive clumps of trees.

'Come closer,' said the Countess, in a kindly, encouraging voice. The man was tanned and weatherbeaten, and the fingers of his gnarled, earth-coloured hands were smooth and shining from the continual handling of tools. The woman was rather pale, the greyness of her skin accentuated by the patches of freckles that covered her face . . . rather awkward too, but very clean and tidy. She kept her eyes on the ground, afraid to look at the splendid lady who would soon be examining her, overwhelming her with embarrassing questions, turning her inside out, like they all did . . . But she watched delightedly the charming picture of the three babies, who, as they played on the grass, already displayed such restrained manners and such easy grace . . .

The couple slowly advanced a few steps and then, simultaneously, both of them with the same mechanical gesture folded their hands on their stomachs.

'Well?' asked the Countess. 'Have you seen everything?'

'Your ladyship is very kind,' replied the man. 'It's a fine

big place . . . a magnificent property . . . There's plenty to do and no mistake . . .'

'And I warn you, I'm very particular . . . Quite fair but very particular . . . I like everything to be just so . . . and heaps of flowers everywhere, and all the year round . . . Of course, you will have some help. Two men in summer, and one through the winter.'

'Oh,' said the man, 'I'm not afraid of work. The more there is, the better it suits me. I'm fond of my job, and I know a good bit about it . . . Trees . . . early vegetables . . . mosaic work . . . the lot. And when it comes to flowers . . . if you're prepared to work, and have a fancy for them, all you need is plenty of water, a good mulching now and then and, saving your presence, your ladyship, lots of dung and manure, and you can grow what you like . . .'

After a pause he went on: 'My wife's very active, as well . . . very handy . . . And she's a good manager. You might not think she was very strong to look at her, but she's got guts and she's never ill, and when it comes to looking after animals, there's no one to touch her . . . Why, in our last place, they kept three cows and two hundred chickens . . . so you can see!'

The Countess nodded her head approvingly . . . 'And how did you like the cottage?'

'Oh, the cottage is all right . . . A bit on the grand side, you might say, for folk like us. We've hardly got the furniture for it. But you live where you've got to live, and that's that . . . Besides, its a good long way from the house, and that's all to the good. The masters don't want their gardeners on top of them, and we don't want to be a nuisance to anybody . . . This way, we can both be on our own, so to speak . . . That's best for everybody . . . There's only one thing . . .'

He paused, overcome by sudden timidity at the thought of what he wanted to say . . .

'Only what?' asked the Countess.

The man still hesitated, and the silence increased his uneasiness. He clutched his cap tightly, twisting it between his great fingers, and eased his weight from one foot to the other. Then, plucking up courage, he said:

'Well, it's like this . . . What I'm trying to say is that . . .

264

well, the wages aren't right for the job . . . They are a bit on the low side. With the best will in the world, we just couldn't manage . . . I reckon your ladyship ought to raise them a bit . . .'

'You're forgetting, my good man, that, in addition to the cottage, you get your lighting and heating, and free fruit and vegetables . . . Not to mention the fact that I allow you a dozen eggs a week, as well as a litre of milk a day . . . That makes an enormous difference.'

'Milk and eggs? . . . free lighting?'

And, looking at his wife, as though to ask her advice, he murmured to himself: 'Well, there's no denying it, that's a bit better . . . That's not bad at all.'

And his wife joined in: 'Well, of course, it would help quite a bit . . .'; adding shyly: 'And I daresay there'll be the usual Xmas boxes?'

'Oh no, I'm afraid not . . . We never do that sort of thing here.'

'And what about the vermin, your ladyship?' enquired the man in his turn. 'Weasels, moles, and the like?'

'No, I don't pay for them, either . . . Though you can have the skins.'

The Countess spoke so sharply that it was obviously no use insisting, and she added quickly: 'And I must warn you, once and for all, that I do not allow the gardener either to sell or give away any vegetables. Oh, of course, I'm quite aware that, if there are always to be plenty for the house, you'll have to grow too many, and that threequarters of them may be wasted . . . But that can't be helped. That's how I wish it to be . . . As long as that's quite understood . . . How long have you been married?'

'Six years,' replied the wife.

'And have you any children?'

'We had one little girl, but she died.'

'Good . . . that's very good,' said the Countess casually. 'After all, you're still both young . . . you've got plenty of time ahead of you . . .'

'Oh, we're in no hurry about that, your ladyship . . . Why bless me, it's a lot easier having another kid than earning a decent wage . . .'

The Countess looked at him severely . . . 'I ought to make it quite clear that on no account will I have children . . . If you did happen to have one I should be obliged to dismiss you . . . immediately. No, no children! . . . Always crying and getting into mischief . . . frightening the horses . . . spreading infection . . . No, I simply couldn't tolerate having children about the place, so don't say you haven't been warned . . . It's up to you. You must take the necessary precautions.'

At that moment, one of her own children who had fallen down came running up to its mother, crying and hiding its face in her dress. She picked him up, rocked him tenderly in her arms, murmured a few soothing words over him, and then sent him back, reassured and smiling, to play with the others . . .

The gardener's wife could scarcely keep back her tears . . . was such happiness, the tender joy of a mother's love, only for the rich, then? . . . Seeing the children, happy once again at their play, she felt such bitter hatred for them that she could willingly have killed them. She wanted to curse this cruel, insolent woman, to strike the selfish mother whose heartless words had just condemned her to forego the happiness of bearing a child. But she restrained herself, and simply murmured:

'We'll take care, your ladyship. We'll do what we can.'

'Then that's understood . . . For I must repeat, with me it's a matter of principle. On this question I am quite adamant.' Then, in an almost affectionate tone, she added: 'Besides, believe me, when you are not rich, you are much better off without children . . .'

And, in an endeavour to please his future mistress, the man concluded: 'That's true, that's very true . . . What your ladyship says is quite right.'

But his heart swelled with hatred, and the wild, sombre light that flashed in his eyes belied the servility of his last words . . . The Countess did not see this murderous gleam, however, for instinctively her gaze had been drawn to the belly of the woman whom she had just condemned to sterility or infanticide.

The bargain was soon struck. She gave her instructions, described their duties in the greatest detail and, as she was about to dismiss them, she said with a superior smile and in a tone which admitted of no reply: 'I assume you are both religious people . . . Here everyone goes to church on Sundays, and receives communion at Easter . . . That is something I am most particular about.'

They set out for home in a sombre mood, neither of them speaking. It was very warm and the road was dusty. The poor woman struggled along, limping a little. Presently, she was out of breath and, sitting down on the side of the road, she put down her bag and undid her corsets.

'Ouf,' she exclaimed, taking a great draught of air. And her belly, freed at last from the tight corsets, resumed its natural, rounded shape, proclaiming that she was guilty of the crime of motherhood . . . And they continued on their way.

A little further on, they entered a wayside inn and ordered a litre of wine.

'Why didn't you tell her I was pregnant?' asked the wife.

'What, and get thrown off the premises . . . same as the last three times?'

'Today or tomorrow, what's the difference?'

There was a silence between them. Then the man muttered: 'If you were a real wife, I reckon you'd go and see old mother Hurlot . . . They say she's got some kind of herbs . . .'

The woman started to cry, moaning through her tears:

'Oh don't say that, love, don't say that . . . It's unlucky.'

'What do you want us to do, then, for Christ's sake? Starve?'

And sure enough, the bad luck came. Four days later the woman had a miscarriage . . . and, after suffering terribly from peritonitis, she died.

When the man had finished telling his story, he said to me: 'So, you see, I am all alone now . . . no wife, no child, nothing. I thought of trying to revenge myself . . . Yes, I thought about it a lot . . . by killing those three kids we saw playing in the grass . . . I'm not a wicked sort of chap, but, I don't mind telling you, I swear I could have strangled that woman's kids with pleasure . . . yes, with pleasure. But there it is . . . I suppose I haven't got the guts. The trouble is, when it comes to the point, we haven't the courage . . . only to go on suffering.'

24 NOVEMBER

Still no word from Joseph. Knowing how careful he is, his silence does not altogether surprise me, though it makes me rather unhappy. Of course, Joseph knows that all letters go to Madame before being passed on to us, and probably he doesn't want to run the risk of her reading his letter, or even knowing that he writes to me. All the same, I should have thought that anybody as resourceful as he is would have found some way of letting me have news . . . He is due back tomorrow morning. Will he turn up, I wonder? I don't mind admitting I'm worried . . . my mind keeps on and on. Why didn't he want me to know his address at Cherbourg? . . . But it's no use thinking about that now, it only gives me a headache.

Here, nothing whatever has happened since Joseph went, even less than usual . . . and the same old, dreary silence. Out of friendship, the verger has been doing his job for him while he is away. Every morning, punctually, he comes to groom the horses and see to the greenhouse. But it's impossible to get a word out of him. He's even more silent, more distrustful, more shifty in his behaviour than Joseph. He's more commonplace as well, with none of Joseph's bigness and power . . . I have hardly seen anything of him, except when I have had to go and give him an order . . . He's another queer fish, all right! The grocer's wife once told me that when he was a lad, he was studying to be a priest, but got kicked out of the seminary for immorality . . . I wonder if it might have been him that raped little Clara? . . . After leaving the seminary he tried all kinds of jobs . . . pastrycook, choirboy, pedlar, lawyer's clerk, domestic service, town crier, auctioneer, bailiff's assistant, and now, for the last four years, he has been the verger here. It's not all that different from being a priest. Anyway, he's got all the slimy, creeping ways of a parson . . . The dirtiest kind of business wouldn't upset him . . . Joseph made a great mistake in having him as a friend . . . But is

268

he really a friend? Or is he just an accomplice?

Madame has got migraine . . . It seems that this happens regularly every three months. For two days she stays shut up in her room, with the curtains drawn and no light, and only Marianne is allowed in to see her . . . She won't have me. These illnesses are the master's great opportunity, and he's making the most of it . . . he's scarcely ever out of the kitchen. Only the other day I surprised him coming out, scarlet in the face and his flies still unbuttoned . . . Oh, but I'd like to see them at it, Marianne and him. It ought to be enough to put you off sex for the rest of your life.

Captain Mauger, who is no longer on speaking terms with me, but just hurls furious glances at me from the other side of the hedge, has made it up with his family, or at least with one of his nieces, and she has come to live with him . . . She's not so bad—a big, fair woman, with a fresh complexion and well-made, though her nose is a bit on the long side. From what people are saying, it looks as though she's going to keep house for him, and succeed Rose as his bedmate. That's certainly one way of keeping your dirty ways in the family.

Rose's death might have been a bad blow to Madame Gouin's Sunday mornings. But she realized that she needed someone to play the principal part, so now she's got the draper's wife to act as ringleader of the gossips and advertise her clandestine talents amongst all the girls in Mesnil-Roy. Yesterday, being Sunday, I paid her a visit. A most brilliant occasion . . . everybody was there. Nothing much was said about Rose, and when I told them the story of the wills there was a general outburst of laughter. Oh, the captain was certainly right when he said 'Nobody is irreplaceable...' But the draper's wife has not got Rose's authority, for she is one of those women about whose private life there is, unfortunately, nothing whatsoever to be said.

How I am looking forward to seeing Joseph again . . . I can scarcely wait to hear my fate, what I have to hope or fear! I can't go on living like this any longer. Never have I felt so disgusted with the mediocrity of the life I'm leading here, with the people I have to wait on, with the bunch of dreary puppets who, day by day, are driving me further round the bend. If I were not sustained by the strange feel-

269

ing that has brought my life a new and powerful interest, it wouldn't be long before I, too, sank into the morass of stupidity and ugliness that surrounds me on every side. Whether Joseph succeeds or not, whether or not he changes his mind about me, I am absolutely determined not to stay here another moment . . . In a few more hours, after one more night of anxiety, my future will be decided!

I shall spend this night reviving once again, perhaps for the last time, memories of my past. It is the only way to stop myself brooding about my present problems, or plaguing myself with dreams about the future. These memories amuse me, yet at the same time they deepen my feeling of contempt. After all, what singular and monotonous faces I have encountered in my life of servitude! . . . When I see them again, in imagination, they no longer strike me as being really alive. They only live, or at least create the illusion of being alive, through their vices . . . Take away their vices, which preserve them like the bandages that preserve a mummy, and they are no longer even ghosts . . . merely dust and ashes . . . death . . .

Consider, for example, the establishment to which I was sent by Madame Paulhat-Durand, with all kinds of excellent references, only a few days after refusing to work for the old gentleman in the country. A young couple, with neither animals nor children . . . an ill-kept house, despite the apparent elegance of the furniture and general display of wealth . . . plenty of luxury, but even more sheer waste. As soon as I got inside the door, one glance was enough . . . I could see immediately the kind of people I had to deal with . . . So my dream had come true! I was going to forget all the misery I had endured . . . and that little beast, Monsieur Xavier, whom I hadn't been able to get out of my system . . . and the nuns at Neuilly, and the heartbreaking sessions at the registry office . . . all those long days of wretchedness and long nights of loneliness or debauchery. Here, at last, was the chance of an easy life, with not too much work and plenty of perks. Delighted at the prospect I made up my mind to keep my wild impulses in check, to restrain my high-spirited outbursts of frankness, so that I might stay here for a long, long time. In the twinkling of an eye all my gloomy thoughts disappeared, and my hatred of the bourgeoisie melted away as though by magic. I was filled with a crazy, vibrant gaiety, my old love of life was restored and I was even prepared to believe that maybe, after all, there was such a thing as a good employer . . . The staff was not large but it was first-class: a cook, a footman, a butler and myself . . . There was no coachman, because they had recently given up their own carriage, and hired one as required from a livery stables . . . They were all very friendly, and on the very first evening, welcomed me by opening a bottle of champagne.

'Crikey,' I exclaimed, clapping my hands. 'They do you proud here.'

The footman smiled, and rattled a bunch of keys before my eyes. It was he who kept them all, including that of the cellar. They trusted him completely.

'You'll have to lend them to me, sometimes,' I said jokingly.

'Well, one day I might,' he replied, with a tender glance in my direction, 'as long as you keep the right side of Bibi . . . You'll have to be nice to Bibi, though . . .'

Oh, he was a treat of a man, and knew just how to talk to a woman. He was called William . . . a nice name!

Throughout the meal, which lasted a long time, the old butler ate and drank steadily, but without saying a word. Nobody took any notice of him, and he seemed to be almost senile. But William behaved charmingly, treating me with the utmost gallantry and gently pressing my foot under the table. When the coffee came, he gave me a Russian cigarette . . . his pockets were full of them. Then, pulling me towards him—I was feeling a bit giddy from the tobacco smoke and rather tight, and my hair was all over the place —he sat me on his knee and began telling me dirty stories in a whisper . . . Oh, but he was a cheeky devil!

Eugenie, the cook, did not appear to be at all shocked by all these goings-on. Anxious and dreamy-eyed, she kept turning towards the door, cocking her head at the slightest sound as though she were waiting for someone, and downing glass after glass of wine with an absent-minded look on her face . . . She was a woman of about forty-five, with a

271

fine bust, wide mouth, full, sensual lips, sleepy, passionate eyes and an air of great good nature. Presently there was a discreet knock at the back door. Eugenie's face lit up, and, springing to her feet, she hurried to open it. Unfamiliar as yet with the habits of the household, I tried to adopt a more seemly position, but, instead of letting me go, William simply clasped me tightly in his powerful arms.

'There's nothing to worry about,' he said calmly. 'It's only the youngster.'

As he was speaking, a young man came into the room, little more than a boy. Slim and fair, with a very white skin, he was the prettiest creature you could imagine, and not yet eighteen years old. He was wearing a smart new suit, which admirably set off his slender, graceful figure, with a pink tie . . . He was the son of the hall porter from next door, and apparently used to come in every evening. Eugenie adored him, she was simply crazy about him. Every day she used to make up a large hamper of food for the lad to take to his parents: soup, a nice cut of meat, bottles of wine, and all sorts of fruit and cakes.

'Why are you so late this evening?' Eugenie asked him.

'I had to keep an eye on the door,' the boy replied in a drawling voice. 'You see, mum had to go out somewhere.'

'Your mother? . . . your mother? . . . Are you sure you're telling me the truth, you bad boy?'

She sighed, and, gazing into his eyes, her hands resting on his shoulders, said dolefully: 'Whenever you're late, I'm always afraid something has happened. I don't like you being late, love . . . You just tell your mother, if this goes on, she won't get anything more out of me.'

Her nostrils quivering, beginning to tremble all over, she went on: 'Oh, but he's my pretty little love, isn't he? That sweet little phiz belongs to me. No one else is going to have it . . . But why didn't you put on your nice brown shoes? I like you to look smart when you come to see me . . . Oh, those eyes, those great wicked eyes, you little rascal! I wouldn't mind betting they've already started looking at other women! And what's that mouth of yours been up to, I'd like to know.'

Smiling, swaying slightly from the waist, he said reassuringly:

'God, no! . . . I promise you Nini . . . it's the truth. Mum had to go somewhere, honest.'

'Oh you bad boy, you! Oh, you wicked boy,' Eugenie went on. 'I won't have you looking at other women . . . Your face and mouth belong to me, and those great eyes of yours! Tell me, do you really love me?'

'You know I do. Of course I do.'

'Say it again, then.'

'Of course I do.'

She flung her arms round his neck, and murmuring words of endearment led him off to the next room.

William said: 'She's absolutely gone on him! . . . And he doesn't half cost her a lot, the little devil. Why, only last week she bought him a brand new suit. You'll never love *me* like that.'

I had been very touched by this scene and felt immediately friendly towards poor Eugenie . . . The lad was like Monsieur Xavier . . . They both had the same kind of moral rottenness . . . and the resemblance made me feel sad, terribly, terribly sad. I could see myself in Monsieur Xavier's room, the evening when I gave him the ninety francs. 'Oh, your little phiz, your darling mouth, your great big eyes!' Yes, they had the same cold, cruel eyes, the same way of swaying their bodies, and the same vicious gleam in their eyes that made their kisses like a drug.

Pushing away William's hands, which were becoming rather too insistent, I said rather primly: 'No, not this evening.'

'But you promised to be nice with Bibi . . .'

'Not this evening.'

And, freeing myself from his arms, I began tidying my hair and pulling down my skirts.

'You don't waste much time,' I said. 'Do you?'

Naturally, I made no attempt to alter the way the house was run. William did the cleaning, if you could call it that —just a flick with the brush or a feather duster, and that was that—and the rest of the time he spent gossiping with me, going through their drawers and cupboards and reading their letters which they left lying about all over the place. I took my cue from him, sweeping the dust under the furniture and making no attempt to tidy up after the master and mistress. If it had been me, I should have been ashamed to live in such a filthily kept house. But they simply had no idea of how to give orders; they were so timid, so afraid of us, that they hardly dared say a word. Occasionally, after some particularly blatant lapse on our part, they might nerve themselves to stammer, 'I think you must have overlooked this.' But we would simply reply firmly, not to say impertinently, 'I beg your pardon, ma'am, but you are mistaken . . . Of course if Madam isn't satisfied . . .', and that would be the end of it. They never dared press the matter . . . In all my life, I have never come across anyone with such a complete lack of authority over their servants, or so simple minded! Honestly, they were absolute mugs!

In fairness to William, it must be admitted that it was he who had managed to fix everything up so nicely. Like many domestic servants, he had one passion, racing. He knew all the jockeys, all the trainers and bookmakers, as well as one or two society people, barons, viscounts and such, who liked to keep in with him because they knew he sometimes got marvellous tips . . . Since the indulgence of this passion demands a good deal of running about, as well as jaunts to the race meetings, it is not particularly well adapted to a restricted, sedentary job like a footman's. But William had managed to arrange things so that, as soon as lunch was over, he was free to get changed and go out. And he didn't half look smart, with his check trousers and patent leather boots, a mackintosh over his arm and a silk hat on the back of his head! . . . Oh, those hats of his! They used to gleam like the water of a pool, in which sky, trees, streets, crowds and racecourses were brilliantly reflected . . . He used to get back only just in time to help the master dress for dinner, and then, later in the evening, he would often go out again to keep some important appointment with one of the many Englishmen connected with racing. On such occasions, I should not see him again till very late at night, by which time he was always a bit tight from drinking too many cocktails . . . Once a week, he used to invite his friends to dinner, coachmen, footmen and jockeys—the latter, the most comical, macabre creatures, with bandy legs and mean, cynical faces. They did nothing but talk about horses, racing and women, and tell the most gruesome tales about their employers, who, according to them, must all have been homosexuals. Then, when the drink had gone to their heads a bit, they would start on politics . . . William used to be completely uncompromising and was violently reactionary.

'Cassagnac's the man for me,' he used to shout. 'There's a real man . . . plenty of guts! They're all scared of him, because when he says a thing, he means it . . . If they're going to start arguing the toss with him, they'd better look out for themselves, the swine.'

Then, when the noise was at its height, Eugenie would suddenly get up, eyes shining in her pale face, and rush towards the door. It would be the lad from next door, surprised to find all these unknown people, seated around the ravaged table, surrounded by empty bottles. But Eugenie would have kept a plateful of titbits for him, and a glass of champagne, and presently the two of them would disappear into another room . . . On such evenings, the baskets for his parents would be sure to contain even bigger and better portions than usual. After all, it was only fair that the good hones souls should benefit from our junketing . . .

One day, when the lad happened to be late, one of the coachmen, a cynical, dishonest sort of lout, who was always invited to these parties, seeing that Eugenie was getting anxious, said to her:

'You don't want to worry yourself . . . He's sure to be here presently, your little pansy.'

Eugenie stood up, trembling, and shouted at him:

'What's that you said? That little angel a pansy? Just you dare to say that again . . . In any case, if that's what the kid likes, he's certainly pretty enough for it, or for anything else.'

'Of course he's a pansy,' the coachman insisted, with a coarse laugh. 'If you don't believe me, go ask Count Hurot . . . He only lives just round the corner, in Mar . . .'

But, before he could conclude his sentence, he was silenced by a swinging blow from Eugenie. At that moment the lad appeared at the door, and hurrying over to him, she said:

'Are there you are, love . . . Come with me, my little lamb!

Hurry up, you don't want to stay with these crooks.'

All the same I think the coachman was right.

William was always talking to me about Edgar, Baron de Borgsheim's famous stud groom. He was proud of knowing him, and admired him almost as much as he did Cassagnac. Indeed, Edgar and Cassagnac were his two great heroes. It would have been risky to pull his leg about them, or even to argue about them. If he came in late at night, William would apologise by saying that he had been with Edgar. Anybody would think that being with Edgar was a duty, not merely an excuse.

'Then why don't you bring this famous Edgar of yours along to dinner one night, and let me have a look at him?' I asked one day.

William was utterly taken aback at the idea. He haughtily rebuked me:

'What? Do you really imagine Edgar would be prepared to dine with ordinary servants like us?'

It was from Edgar that William had acquired the art of giving his hats their incomparable sheen . . . On one occasion, at the Auteuil races, Edgar had been approached by the young Marquis de Plérin.

'Tell me, my dear fellow,' said the Marquis, 'How do you manage to keep your hat so splendidly?'

'My hats, my lord?' replied Edgar, flattered by this attention, for at that time young Plérin, thanks to swindling the bookmakers and cheating at cards, was one of the most distinguished figures in Parisian society. 'Why, once you've got the hang of it, it's as easy as picking winners . . . What I do is this. Every morning I send my valet for a quarter of an hour's run, to make him sweat . . . Sweat contains oil, you see . . . Then he mops up his sweat with a silk handkerchief rubs it into my hats, and finishes them off with the iron. Of course, you need a healthy, clean sort of chap . . . auburn haired for preference—if they are too fair they tend to smell a bit. Some kinds of sweat are better than others . . . As a matter of fact, only last year the Prince of Wales asked me the same question.'

And as the young nobleman was thanking him, Edgar

surreptitiously shook hands with him, and whispered confidentially:

'You want to back Baladeur for the next race, your lordship . . . seven to one . . . He's a cert . . .'

In the end—honestly, it's quite ridiculous when I come to think of it—I myself even began to feel flattered that William should have such an acquaintance . . . For me, as well, Edgar was becoming as marvellous and inaccessible as the Kaiser Wilhelm, Victor Hugo or Paul Bourget . . . Perhaps that is why I feel it is worth while giving a brief sketch of this illustrious . . . no, this historic, figure.

Edgar was born in London, in a terrible slum, between two belches of whisky. While still a lad, he was running wild, begging and thieving, and being sent to prison. Later on, when he had acquired the necessary moral deformaties and sufficiently depraved instincts, someone picked him up and gave him a job as groom. Promoted to the stables, it was not long before he had picked up all the greedy cunning, all the vices, that are to be learnt by serving in the 'best houses'; and he became a stable lad at the Eaton stud. There he used to swank about, wearing a Scotch bonnet on the side of his head, a plaid waistcoat and a pair of white breeches. Almost before he was fully grown, he was already a little old man with skinny limbs, a wrinkled face, red in the cheeks but yellow at the temples, a tired, grimacing mouth, and thinning hair, brushed over one ear in a greasy curl. In a society which delights in the smell of horse-dung, Edgar soon ceased to be an anonymous workman or peasant, and almost passed for a gentleman.

At Eaton he was taught his job thoroughly. He learnt how to groom a well-bred horse, how to look after it when it was sick, and all the minute and complicated spongings and subtle polishings, all the arts of pedicure and make-up which are used to beautify both racehorses and mistresses, and to increase their value . . . In the bars he was soon on familiar terms with all the well-known jockeys, famous trainers, paunchy baronets and good-for-nothing dukes, who constitute the flower of this dunghill society. He would like to have been a jockey himself, for he knew all about pulling a horse and was up to all the deals that could be arranged with the bookmakers. But he put on too much weight . . . despite his skinny, bandy legs, he developed a pot belly. Thus prevented from sporting racing colours, he found consolation in a head-coachman's livery . . .

Today, at forty-three, Edgar is one of the five or six stud grooms in England, Italy and France who is admired throughout the fashionable world. His name is continually mentioned in the sporting press, and is even to be found in the gossip columns of fashionable papers. His present master, Baron de Borgsheim, takes more pride in being his employer than in any of the financial transactions by which he succeeds in ruining thousands of little shopkeepers. He boasts of 'my stud groom' with the same flatulant air of superiority that an art collector might congratulate himself on 'my Rubens'. And, indeed, the lucky baron has reason to be proud, for the fact that Edgar works for him has vastly increased the esteem and respect in which he himself is held. It is to Edgar that he owes his invitations to those exclusive drawing-rooms from which he had previously been excluded. It is Edgar who has enabled him to over-come the last strongholds of anti-Semitism, and in the clubs they do nothing but talk about the baron's 'famous victory over England'. The English may have succeeded in depriving us of Egypt, but at least the baron has won Edgar from the English, and thus restored the balance of power. If he had conquered India, he could scarcely have been more highly proclaimed. But all this admiration has resulted in considerable jealousy. Many people would be only too happy to seduce Edgar from his master, and this gives rise to every kind of intrigue and corrupt machination as though Edgar were some infinitely desirable woman. As to the papers, their respectful adulation has reached such a pitch, that they are no longer quite sure which of the two is the distinguished stud groom and which the inter-nationally famous financier . . . The two of them have become confused in a mutual apotheosis.

If you have ever had the curiosity to mingle with the aristocratic crowd, you will certainly have met Edgar, for he has come to be regarded as one of the brightest ornaments of society. A man of average height, and very ugly, with that comical ugliness peculiar to Englishmen, he has an unconscionably long nose, with the doubly royal curve that distinguishes both Jews and Bourbons. A short upper lip reveals a number of decayed teeth, interspersed with ugly gaps. His complexion comprises every tone of yellow, but is relieved by scarlet splotches on the cheeks. Without being as enormous as the majestic coachman of the past, he nevertheless has a comfortable, evenly disposed layer of fat that fills out all the normal hollows of the human frame. He walks with a hopping movement, the upper part of his body slightly inclined forwards and his elbows projecting from his sides at the regulation angle. Disdaining to follow the fashion, he attempts to create it by wearing very expensive, but quite fantastic, clothes. His blue overcoats, always too new-looking, are lined with silk and cut much too tight. His trousers, in the English style, are too light, his ties too white, his jewels too big, his handkerchiefs too scented, his boots too polished, his hats too shining . . . For a long time now, the unusual and striking brilliance of Edgar's headgear has been the envy of every young toff!

Each morning, at eight o'clock, Edgar arrives at the Baron's and descends from his motor car, wearing a small bowler hat and knee-length mackintosh, with a huge yellow rose in his buttonhole. The grooming has just been completed. Prancing round the yard with a bad-tempered expression on his face, he goes into the stables to begin his inspection, followed by a string of anxious and respectful grooms. Nothing escapes his suspicious eye, a bucket out of place, a dirty mark on a steel chain or a scratch on the silver and brass . . . He grumbles, loses his temper, threatens to sack them, in a hoarse voice, still thick from drinking too much poor quality champagne the previous night. He visits every loose-box, and runs his white-gloved hand over the horse's mane and withers, belly and legs. If there is the least trace of dirt on his gloves, he starts abusing the grooms with a flood of foul language and horrific oaths, furiously waving his arms in the air. Then he minutely examines the horses' hoofs, sniffs the hay in the marble mangers, makes sure that the litter is clean and carefully studies the form, colour and consistency of the dung, with which he always has some fault to find.

'D'you call that dung, my God?' he shouts. 'Why, a bloody

279

cab horse would be ashamed of it . . . If it's like that again tomorrow, I'll damn well make you eat it, you dirty lot of bastards!'

Occasionally, delighted at the prospect of a chat with his stud groom, the Baron arrives on the scene, but Edgar scarcely deigns to notice his master's presence. To the Baron's timid enquiries he replies briefly, in an ill-tempered voice. He never addresses him as my lord, but, on the contrary, the Baron feels tempted to refer to him as 'your honour'. And so afraid is he of upsetting Edgar that, before long, he discreetly withdraws.

Having completed his tour of the stables, coach-houses and harness-rooms, and issued his orders for the day like a military commander, Edgar climbs back into his motor car and drives rapidly towards the Champs-Élysées, where he pays a quick visit to a small bar, filled with racing men and weasel-faced tipsters, who show him confidential reports and whisper mysterious messages in his ear. The rest of the morning is devoted to the shops, where he places orders and picks up his own commission, and to the horse-dealers, with whom he engages in the following conversation:

'Well, Mr Edgar?'

'Well, Mr Poolny?'

'I've got a buyer for that pair of bays of the Baron's.'

'They're not for sale . . .'

'There'll be fifty quid in it for you.'

'No.'

'A hundred then, Mr Edgar.'

'I'll have to think about it, Mr Poolny . . .'

'There's another little matter, Mr Edgar . . . I've got a magnificent pair of chestnuts for the Baron . . .'

'We aren't looking for any, just at the moment.'

'There'll be fifty quid in it for you.'

'No.'

'A hundred then, Mr Edgar.'

'I'll have to think about it, Mr Poolny.'

A week later, having effectively ruined the paces of the Baron's pair of bays, and having convinced the latter that it would be a good thing to get rid of them as soon as possible, Edgar sells them to Poolny and, at the same time, buys the magnificent chestnuts from him. Poolny does very well out of the transaction: having turned the bays out to grass for two or three months, he will almost certainly be able to sell them back again to the Baron some two years later.

But, by midday, Edgar had finished with work, and would go home to lunch at his flat in Euler Street, for he did not live at the Baron's and was never expected to drive him anywhere. His ground-floor flat was filled with plush furniture in the most ghastly taste, with English lithographs on every wall, of hunting scenes, steeplechases and Derby winners, as well as a selection of portraits of the Prince of Wales, one of which was signed by the Prince. A collection of riding canes, whips, hunting crops, stirrups, bits and coaching horns was arranged as a kind of trophy around an enormous polychrome bust of Queen Victoria standing on a gilt pediment. For the rest of the day, Edgar was free to devote himself to business and pleasure, tightly buttoned up in his blue overcoat and wearing one of his glistening hats. His business affairs were extensive, for in addition to being in partnership with a bookmaker and a well-known photographer of horses, he also had three horses in training near Chantilly. Nor was there any shortage of pleasure, for some of the best known tarts used to find their way to Euler Street, whenever they were on the rocks, as they could always be sure of finding there a cup of tea and a loan of five louis.

In the evening, after putting in an appearance at the Ambassadors, the Circus, or Olympia, very correct in a black-tail coat, Edgar would repair to a bar called 'The Old Man', here he would sit boozing for hours, in company with coachmen who behaved like gentlemen and gentlemen who behaved like coachmen . . .

And every time William told me one of these stories about Edgar he would conclude by saying, in an admiring tone of voice:

'No, you can say what you like, but Edgar's a fine chap!'

The master and mistress belonged to what is usually called high society, that is to say the master, though penniless, was of noble birth, though nobody could say exactly where his wife had sprung from. There were all

281

kinds of stories, some worse than others, as to her family background. William, who was very well up in society gossip, maintained that she was the daughter of a retired coachman and an ex-chambermaid who, as a result of scraping and swindling, had managed to get together a small sum of money, enough to set up as moneylenders in one of the poorest parts of Paris, where they had rapidly succeeded in acquiring a huge fortune by lending money to tarts and domestic servants . . . They must have been in luck!

To tell the truth, though she was pretty and elegant, Madame had the most curious manners, and some of her personal habits I found most unpleasant. She liked eating boiled beef and fried cabbage, the pig . . . and, for a special treat, used to pour her wine into the soup, like cabbies do. I often felt ashamed for her . . . Sometimes, when she was quarrelling with the master, she would so far forget herself as to call him a shit, at the top of her voice. When she lost her temper, it seemed to stir up all her native filth, unpurged by the too recent acquisition of wealth, and, like some filthy scum, words would rise to her lips . . . well, words that I, with no pretence of being a lady, am really ashamed of using . . . But there it is . . . People simply have no idea of the number of women there are, who, in their own homes, though they look like starry-eyed angels and wear dresses costing three thousand francs, use the filthy language and gestures of the lowest streetwalkers.

'Fine ladies,' William used to say, 'are like the most delicious sauces: never enquire what they're made of . . . If you do, you'd never want to sleep with them.'

William was full of such cynical aphorisms, but, as he had taken a real fancy to me, he would put his arm round my waist and add:

'Maybe a pretty little piece like you doesn't flatter a man's vanity so much maybe . . . But it means a lot, all the same.'

It is only fair to say, however, that the mistress used to work off all her bad temper and filthy language on the master . . . With us, as I have mentioned already, she was much too shy . . .

Despite the utter chaos of her household, and the frantic waste that she was prepared to put up with, Madame was in some ways extraordinarily, and quite unexpectedly, stingy. She would argue the toss with the cook over two-pennyworth of salad, try to cut down on the staff's laundry, kick up a row over a bill for three francs, and carry on an endless correspondence with the railway company about the repayment of fifteen centimes, which she claimed they had overcharged for delivering a parcel. She never took a cab without having a row with the driver over the fare, and usually managed to cheat him as well as not giving him a tip . . . This didn't prevent her from leaving her money lying about all over the place, as well as her jewellery and keys. She would ruin the most expensive dresses and exquisite lingerie in no time, but, nevertheless, allowed herself to be preposterously swindled by the most exclusive shops and settled the accounts presented by the old butler without batting an eyelid . . . as indeed, the master did, with those prepared by William. And yet, God only knows how much those two used to twist them! I sometimes used to say to William:

'Really, you fiddle much too much . . . One of these days you're going to get into trouble.'

To which he would reply, without turning a hair:

'Just you mind your own business . . . I know what I'm up to, and exactly how far I can go. If you work for people as stupid as these two, it would be a crime not to take advantage of them.'

But his endless swindles did not benefit the poor fellow much, for all the money he succeeded in making simply went to swell the profits of the bookmakers, in spite of all the marvellous tips he used to get.

The master and mistress had been married for over five years. At first, they used to go out a great deal, and were always giving dinner parties. Gradually, however, they cut down both their visits and their invitations, and lived pretty much on their own, supposedly because they were jealous of each other. She accused him of flirting with women, and he maintained that she was always running after men. They were very much in love . . . that is to say, they spent most of the time quarrelling, like any petty-bourgeois couple. The fact of the matter is, Madame was by no means a social success, and was frequently snubbed because of her bad manners. On such occasions, she accused her husband of not backing her up, while he blamed her for making him look ridiculous in front of his friends. They refused to admit the bitterness of their feelings for each other, and found it simpler to attribute their constant bickering to their being in love.

Each year about the middle of June, they used to go to the country, to Touraine, where Madame had a magnificent country house. In addition to the usual staff, they employed a coachman, two gardeners, a second chambermaid and women to look after the livestock . . . There were cows, peacocks, chickens and rabbits . . . It must have been wonderful, but when William used to describe the kind of life they led there, he always spoke in the sourest and grumpiest way. He couldn't stand the country, and was bored to tears by the endless trees and fields and flowers. He was a real Parisian, and the only kind of nature he really approved of was bars, racecourses, bookmakers and jockeys.

'Can you imagine anything more utterly stupid than a chestnut tree?' he often used to say to me. 'Look . . . Edgar's a smart, intelligent fellow, but does *he* like the country?'

'Oh, but think of all those huge beds of flowers,' I would say enthusiastically, 'and all the birds.'

'Nonsense,' he would sneer. 'The only proper place for flowers is on a pretty woman's hat . . . And as for birds, just think how they wake you up in the morning . . . worse than a lot of screaming kids. No, no . . . I can't stand the country at any price. The only people it's any good for are the peasants.'

Then, drawing himself up and striking a noble attitude, he would proudly conclude:

'What I need is sport. I'm a sportsman, not a peasant.'

Nevertheless, I was happy, and longed for June to come. Oh, the daisies growing in the meadows, and the little footpaths through the woods, and the fluttering leaves . . . And then the birds' nests that you find in the clumps of ivy, hanging from old walls . . . And the nightingales singing in the moonlight, as you sit on the wall of a well, covered with maidenhair fern and moss and honeysuckle climbing all over it, holding hands and talking quietly to one another . . .

And the great bowls of warm milk, and the big straw hats, and the baby chicks, and going to mass in the village church, and the sound of the bells, and all the rest of it . . . Why, it makes you feel as though your heart would burst with happiness, like those lovely songs they sing in the cafés in Paris! . . .

Although I enjoy a bit of fun, at least I am a poetical creature. Old shepherds, harvest time, birds chasing each other amongst the branches, the sound of the cuckoo, streams chattering over the white pebbles, and all those handsome fellows, with their faces burnt the colour of ripe grapes by the sun, and great, healthy limbs and powerful chests . . . things like this fill my mind with charming dreams . . . I have only to start thinking of them, and I almost become a little girl again, and their candid innocence floods my soul, refreshes my heart, like the gentle rain that revives a flower too long exposed to the burning sun and withering wind . . . One evening, as I was lying in bed, waiting for William to come to my room, I felt so moved by all the happiness that was awaiting me that I began writing a poem: but as soon as he got back from the frowsty bar where he had been spending the evening the smell of gin when he began kissing me drove away all thought of poetry and put an end to my dreams. I had no desire to show him what I had written. What would have been the use? He would only have laughed at me, and probably he would have said:

'Edgar's a marvellous fellow . . . but does *he* write poetry?'

My poetical nature was not the only reason why I felt so impatient about getting to the country. The long period of poverty I had been through had thoroughly upset my digestion, and the present over-abundance of rich food that I was getting, on top of all the champagne and Spanish wine that William insisted upon my drinking, was not improving matters. I was really ill. When I got out of bed, first thing in the morning, I often felt giddy, and during the day my legs were like lead and there was a continual hammering in my head . . . If I was to get better, I badly needed to lead a more tranquil existence.

Unfortunately, however, fate decreed that this dream of

health and happiness was to come to nothing . . . 'Oh shit!',
as Madame would have said.

The scenes between the master and mistress always used
to start in Madame's boudoir, and they always started over
nothing . . . the more futile the pretext, the more violent
the row. Then, having emptied their hearts of all the
accumulated bitterness and anger, they would sulk for a
week on end. The master would retire to his study, where
he would devote himself to playing patience and re-
arranging his collection of pipes. Madame would stay in her
bedroom, and spend hours stretched on a couch reading
novelettes, occasionally interrupting her reading by a furious
attack of the drawers and wardrobes, sorting out her clothes
as though she were sacking the place . . . They only met for
meals. At the start, before I had got used to the way they
carried on, I used to expect them to begin throwing the
plates at each other . . . Unfortunately, however, nothing
like that ever happened. On the contrary, at such times
their manners were always at their best, and Madame even
did her best to behave like a lady. They would talk to each
other as though nothing at all had happened, rather more
formally than usual, and with a cold, stiff politeness . . .
they might have been dining at a restaurant. Then, as soon
as the meal was over, they would go off to their respective
rooms, both preserving an air of mournful dignity. Madame
returned to her novels and tidying up, the master to his
patience and his pipes. Sometimes, though not often, he
would go off to his club for an hour or two . . . They used
to keep up a furious correspondence, continually writing
notes to each other, which I had to take. I spent the whole
day like a postman, running between the mistress's bedroom
and the master's study, delivering terrible ultimatums,
threats, pleas for forgiveness, and tearful reconciliations . . .
It was enough to make you die with laughing.

After a few days of this they would make it up, as though
there had never been any real reason for their quarrel.
Then, after floods of tears, off they would go to a restaurant
to celebrate, and the following morning they would stay in
bed late, exhausted by love-making . . .

It didn't take me long to realize that all this was just play acting, poor fools, and that though they threatened to leave each other they never had the least intention of doing so. They were firmly bound to one another—he by self interest, she by vanity. The master held on to Madame because she had the money, and Madame clung to the master because of his name and title. But, because fundamentally they couldn't stand each other—and all the more so because they were aware of the sordid bonds that kept them together—they felt obliged to have it out now and then, to express, in words as ignoble as their hearts, all the shame and bitterness they felt.

'Whatever purpose do such creatures serve?' I would say to William.

'Bibi's!' he would reply. He always found the most apt and definitive answer for every occasion.

And, as an immediate and practical demonstration of how right he was, he would produce a magnificent Corona Corona, stolen that morning, carefully cut the end, light it with the utmost satisfaction, and, between puffs of fragrant smoke, declare sententiously:

'You should never complain about the stupidity of your employers, my dear Célestine . . . It is the surest guarantee of happiness that we poor devils can ever hope for. The stupider the boss, the happier the servants . . . Run and fetch me a glass of brandy love . . .'

Lying back in a rocking-chair, his legs crossed, the cigar stuck in his mouth and a bottle of old Martell within reach, he would slowly and methodically spread out *L'Autorité*, and continue with the utmost good humour:

'You see, honey, it is essential to keep the upper hand of the people you work for. That's the whole secret . . . God knows, Cassagnac's a tough kind of bloke . . . God knows, he suits me down to the ground and I have the greatest admiration for the old devil . . . But I'll tell you one thing: I wouldn't work for him, not for anything in the world. And what goes for Cassagnac goes for Edgar as well. You mark my words, and try to profit from them. Working for intelligent people, who know their way around, is simply a waste of time, my little beauty.'

And, after a silence, during which he continued to savour the aroma of his cigar, he added:

'When you think how many servants there are, who spend their lives arguing the toss with their employers, plaguing the life out of them, threatening them . . . yes, even wanting to kill them . . . you can't help feeling what fools they are! Because what then? Do we kill the cow that gives us milk and the sheep that gives us wool? Of course not. We milk the one and shear the other . . . and we do it skilfully . . . gently.'

And then he would immerse himself silently in the mysteries of conservative politics.

All this time Eugenie was still wandering around the kitchen, lovesick and dreamy. She did her work mechanically, as though she was sleep-walking, far away from the couple upstairs, far away from us and from herself, her eyes regardless of their foolishness and of ours, her lips forever murmuring unhappy words of love and adoration.

I don't know why, but all this used to make me feel sad, so sad I could have cried . . . Yes, somehow that strange household, where everyone, the silent old butler, William, I myself, seemed to me like restless, futile ghosts, filled me with a heavy, indescribable melancholy.

The last scene I was present at was a particularly funny one . . . One morning, the master happened to come into the boudoir, where I was helping Madame try on a new pair of corsets . . . hideous things, made of mauve satin, with small yellow flowers and yellow laces. But then, taste was scarcely her strong point.

'What?' said Madame, in a gay, reproachful voice. 'So that's the way you enter women's bedrooms . . . without even knocking.'

'Women's?' cooed the master. 'But you're not *women*.'

'Well, if I'm not, I'd like to know what I am, then.'

The master screwed up his mouth—God, what a fool he looked!—and murmured with an affectation of tenderness:

'But you're my wife, of course . . . My sweet little wife. Surely it's not a crime to visit one's own little wife.'

Whenever the master behaved like a love-sick idiot, it usually meant that he was hoping to cadge some money, as Madame realized. Already suspicious, she replied:

'I'm not so sure . . . You and your "little wife", indeed! . . . I'm not sure I want to be your "little wife" ' . . .

'What? . . . You're not sure? . . .'

'How can you ever be? . . . Men are such funny creatures . . .'

'But of course you're my little wife, my one and only darling little wife.'

'Get along with you . . . And I suppose you're just my own great big baby?'

While I was lacing her up, Madame stood with her hands raised above her head, regarding herself in the mirror and stroking the tufts of hair in her armpits . . . I could have laughed. All this 'little wife, big baby' stuff was enough to drive you round the bend. And they looked such utter fools . . . the pair of them.

After glancing into the bathroom and picking up some petticoats and a pair of stockings, the master began fidgeting about with all the brushes and flasks and pots of cold cream. Then, taking up a fashion magazine that was lying on the dressing table, he seated himself on a kind of plush stool and asked:

'Is there a puzzle this week?'

'I expect so.'

'Have you solved it?'

'No, I haven't.'

Seeing that he had become absorbed in the puzzle, Madame said rather drily:

'Robert.'

'Yes, darling.'

'Haven't you noticed anything?'

'What? In the puzzle?'

Pulling a face and shrugging her shoulders, she said 'No, not in the puzzle . . . Haven't you really noticed anything? But there, you never do notice anything.'

The master gazed vacantly round the room, from the carpet to the ceiling, from the bathroom to the door, with a ludicrously vacant expression on his face.

'What on earth are you talking about? Do you mean there's something new, here in this room, that I haven't noticed? I can't see anything, on my word of honour.'

'Then you simply don't love me any more, Robert,' Madame groaned.

'Not love you? . . . Surely, that's coming it a bit thick!'

He stood up, waving the magazine.

'Not love you?' he repeated. 'Where on earth do you get that idea?'

'Oh, I'm sure you don't, because if you did, there's one thing you certainly would have noticed . . .'

'But what?'

'Can't you see I am wearing a new pair of corsets?'

'Corsets, what corsets? . . . Oh, now I see. To tell you the truth, I hadn't noticed them. I must be going crazy . . . Oh but aren't they sweet . . . perfectly ravishing . . .'

'Yes, it's all right to say that now, but you don't care tuppence . . . It's me who's crazy, wearing myself out trying to make myself look nice for you . . . and you don't care in the slightest . . . Anyhow, what do I really mean to you? Nothing, less than nothing! You come in here, and all you do is read that beastly magazine . . . The only thing you're interested in is that ridiculous puzzle . . . Oh, it's a nice life you lead me. We never see anyone . . . we never go anywhere . . . we just live here like savages without any money . . .'

'Come, come, now, I implore you . . . Don't get all worked up. Look here! . . .' And he tried to put his arm round her waist and kiss her.

But she angrily pushed him away.

'No, leave me alone . . . you get on my nerves . . .'

'But, see here, darling, my own little wife . . .'

'You get on my nerves, d'you hear? Leave me alone . . . Don't come near me . . . You think of nobody but yourself, you great lout . . . You never do a thing for me . . . You're just a pig, there!'

'Whatever are you talking about? This is all nonsense. Look, it's no good getting in such a tizzy . . . All right, then, I'm in the wrong . . . I ought to have seen them straight away . . . they're very pretty corsets . . . I just can't understand why I didn't! . . . Look at me, love. Smile at me . . . God, yes, they really are sweet, and they suit you perfectly.'

But the master was trying too hard. He was even getting on my nerves, though their quarrel did not concern me in the slightest. Madame was stamping her foot, growing more and more hysterical. Her lips were pale, and her hands clenched, and she kept repeating:

'You get on my nerves . . . you get on my nerves . . . you get on my nerves . . . Is that clear? . . . Get out!'

The master went rambling on, but he, too, was beginning to get annoyed.

'Now, sweetheart. you're being unreasonable. All this over a pair of corsets. They've simply no connection . . . Come, look at me, darling, smile at me . . . It's stupid to get so worked up about a pair of corsets . . .'

'Oh, for Christ's sake, get out,' she shouted in a voice like a washerwoman's. 'Go on, get out and leave me alone.'

I had finished lacing her up. At these words I stood up, delighted that they had both completely given themselves away in front of me and, later on, would feel humiliated. They seemed to have forgotten that I was there, and anxious to see how the scene ended I made myself as inconspicuous as possible, not saying a word . . .

It was now the master's turn. Having contained himself as long as he could, he suddenly lost his temper and, screwing the magazine up into a ball, flung it with all his strength at the dressing-table mirror and shouted:

'Oh, for heaven's sake, this is really impossible! It's always the same. You can't say a word without being treated like a dog . . . And always the same coarseness, the same filthy language . . . I've had just about enough of this kind of thing. I'm absolutely fed up with you behaving like a fishwife . . . And shall I tell you something? Those corsets are simply impossible . . . Nobody but a whore would dream of wearing them!'

'You swine!' Her eyes bloodshot, her mouth foaming and her fists clenched, she bore down upon the master, in such a fury that when she tried to speak her words almost choked her . . .

'You swine,' she managed to bring out at last. 'And you dare to speak to me like this. Why, it's unforgivable . . . Who was it that picked you up out of the gutter . . . a fine, broken-down gentleman, up to his eyes in debt, blackballed by his club? . . . You were glad enough when I pulled you out of the shit! . . . I suppose you think I did it just for your

291

name, your title? A fat lot they counted, when the money-lenders wouldn't even advance you another sou . . . Well, you can take your title back and wipe your backside with it . . . Talk about your noble ancestors . . . why, wasn't it I that bought you in the first place? And haven't I been keeping you ever since? Well, you're not getting another penny out of me! And as to your ancestors, you cheap skate, just you try hocking them, and see if you can raise ten sous on the whole thieving pack of them . . . There's going to be no more of all that, you understand. Never, never! . . . So you'd better take up gambling again, you cheat . . . or find yourself a whore, you ponce!'

She was really terrifying . . . Trembling with fear, his body sagging, not knowing where to look, the master recoiled before this flood of filth . . . As he reached the door, he caught sight of me and fled, while Madame went on shouting after him down the corridor, in a still more terrible voice:

'A ponce, that's all you are!'

Then she sank down on the couch, overcome by a terrible attack of nerves, which I only managed to calm by making her inhale ether . . .

Eventually she returned to her novelettes and started tidying her drawers again, while the master became more absorbed than ever in his complicated games of patience and yet another rearrangement of his pipes . . . And the correspondence started all over again . . . shyly at first, and at long intervals, though before long it had become as fast and furious as ever. I almost ran myself into the ground, hurrying backwards and forwards between the bedroom and the study, carrying their ridiculous notes . . . Oh how I laughed!

Three days later, as she was reading one of the master's messages written on pink paper stamped with his coat of arms, Madame suddenly turned pale and asked me breathlessly:

'Célestine, do you believe the master really means to kill himself? Have you seen him with a revolver? My God, what if he were to commit suicide!'

I just burst out laughing, straight in her face . . . I didn't do it on purpose, but I couldn't help myself. I simply couldn't stop. My laughter just grew louder and louder. It was choking me. I thought I should really die of laughing.

For a moment she looked absolutely bewildered. Then she said:

'What on earth's the matter with you? What are you laughing about? Be quiet . . . Will you shut up, you wicked girl.'

But it was no use. I just couldn't stop. At last I managed to stammer out:

'Oh no . . . it's really too funny, this nonsense of yours . . . Too stupid, ha-ha, ha-ha-ha. Oh, but it's ridiculous!'

Naturally, that evening I had to leave the house, and, once again, I found myself in the street. What a bitch of a job, what a bitch of a life!

This was a bad blow, especially as I realized—though too late—that I could never hope to find such a good situation again . . . It had everything: good wages, all kinds of perks, easy work, and plenty of freedom and amusement. All I had to do was to let myself drift along. Any other girl, not a crazy idiot like me, would have managed to save up a nice bit of money, and fixed herself up with a handsome trousseau. In five or six years or so, who knows, I might have got married, bought a little business, had my own place, with no fear of being hard up . . . happy, almost a lady . . . As it was, I had to start the whole wretched business all over again, submit once more to the mercies of chance . . . I was vexed by what had happened, furious with myself, with William, Eugenie, Madame, everybody. What is so curious, and hard to explain, is that, instead of hanging on to this place by hook or crook, which, with a woman like Madame, would have been quite easy, I allowed myself to behave more stupidly than ever; and even, by my sheer impertinence, made the position irreparable when it could quite well have been patched up . . . Isn't it strange, the things that sometimes go on inside you? It just isn't possible to understand them. It's as though you were seized by a kind of madness that shocks and excites you so that you start shouting and insulting people, though you haven't the least idea where it comes from or what it is. Dominated by such madness, I had treated Madame absolutely outrageously. I had jeered at her parents, and drawn attention to the ridiculous lie she was living. I had treated her worse than anybody would dare treat a whore, and had said the filthiest things about her husband . . . It frightens me to think about it, and it makes me ashamed as well . . . These sudden outbursts of shamelessness, this intoxication with filth, that sometimes drives me almost to the point of murder, and makes me feel that I'm going out of my mind . . . What stopped me strangling her, killing her, I simply don't know . . . Yet, God knows, I'm not a bad woman. Now, later, when I think about that poor creature and remember the wretched, muddled kind of life she was leading with that miserable weakling of a husband, I feel immensely sorry for her . . . I only hope she had the strength of mind to leave him, and that now she has found some kind of happiness . . .

Immediately after that terrible scene I went downstairs to the pantry, where I found William, lazily polishing the silver and smoking a Russian cigarette.

'What's up with you then?' he asked me, as calm as you like.

'I've got to leave . . . I'm giving up the job this evening,' I panted, scarcely able to speak.

'You don't say! . . . What on earth do you want to leave for?' said William without the slightest trace of emotion.

I described the scene with Madame in short, breathless sentences, trying to imitate the way she spoke, but William remained completely indifferent. He merely shrugged his shoulders and said:

'But this is absolutely ridiculous . . . No one can be as stupid as that.'

'Is that all you can find to say to me?'

'And what else do you expect me to say? I tell you, it's silly, and that's all there is to it.'

'And what about you? What are you going to do?'

He glanced at me from under his eyebrows, and there was a mean sneer on his lips. Oh how ugly he looked now that I was in trouble! What a hideous, cowardly expression he had!

'Me?' he said, pretending not to understand that my question was an appeal to him.

'Yes, you . . . I asked you what you're going to do . . .'

'Nothing . . . there's nothing I can do . . . I shall just go on as I am . . . But you're mad, my girl. You should never have done it!'

I burst out: 'So you're prepared to stay on with these people when they've given me the sack?'

He got up, relit his cigarette which had gone out, and said coldly:

'Oh, we won't have any scenes, if you don't mind! I'm not your husband you know . . . If you've chosen to make a fool of yourself, that's your look out. It's not my fault . . . What d'you expect? You'll just have to put up with the consequences . . . That's life!'

'So you're going to let me down?' I said indignantly. 'Then you're a miserable swine, like all the rest of them . . . Do you hear? . . . A miserable swine!'

William merely smiled in his superior manner.

'Don't start talking a lot of nonsense . . . When you and I got together, I never made any promises and nor did you . . . We just happened to meet, and we just fell for each other . . . Very good. Now you've got to go, so we break it off . . . and that's all right, too. That's life.'

And he added, sententiously: 'You see, Célestine, in real life, you have to learn to behave . . . You need what I call organization. You don't know how to behave, you can't organize . . . You let yourself be carried away by your feelings, and in our job we can't afford feelings . . . Just you remember what I've told you . . . That's life.'

I could have thrown myself on him and scratched his face with my nails—his unfeeling, cowardly, flunkey's face —if a sudden burst of tears had not brought relief to my exhausted nerves. My anger disappeared, and I implored him:

'Oh, William, William, my dear little William, if only you knew how miserable I feel!'

He made some attempt to restore my morale, and, I must say, he employed all his powers of persuasion and philosophy. For the rest of that day he overwhelmed me with noble thoughts and grave, consoling aphorisms, in which the same alternatively irritating and soothing phrase continually recurred . . . 'But that's life . . .'

I must, however, do him justice. That last day he was charming, though rather pompous, and he did things handsomely. In the evening, when we had had dinner, he loaded my trunks on to a cab and took me to a lodging house that he knew, where he paid a week in advance for me and told them they must look after me properly. I wanted him to spend the night with me, but he had an appointment with Edgar.

'I can't very well let him down, you know . . . And now I come to think of it, perhaps he may know of a situation for you . . . If Edgar was to find you a place, that would be marvellous.'

As he was leaving, he said:

'I'll come and see you tomorrow. So be a good girl, and don't get up to any more of your nonsense . . . That get's you nowhere . . . The one thing you have got to get into your head, Célestine, is that life's like that . . .'

The next day I waited for him in vain. He never came. 'I suppose,' I said to myself, 'that's life.'

The following day, however, as I was still anxious to see him, I went back to the house. There was no one in the kitchen, except a tall, fair-haired girl, extremely cheeky and a bit wild, and prettier than me.

'Isn't Eugenie about?' I asked.

'No, she's gone out,' the tall girl replied drily.

'And William?'

'He's not in, either.'

'Where is he?'

'How should I know?'

'I want to see him . . . Go and tell him I'm here.'

The tall girl looked at me disdainfully:

'What's that? . . . I'm not paid to wait on you, you know.'

The position was only too obvious . . . And as I was tired of struggling, I took myself off . . . 'That's life . . .'

I couldn't get the phrase out of my head. It went on and on, like the words of some popular song. As I turned away, I couldn't help remembering how gaily I had first been made welcome in that house . . . The same scene must have taken place all over again . . . the uncorking of the champagne . . . William taking the fair girl on his knee, whispering in her ear: 'You must always be nice to Bibi . . .'

all the same words, the same gestures, the same caresses . . .
and Eugenie gazing adoringly at the porter's son and taking
him off into the next room . . .

For more than an hour I walked up and down outside the
house, hoping to see William, either coming in or going
out . . . And all the time the ridiculous little phrase kept
running through my head . . . I saw the grocer's boy go in,
and the little dressmaker, with two big cardboard boxes,
and the delivery man from the Louvre; and I saw the
plumbers coming out, and all sorts of other people . . .
ghosts, ghosts, ghosts . . . I was afraid to visit the porter's
lodge next door, in case she should be unpleasant to me.
And, besides, what could she have told me? At last I decided
to give up, and went away pursued by the irritating refrain:
'That's life.'

The streets seemed unbearably sad. The passers-by were
like creatures from another world. When, in the distance, I
caught sight of a man's hat, shining like a beacon in the
night, my heart suddenly leapt . . . But it was not William . . .
In the heavy, leaden-coloured sky there was no gleam of
hope.

I got back to my room, disgusted with everything . . . Oh
men, men, men! They're all the same . . . coachmen, footmen, toffs, parsons, poets . . . Nothing but a lot of swine!

Well, that's the last of my memories I mean to write
about. Not that I haven't got plenty of others . . . I have.
But they're all so much alike, and I'm tired of continually
describing the same events, the same monotonous succession
of faces, hearts, phantoms. Besides, I am distracted from
the ashes of the past by my preoccupation with the future . . .
I could have told a good deal more about the time I was
with the Countess Fardin . . . But what's the use? I'm sick
and tired of it all . . . It was there, that, for the first time I
encountered the type of vanity that most disgusts me,
literary vanity, and the lowest of all forms of stupidity,
political stupidity . . .

It was there that I met Monsieur Paul Bourget, at the
height of his fame—need I say more? . . . He is precisely
the kind of philosophizing, poeticizing, moralizing writer
that suits the pretentious nullity, the intellectual snobbery,

the fundamental untruth of that social stratum for whom everything is artificial: elegance, love, cooking, religious feeling, patriotism, art, charity . . . yes, even vice itself, which, on the pretext of literature and good manners, decks itself out in tawdry mysticism and hides behind a mask of sanctity . . . A world in which there is but one genuine desire . . . the ruthless desire for money, a desire that adds an odious and savage quality to the absurdity of these puppets, and is the one indication that the pathetic phantoms are living human beings.

It was there, too, that I met Monsieur Jean, another psychologist and moralist: the psychologist of the pantry, the moralist of the backstairs, and, in his own way, scarcely more of an upstart and a simpleton that the one that rules the roost upstairs in the drawing-room. Monsieur Jean empties people's chamber-pots, Monsieur Bourget their souls . . . In terms of servility, there is not so much difference between the kitchen and the drawing-room as is sometimes supposed! . . . But, since I have put Monsieur Jean's photograph away at the bottom of my trunk, I may as well let the memory of him remain buried at the bottom of my heart, beneath a thick layer of oblivion . . .

It is two o'clock in the morning . . . The fire has gone out, the lamp is beginning to gutter, and I have no more wood or paraffin. I am going to bed . . . But my brain is too feverish to let me sleep. I shall dream of what is advancing to meet me, of what will happen tomorrow . . . Outside, the night is silent and tranquil. The earth lies frozen hard, beneath a sky glittering with stars. And, somewhere within that night, Joseph is on his way home . . . Through the darkness I can see him, yes, really see him, sitting in a third-class carriage, grave, thoughtful, huge. He is smiling at me, drawing closer to me, bringing me at last peace, freedom, happiness . . . Will it really be happiness? Tomorrow I shall know.

It is eight months since I last wrote anything in this diary, I have had so many other things to think about; and exactly three since Joseph and I left the Priory and settled at Cherbourg, in the little café near the harbour. We are married; business is good; I like the work; and I am happy. Born by the sea, now I have returned to it, and though I used not to miss it, I am glad to be back there all the same. Here, it is not like the desolate country at Audierne, the infinite sadness of the cliffs, the terrible splendour of those sombre, roaring beaches. There is nothing sad about Cherbourg, on the contrary, everything is full of gaiety . . . all the cheerful din of a military town, all the picturesque bustle and motley activity of a naval port. All around you are people making love, indulging in wild riotous sprees . . . crowds intent upon pleasure, between two spells of exile . . . an absorbing, ever-changing spectacle, and the smell of tar and seaweed that I have known and loved since childhood, though in those days, I must say, I never found it particularly sweet. Once again I meet lads from home, serving in the navy . . . not that we have much to say to each other, and I have never dreamt of asking them for news of my brother . . . That's all so long ago. For me, it's as though he were dead. Good morning . . . Good evening . . . How are you? . . . When they aren't drunk they're too stupid, and when they aren't stupid, they're too drunk . . . And they all look the same . . . heads like old fishes . . . and no more feeling for me than I for them. Besides, Joseph doesn't like me being too familiar with ordinary sailors . . . lousy Bretons, who haven't a penny to bless themselves with and get tight on cheap spirits.

But I must briefly describe what happened before we left the Priory. As you will remember, Joseph used to sleep in the stables, in a room over the saddle room; and every day, summer and winter, he used to be up at five o'clock in the morning. Well, on Christmas Eve, exactly a month after he got back from Cherbourg, the first thing he saw was that the kitchen door was wide open . . . 'What?' he thought. 'Surely they aren't up already? . . .'

Then he noticed that a square hole had been cut in the glazed panel of the door, near the lock, large enough for a man to get his arm through. The lock had been expertly forced, and a few bits of wood, tiny pieces of twisted iron and splinters of glass were scattered about on the ground . . . Inside, all the doors, so carefully bolted every evening under

Madame's personal supervision, were also open. It was obvious that something terrible had happened . . . By this time, feeling very worried—I am repeating exactly what Joseph told the examining magistrate—he hurried through the kitchen into the passage, which leads to the apple room, bathroom and hall on the right, and, on the left, to the pantry, dining-room, morning-room and, at the far end, the drawing-room. The dining-room was in a shocking state—furniture overturned, the sideboard ransacked from top to bottom, all its drawers, as well as those of the two dumb-waiters, emptied on to the floor, and, on the table, in the middle of a jumble of empty boxes and objects of no value, a candle, still burning in a copper candlestick. But it was when he got to the pantry that he realized how serious the situation was. There, as I think I mentioned earlier, there was a deep cupboard, fastened by a very complicated lock, the combination of which was only known to Madame. It was here that the famous silver was kept, in three heavy cases, protected by steel bands and corner-pieces, which were bolted to the bottom of the cupboard and secured to the walls by solid iron brackets. Well, these three cases had been wrenched from their mysterious and inviolable tabernacle, and were standing in the middle of the room, empty. Directly he saw this, Joseph raised the alarm, running to the bottom of the staircase and yelling with all the strength of his lungs:

'Sir! Madame! Come on down, quick . . . We've been robbed, we've been robbed!'

There was an immediate rush, a terrifying avalanche of people. Madame in her nightdress, with only a light shawl round her shoulders; the master still trying to tuck the ends of his shirt into his trousers . . . and both of them, pale, dishevelled, with an expression of bewilderment on their faces as though they had been woken up in the middle of a nightmare, were shouting:

'What's the matter? What's the matter?'

'We've been robbed, we've been robbed!'

'What's been stolen? What's been stolen?'

In the dining-room, Madame started wailing, 'Oh my God, my God!' While the master kept on bawling 'What's been stolen? What's been stolen?'

Joseph led them to the pantry, and there, at the sight of the three open cases, Madame threw her arms in the air and shrieked:

'It's my silver! Oh my God! Is it possible? My silver!'

And, taking out the empty compartments, turning the cases upside down, bewildered, horrified, she sank to the ground . . . It was all she could do to mutter in a childish voice:

'They've taken the lot! Everything, everything, everything—even the Louis Sieze cruet!'

She continued staring at the cases, as though she were gazing at her dead child, while the master, scratching the back of his neck and rolling haggard eyes, could only moan, in the obstinate, faraway voice of someone going out of his mind:

'Well, I'll be damned . . . Well, I'll be damned!'

Not to be outdone, Joseph stood there with a ghastly expression on his face, yelling:

'The Louis Seize cruet! The Louis Seize cruet . . . Oh, the bandits!'

Then, suddenly, there was a tragic silence, a long moment of prostration, like the protracted deathlike silence, enveloping things and people alike, that succeeds the crash of a great earthquake, or the thunder of a mighty cataclysm . . . And the swaying lantern that Joseph was carrying lit up the whole scene, the deathly faces and the empty cases, with its trembling, sinister red beams.

I had come downstairs at the same time as Madame, when the alarm was first raised. Despite the highly comical spectacle they presented, my first reaction was one of compassion. I felt that I, too, was involved in this disaster, and I, too, shared their grief, like one of the family. So upset was I by the sight of Madame's utter collapse, that I wanted to console her . . . But it was not long before this fellow feeling—or was it just instinctive servility?—was dissipated.

The very violence of the crime had something impressive about it, a quality of almost religious retribution which, while it certainly scared me, also left me with a feeling of admiration that I find it hard to explain. No, it was not exactly admiration, for admiration is a moral feeling, it produces a sense of spiritual exultation, whereas what I felt only

301

affected me physically . . . It was a savage shock, experienced by my whole body, distressing, yet at the same time delightful, painful yet rapturous, a kind of sexual violation . . . It is a curious thing, probably quite personal, and perhaps horrible—and I don't pretend to understand what causes such strange and powerful feelings—but, with me, any crime, especially murder, is in some mysterious way closely related to love . . . Yes, that's it . . . a splendid crime excites me in the same way as a fine specimen of a man.

I ought, perhaps, to add that this atrocious and powerful feeling of pleasure, which replaced my first instinctive, but quite inappropriate sense of compassion, was itself quickly transformed, by the thought that almost immediately struck me, into wild, mocking gaiety. 'Here are these two creatures,' I said to myself, 'living like moles, like grubs . . . Willing prisoners, they have voluntarily shut themselves up in this inhospitable gaol, suppressing all the joy of life, everything that might be a source of happiness, as though it was superfluous, and denying themselves whatever might have excused their wealth, pardoned their human futility, as though it were mere filth. Too mean to spare a crumb from their table for the hungry, too heartless to give a thought to the sick, they have preferred to do without happiness, even for themselves. Why, then, should I feel pity for them? What has happened to them is simply what they deserve. By robbing them of some of their wealth, by stealing their buried treasure, the thieves have merely restored the balance . . . My one regret is that while they were about it, they didn't strip these two evil creatures naked, leave them as destitute as the tramps who have so often begged in vain for bread, as the sick whom they have left to die by the roadside within a few yards of all this accursed wealth.'

This idea, that the Lanlaires might have been obliged to trail their lamentable rags and bleeding feet through all the misery of the gutter, begging their bread at the implacable doors of the rich, enchanted and delighted me. And my delight became all the more immediate, more intense, more filled with hatred, at the sight of Madame, slumped over her empty cases, deader than if she had really died, because she was conscious of being dead—for what death could conceivably be more horrible, for a creature who had never in her life loved anything, but had always assumed that money could buy everything, even the things without price, pleasure, charity, love . . . This shameful grief, this sordid dejection were my revenge for all the humiliations and brutality I had suffered, which she had inflicted upon me with every word she uttered, every look she gave me . . . And I delighted to the full in this savage revenge. I would have liked to shout aloud, 'Well done, well done!' But, above all, I would have liked to know these admirable, these sublime, thieves, that I might thank them in the name of all the beggars in the world, that I might embrace them as brothers. Oh, honest thieves, beloved figures of justice and of pity, what a succession of powerful and delicious sensations you have enabled me to experience!

It was not long, however, before Madame succeeded in pulling herself together . . . Her violently aggressive nature soon reasserted itself . . .

'What on earth d'you think you're doing?' she said to Monsieur Lanlaire, in an angry and supremely contemptuous tone of voice. 'What are you waiting for? If only you could see what a fool you look, with that great puffy face and your shirt all over the place! Do you think that's going to get us back our silver? Come on, wake up and get a move on! Try to realize what's happened. Why don't you call the police? They should have been here long ago . . . Oh my God, what a man!'

The master hung his head, and was about to leave the room, when she called him back.

'How is it you never heard anything? The whole house is turned upside down, doors forced, locks broken, cases gutted, and yet you never heard a sound, you great, good-for-nothing blockhead.'

'But neither did you, my love,' he replied, summoning up all his courage.

'Me? But that's quite different . . . Really, you're infuriating. For heaven's sake, get out of my sight.'

And, as her husband went upstairs to get dressed, she turned her anger against us.

'And what about you? What's the good of staring at me like that, you boobies? I suppose it's all the same to you whether your employers are robbed or not? Do you mean to tell me you heard nothing, either? Oh, it's marvellous to have such servants . . . All you ever think of is eating and sleeping, you lazy brutes!'

Then, turning to Joseph and addressing him directly, she said:

'Why didn't the dogs bark? Tell me . . . why?'

Her question seemed to disconcert him, but only for the flash of a second. Quickly recovering, he replied in the most natural tone of voice:

'I don't rightly know, ma'am, but it's quite right . . . the dogs ought to have barked. It's funny they didn't, and that's a fact!'

'Did you let them off the chain?'

'Certainly I did, like I do every evening . . . But it's a funny thing they didn't bark . . . Makes you think. The thieves must have got to know the place, and the dogs . . .'

'All the same, Joseph, how comes it that you didn't hear anything? You're usually so careful . . . so sensible.'

'True enough, I never heard a sound . . . And there's another thing that makes it seem as though there was some funny business . . . I'm not a heavy sleeper . . . As a rule I hear if a cat runs across the garden . . . No, it's certainly not natural, especially those damned dogs . . . But there it it, there it is!'

But Madame cut him short:

'That'll do . . . You're a pack of fools, the whole lot of you . . . But where's Marianne? What's happened to her? Why isn't she here? . . . I suppose she's still sleeping like a log.'

And leaving the pantry, she went to the foot of the staircase and started calling: 'Marianne, Marianne!'

I looked at Joseph. He was still staring at the empty cases with a grave, intent expression on his face. But there was a mysterious look in his eyes . . .

I shall not attempt to describe that day in detail, with all its fantastic goings on. The District Attorney, summoned by special messenger, arrived in the afternoon and began

304

his enquiry. Joseph, Marianne and I were interrogated in turn, the first two more or less formally, I, with an insistent hostility that I found most disagreeable. They went up to my room, and searched through all my drawers and trunks. All my correspondence was minutely examined, but, by the greatest piece of luck, my diary escaped their attention, for a few days previously I had sent it to Cléclé, who had written to me most affectionately. Otherwise, the examining magistrate might have found sufficient evidence to charge Joseph, or at least, to suspect him . . . Even now it makes me shudder to think of it . . . Needless to say, they also carried out a thorough search of the garden paths, flower-beds, walls, gaps in the hedge and the little courtyard leading to the alleyway, hoping to find footprints . . . But the ground was so dry and hard that they failed to discover the slightest clue. Gateway, walls, gaps in the hedge, they all jealously kept their secret. As had happened with the affair of the rape, the entire neighbourhood flocked to the scene, demanding to give evidence. Someone had seen a fair-haired man that he 'didn't at all fancy'; someone else a dark man who 'looked funny'. In short, the enquiry led nowhere. There was not even a suspect . . .

'We shall just have to wait,' the District Attorney declared mysteriously as he was leaving. 'Perhaps the Paris police will be able to put us on their trail.'

Throughout that exhausting day, what with all the coming and going, I scarcely had time to consider the consequences of this drama, which, for the first time, had brought some life and animation to this dreary Priory. Madame never let up for a moment. She kept us continually on the run . . . quite pointlessly, as it turned out, for she herself had lost her head . . . As to Marianne, she seemed not to notice that anything out of the ordinary was going on. Like poor Eugenie, she was intent on her own thoughts, and they were far away from what preoccupied the rest of us. But, when-ever the master appeared in the kitchen, she immediately began to behave as though she were drunk, staring at him ecstatically . . .

It was not until the evening, after we had eaten our dinner in silence, that I was able to think about things. It had struck me straight away, and I was now more convinced than ever, that Joseph was in some way involved in the robbery. I like to think that some clear connection might emerge between his visit to Cherbourg and the preparation of this bold and incomparably well-executed plan. And I recalled the answer he had given me the night before he set out:

'It all depends on some very important business . . .'

Although he did his best to behave naturally, his gestures, his silence, his whole attitude, betrayed an uneasiness, imperceptible to anybody but myself. This presentiment was so satisfying that I made no attempt to reject it. On the contrary, I indulged it to the full . . . When for a moment Marianne happened to leave us alone together in the kitchen, I went up to him and, stirred by an inexplicable emotion, asked him, in a tender, coaxing voice:

'Tell me, Joseph, it was you who raped little Clara, wasn't it? And now you've stolen the silver . . . Yes?'

Surprised and dismayed by this question, Joseph looked at me . . . Then, suddenly, without replying, he drew me towards him and planted a kiss on the back of my neck like a blow from a club.

'We won't talk of such things,' he said, 'in the first place because you're going to come away with me, and, in the second, because you and I are the same kind of people!'

I could not help thinking of a Hindu idol, terrifyingly beautiful, that used to stand in the small drawing-room at Countess Fardin's . . . At that moment, Joseph looked exactly like it.

The days went by, and gradually turned into months . . . Naturally, the examining magistrates failed to discover anything, and finally abandoned their enquiries. In their opinion, the robbery was the work of burglars from Paris . . . Paris has a broad back!

This negative result infuriated Madame, and she roundly abused the magistrates for their failure to restore her silver. But she did not give up hope of getting back 'Louis XVI's cruet', as Joseph called it. Every day she had some new, cockeyed proposal, which she conveyed to the magistrates. But they soon became so fed up with her nonsense that they didn't even trouble to reply . . . And in the end I felt convinced that Joseph was safe, for I had always been terrified lest some catastrophe might befall him.

Meanwhile, Joseph had once again become the silent, devoted, family servant . . . 'A perfect treasure'.

I could not help smiling at the thought of the conversation I had overheard on the day of the robbery, between Madame and the examining magistrate, a dried-up little chap with thin lips and a bilious complexion, and a profile like the edge of a scimitar.

'You don't suspect any of the servants?' asked the magistrate. 'Your coachman, for example?'

'Joseph?' Madame had exclaimed in a shocked voice. 'Why he's been with us more than fifteen years, and is utterly devoted to us! He is honesty itself, a perfect treasure! He would go through fire and water for us . . .' Then, frowning a little, she had thoughtfully considered the question, and added:

'Of course, there's the girl . . . my chambermaid. I really know very little about her. For all I know, she may well have criminal connections in Paris. She often writes there . . . And I've several times caught her drinking the table wine and stealing fruit . . . A girl who would do that, is capable of anything . . . One should never get servants from Paris . . . She's certainly a peculiar girl.'

Can't you just see the old cat?

It's always the same with these suspicious types . . . they distrust everybody except the one that is actually robbing them . . . For I was more and more convinced that Joseph had been the ringleader in this business. For a long time I had been watching him, not in any unfriendly way, you understand, but out of curiosity, and I was quite certain that this faithful and devoted servant, this 'absolute treasure', was pilfering everything he could lay hands on. He stole hay, coal, eggs . . . all the little things, that it would be impossible to trace when they were resold. And his friend, the verger, certainly didn't come to the saddle-room every evening for nothing—nor just to discuss anti-semitism. A man as shrewd, patient, prudent and methodical as Joseph was certainly aware that small daily thefts add up to a considerable annual sum. And, indeed, I'm quite sure that in this way he must have trebled or quadrupled his

wages . . . which is not to be sneezed at. Of course, I realise
that small-scale pilfering like this is a very different matter
from an audacious robbery like the one on Christmas Eve,
but that only goes to prove that he was also capable of
working on a grand scale . . . Nobody's going to tell me that
Joseph didn't belong to some gang or other. Oh, how I
should have liked, and, indeed, would still like, to know
for certain!

Ever since that evening when the savagery of his kiss
was almost an admission of guilt, Joseph had repeatedly
denied it. However much I twisted and turned, tried to trap
him, coaxed him, caressed him, he never gave himself away
again . . . And he continually played up to all Madame's
crazy hopes, reconstituting the details of the crime, entering into all her plans, thrashing the dogs for not having
barked, and even shaking his fist at the chimerical robbers,
as though he could actually see them just disappearing over
the horizon. I no longer knew where I was with this
impenetrable man . . . One day I believed him to be guilty,
and the next I was sure he was innocent. It was all terribly
exasperating.

In the evenings we used to meet as usual in the saddle-
room.

'Well, Joseph?'

'Ah, so there you are, Célestine!'

'Why do you never talk to me these days? You seem to
be running away from me . . .'

'Running away from you? Whyever should I do that, for
God's sake?'

'Yes, ever since that famous day . . .'

'Say no more about it, Célestine . . . You've got some
wicked ideas in your head,' he would say, sadly shaking his
head.

'Oh come on, Joseph, you know very well I was only
joking . . . How could I still love you if you'd committed
such a crime, my little Joseph . . .'

'Always trying to wheedle me . . . You shouldn't do it.'

'Well, when are we going to leave? I simply can't stick
this much longer.'

'Not just yet . . . We must wait a bit.'

'But why?'

'Because it wouldn't do . . . not straight away.'

Somewhat piqued, I said irritably:

'That's not very nice! . . . You don't seem to be very anxious to have me.'

'What?' cried Joseph, his eyes lighting up. 'If only it were possible, my God! I'm crazy about you, crazy!'

'Well then, let's leave . . .'

But he wouldn't budge, and he refused to explain himself further.

Naturally I thought:

'So I was right, after all . . . If he really did steal the silver, he just couldn't leave straight away and set up in business. It might arouse people's suspicions. He's got to wait until the whole mysterious affair has been forgotten.'

Another evening I suggested:

'Listen, my love, I've thought of a way we could arrange it . . . If we were to have a row with Madame, we could force her to give us both the sack . . .'

But he protested strongly:

'No, no, that wouldn't do, Célestine . . . I like the Lanlaires . . . They've been good masters to me, and we've got to treat them properly. When we leave here, everything's got to be on the level. We want them to be sorry we're going . . . really upset about it.'

And, with a grave air of sadness that betrayed not the slightest hint of irony, he insisted:

'Don't you realize? It's going to be a big blow for me to leave here . . . After fifteen years in a place, you can't help getting attached to it . . . What about you? Don't you mind at all?'

'Not in the slightest,' I laughed.

'Well that's not right . . . not right at all . . . After all, bosses are bosses and you ought to treat them right . . . You mark my words, and just behave properly, treat them decently, work well . . . No, don't answer me back . . . After all, Célestine, we owe them something . . . especially Madame.'

I accepted Joseph's advice and, during the month that we still had to remain at The Priory, I determined to become a model chambermaid . . . I, too, would be an 'absolute treasure'. I did everything I possibly could to keep on good terms with Madame, and gradually she became more human, almost like a friend to me. But I don't think it was only the pains I took that brought about the change in her character. Her pride had been wounded and she had lost all reason for living. Like someone overwhelmed with grief, shattered by the loss of a uniquely beloved being, she had given up the struggle, and become a gentle, plaintive creature, demanding from those around her little more than consolation, pity, trust. The hell of The Priory was transformed for everybody into a real paradise . . .

One morning, in the middle of this peaceful family life, this domestic bliss, I informed Madame that I must give notice. I invented a romance . . . I was going home to get married, to a decent fellow who had waited for me a long time. In the most affecting terms, I spoke of my concern and regret, of all her kindness to me, and so on. Madame was quite overcome . . . did her best to persuade me to stay, out of affection as well as from self-interest . . . offered to raise my wages, to give me a fine bedroom on the second floor. But, realizing that I'd made up my mind, she eventually resigned herself.

'I've got so used to you now,' she sighed. 'Oh, I never seem to have any luck . . .'

But it was much worse, when, a week later, it came to Joseph's turn, and he had to explain that he was getting too old and tired, that he couldn't go on working for them any longer and needed a rest.

'What Joseph,' said Madame, 'you as well? But this is too much . . . There must be a curse on The Priory. Everyone's forsaking me, everyone.'

Madame wept, Joseph wept, Monsieur Lanlaire wept, Marianne wept . . .

'We're all going to miss you terribly, Joseph. Our regrets will go with you.'

But, alas, it was not only their regrets that were going with him. It was also their silver!

Once I was away from the place, I felt bewildered. I had no scruples about enjoying Joseph's money and the stolen silver . . . No, it was not that. After all, where is the silver that has not been stolen? . . . But I was afraid lest the feeling I had for him should turn out to be only a fleeting curiosity. The ascendancy that Joseph had won over me, over my mind as well as my body, perhaps might not last . . . Perhaps it would turn out to be no more than a momentary perversion of my senses? There were even times when I wondered whether it was not just my imagination, always so prone to fantastic dreams, that had created the Joseph that I saw, whether he was not merely a simple brute, a peasant, quite incapable of real violence, of splendid crime . . . I was scared of what my decision might lead to . . . Besides, and this is something I simply cannot explain—I could not help regretting that I should no longer be working for other people . . . In the past, I had always believed that I should be delighted to be free. Yet now it had come to the point, I found that I was not . . . Being a servant must be something in the blood . . . What if I were suddenly going to miss all the bourgeois luxury I had become accustomed to? I imagined my own little home, severe and cold like any worker's, the dull life I should lead, deprived of all those pretty things, all the lovely materials I so enjoyed handling, all the charming depravity it had delighted me to minister to . . . But there was no going back.

Oh, whoever would have imagined, on that grey, rainy day when I first arrived at The Priory, that I should end up with this strange, silent, morose man, who regarded me with such disdain?

Now that we have actually taken over the little café, Joseph has become much younger. He is no longer bowed and clumsy. He walks from table to table, moves swiftly from one room to another, with an elastic step and upright carriage. His shoulders, which used to frighten me, have become kindly; the back of his neck, which I once found so terrible, now has something soothing and fatherly about it. Always well-shaven, his brown skin, shining like mahogany, dressed in a smart beret and a scrupulously clean blue blouse, he looks for all the world like a retired sailor, an old sea dog, who has seen the most extraordinary sights and visited the most exotic countries. What I most admire in him is his moral tranquility. There is no longer the least trace of anxiety in his eyes. One can see that his life rests upon solid foundations. More strongly than ever, he stands for the family, property and religion, supports the Fatherland, trusts in the army and navy . . . I find him marvellous.

When we got married, Joseph settled ten thousand francs on me . . . The other day, when the marine assessor knocked down a wreck to him for fifteen thousand francs, he paid on the spot, and he has already sold it again at a considerable profit. He also has a small banking business, that is to say, he lends money to the fishermen; and now he is thinking of expanding, by buying the house next door. We shall turn it into a cabaret.

It intrigues me to find that he has so much money, though what his fortune actually amounts to I really don't know. He doesn't like me to talk about it, any more than he likes me talking about the days when we used to be in service . . . You would imagine that he had completely forgotten the past, and that his life only really began the day when he took over the café. When I question him about what torments me he seems not to understand what I'm saying, and a terrible light comes into his eyes like it used to . . . I shall never know anything about Joseph, never understand the secret of his life. And perhaps it is this unknown quality that binds me to him.

Joseph supervises everything and nothing ever goes wrong. We have three waiters to look after the customers, and a maid who does the cooking and housework, and it all runs like clockwork . . . True, she's the fourth we've had in three months, but they're so tiresome, these Cherbourg girls, and such shocking thieves! . . . It's incredible, really disgusting!

As for me, I am in charge of the till, and sit enthroned behind the bar, amid a forest of glittering bottles. I am there to be looked at, and to chat with the customers. Joseph likes me to be dressed up to the nines; he never refuses me anything that might improve my appearance and, in the evening, he likes me to show off my bosom by wearing a saucily *décolleté* dress . . . My job is to arouse the customer's interest, to keep them happy by displaying my physical charms. Already there are two or three quartermasters, two or three engineer warrant officers, all well breeched, who court me assiduously. Naturally, in order to please me, they spend freely. Joseph makes a great fuss of them because they're all heavy drinkers. We also have three paying

312

guests. They eat with us, but of course the wine and liqueurs they drink in the evening are extras, so that everybody does well out of it. They treat me with the greatest gallantry, and I do my best to keep them on tenterhooks. But I don't think Joseph would like it if I went any further than encouraging their lovesick glances, suggestive smiles and meaningless promises . . . Anyway I wouldn't dream of it. In any case, Joseph suits me fine, and I wouldn't exchange him for anybody in the world, even an admiral of the fleet . . . He's a real man, all right! There aren't many young fellows that could satisfy a woman like he can . . . The funny thing is, though he's really quite ugly, for me there's no one as handsome as he is . . . He really does something to me, and that's the truth! . . . And when it comes to making love, the old monster, there's nothing he doesn't know, and he's very inventive . . . When you think that he's spent his whole life in the country, that he's really only a peasant, you can't help wondering where he learnt it all.

But Joseph's greatest triumph is in politics. Thanks to him the café—with its golden sign, 'To the French Army', all lit up at night—is now an official meeting place for all the best-known anti-semites and rowdiest patriots in the town. The latter have the most tremendous booze-ups, fraternising with all the N.C.O's and warrant officers. There have been one or two pretty serious rough-houses already, and, on several occasions, the N.C.O's have drawn their swords and started threatening to do in the traitors . . . The evening Dreyfus arrived back in France I thought the whole place was about to go up in smoke . . . everybody shouting 'Long live the Army', 'Death to the Jews' . . . Joseph was already very popular, but that evening they all went crazy about him. He stood on a table, yelling out at the top of his voice:

'If the traitor's guilty, send him back again . . . If he's innocent, shoot him!'

And everyone joined in: 'That's right, shoot him! Long live the army!'

There was tremendous excitement, with everyone shouting, banging their fists on the tables and rattling their swords. When someone tried to protest, there was an outburst of booing, and Joseph hurled himself on the poor chap, hitting him a terrible blow that split his lip and

313

knocked out five of his teeth . . . Then the rest of them started beating him with the flat of their swords and tearing his clothes to shreds, till in the end, covered with blood and half dead, the poor fellow was chucked out into the street, with everyone yelling 'Long live the army', 'Death to the Jews'.

Sometimes the atmosphere gets so murderous that I feel scared amongst all these animal faces, distorted with drink. But Joseph reassures me:

'You don't have to worry,' he says, 'It's good for business.'

Yesterday, when he got back from the market, he announced gaily:

'There's bad news . . . Everyone's talking of war with England.'

'Oh my God,' I exclaimed, 'what if they bombard Cherbourg?'

'No, no, they'll never do that,' said Joseph. 'But I've been thinking . . . I've got an idea, a marvellous idea.'

I felt sure he had thought up something really monstrous, and couldn't help trembling. But all he said was:

'The more I look at you, the more it strikes me you don't look like a woman from Brittany . . . No, you're not a real Breton . . . You're more like an Alsatian . . . Now, an Alsatian woman behind the bar, that would be something to look at!'

I felt completely let down . . . I was expecting him to propose something really terrible, and the idea that I was to be involved in some daring enterprise flattered my vanity . . . Whenever I saw him looking thoughtful, my imagination always flared up immediately and I began dreaming of nocturnal expeditions, burglaries, drawn knives, people gasping out their last breath in the forest . . . And, after all that, here he was just thinking about a new kind of advertisement, a trivial, vulgar advertisement.

Hands in pocket, swaggering about in his blue beret, he went on:

'Don't you realize? . . . If there's a war, just think what a fine patriotic effect it would have . . . a pretty, smartly turned out Alsatian girl behind the bar . . . There's nothing like patriotism for getting people tight . . . Isn't it a splendid idea? I could get your picture in the papers . . . Maybe on the hoardings . . .'

'I prefer to remain a lady,' I replied rather drily.

Whereupon we began arguing, and for the first time we both lost our tempers.

'You didn't put on such airs when you were sleeping around with every Tom, Dick and Harry,' cried Joseph.

'And what about you? Why, when you . . . But there, let's drop it, or I shall be saying too much . . .'

'Whore!'

'Thief!'

At that moment a customer came in . . . We immediately changed the subject, and that night we kissed and made up . . .

I'm going to have a lovely Alsatian costume made . . . all silk and velvet. When it comes to the point, I can't deny Joseph anything. I may occasionally rebel, but I belong to him, he possesses me like a demon. And I'm happy to belong to him . . . I know that I shall always do whatever he wants me to, always go as far as he tells me to . . . even if it means committing a crime!